SWORD OF THE SPANIARD

SWORD OF THE SPANIARD

Michael Scott Bertrand

Sword of the Spaniard
by Michael Scott Bertrand
Copyright © 2018
by Michael Scott Bertrand
First Edition

Published by Hyde & Silver

Cover art by Alan Flinn
Interior illustrations by Gustave Doré and Frederick Catherwood
ISBN 978-0-9996531-1-1
Also by Michael Scott Bertrand:
Flying Conquistadors

For anyone lost

A NOTE TO THE READER

This is a work of fiction. However, within these pages you will encounter characters based on real-life individuals. As was the case with *Flying Conquistadors*, I have taken tremendous creative liberties with these characters. Please view them as the caricatures they are intended to be.

On a related note, this is not a history book. In these pages I have used broad brushstrokes to simplify complex historical events, such as the Conquest of the New World and the Spanish Inquisition. I have plucked selective facts out of the historical record and spun them together in ways that would make an academic vomit. Accordingly, please enjoy the story …but don't believe a word of it.

Contents

1

LEAVING CHICHEN ITZA

octor Morley likes to tell visitors that there are ninety-one steps on each side of El Castillo. As the pyramid has four sides, each with ninety-one steps, that adds up to three-hundred and sixty-four steps. Then there is the top platform, where the high temple sits. If you count that as another step it all equals three-hundred and sixty-five steps.

A perfect year. One step per day.

Doctor Morley's take was that you could climb the pyramid and sit on a different step each day. That way you would have a fresh perspective on the ruins—and perhaps life—daily.

Which I thought was bullshit, for two reasons:

Number one, we all know the Mayans didn't build the Pyramid of Kukulcan for scenic viewing purposes.

Number two, I had tested Doctor Morley's perspective theory over and over … and it didn't work. I had been climbing this goddamn pyramid every single day for the past two months, to get away from everyone and smoke my cigarettes in peace. I had moved around and sat on every goddamn step and looked at things from every direction possible.

But my perspective—on life, that is—hadn't changed one bit. I was still seeing things the same way. The same thoughts, the same scene … they all kept playing over and over again in my mind:

The cave. Lindbergh. The sword, the pistol. The flash of light, that awful sound. The Dead Writer.

I took a deep drag off my Campeone. On the inhale I prayed for inner peace. On the exhale I achieved nothing of the sort, the memories of all that awfulness lodged in my frontal cortex.

So I tried again without the Campeone, taking a long, smoke-less breath deep into my lungs. Then, on the exhale, I attempted to calm myself by humming a little bit of *Habanera*:

"Bum-bum-bum … ba-da bum-bum … ba-da-da rumpa-tumpa-rum-bum-bum."

And that seemed to do the trick. I found myself transported back to a happier time, that night we had the talent show on the ball-court. The night I spoofed Doctor Morley with a version of Bizet's finest and first got to know Oliver. Before everything got so batshit crazy.

Then I got back to my smoke and my epic view. I was going to miss this spot, even if the trip was only for a month. The pyramid was my place to be alone … and alone was my preferred state of being.

I took a deep drag and watched some workers below, trying to re-position a large stone on the Platform of the Eagles and Jaguars. The sun had not been up that long but already the humidity was thick and the men kept stopping to wipe their brows.

I wouldn't miss the heat, that's for sure. It would be good to be away from the Yucatán. Spain would be cooler,

I assumed. And getting out of here would allow me to forget what happened ... hopefully.

A shout came from below:

"Wendy!"

It was Tatiana. I saw her out of the corner of my eye. She was standing next to one of the carved serpent heads at the base of the south steps. She was looking up, using a hand to shield her eyes from the sun. I figured if I ignored her I could buy myself another minute of solitude.

"Wendy!" she hollered again. I kept my gaze locked on the horizon for a moment but it was no use.

"Oh, stop that! I know you can hear me!" she yelled next.

I gave her the one-minute finger and took one last glorious drag off my Campeone. I snuffed it out on the step, then dug in my shoulder bag for the stinky little tin I carried for spent cigarette butts. Doctor Morley didn't like to find butts on top of his cherished pyramid. I had learned that lesson the hard way.

"Don't make him wait!" came another shout.

I gave the gods above a big eye roll. I opened the tin and dropped the butt in it and stashed the tin back in my shoulder bag. I pushed myself up and brushed my bum off and started down.

"Hustle, sweetie. He needs you," Tatiana repeated, as if I hadn't gotten the hint. I hollered back:

"He told me we weren't leaving until after eight!"

"He needs you to talk with a visitor," came the response. "Come on, let's go. He's getting impatient."

"Impatient. Shocking," I muttered.

I grabbed hold of the rope that ran down the center of the steps and began my steep descent. I knew there were visitors staying at the Hacienda, but I hadn't seen them and couldn't imagine what they wanted with me.

Perhaps they were here from the Carnegie Institution. Perhaps they were going to dis-invite me from the trip and I wouldn't be going to Spain after all. Maybe they had realized I was a miserable wreck and poor company and more in need of a firing than a trip to Europe.

I tried to shake that thought. I focused on the steps and used the rope to steady myself as I climbed down.

A foreman had come to talk with Tatiana and with her distracted I paused to take a last look over the ruins. The ancient complex looked like a construction site, even at this early hour. Over by the Temple of the Warriors, a dozen men were trying to hoist a column into position. Doctor Morris was supervising them. He was holding a clipboard with one hand and pointing with his other, looking quite ready to become boss upon Doctor Morley's departure. Beyond them, another team was picking grass and weeds from a series of steps near the ruins of the market.

As I neared the bottom the foreman who had been talking with Tatiana turned to me and tipped his sombrero.

"Tenga un buen viaje," he said. "Have a good trip, señorita."

"Gracias, Adolfo," I replied. "No me iré por mucho tiempo. I won't be gone long."

"Ah, muy bien," Adolfo said. Then he tipped his cap a second time, turned and walked off in the direction of Doctor Morris.

I came off the last step and onto terra firma. Tatiana was giving me a funny look.

"Up there praying?" she asked.

"You better believe it," I answered. "Praying for peace and serenity."

"Ha! Good luck with that. Did you wish for a flying unicorn too?"

"I did, actually. So how's my travelling companion doing?"

"You know the answer to that," Tatiana said as we started walking. "Rattling off orders like he's the new Napoleon."

"That's an actual malady, you know. What does he want from me?"

"There's a lawyer here. They want you to sign something."

"A lawyer? Sign what?"

"I'll let them explain it," she said and changed the topic. "So ... I see you're still smoking those wretched Marlboros. You better not have left any butts up there."

"They're Campeones. And rest assured there are no butts on his precious pyramid."

"Good. He hates that."

"Trust me, I know," I replied.

We came onto the dusty road that bisected the ruins and led toward the Hacienda. As we walked we heard a familiar rumble approaching from behind us: Señor Peon's truck was coming in on the road from Merida.

As he drove through the site all the workers stopped for a moment and some of them waved their hats. Señor Peon slowed his truck and leaned out and waved back. Then he honked the ridiculous horn on his truck, to more cheers from the workers. It was a silly scene that repeated itself every time he arrived, which was most every day.

Señor Peon slowed his truck as he passed us. He had an elbow out the window and a great smile on his weathered face.

"Hola, señor!" we said in accidental unison, like dopey schoolgirls.

"Buenos días, señoritas. Te veo pronto," he said as he rolled by.

He kept motoring down the road, toward the Hacienda. More workers stopped to wave and Señor Peon honked his silly horn again.

Tatiana and I walked in silence for an all-too-brief moment, then she took an audible breath in and spoke.

"Wendy," my mentor said, her tone lower and more serious. "There's a ... delicate matter I'd like to discuss before you leave ...,"

"I know, ease up on the smoking," I said, cutting her off, knowing full well that wasn't what she was talking about.

"You know that's not what I'm talking about," she confirmed.

"The reading? My Twain addiction?" I went on, trying to avoid the discussion. "Or my shoes ... too clunky for the city?"

"Hardy-har. You know what I'm talking about, sister," she said. "It's ... the brooding. And the drinking."

"The *brooding*?" I protested, expecting her second accusation but not the first. "I don't *brood*."

"Oh, yes you do. You brood, you mope around, you snap at people all the time, you scurry up your pyramid to smoke your stinky cigarettes all alone. Ever since the incident you've been, well ... anti-social. Do you know what that term means, anti-social?"

"I do, and I'm not," I snapped. "Besides, you can't be both a drunk and anti-social."

"I didn't say you were a drunk. I said I wanted to talk about your drinking."

"No, you said I was brooding. Brooding and being a drunk are two sides of the same coin."

"They don't have to be," she said.

I opted to bite my tongue, a skill I had been trying to develop with little success. Tatiana looked over and studied me. Her look was one of both pity and misunderstanding.

We came under the trees lining the road to the Hacienda. It was much cooler. Light was filtering through the leaves and there were birds tweeting overhead. From far off I could hear the caw-caw of a parrot. It was lovely and peaceful until Tatiana opened her mouth and ruined it:

"I'm worried about you, Wendy," she said. "You went through something awful. Our hearts break for you. But ..."

"But … what?"

"Well, I worry that you've allowed a horrible, traumatic event to become even worse. You need to …"

"Get over it?" I said, stopping and wheeling around to face her. "That's what you're going to say, right? Get over it?"

I had my hands on my hips. I realized I was biting my lower lip, another bad habit. Tatiana was looking at me with a very serious look, but then one side of her mouth curled up. She started to nod her head.

"My goodness, look at you," she said. "You need to stop this, Wendy. Look at yourself! You look like you're gonna take a swing at me! Stop biting your lip!"

I took a deep breath. I closed my eyes for a second and tried to calm myself down.

"We love you, sweetie, you know that," Tatiana said while my eyes were still closed. "But your emotions are always bubbling right under the surface of your skin. You need to relax. Stop being so … touchy."

She was right, I knew that, but I still hated to hear it. I could feel a tear welling up in one eye. I used my will power to stop it. Crying was for weak people.

"You need to come to terms with what happened," she went on. "Otherwise it's going to continue to haunt you. And you deserve better than that."

My eyes were open now. The rogue tear had retreated upstream.

"That sure as hell sounds like 'get over it' to me," I grumbled.

Tatiana let out her famous half-laugh of frustration. I deserved that, too.

"I'm sorry, Tat," I said. "It's been tough."

She didn't respond but gave me an understanding nod. We started walking again and for a glorious minute we strode in silence down the familiar dusty road. Again, Tatiana ruined it.

"Since you're already pissed off, I'll circle back to my first point," she said. "You need to take it easy over there. Morley would drive the Pope to drink. But you need to watch out for yourself."

"I always watch out for myself."

"There's a big difference between getting drunk at the Hacienda and getting drunk in Madrid."

"Better wine?"

"Well, of course," she relented. "Better wine, better food, better men. But you shouldn't overdo it on any of them, alright? Have fun, see the sights ... but remember the task at hand."

"Mm-hm," I said. "The great and mysterious treasure of Tenochtitlan. How could I ever forget?"

Now Tatiana stopped and glared at me.

"Oh, stop that. Such attitude. That's what I'm afraid of, you know. You'll use that mocking tone of yours and piss everyone off," she said with a wag of her finger. "And as we've discussed, many times before, what you or I believe—or don't believe—doesn't matter. It doesn't matter one bit. Alright?"

I looked at her and smiled and nodded. Yes, we had talked about this many times before. I knew her thoughts on all this and she knew mine. I had come to believe it was all silly rubbish, a fool's errand, a snipe hunt. Tatiana, ever the wise one, thought I should keep my mouth shut.

"But back to my point," she said, now reaching out and laying a sympathetic hand on one of my crossed arms. "About, you know, the brooding … and the drinking …,"

"Actually, I think people drink and only *after* do they brood," I interjected. I uncrossed my arms, her hand fell away and we started walking again.

"Whatever. All I'm saying is take it easy. Don't get all mopey and then sauced and then … you know, party all night long …," Tatiana continued, waving her arms in the air. "… And then expect to be able to do the things your boss expects of you. You know how demanding he can be."

I thought about that for a second, and couldn't resist a smart-ass answer.

"So you're saying if I'm mopey, then I get sauced, I get to party all night long?" I said. "That sounds rather pleasant."

"It's pleasant as its happening. It's not pleasant the next day," she said. "And Sylvanus could make anyone's hangover ten times worse."

"I'm joking. I get it. Take it easy."

"Right. Take it easy."

She went quiet, which was good since I had no appetite to discuss the matter further. The two of us walked without talking for a little bit. Then, to break the silence, I spoke up:

"You know, I've never been to a party where people do that."

"Do what?" Tatiana asked.

"Wave their hands in the air like that," I said.

"Like this?" Tatiana said, raising her hands high up above her head again and wiggling her fingers. "Oh, those are the best parties there are!"

"Do they have parties like that in Spain?"

"I hope not while you're there, my dear," came the answer.

We both laughed. Tatiana patted me on the back and we walked the rest of the way to the Hacienda without further awkwardness.

***

Señor Peon's truck was out front. Señor Peon himself was holding the door open for two houseboys coming out of the Hacienda. They were carrying Doctor Morley's bags.

"So much for leaving sometime after eight," I muttered.

"You know Vay. When he says eight, he means seven-thirty," Tatiana replied.

Señor Peon turned and saw us approaching. He held the old wooden door open for us.

As we passed inside he said to me, in a whisper, "You are ready for your big adventure, no?"

"As ready as I'll ever be," I whispered back.

"You and him together for a whole month ... es loco, no?" Señor Peon added.

"Muy loco, amigo, muy loco," I replied.

Señor Peon unfurled his broad smile and tipped his hat as he closed the door behind him.

It was cool and dry inside and walking into the Hacienda always felt good. I followed Tatiana down the main hall and past our makeshift library. She turned around to make sure I was behind her and hadn't run off.

The door to the dining room was closed. She gave a rap of her knuckles as she opened it.

Doctor Morley was sitting at the longest table, jabbering away at another man whose face I couldn't see yet. They had a collection of papers in small piles in front of them. Doctor Morley didn't stop talking when we walked in, which was typical of him, but the other man noticed us, stood up and smiled.

"Hold on, Sylvanus, hold on," the guest said. "It's hard to keep up with you. You really need to write more of this down."

Then he extended his hand to me and said:

"Now ... this must be Miss Willowtree."

"Willoughby," I corrected him.

"Oh, that's right, Miss Willoughby. I should have remembered that. My apologies. Please, have a seat," he said, motioning to a chair on his side of the table.

The lawyer's clothes looked fancy. He was wearing cufflinks and cologne. His hair was combed back and pressed down. I would have bet a dollar he was from New York.

I took my seat. Doctor Morley was mumbling reminders to himself and writing them down in his notebook. He still hadn't acknowledged my presence. But when Tatiana sat down next to him he leaned over toward her and started whispering something to her. I was growing more and more nervous.

The lawyer scooted his chair forward and cleared his throat. That got Doctor Morley's attention. My boss stopped his murmuring and looked over the table to me.

"Ah, yes," Doctor Morley began. "Wendy, this is ...,"

"Benjamin Bow," the other man said, cutting Doctor Morley off.

"Right," Doctor Morley chimed in. "And Ben is here on behalf of the Metropol ..."

"*Ahem* ... I'm here on behalf of a variety of partners," Mister Bow said, interrupting Doctor Morley again and giving him a glare.

"A variety of partners. Right," Doctor Morley said, then he smacked his lips in his funny way. "You know ... perhaps it's best I just let Mister Bow do the talking."

"Much appreciated, Sylvanus," the man replied, making my boss wince.

The lawyer scooched his chair toward me, leaned forward and looked me in the eyes. He gave me a very fake but very professional smile.

"Miss Willoughby," he began. "Let me start by saying I'm very impressed with what I've seen of your artwork. Especially those drawings of the Mayan priests on the pyramid, with all the people gathered below. It's quite ... engrossing."

I was never comfortable with compliments and I especially disliked clumsy ones.

"Engrossing. That's lovely. Thank you."

"Perhaps spellbinding is a more appropriate word," he went on. "Sylvanus showed me a large illustration that you did of the big pyramid, as it looked during the time of the Maya, when it was painted red and yellow. It was stunning, really."

"Thank you."

"Now, Wendy ... may I call you Wendy?"

"You may."

"Wendy, my role in ... um ... matters like this is to handle the boring stuff. Paperwork. You know."

"For Carnegie?" I asked.

Mister Bow smacked his lips and paused before responding.

"Well, yes, for the Institution ... along with certain partners of theirs."

"What partners?" I inquired.

The lawyer took a deep breath. "Like I said, a variety of partners."

"Pan American?"

"Pardon?"

"You heard me: Pan American. Do you represent them too?"

"Pan American? Well ... no, I don't."

I studied his suspicious New York City eyes for a moment. The way he said it was dodgy.

"And ... what about Juan Trippe?" I said, confident he would break. But he didn't.

"No and no," Mister Bow replied. "I don't represent Juan Trippe and I don't represent Pan American."

As I glared at him he anticipated the exact question I was about to ask. He said:

"… And, to save us both some time, I don't represent Colonel Lindbergh either."

Then he stared at me and smiled and didn't blink. I stared right back, with no smile. I still wasn't sure I believed him—out of principle I don't trust lawyers—but I didn't push it.

The lawyer took off his glasses and placed them on a stack of papers. He let out a sigh.

"You know, Wendy … let's start over, alright?" he said. "And I'll begin. I'll begin by saying what I should have said to you the moment you walked in that door: I am very, very sorry you had to go through what you went through. I'm not privy to all the details, but ..."

"Would you *like* to know the details, Mister Bow?" I interrupted.

His mouth was stuck half-open and his eyes were like saucers.

"No. No, I … I just hope that ... that you're finding the support and guidance you need. That's all," he stammered. "Everyone needs a little help from time to time."

I didn't dignify his amateur psychoanalysis with a response. I glanced over to Doctor Morley, who was squinting at me, and then to Tatiana. She gave me one of those looks that told me I was being naughty and needed to behave.

I took a deep breath and motioned to a stack of papers the lawyer had in front of him.

"I assume you want me to sign something?"

Mister Bow seemed relieved our little battle was over. He looked down at the papers then straightened up in his chair. He picked up his pen and tapped it on the table.

"Ah, yes, indeed. We have been very remiss in not doing this sooner, but better late than never." he went on. "Now, Miss Willoughby ... sorry, Wendy ... Doctor Morley tells me you're originally from Vermont?"

I nodded.

"Never been myself. I hear its cold up there."

"Only in winter," I said, returning one stupid comment with another.

"Only in winter. Huh. Right, right," he said. "And where'd you go to school?"

I hadn't gone to college and that bothered some people so I always tiptoed around this topic.

"Saint Johnsbury," I said.

"Is that a college?" he asked.

"It's ... an academy."

"An academy, okay. But, Wendy, you've got a pretty good way with words, am I right? You can read a document or a contract and understand it, can't you?" Mister Bow went on.

"I guess it depends on what I'm reading."

The lawyer reached down to one of the piles of papers and slid them in front of me.

"This document here is what we call a do-no-disclose agreement. It means you can't talk to anyone about what you're doing on this trip," Mister Bow said. "That means all your work with the Codex, or any other work you do for the Carnegie Institution on the trip, is not to be discussed. At all. With anyone. For any reason. *Ever.*"

And with that short explanation he reached out to hand me the pen. As he reached for the inkwell I glanced over at Doctor Morley. He, in turn, arched his eyebrows and looked at me over his glasses.

"You have to sign," my boss said. "If you don't, I can't take you."

I didn't like to sign anything other than my art. I turned back to Mister Bow.

"So ... if I want to write a book about my trip to Spain, thirty years from now, I can't?" I asked.

Mister Bow gave me another smile, real this time.

"A book?" he said "Miss Willoughby, I've been to Spain several times myself. And if I can give you a piece of advice, only Spaniards understand Spain enough to write a book about the place. When Americans try, they come off looking like ignorant asses. Don't do it."

"So you're saying don't do it ... but it's still okay to do it?"

"To do what?"

"To write a book. About Spain. You're saying that's permissible."

The lawyer let out a can-you-believe-this laugh and made a bewildered face to Doctor Morley.

"Perhaps I'm making myself less than clear?" Mister Bow said. "The answer is no. You can't write a book, at least not about this trip or your work for the Institution. Again, by signing this document you promise you will never divulge information pertaining to this journey to third parties. If you do, there will be consequences."

"Consequences. Like what?" I said, knowing I should shut up but unable to do so.

The lawyer took another, deeper breath. Doctor Morley sighed in fraternal frustration and looked to the ceiling.

"*Significant* consequences," Mister Bow finally said, oh-so-serious.

"Just sign the damn piece of paper, Wendy," Doctor Morley growled.

"I want to read it first."

"Please do. But it's non-negotiable," Mister Bow shot back.

Then he and Doctor Morley both stared at me. Tatiana was trying to avoid eye contact. To hell with them, I was at least going to read it. The two men groaned as I picked up the papers and began to flip through them.

The document was five pages long. The print was tiny. There were lots of 'whereases' and 'heretofores' and 'accordinglys.' There were repeated references to the 'Institution' and the 'Museum' and the 'Coalition.' The words 'shall not' appeared over and over and over again.

I scanned every page, knowing full well it was making the men furious. I came to the last page and read the last paragraph. I paused on the final sentence and read it out loud:

"This agreement also pertains to any and all information acquired during, or related to, the so-called 'Yaxchilan Incident.'"

I looked up at Mister Bow.

"Does this mean I can't talk to people about what happened in the jungle?"

Mister Bow looked over at Doctor Morley then back to me. He said:

"The jungle? Well, yes. At least as it relates to ... you know. The project, as it were."

"I don't think that 'incident' was really part of the 'project' ... do you?"

"Well, yes, I do," the lawyer said. "Your discoveries toward the end of that ... incident ... were very much relevant to the, um, project."

"I thought you said this was about our trip to Spain."

Mister Bow pursed his lips. "Well, it is. But it's also about the broader project, of course."

"Stop calling it a 'project.'"

"The mission, then," the lawyer shot back.

"The mission," I said. "You mean ... the treasure."

That pissed Mister Bow off. He furrowed his eyebrows and made a little sucking sound with his lips and leaned back in his chair. He tapped his fingers on the table and looked first at me and then over to Doctor Morley. But I wasn't done talking.

"And what about Lindbergh?" I said, knowing full well the answer. "Does this mean I can't say anything about him? Or what he did?"

Mister Bow took a breath.

"Again, he is not my client. Colonel Lindbergh has his own lawyers and I'm not one of them," he said. "As you can see on the signature page, he is not a party to this agreement. But I would caution you, Miss Willoughby ... I went to school with some of Colonel Lindbergh's lawyers and they're very, very good."

What a lousy answer. Now I really didn't want to sign it. But the moment was at hand. I looked over to Doctor Morley and then Tatiana and they were both giving me you-better-sign-that-damn-thing looks.

And I wanted to go. I had been miserable and angry for too long. I knew deep down the trip would almost certainly do me some good. I had dreamed of going to Europe since I was a little girl; I wanted to see the museums and the architecture and the palaces. I wanted to soak in the culture, by which I mean I wanted to get liquored up at some picturesque sidewalk café. So I swallowed the remainder of my pride and pulled out the signature page. Without another snarky word, I dipped the pen in and scrawled out my name.

"Initial all the other pages too, please," Mister Bow said.

Damn lawyers. I flipped page to page, putting 'WW' on the bottom of each one. As I made my final mark Mister Bow spoke again:

"And remember, as the saying goes, loose lips sink ships."

I put the pen down and glared at him.

"That's not the thing to say to someone about to get on an ocean liner," I said.

"Oops, sorry, figure of speech," the lawyer replied, a satisfied grin on his steak-fed mug. "Thank you, Miss Willoughby, for your understanding."

"My pleasure," I lied.

Then Doctor Morley motioned to Tatiana, and she motioned to me. She and I got up to leave. Doctor Morley stayed in his seat, but Mister Bow stood up reached out his hand.

"I hope you have a safe and productive journey," he said. "If you have the time, make sure you visit the Prado. It's remarkable."

At last he was speaking a language I could appreciate.

"It's on my list," I replied, which was the truth. I gave him a polite nod-and-smile and followed Tatiana out to the hallway.

As we walked out and Tatiana closed the door I overheard Doctor Morley grumbling to Mister Bow:

"The Prado? She doesn't need sightseeing tips, Benjamin ... keeping her focused is hard enough as it is."

***

Tatiana walked with me to my cottage. In preparation for my departure I had spent some time tidying up the place, which was usually an absoluter disaster. It was, I'm proud to say, the cleanest it had been in well over a year.

She insisted on going through the clothes I had packed, all my shirts and dresses and privates. She was sweet and wanted to make sure I had everything.

"Don't forget something red. You'll want to wear red in Seville, when you go to the Exposition," Tatiana said.

"Why red?" I asked. She looked at me like I was a moron.

"Because it's Seville, Wendy!" she exclaimed. "*Carmen*! Matadors! Barbers! You have to wear red!"

I didn't understand what barbers had to do with it, but I took her advice. I traded out one of three tan skirts for a long-sleeved dress I had considered packing.

"Goodness," she said when she saw it. "That's more of a burgundy, isn't it? And haven't you got something that's a little more, you know, modern?"

"Hmph! No," I replied. "This is the nicest thing I have, thank you very much."

"Oh, don't take it that way. It's a city, alright? Cities are always fancy," she said. "But anything looks good on you, I should stop nitpicking. Now, what else do we have?"

We continued our review of my luggage. As Tatiana was re-packing my clothes she kept ticking off travel tips. She was like a big sister to me.

"Big cities can be dangerous," she warned. "Remember that. You'll have to be careful."

"What's that supposed to mean?"

"We both know what I mean," she replied. "Don't be walking down any dark alleys all dolled-up and wall-eyed. That's just asking for trouble."

"It shouldn't be."

"No, it shouldn't be … and perhaps one day it won't be. But for now it's an unfortunate truth you must be aware of," Tatiana said. "You remember what I told you, right? How to protect yourself against any aggressive male, big or small?"

"Kick them," I answered.

"Where?"

"In the nuts."

"Damn straight. Dead center, right between the legs. The harder the better," Tatiana deadpanned.

"I don't think I have the heart," I said.

"But if it's your only option you can't be afraid to use it," she advised. "A firm kick to the balls will drive any male attacker away ... but you have to have the courage to make that kick."

"Tatiana, please ...,"

"And like I said, the harder the better. Bring that foot up firm and fast," she said, doing a half-kick.

"Oh, stop."

"Just making sure you're prepared for whatever comes your way. Now, where's your passport?"

"It's in my shoulder bag."

"Is that the best place for it?" she asked.

"Well, I suppose it is. I'll have my shoulder bag with me every day, the entire trip."

"I suppose that's alright. Don't lose it, okay? You'll probably need it here in Progreso, when you board the ship. Ask Fernando on the ride, he'll know. Now, money ... Vay will give you some money once he exchanges his dollars. I suspect he'll do that on the boat, exchange rates be damned. He won't have the patience to wait until he gets to Madrid.

Make sure he gives you what he's supposed to give you, okay? And you have some of your own American money too, right?"

"Yes."

"How much?" she asked.

"About seventy-five, I think."

Tatiana gave me a big smile. She reached into her shirt pocket and pulled out a twenty dollar bill.

"Here's some extra," she said. "A month is a long time to be away. Don't thank me, just toast to my generosity in some classy place, okay? Now, where are you keeping your dinero?"

I patted my tummy.

"My secret hiding place," I confided. I undid two buttons on my shirt so I could access the money belt hidden around my waist. I fished around until I found the zipper, then I tucked the twenty in with my other bills.

"Ooh, that's a nice one," Tatiana said as she watched me. "Very discrete. You're keeping all your money in there?"

"I think so," I said, re-doing my buttons and smoothing my shirt. "There, look. You can't even tell I have it on, can you?"

"No, I can't. But shouldn't you be keeping some spending money in your bag? Otherwise you'll have to show your clever little belt every time you need a bill. That defeats its purpose, doesn't it? Before you get to Havana you should make sure to do that."

"I will."

"Good, good. Alright, let's go through your art supplies."

We had been through my supplies twice before, but I knew she wouldn't rest until we did it again. I went to pull my drawing kit out of the suitcase. As I lifted it I caught sight of my two letters from Moses, which had been laying underneath the kit. I didn't want Tatiana to see those and ask questions, so I snatched them both up before she spied them. I tucked them under some papers that I was supposed to review before the trip, which I had not.

I laid my art kit on the bed next to my empty notebooks. I undid the latches to the kit and opened it. Tatiana started going through it like a teacher on the first day of school:

"Notebooks, check. A ruler, check. Protractor, check. Pencils, erasers, check, check. Charcoal. Is this all you have? I suppose that's enough. Now those pencils. Let's count the blue pencils again, you'll be shocked at how blue the Codex is. Orange, too. Ooh, that little sharpener, do you still have that?"

"Yes, ma'am."

"Good, good. Oh … did I ask you about a hat?"

"Lordy, you're thorough. Yes, I have a hat,"

"Shoes?"

"Three pair."

"I mean *nice* shoes, Wendy," she said, trying but failing to be subtle. "Not those clunky boots you like to wear around the ruins."

"My boots are made for walking. They're very comfortable."

"And not fit for a fancy dinner on a ship or in a hotel! Show me the others you're bringing."

I dug down and pulled out my red platforms and a black pair with modest heels. I held them up for her approval.

"Oh, those red ones are pretty. Those should work fine. You'll be with Veronica Shetty, you know. Have to keep up."

"I have no desire to keep up with Miss Shitty."

"It's *Shetty* … not *Shitty*," Tatiana said, smirking. "You really have to stop saying it like that."

"But it fits her so well!" I explained, which was true. "She should just change her name to Veronica Shitty and make it easier on everyone."

"If you don't stop saying it like that, you're going to slip up and say it to her face," she said. "And if you piss her off, you piss off the powers that be."

"Doctor Morley or the Institution?"

"Both and then some."

"I'll do my best," I said. "Here, I'll practice. Good morning, Miss Shh-Etty."

Tatiana giggled. Then I said it again, even slower, and the slower I said it, the more it sounded like 'Miss Shitty.'

"No, it's like this: Sheet-Tee," Tatiana said, which sounded even worse.

We both laughed and kept making fun of Veronica's crappy last name as we finished the inventory of my bags. Tatiana tried to imagine how our poor victim would respond if I called her Miss Shitty to her face.

"Ah, Miss Willoughby, as usual your manners are as horrid as your shoes!" Tatiana said in a too-proper English accent.

"You sound just like the real thing," I remarked.

"Excuse me while I light my very expensive cigarette," she went on, keeping up with her impression. "They're Turkish, you know. A blind man rolls them for me at the Istanbul bazaar. I'd offer you one, but they're much too sophisticated for you."

Her voice was spot on. She sounded like the real Shitty. We got laughing so hard we started crying.

***

Twenty minutes later there was a small gaggle in front of the Hacienda to see us off.

My colleagues and former roommates Susan and Emily were both there. They gave me big hugs and as Emily hugged me she slipped me a little flask. She whispered that it had Widow Watson's whiskey in it—my absolute favorite. It was such a beautiful gesture I hugged Emily a second time.

I said good-bye to Doctor Morris then good-bye to David, the lucky dolt of a researcher that I went too far with one night. Next I gave a big hug to Jimmy Chan, the cook, and Tarsisio, our major domo. Then I gave one last big hug to Tatiana. She pulled me close to whisper in my ear:

"Don't go starting any wars, alright?"

"I never start them, I only participate in them," I reminded her.

After Señor Peon loaded our bags into the back of truck he came around to hold the door open. Without discussion I shimmied my ass to the middle of the seat. I'd be stuck there, between the driver and Doctor Morley, for five hours, all the way to Progreso. I thought about asking to sit in the back, under the tarp, but I knew they wouldn't let me sit back there alone.

Doctor Morley was having a few final words with Doctor Morris and Tatiana:

"The Thompsons will be here Friday. Make sure Tarsisio has their cottage clean and ready to go," he instructed. "Keep everyone on time … and please, please, don't let any teams work around El Caracol unless one of you is present."

"Fear not, the world will stop spinning until your return," Doctor Morris said as they shook hands.

"As it should, as it should," Doctor Morley said. "Oh, and make sure Jimmy comes up with something special for the Thompsons that first night? Perhaps the duck again?"

"The dinner menus should be the least of your concerns, Vay," Tatiana said. Then she gave Doctor Morley a hug and a peck on the cheek.

Doctor Morley donned his pith helmet and shook hands with Doctor Morris. Then he got in the truck and gave a great enthusiastic wave out the window. Everyone waved back and then hip-hip-hoorayed as we drove away from the Hacienda.

Then we bounced down the dusty road until we came out of the trees and into the ruins. Doctor Morley asked Señor Peon to slow down so he could wave again. All the workers stopped and perched their tools and clapped and cheered. They looked very, very happy. I'm sure Doctor Morley assumed they were excited for him, but I knew the truth: the workers were ecstatic that the boss was leaving.

***

For four and a half dreadful hours I had to sit between Doctor Morley and Señor Peon and listen to them rattle on and on about their grandiose ambitions.

Señor Peon had been bringing travelers from Merida out to see the ruins. He and his family had grand plans for a new hotel near the Hacienda, so folks could spend the night and have a good meal. That got Doctor Morley babbling on about doing more excavations to get the site ready and safe for more visitors. As the two of them babbled away they became more and more animated and annoying. At one point I even drooped my head and feigned being asleep to try to get them to shut up. It didn't work. When we arrived in Progreso, and I was released from my middle-seat prison, I was so happy to be out of that damn truck I could have kissed the ground.

The liner was already there, connected to the pier by a single gangplank. It was larger and much taller than I expected. Señor Peon unloaded our suitcases and carried them to the edge of the pier and left them with a young man in a Ward Line jacket. Then he said good-bye to us and suddenly it was only me and Doctor Morley.

I studied my boss for a moment. This short, overdressed, determined man who dominated my waking hours was scanning the ship from end to end. He looked a bit off. He gulped, like his tummy was acting up.

"Why does travel always involve so much ... *travel?*" he said in a low voice, more to himself.

My eyes followed his gaze up to the tons of steel that would float us across the deep, dark ocean. It looked big and old and heavy. I didn't much care for ships and this was the part of the adventure I had been dreading most. As we stood looking up in the hot sun, all my fears and anxieties began to percolate inside me.

Then we started up the gangplank, at the end of which stood a broad-smiled attendant. As I climbed the gangplank I could feel the contents my stomach rising in proportion to my elevation. It all bubbled up into my chest, then into my throat and I knew where it was going next.

Doctor Morley was coming up the gangplank just in back of me. The attendant was now only a few steps in front of me, still smiling, waiting to welcome us aboard.

I tried to smile back. Then I could feel my innards rushing up to say hello. I knew it was helpless. I grabbed the railing and barfed into the Gulf of Mexico.

I was shocked and embarrassed, Doctor Morley more so. I used a hand to wipe the nastiness off my lips, tried to compose myself and then looked up to the attendant. He still had the same goofy smile.

"Welcome aboard the Orizaba, ma'am!" he said, in English. "And don't worry ... vomiting before boarding is good luck!"

And he laughed, as if he was being funny. His poor humor made me lightheaded and for a second I thought I might lose my innards again, on him. The attendant noticed and hailed to another crew member. In a flash someone rushed up with a wheelchair. They slid it under me and I sat down.

"I'm ... I'm just nauseous," I tried to explain.

The first attendant asked for my passport. I pulled it out of my bag and gave it to him. He looked at it and then consulted a list and then barked a cabin number to the attendant who had brought the wheelchair over. Another attendant came up and took my bags. Before I knew it, I was being wheeled away from Doctor Morley and down the deck.

The first attendant maneuvered the wheelchair through a tight door, then backed me into a little lift that brought us down to a lower level. Then he wheeled me down a long hallway and right up to the door of my cabin. The second attendant—the one carrying my bags—fumbled for the key, unlocked the door and pushed it open.

Then the two of them, together, hoisted me out of the chair. They carried me over the threshold like I was the luckiest bride in the world ... and then dumped me on the bed like a lifeless corpse.

"Disfruta tu viaje," one of them said on the way out the door.

Enjoy your voyage. My tummy did a cartwheel, as if to say it had no intention of letting me enjoy a damn thing.

2
ABOARD THE ORIZABA

That night, while I was asleep, awful memories awoke in my head.

There I was, back at Yaxchilan, in the cave. Lindbergh had confronted us. His eyes were bloody and he was wild with anger. I could hear Mister Trippe trying to calm him down. I could see Oliver pulling out his little penknife and trying to talk sense into the madman. I could feel the rush of air as Lindbergh fired the flare gun, sending the bats into a tizzy. Then he turned to the writer and…

… I startled myself awake. It was just another bad dream, I told myself. But then I opened my eyes and all I could see above me was a long body-length wooden board. Then my hand brushed against soft fabric hanging to my side. Terror washed over me: I was in a coffin. I had been buried alive! I thrashed out in panic.

In the midst of my thrashing I kicked the bed curtain back. Only then did my beleaguered brain remember we had boarded a liner the previous day. What I had assumed was the lid of my casket was, in fact, only the bottom of the upper bunk.

I sat up and surveyed my small, dark quarters. Then I rose and threw open the curtain covering the small porthole. The sun was in front of the boat, on the other side and still low. I fumbled along the wall to find the electric wall lamp.

The light revealed a modest but efficient cabin. There was a compact armchair, bolted to the floor. There was a little bureau, which also served as the nightstand and the cabin's lone table. There was a miniaturized porcelain sink crammed into the corner, and in front of it—to the side of the armchair—was an undersized john.

It was a fine cabin, I suppose. I had envisioned my first transatlantic voyage being opulent and luxurious, like the Titanic—without the sinking, of course. But I wasn't paying and could never afford this journey on my own, so I was in no position to complain.

I found my luggage and my shoulder bag stashed in the narrow closet. I freshened up, put on fresh clothes and double-checked the dinero in my money-belt. Then I went to find Doctor Morley.

***

The interior corridors were narrow with dim lighting and low ceilings. The carpeting was worn through in many spots. There was a musty odor that permeated the entire ship. The Titanic this most certainly was not.

It took me several minutes to find my first crew member, an unsmiling bursar. I asked where I could find Doctor Morley's cabin. He sighed, took out his passenger list and with a perturbed look scanned the first page, then the second. Finally he found it on the third:

"Morley. Silv ... Sy ...," he said, struggling with the first name.

"Sylvanus, that's right."

"Hmph. Third class. 342."

He said it in a snooty, harrumphing way and I gave him a good stare for that because I wasn't in the mood. He got my drift and directed me back the way I came.

When I found Doctor Morley's cabin I knocked.

"Vete, vete … Go away," came a tired voice.

"It's Wendy. Are you alright?"

There was a pause before he responded:

"Good to know you're alive."

"Thank you, it's good to be alive," I said. "But you don't sound so good."

"Just an upset tummy. I'm fine."

"Well, I know what it's like to have an upset tummy. Can I come in?"

There was another pause, then an audible groan followed by some shuffling around. The lock clicked and he opened the door.

When I saw the color of his face I flinched. His skin was a sickly white, almost translucent, but there was a hint of green to him, too.

"You're seasick," I said.

"No I'm not," he said. "Just tired."

He was wearing an untucked dress shirt over wrinkled suit pants. He staggered to the armchair and plopped himself down. As he sat he let out an ugly, nasty-smelling burp. He said:

"Our big adventure isn't off to much of a start."

"I've had enough big adventures lately," I replied. "Goodness, you smell worse than you look. You need to get back in bed."

"Stop your nursing. I'll have my sea-legs soon enough," he said, and burped again. "Sorry, my stomach is still getting used to the motions of the boat."

"Right, that's called being seasick," I told him. "Have you been ... feeding the birds?"

"Why would I feed birds?"

"It's an expression. Have you, you know ... lost your lunch? Tossed your cookies? Barfed?"

He let out another foul burp before he answered.

"That's confidential information ... but yes."

"That's good. Have you had something to drink? Or eat?"

"No and no."

"Well, get up. Let's find you a seltzer or a glass of water and some food," I said. "Trust me, moving around works wonders."

He groaned and griped but then he pushed himself up. He tucked in his shirt and tied his necktie and adjusted his belt. He matted his thinning hair down in the mirror. Then, even though he had fixed his hair, he grabbed his pith helmet and put it on.

"No sombrero?" I asked, a reference to the oversized, floppy laugh-getter he wore around Chichen Itza.

"The pith is better for travel," he answered. "Sturdier. Better ventilation."

"You're not going to wear that in Madrid, are you?"

"Ab-so-lute-ly," he replied, with a serious face. "Pith helmets are this year's hottest new fashion trend."

My seasick boss checked his tie one last time then stutter-stepped his way out the door.

***

Moving around did *not* work wonders on Doctor Morley.

As we made our way up to the main deck we experienced more of the pitch and roll of the liner. Doctor Morley tried to babble on as we climbed, but then he became silent. Then we finally came onto the main deck and he caught view of the heaving, spraying, unrelenting waves. He made an awful face and put a hand to his mouth. He sprinted to the railing, leaned over and did some heaving and spraying of his own.

When that was all over, I guided him to a bench protected from the wind. It had a partial view of the ocean, which made Doctor Morley groan again. I told him to stare at the floor. He did, which helped him catch his breath. Then he pulled a handkerchief out of the pocket of his trousers, wiped his mouth and said:

"When I was no more than five or six my mother took me on a train for the very first time. It was a special, going from our hometown all the way to the State Fair. The train was overflowing with happy families and excited children. The railroad had even hired a clown for the occasion.

"Well ... when we boarded I was just fine. I was having fun. Everyone was laughing. Then the train started rolling and right away my stomach turned inside-out. I told my mom I needed to get off, immediately. She told me we couldn't. Mind you, we hadn't gone a half-mile yet. And I *so* needed to throw up … but I kept it down. I didn't want to humiliate myself or, worse, my mother.

"And that dumb clown had been going up and down the aisle, entertaining the kids and whatnot. He was behind me and decided this was a good time to scare someone. So he grabbed my shoulder and yelled '*Boo!*' right in my ear. I turned and, without warning, began to vomit on him. Then, realizing what was happening, I turned the other way … and continued to vomit all over my mother."

Doctor Morley paused and sighed then kept going:

"The odor of my upchuck caused a near-riot. The children all began to shriek and gag and cry. That got all the mothers mad. They started yelling up to the attendants, telling them to stop the train.

"I was extremely upset, as you might imagine. My mother was horrified. Her dress was drenched with my vomit. Then the engineer stopped the train and made us get off. Told us we were ruining everyone's special day."

"Made you get off?" I remarked. "At the next station?"

"No. They told us we had to get off right then and there. In the middle of a cornfield. They ushered us out of our seats, quite forcefully. Several children made fake barfing noises to tease me as we left. Then the train took off … and my mother and I, both vomit-splattered, had to walk all the way home."

"That's horrible!"

"Isn't it? I've been uncomfortable with travel ever since. Trains, long motorcar rides over unfamiliar terrain, those damn aeroplanes … they all bring out the worst in me. Literally."

"My goodness," I said. "Poor thing. Kicking a child off a train. How awful."

"I am forever scarred," Doctor Morley said with a half-chuckle.

We sat in silence for a moment, but I know talking had made him feel better. Doctor Morley liked to talk. When he spoke next I could see some color was returning to his face and he was able to view the ocean without consequence.

"Wendy, I wanted to thank you for ... well, I should thank you for many things, I suppose," he said. "For coming along on this journey and abiding by all the, ahem, necessary ... precautions."

He was stammering a bit. I picked up he was referring to the signing ceremony back at Chichen Itza.

"You mean the blood oath?" I said, trying to be friendly about it. "Feel like I've joined Tom Sawyer's gang or something."

He gave a little laugh at that. "Me too," he said. "And I suppose I should mention our cabins. This is a lean operation, to put it mildly. And this route, going from Progreso to Havana to Cadiz, was a bit more expensive than going up through New York. Several days shorter, though, that's why I picked it. But then it came down to a choice between one shared second-class cabin or two separate third-class cabins. I thought we'd both prefer the privacy, even if it means somewhat less opulent accommodations."

"You made a wise choice," I said, which he had.

"Good, good, I think I did too," Doctor Morley said. "Now, you do know that Veronica Shetty will be meeting us in Madrid ..."

"How could I forget?" I said. Then, out of instinct, I added, "Will she be flying in on a thundercloud, or does she just appear in a cloud of smoke?"

"Ah-ha-ha. Witty," Doctor Morley replied. "Needless to say, if you pop off like that to her face it won't be pleasant for anyone. Trust me. So, as I was saying, she'll be meeting us in Madrid. She's at a different hotel, be grateful for that. She'll be coming in from Vienna. My understanding is th ..."

"Do you think she's a witch?" I interjected.

Doctor Morley lowered his chin so he could look at me over his glasses. "Enough. I can't make you like her, but you do need to keep your tongue in check. Alright?"

"If she's a witch she probably floats. We should dunk her in a river to find out."

"Quite the comedian you are. Now, if ...,"

"A she-devil!" I exclaimed, slapping a hand on my thigh. "A good old-fashioned she-devil, right out of ..."

"*E-nough!*" Doctor Morley growled, his teeth gritted, his face now flushed red. "I've got too many headaches already. I don't have time for ... for ... potential bickering from the ladies."

My jaw clenched and my spine stiffened. Bickering ladies? I had some choice words for him, but this time I caught myself and apologized instead.

"I'm sorry," I said, then I shut up. Doctor Morley let out a big breath and continued:

"Jim Thatcher, too. You've seen him around the ruins, I'm sure. Big man, small glasses. He'll be working with me at the Library, at least that's my current understanding. As for Veronica, I'm not sure what exactly she will be doing with you or myself—if anything. She likes to think of herself as management and everyone else as her laborers, if you know what I mean."

"I'm shocked."

"Yes, sure you are. It's the price I pay, though. Anyhoo, she might very well come over to the Museum to check on you, so be prepared and be on your best behavior. I don't want to have to break up any cat fights," he said.

I felt my claws spring ... but again my better angels won out and I maintained control. Then we sat there in silence and I, at least, watched the waves. The sun was to our back. There was no land in sight. I hoped the next words my boss said wouldn't tick me off. It was wishful thinking.

"Wendy," he said, in a lower and more-serious voice. "There's a ... somewhat delicate matter we should discuss ..."

He paused mid-sentence. My head spun toward him. Those sounded like Tatiana's exact words. Were they ganging up on me? As he continued I steeled myself and readied my response.

"... It's about, well, what we're looking for," he said, surprising me.

"That's not what I expected you to say."

"What did you expect me to say?"

"Never mind," I said. "Continue."

This was a notable moment. Doctor Morley didn't ever talk about *what* we were looking for. He talked all the time about *how* we were going to find it … but he never talked about *what* he expected to find.

Then, just as he was about to say something, two men came walking down the deck. They were talking in Spanish, not paying a lick of attention to us. Doctor Morley paused and waited for them to pass before continuing:

"I'm well aware that you have some doubts about the existence of what it is we are seeking. Tatiana has her doubts too, as I'm sure you know. And trust me, I have days where I'm convinced this whole thing is, to put it mildly, a wild goose-chase and an endeavor not worthy of my limited time."

That was a welcome confession. I had found it increasingly hard to believe that Doctor Morley believed in something that was, in a word, unbelievable.

"But circumstances being what they are, this is a mission we cannot take lightly," he went on. "There are financial repercussions to all this. I can't go into too much detail, but what we are being asked to do is critical to the Institution and to our work back home. Not just at Chichen Itza, but at sites throughout Mexico and Central America. And as much as I wish I were in charge, calling the shots as they say, the truth is I am not.

"So I find myself in a situation where I have to overlook the remarkableness of our quest and what we hope to find. Instead, I focus on the individual tasks needed to get there. First and foremost, that means your work with the Codex and my work in the Library.

"And my suggestion to you is a simple one: Let's just do our job and do it well. Then we can move on to Seville for the Expo. I do have a presentation to make, you know. I can't be spending all my time in Spain looking for the ... the ..."

He stammered and then pursed his lips together. I finished his sentence for him.

"The ... treasure?"

Doctor Morley nodded and said:

"Yes ... the treasure. That damn, damn treasure."

***

I knew he had work for me to do. But he didn't bring it up that afternoon, and I'll be damned if I was going to mention it.

Instead we learned about our ship, then learned our way around it.

A bursar informed us that the Orizaba had been built as a troop carrier during the latter parts of the War. After that the Ward Line had converted it to passenger service, with capacity for over a thousand. It still flew under the American flag and the majority of crew members looked and sounded American. The remainder appeared to be Spanish, which made sense as all the ship did was sail back and forth between Mexico, Cuba and ports in Spain.

There were forward and aft seating areas on the main deck. Between the seating areas, still on the main deck, was a fitness area filled with stupid-looking exercise machines. Near that was a big space where annoying people were playing annoying games. Several too-serious men were playing tug of war on one side, while on the other two dopey men were trying to play badminton with two beautiful women. Everyone was smiling. I hated them all.

Inside there were three dining rooms and a handful of small lounges. There was a barber shop and a beauty parlor and a little store. We spotted three card rooms, too, and a nice quiet deck that looked over out over the stern.

We returned to eat in the third-class dining room. It had large windows and a high mosaic ceiling and it all looked lovely, but the experience went downhill from there. The chairs, bolted to the floor, were achingly uncomfortable. It took over five minutes to flag down a waiter, then another five to get a drink. I started with a glass of wine, which tasted rancid. Then I had the salmon aspic, which was awful, and my boss—ignoring my admonitions—ordered the split-pea soup. By now the ship had begun rolling again; I could tell by Doctor Morley's uncharacteristic silence that his seasickness had returned. Sure enough his face began to turn the color of his soup. I told him again that he needed to go back to sleep and, for once in his life, he agreed with me.

He retired before six; I took a stroll around the main deck and then decided to retire as well. I sat in the lone chair in my cozy cabin and wrote in my journal. Then I took a couple of strong belts from my flask of Widow Watson's Whiskey and pulled out my letters from Moses.

Now, I had only met Moses Hardwick once before … and it was under much different circumstances. He was one of the Pan American pilots who found us out in the jungle.

I had exchanged addresses with him in Merida, right after Oliver quit his job with the airline and went off on his own. I had given Moses instructions on how to write to me at Chichen Itza and he gave me his address in Key West. We had both promised to let the other know if we heard anything from Oliver.

I had written him first, not because I had news but because I was curious if he did. I got his reply about a week later and his answer was no, nobody had seen or heard from Oliver. But there was something about that first letter that spoke to me. In it Moses talked about what it was like during the search for us, when everyone was fearing the worst. He told me how sorry he was that I had been dragged into such madness.

So I had written him a second time, to tell him how much I appreciated his kind words and sympathy. And I had felt comfortable enough to let him know how difficult life had been since the incident. I thanked him, once again, for saving me.

Ten days later I got his response, now and forever known as the Second Letter from Moses. It was one hell of a letter, one of the finest I have or probably will ever receive. In it Moses informed me that he had heard from Oliver, news that gave me great relief. He also inquired about me and how I was doing. Then Moses ended his second letter with a message that could have been delivered from a pulpit:

The best way to get over something is to live your life the way it deserves to be lived. Run and dance and play and smell the flowers and do the things you want to do. Wake up every day and remind yourself how lucky you are to be alive. Because you are, in more ways than one.

The Second Letter of Moses came to occupy a special place in my heart. It wasn't very long and the handwriting was a bit sloppy … but I read and re-read its magical words over and over again. I suspect I put more thought into the language than the author himself had. Somehow this man, whom I had met only briefly, had become my pen-pal preacher. His surprising sermon gave me a little bit of hope that I might someday overcome the demons and doubts that had been consuming me.

So I ended my first full day on the Orizaba sipping my whiskey alone in my cabin, re-reading my gospel-like letters. Buzzed and refreshed, I got into bed feeling warm and optimistic. As my eyes got heavy I did everything I could to keep my positive thoughts afloat and my dark memories at bay.

It was foolish thinking, of course. Soon the demons and doubts—along with that damned Dead Writer—were knocking on my mind's door again.

***

By the next morning Doctor Morley's energy had returned with a vengeance. He inhaled an entire Orizaba breakfast special then barked for another serving. Then, after a too-brisk walk on the deck, we went to his cabin. He had me sit in the armchair and then he pulled a well-worn leather folder out of his bag. He set the folder on the little table, unzipped it and began to pull papers out.

There were maps, all kinds of maps. Maps of the Yucatán, maps of Central Mexico, maps of Guatemala and maps of the Honduras. There were archaeological site plans, some of which looked professional and precise; others were less-so and appeared to be torn from field journals. There were several letters, some in Spanish and some in English. Many of the letters were on old, brittle, yellowed paper and a few looked to be parchment.

"My word. What's all this?" I asked.

"Your assignment for the voyage," Doctor Morley replied. "Homework, if you will."

I looked again at the odd assortment. "My … assignment? What, you want me organize it?"

Doctor Morley took a great, theatrical breath in.

"*Inhale it,*" he said with a flourish worthy of a stage actor.

"Come again?"

"Inhale it. Swim in it. Burn these images into your mind."

"Enough metaphors. Why?"

"So when you come across something important, you will be able to say, 'Aha! This is something important!'"

"I'm not following."

Doctor Morley reached down and began flipping through his collection. He pulled out a folded-over piece of paper and opened it. It was two large photographs, taped together like a book, with interleaving so the photos wouldn't stick together. He removed the interleaving and laid the photographs out on the table so I could see the entire image.

It was a photograph of a map. A near-ancient map, from a time before men had discovered how to properly draw a map. Dark lines representing rivers snaked past cartoonish trees and villages. Some rivers bled into the grey ocean on one side of the image, while others retreated into the black mountains on the opposite side. Scattered around the central circular image was an abundance of small, almost miniscule, Spanish writing. Along the outermost edges, in a larger font, were the words "Norte" and "Oeste" and the other compass points. It may have been a peculiar map, but it was a map all right.

"Recognize this?" Doctor Morley asked.

"Not at all."

"It's the Tabasco region. From the time of the conquests, before they perfected the art of mapmaking, as you can see. I've never seen the original—it's in Seville, believe it or not—but my understanding is that this outer part and all these rivers are colored blue. The interior is green, the mountains black and purple.

"Now, let me orient this right …," he said, reaching out with both hands and rotating the two photographs. "… This up here is the Gulf of Mexico. Over here, the mountains, this is the Chiapas region. And all these little squares with crosses over them, those are individual Spanish missions. I'm sure you figured that out.

"Now, they may not have been that precise, but all the larger rivers are here. This big area up here is the Terminos Lagoon, and there's the Mecoaca Lagoon. Villahermosa would be down here somewhere, to the south, off the map. Lovely there. Have you been to Villahermosa?"

"No," I said. "But I think I flew over it."

"Well, you should visit sometime," he said, not looking up at first. Then he must've thought about what I had said because he turned his face to me and his expression was different.

"Oh," he said. "*Flew over*, yes, we both did I suppose. Sorry, your reference … *flew over* my head, ha ha. But speaking of that, see this short river here that runs into the mountains? That's the Usumacinta. If you were to follow it past these mountains it would take you south toward Guatemala. Take it far enough and you'd run right into Yaxchilan."

As he said that word, the name of that awful place, I felt a shiver run up my spine.

"Safe to say I won't be going back," I offered.

"Well, I guess you and I are cut from different cloth then," he said. "I can't *wait* to return to Yaxchilan."

And as he said the name of that terrible place a second time, my whole body seized up. The entire incident in the jungle replayed itself in my mind, at lightning speed. I closed my eyes to make it stop. Doctor Morley didn't notice.

"When I said I want you to burn these images into your mind, this is what I'm talking about," he kept on, oblivious. "I want you to know this map like the back of your hand. Memorize it."

I opened my eyes and looked back to the table. Memorize this?

"Memorize *this?*" I repeated, out loud this time. "An old, incorrect map? And this writing ... it's too small, nobody could make that out!"

Doctor Morley looked to me, his face lit up, and then he stood up. He walked to his armoire, rummaged around a bit, and came back with a small velvet pouch. As he sat back down he opened the pouch and showed me what was inside: a magnifying glass.

"I came prepared," he said, a smug look on his face.

"Oh," I said. "Wonderful. Thank you, oh so much."

I would spend the next two-and-a-half hours working my way through Doctor's Morley's portfolio. The old maps were of interest and I did what I was told and, well, stared at them.

But I can't say I was "inhaling" the documents quite the way my boss wanted me to. Instead, I found myself daydreaming about new places, new people and perhaps a new life.

3

THE BARTENDER AND THE POET

Another restless night gave way to another early morning. I tried and tried to fall back asleep, but by seven o'clock Doctor Morley's knuckles were rapping on my door. After a tasteless breakfast, during which the boss ticked off a thousand things-we-must-do, it was off to his cabin. There I was to spend several hours combing through his portfolio, again.

So I stared at the old maps ... and once more found daydreaming made the task go faster. I imagined myself walking the ancient roads on the map, travelling to new villages, meeting new people. I dreamed of floating away on the ribbons of blue, riding them into the mountains and far, far away.

Next I tried to decipher some of the old letters. The majority of them were written in Spanish, but a handful were in Latin and two were in Italian. I relied on my Spanish to figure out the Italian and guessed on the Latin. Most of the documents were religious in nature. All were excruciatingly boring.

After a full day of appearing to work, I was ready for a drink. I was ready to be alone, too ... but Doctor Morley failed to pick up on my nonverbal cues. He suggested we leave the cabin and take a walk on deck, together.

"To clear our minds," he said, as if that were something a walk could achieve.

I agreed then, within two minutes of our arrival on deck, Doctor Morley started complaining about the heat. Mind you, he was wearing a full wool suit with the bottoms of his pants tucked into tall leather boots. His tie was cinched tight around his skinny neck and he was wearing his pith helmet. A cold-blooded reptile would have been hot in that outfit.

"Why don't you take off your jacket" I offered.

"On a liner? Not a chance. I don't want to be underdressed," he answered.

We couldn't find any open seating on the main deck, so we wound down to the quiet deck we discovered our first day aboard. There was no one else there, a welcome surprise. We pulled two Adirondack chairs closer to the railing and sat down, then we relaxed and admired the view. The water churned up by the boat cut a long white streak through the ocean, leaving a curved tail that stretched all the way to the horizon.

By and by Doctor Morley felt the need to talk, ruining this otherwise tranquil moment:

"You know, back at Harvard, we used to play a drinking game called 'three questions,'" he began.

"A drinking game? I'm in," I replied.

"Ha. Yes. Well, I was thinking we could play a … somewhat modified drinking game. You know, without the booze," he said.

I gave him a cold look. "And what's the point in that?"

"Well, we're going to be spending a lot of time together … 'three questions' would be a good way for us to get to know each other."

"Don't we know each other well enough?" I replied. "And why do it without alcohol? I'm sure a waiter will come by."

He turned to me, squinting his eyes and pursing his lips. "Because it's only four in the afternoon, that's why," he said.

I was about to offer my opinion of such rules, but he cut me off before I could speak.

"Pretend you have a drink in your hand, if you must," he said. I looked over and he was holding his hand with one thumb and a pinky sticking out. He lifted his imaginary drink to his lips and took an imaginary sip, then he smacked his lips and smiled.

Good frickin' lord. I pulled my shoulder bag onto my lap and started digging around for a Campconc. Imaginary cocktails didn't cut it in my world but I needed something. Doctor Morley watched me go through the motions of getting my cigarette and lighter out. As I lit up, I looked at him and he was staring at me.

"Want one?" I asked.

"I'm fine with my drink, thank you," he said, and took another idiotic imaginary sip.

I took a deep, real drag and watched the churning water behind the ship. I tried to think of what I wanted to ask Doctor Morley for my first question. He went first:

"I remember you're from New England. Vermont, correct? What town?"

"Ha. You'll laugh when you hear it."

"Of course not."

"Yes you will. It's Bittyville. Bittyville, Vermont."

Doctor Morley let slip a little giggle.

"See? I knew you would laugh," I said.

"*Bittyville?* Come on, that's not a real name …,"

"It's quite real! I'm from East Bittyville, actually."

He giggled again. "Yes, don't want to confuse East Bittyville with Bittyville proper. That's quite a name for a town to live up to."

"Don't I know it."

"So, what's life like in East Bittyville? That's a follow-up question, by the way, not a new one."

"Can you do that?"

"Of course, as long as I take a drink," he said, and lifted his thumb to his lips again.

"What's Bittyville like? Well, it's not very big, as you might imagine. Lots of farms … goat farms, especially. But it's beautiful and peaceful and everybody knows everybody. One of those places."

"Do you miss it? Same question."

"Hmph. Seems like that's your third and last," I said.

"My first was an easy question," Doctor Morley replied. "Big difference between Chichen Itza and East Bittyville, I would suppose. You must miss it."

"I do. I miss the change of seasons."

"And your family, I would guess," he said, and then he waited for me to answer, which I was in no hurry to do.

"That's a longer story," I said. "Isn't it time for me to ask something?"

"Well, I'm trying to find out about family. It's tied to my first question."

"No, your first question was about my hometown," I said. "Asked and answered. My turn."

Doctor Morley took a deep breath and nodded.

"Alright, very well. Fire away."

I hadn't planned to ask him anything too personal. But he had brought up my family, which was a touchy subject. I used my first question to fire a warning shot across his bow.

"Tatiana told me you used to be married," I said. "What happened?"

My question had the intended effect. Doctor Morley gave me a shocked look and squirmed in his chair. I could tell that he, too, didn't care to be on the receiving end of overly-personal questions.

"Well, well," he said. "Not many people know that."

He was quiet again for a minute. He stared out over the white ribbon of water trailing the ship. Then he started to talk:

"Guess it's hard to keep some things a secret. Yes, I was married. To a very sweet girl. A very sweet girl that deserved better than I could provide. Her father was a U.S. Senator, did Tatiana mention that? No? Well, a powerful man he was ... but he didn't care for me. Oh no, the good Senator didn't care for me one bit. Thought I wasn't of the right caliber for his little princess.

"And know what? He was right. I was young and selfish. And young, selfish me wanted to be digging in the dirt somewhere. I didn't have the acting chops to pretend I was some upper-crust ninny."

The words 'upper-crust ninny' made me chuckle. Doctor Morley turned to me and he smiled, too.

"It's like her entire family wanted me to play a role, to be someone other than the person I wanted to be," he went on. "Do you know what that's like? Her name was Alice, by the way. Such a sweetheart. I heard she got remarried, some rich bloke. I suspect he's better at high-society chit-chat than I am, which should make her pa-pa happy. I hope she's happy as well."

His voice had become lower and his gaze seemed distant. I was about to say something when he piped up again, sounding cheerier:

"But I've met someone else. Haven't told anyone that, so keep it quiet."

"Well, well," I said. "Good for you. Is it … someone at the camp?"

"The camp? Good gracious, of course not. A woman from New Mexico."

"And does this woman from New Mexico have a name?" I said. "That's not a new question."

Doctor Morley turned to me and a broad smile came across his lips.

"Frances," he said. "Her name is Frances."

"She must be lovely."

"That she is," he answered, still smiling. "That she is. Okay, my turn."

I crossed my fingers that he wouldn't ask anything family-related. Most any other topic I could handle.

"Alright ... so," he said, shifting in his chair and crossing his legs. "Do you enjoy what you do? That is, do you enjoy your work with the Institution?"

Those were two separate questions with two very different answers. I had to be careful.

"Well, yes, of course," I said. "I consider myself quite privileged to have the opportunity. I could be picking apples back in Bittyville, you know."

Doctor Morley laughed. "Ha! Yes, very true. But my question was ... do you *enjoy* it?"

"Enjoy it? Why, yes, of course," I said, trying not to make eye contact as I fibbed.

The sad truth was I didn't enjoy much of anything these days. But I didn't want to give him time to dissect my thoughts, so I started to think about my next question. All I could think of was an obvious one I shouldn't ask. Then, without warning, that one question shot out of my stupid mouth:

"You were a spy."

I didn't even ask it like a question, which might have come off better. I just said it, then looked over to Doctor Morley. His eyes had become tiny slits. His lips were so firmly clenched together they were turning white.

"Pardon me?" he asked.

A wave of regret welled up in me. But I had said it, there was no turning back, and I had wanted to know the answer to this for a long time. So I dug in.

"In the War. Some ... some of the men at camp. They said ...,"

"Uh-huh. Which men at camp?" Doctor Morley scoffed.

"Well, I can't remember, but …,"

"Mm-hm."

"… But they said that you had served. You didn't go to France, but you served. As …,"

"As what?"

"Well, like I said … as … as a spy."

I had said it already, but when I said it that second time Doctor Morley turned to face the ocean. I had crossed a line, or at least I thought I had. He sat there and stared out over the horizon and didn't say anything for a solid thirty seconds.

"Is that the term they use … a spy?" he finally said. "That makes it sound much more exciting than it really was."

"So it's true then."

"That I served my country during the War? Yes, that's true," he said.

I made a decision to stay quiet to see if he would keep talking. I was right, he did.

"I'll tell you this, but you can't repeat it … and you have to give me your word on that. Okay?" he continued, and I nodded. "Good. Now, here's the real truth: I didn't fight. I never had to fire a gun. I was never in a foxhole. I spent the War watching the coasts of Mexico, Guatemala and the Honduras for German submarines that never came."

"That sounds … exciting," I said.

"It wasn't," he said. "And I don't like to talk about it."

"Why? You should be proud of what you did."

He scoffed. "Bull. While my classmates were dying in a trench in Belgium—quite literally—I was a half a world away. They carried bayonets ... I carried binoculars."

"Oh, don't be so dramatic. You served. That counts."

"I suppose. For the record: I did get shot at a few times," Doctor Morley offered.

"Well, see, that's exciting!"

"Those were mostly over misunderstandings, but that's a whole other story," he said. "Enough on that. Don't repeat any of it, alright?"

"Of course not."

"I mean that. We spies, we'll do anything to protect our secrets. Got it?" he warned, with a wink. "Now, my turn ... this is my second, correct?"

"Third and final."

"Is it? Well, I better make it a good one then," he said. He thought for a moment, then scratched this chin, then thought some more, then spoke.

"Tell me, have you heard anything from our friend Oliver?"

I wasn't expecting that.

"Oliver ...?" I said, trying to play dumb.

"Oh, come now, you know who I mean. Oliver Wheelock. The man we went to hell and back with," Doctor Morley said. "That day we left Merida, when he quit and walked off ... you talked with him. Have you heard from him since?"

"Oh ... *that* Oliver. No, I haven't. Not directly."

That last part had slipped out, my tongue chasing it and trying to drag it back in.

"Not *directly*? What does that mean?" Doctor Morley asked.

"You've already had your three questions," I said.

"That wasn't a question. That was me trying to understand your answer. So you have heard from him?"

"Well, in a way I suppose ..."

"Now you sound like the spy. What did you hear? Did you get a letter? A telegram?"

"I ... I've exchanged some letters. Not with him, with someone that heard from him. But, like I said, *I* haven't heard from him. Not directly."

"Mm-hm. And who is this mysterious individual who *did* hear from him?"

"Um ... one of the pilots that found us in the jungle," I said.

Now Doctor Morley went quiet. I stared at him, he stared at me. He was using my own trick against me: remaining silent in hopes I would say more. I did.

"Moses. The pilot named Moses," I volunteered.

"Oliver wrote the pilot a letter?"

"No. Oliver wrote his mother, actually. Then she told Moses about it."

"I see. And ... what did he have to say?"

"Uh ... that he was safe and doing well. He regretted not having better shoes."

"And ... where is he?"

"I'm not sure of that. I'd be surprised if he's even left Merida. He likes his cantinas, that man."

I snickered and hoped Doctor Morley would snicker too. He didn't.

"But you're not sure. So ... what are his plans?"

"His plans?" I said, acting like I didn't have any idea.

"Yes, his plans. His itinerary. His destination. Where is he going? He must have told someone where he's going, right?" Doctor Morley demanded.

"I don't have the slightest clue," I lied. "I think he was just looking for an adventure."

"An adventure. I see. Tell me, that last time you saw our man Oliver ... did you two discuss what you and he found at Yaxchilan? The headdress and all that?"

"The ... um ... at Yaxchilan? No, of course not," I said. That was sort of truthful, which was close enough.

"And when was this?"

"When was what?"

"The letter. When did Abraham hear from the mother about Oliver's letter?" he asked.

"Who's Abraham?"

"The pilot."

"Moses."

"Close enough. I'm trying to figure out how long this was after our return."

"Not long after," I answered. "A couple of weeks, at most."

"And that's all you've heard from him? I mean, of him?"

"Yes," I said. That was honest.

"Well, if you should happen to hear more, let me know *immediately*. Understood?" Doctor Morley said.

I nodded. He was quiet and the uncomfortable topic was over. Then we sat in silence for a bit and looked out to the endless horizon. I had a vigorous debate within my mind about whether I should ask my final question. But I needed to know whether he was suffering like I was.

"Do you ever think about what happened?" I asked. "In the jungle, I mean."

He turned to face me and I knew I had wasted a question. I could read his emotionless expression. He knew what kind of answer I wanted and I could tell I wasn't going to get it. He took a big breath in, looked out over the water and then let out a big sigh.

"Hoo boy," he said. "Of course I do. Quite often. Keeps me up at night."

That was refreshing. At least we had insomnia in common. He continued:

"But during the day I have to move forward, you know? People depend on me and, in a way, I depend on them. Getting back to normal has been good for me."

My cigarette had burnt down to the nub. I tossed it on the deck and smooshed it with my shoe and thought about what he had said.

"Normal?" I said. "Everything is all so far removed from normal. Don't you agree?"

"Alright, instead let's say I'm doing my best to work my way back to normal. Is that a better choice of words? Oh, don't shake your head like that, this was your question. And my answer is that yes, I think about it but no, I don't let it control me. How's that old saying go, give me patience to understand that I can't control everything? Can't quite remember how it goes, but you get my drift. I can't erase the past, I can't erase what happened, so I ...,"

"But others are!" I interjected. "Others *are* trying to erase the past. All those lies they made up about Lindbergh and how he was injured, and what ... well, all of it. It's ... fake news."

"That's such an idiotic expression," Doctor Morley said.

"Well, that's what it is," I said. "A web of lies, spun to protect a monster."

My boss exhaled and said nothing so I kept going:

"And it's Pan American that's leading the charge," I said. "That's where the lies started, believe you me. That turd that was with us, Mister Trippe."

"Juan."

"Screw Juan. Screw Juan Trippe and screw Pan American and screw the newspapers and screw anyone that's been complicit in this frickin' charade."

"Oh, calm down."

"Don't belittle me, I'm fired up about this," I said, and I was. "I understand staying quiet about ... well, about our current undertaking. But I shouldn't have to be quiet about Lindbergh, or about what he did to the Dead Writer."

Doctor Morley's face scrunched up.

"The who?"

I realized that I had used a name confined to my head in actual conversation, where it didn't belong.

"The head writer, sorry," I said. "We shouldn't have to pretend that …"

"I thought you said 'the dead writer,'" Doctor Morley said, cutting me off.

"What? No, no, the head writer for that magazine. We shouldn't …"

"No, you said 'the dead writer.'"

"Well, you misheard me."

He gave me a look which suggested he didn't believe me. But I kept going anyways:

"Phonies. That's what they all are, a bunch of phonies. And the world needs to know. The world needs to know the truth. Lindbergh should be behind bars—or worse— for what he did. And I've got half a mind to tell everyone myself."

"Don't," Doctor Morley said, in a heavy voice.

"And why not?" I huffed.

"Because Charles Lindbergh is a powerful man, as is Juan Trippe," he said. "And behind them are men that have the ear and pocket of every reporter in New York. You'll be regarded as nothing more than squirrel food."

"Squirrel food?"

"Nuts. They'll think you're nuts," Doctor Morley replied. "Poor expression."

I didn't ask anything else. I didn't need to. He had said all I needed to hear.

We sat in silence for a few minutes and then Doctor Morley said he had to go to his cabin. I doubted that was true … but if he wanted to get away from me, more power to him.

After he left I sat there and stared at the long ribbons of churned-up water trailing the liner. They seemed to stretch all the way to the edge of the earth. They made me think of how far I had travelled, only to find myself utterly and hopelessly lost.

***

Over dinner I picked at my food and counted the minutes before I could have a stiff drink. I hadn't had a drink since we had boarded, except for whiskey, which didn't count as I was in my cabin and alone at the time.

After Doctor Morley retired, I returned to my room and gussied myself up. Then I went to explore the nightlife aboard the Orizaba.

There were three main lounges. The Gentlemen's Lounge was one floor below the main deck on the port side. It had dark tables and dark chairs and reeked of cigar smoke. It also had a large sign by the door indicating women were not allowed and directing said females to the Ladies' Lounge, one deck below.

The Ladies' Lounge was pathetic. All the tables had white tablecloths and all the ladies had white hair. There were several women knitting, no doubt out of boredom. There were white-coated waiters scurrying about, pouring tea into silly little white teacups. It was so god-awful I didn't even break stride and walked right on by.

I knew there was a Third-Class bar another deck down and toward the stern. I had avoided it, thinking I was somehow better than my Third-Class status. But it was my only option … and it turned out to be just what I was looking for.

It was called The Black Dog. When I walked in the joint was lit: the tables were filled—with both men and women—and everyone was laughing and smiling and drinking. Against one wall there was a piano player and a bleary-eyed gang was singing *Danny Boy.*

I made my way to the long bar. As I arrived a nice man was getting up to leave and offered me his stool. I sat, adjusted myself and looked up to see an absolutely gorgeous bartender.

He had dark hair, olive skin and a crooked bow tie. That was set off by a white jacket, white shirt and teeth as brilliant as the morning sun. He had perfect lips, too.

"Buenas noches, bonsoir, good evening," he began, placing a small napkin in front of me.

"Good evening," I purred.

"I should've guessed, you only needed the good evening," the bartender said, clearly American. "What'll you have?"

I'll have you, I thought. "A whiskey, please," I said instead.

He arched an eyebrow and tilted his head as if to say oh-is-that-so. I smiled my sweetest smile and batted my eyelashes as if to say you're-damn-straight.

"Whiskey! A woman after my own heart," he declared, then he turned to the booze bottles behind the bar. "Let's see, the house stuff is kicked … whiskey … ah, here we go."

He turned back around and in his hand he held a bottle of Widow Watson's. My entire body trembled with shock and wonder. Was this an epiphany? Was God a bartender?

"You won't believe this, but that's my ab-so-lute fave," I said. "A double, please."

"One double coming up, Miss ...,"

"Wendy."

"Alright, Miss Wendy." he asked as he used tongs to plunk cubes in a glass.

"Wendy's my first name, actually. Oh, and straight up, please."

Now he nodded as if to say well-well-well and I giggled. He dumped the ice back in his ice bucket, poured me a triple and placed it on my napkin. Then he darted his eyes around the room, edged closer to the bar and pulled out a second glass. He gave me a wink and an I-think-I'll-join-you look and poured himself one.

"To you," he whispered, then he tapped his glass on the bar, raised it to his lips and drank. I did the same, tapping my drink for some unknown reason and then chugging the entire thing. Our empty glasses hit the bar at about the same time.

The bartender's eyes were wide as platters.

"Wooh, hot damn ... ain't that the elephant's eyebrows," he said, looking pleased but keeping his voice low. "Another?"

I nodded. I would do whatever he asked of me. He poured two more, but before we could drink them someone yelled to him.

"Don't you go anywhere," he said with a knowing grin. Then he walked to the other end to help another customer. I sat and took a small sip of my whiskey and watched him. Before I took my second sip he had returned.

As he worked and I drank we got to know each other. His name was Thomas. He had been working for Ward Line for three years. He had been everywhere, but he hadn't seen much of the places he had been because he was always working. Someday, when he had enough money saved, he would go back to those places and do them right. Then he was going to see the rest of the world, too. On about his third drink, and my fourth, he rattled off his itinerary to me.

"Egypt, to see the pyramids, of course. Then to the Holy Land. And I talk to people here on board that have been all the way to India. It's like a whole other planet, they say."

It all sounded wonderful. He sounded wonderful.

And then we talked about me. At first he thought I was pulling his leg about what I did and where I was from. I told him about smoking cigarettes on the pyramid and his face scrunched up.

"Oh, now I *know* you're joking," he said, and it was a delight to convince him otherwise.

He had seen pictures of Chichen Itza and he had some good questions. He asked me several times if I knew of any tombs overflowing with priceless riches, which I did not. Then he suggested we go hunting for treasure together. That hit a little close to home, so I turned the conversation back to him.

Over the course of the next two hours Thomas and I connected. The bar was crowded and he was busy but time and time again he returned to me. We would talk and I would look into his blue eyes and the piano was playing and it was all just delightful.

At one point during our flirting I was overcome with a marvelous thought: Thomas should ravish me. After he finished with his work, of course, which I hoped was soon. Then he could take me back to my cabin, press me up against the wall and kiss me all over. He could use his fingers and his mouth to remove my clothing, every last bit of it. I could do the same for him. Then he could throw back the curtain on my bed, toss me into the bottom bunk and have me all night long.

Thomas' smoky, seductive gaze suggested he was thinking along the same lines.

After he had poured me my umpteenth drink a waiter came up and tapped Thomas on the shoulder. He gave me the one-finger I'll-be-right-back signal and followed the intruding waiter away. My eyes followed those two to the back corner of the room, where they huddled with a third man. Thomas shook his head at something this other man said and then walked away with a dismissive wave of his hand. He caught me looking, smiled and came back to me.

"Everything alright?" I asked.

Thomas shook his head. "Ah, it's nothing," he said. "Some fag tried to kiss one of my bunkmates."

His smile had disappeared. With that crude comment his halo vanished as well.

"Pardon me?" I said, hoping I had misheard. I hadn't.

"Frickin' guy cornered my buddy outside the upstairs lounge, planted one right on him. Went for the lips, too. Only got his cheek, but it was close."

"How fortunate."

"Right? He'll be fine, though," my fallen hero said.

"What happened to the other man?" I asked. I was hoping my evil glare would provide him some clue that I didn't care for unbridled machismo. He didn't get the hint.

"Who, the fag? He learned a lesson, that's what happened to him."

With that, Thomas gave me a don't-you-agree-with-me look … which met with my no-I-do-not stare. He turned away to serve someone and as he poured he looked back toward me. We shared one of those the-magic-is-gone moments. Then I looked away and finished my drink. When he returned he got right to the point:

"Listen, I think maybe I've upset you," he said. "I'm sorry I told you that stuff. It's nothing you need to know about."

Then he looked at me with his puppy-dog eyes and waited for me to speak.

I had plenty to say, but all I said was "Check, please."

He pursed his lips and took a deep breath. "Listen, Wendy, I'm …,"

"Check. Please."

He exhaled in frustration. "There's no charge," he said. "It's on me."

"I'm not comfortable with that," I said. "Tell me how much."

"Ma'am, I ...,"

"How much?" I repeated, in an unpleasant voice.

He looked at me with a dumb look. "A dollar, I guess."

I glared at him and as I glared it dawned on me all my money was in my money-belt. I scowled and hunched over and, trying to be discreet, undid a button on my blouse. Then I fumbled around trying to adjust the belt so I could reach the zipper. I unzipped it, pulled out a fold of bills and peeled off a dollar. Then I handed it to Thomas, who had been standing there watching the whole pathetic exercise.

"Thanks," he said. I turned to walk away. He spoke one last time:

"You know, I should keep my mouth shut," he said. "But ... what's the point of a hidden money-belt if everyone can see you pulling your money out of it?"

I stopped and shot a final nasty look at him.

"You're right," I said. "You should keep your mouth shut. Asshole."

I got up from my stool, smoothed my skirt and adjusted my shoulder-bag. Then, without turning back, I marched through the happy crowd and exited The Black Dog.

I was fuming. Mankind, I thought, disgusted me. To be more precise, the men of mankind disgusted me. All of them. Never what they appear to be. Nothing but posers, charlatans.

I needed a smoke. I made my way up the stairs, down the corridor and opened the door to the secluded quiet deck. A gust of salty air hit my face.

The quiet deck was even more peaceful at night. I was glad to be alone. I went to the railing and gazed out into the endless void of the dark ocean. The water seemed calm, and the stars reflected off the water. It was hard to tell where the sky ended and the earth began.

I pulled my shoulder bag over, opened it and dug around for my Campeones. When I located them I turned my back to the wind, cupped my hand and tried to light my smoke. It took several tries.

I took a deep drag in and wandered back to the railing. As I exhaled I looked down and watched the grey waves churning up and then disappearing back into the black water. My eyes followed the waves toward the aft of the ship. Only then did I notice a man farther down, looking right at me.

He was standing on the ocean side of the railing.

My heart jumped, then I froze. I wanted to yell but I was afraid I would startle him and make him fall.

He was still looking at me. I had to say something:

"Oh. Oh my. Please … whatever you're about to do, please don't."

The man on the wrong side of the railing said nothing. He looked terrified and at ease at the same time, if that were possible.

I looked behind me, hoping against hope someone else was present. But it was just the two of us, alone on the quiet deck.

Then I looked at him again and realized how precarious his position was. He was holding on to the railing, but only the tips of his shoes were touching the deck. His heels hovered over the dark sea, some thirty feet down. I knew a big wave or a stiff gust of wind could knock him right off.

My options raced through my mind. I could run away, go and find someone, bring them back. Or I could yell. Or I could race toward the poor man and grab him.

Any of those options, I realized, could end in disaster. So I decided I should try talking to him again. I said the first thing that popped into my mind.

"Would you … would you like a cigarette?" I asked.

The man stared back at me. I worried I had offended him by not saying something more appropriate to the occasion. Then, in a meek voice, he answered me:

"Um … yeah. Yeah, that'd be nice. Thanks."

My body shook. I took my first tentative steps toward him. As I neared him I could see his worried eyes. He was scared.

He wasn't a big man. Dark hair, skinny, average height. He was wearing suspenders and a striped tie. The tie and his thin hair were flapping in the breeze.

I pulled out a Campeone for him.

"I … I'm not sure how to handle this," I said. "Would you like to light it yourself, or …,"

"You can light it. Please and thank you," the man replied.

As he said that I got a better look at him. One side of his face was bruised. His eye on that side was swelling up. It dawned on me this was the individual my bartender had been talking about.

I held my own lit cigarette in one hand and put the new one in my mouth. Again the wind foiled my efforts, so I had to turn my back on the poor man as I tried to light his smoke. When I succeeded I turned back to him. He gave me a smile. I stepped forward and reached out with the lit Campeone.

The man stared the cigarette. He pulled himself tight against the railing and hung one elbow over. Then he scared the crap out of me: he took his other hand off the railing, so he could take the cigarette, and stumbled. He caught himself just in time. His face, for the briefest of moments, had a look of sheer terror. Then he turned back to me and faked a smile.

"Sorry," he remarked. "Slippery shoes."

"It's ... it's nothing to apologize for," I told him.

He reached out again. I handed the cigarette to him. He pinched the Campeone with two fingers and then put it in his mouth. He proceeded to take a deep drag, again holding on to the railing with one hand. As if matters weren't frightening enough, he then stood up straight and leaned back. He exhaled upward, sending a cloud of smoke into the blanket of stars. Then he just stood there, smoking, on the wrong side of the railing.

"Since I gave you that, I don't suppose you'd come back over to this side," I said.

It was as if he didn't hear what I said at first. Then, without looking at me, he spoke:

"I didn't think anyone came to the quiet deck," he said. "What's your name?"

"Wendy," I answered. "What's yours?"

"Hart," he said. "No 'e,' just h-a-r-t."

"Hart. Alright," I said. "I'd like to help you, Hart."

My words seemed to pass through him. He didn't answer. He took another drag from his cigarette, and I could see his hand tremble. Then he left the Campeone dangling in his mouth and looked up at the stars and spoke again.

"You ever wonder why, Wendy?"

I turned to scan the deck. We were still alone. I prayed for someone to come along to help me.

"Why what, Hart?" I said, realizing it may be up to me and me alone to stop him from jumping.

"Why? Why do we have to go through it, you know? All this pain ... for what?" he asked. "Why make us suffer like this?"

It was a question I had asked myself many, many times. I tried to think of what to say. I was at a loss for words. Next he asked:

"Who are you, Wendy?"

From the way he said it, it seemed like he was expecting a profound answer. I didn't have one.

"I'm an artist," I said. "Well, sort of."

"Huh! No kidding," he said. "Well, guess we've got the arts in common. I'm a poet. Sort of."

As he spoke I took a small step toward him. One side of my brain told me I might be able to grab his arm and yell for help. The other side of my brain was trying to talk me out of it, fearing such a move would only seal his fate.

"A poet," I said, preparing for another small step. "I love poetry, Hart. Would you ... would you ... recite one of your poems for me?"

"I will if you stay over there."

I froze. I didn't say anything. He began, with a grand flourish of his arm toward the ocean:

"Oh, rivers of infinite blackness, ye flow from the eternal voids beyond. Relentless, unforgiving, you flood my defenseless soul."

Then his voice became more dramatic and louder, like an actor's. He waved again to the ocean.

"Oh, rivers of darkness and despair, ye wash away the good of this world! In your wake exists only the raw, bare, unforgiving surface of this pitiful rock."

Then he finished in a lower voice.

"Oh, rivers of destiny, take me away from this godawful place."

Then he stopped. He was looking down, past his shoes, at the water. I struggled with what to say.

"That's a ... a very nice poem, Hart," I said. "Do you have any others I could hear?"

He laughed at that. Then he turned so I could see his face. He was smiling.

"Nice try," he said. "Say, Wendy ... you ever been to New York?"

I couldn't determine whether the situation had gotten worse or better. I felt it best to keep him talking. He took a drag off his cigarette as he waited for my answer.

"Well, yes," I began to say. "But I haven't been in a long ...,"

He cut me off. "If you go, make sure you go to the Carnegie Deli. Seventh Avenue, midtown."

It was an odd statement. I took a step forward, readying myself to lunge out and grab him. I kept eye contact.

"Carnegie Deli," I said, waiting for him to start talking again.

"Yeah, Fifty-Fifth and Seventh. Near Times Square," he said. "Best corned beef on the planet."

Then he took one more drag off his Campeone. He looked at me, smiled … and let go.

It happened so fast. I heard the splash before I made it to the railing.

"No! No!"

I kept yelling, looking for some sign of life in the black water.

"Hart! Hart!"

But it was too late. He was gone. I screamed as loud as I could:

"Help! Man overboard! Man overboard!"

4

DARKNESS AND DESPAIR

The next few hours were a blur. A horrible, awful, nightmarish blur.

A minute after I screamed, an officer came barging onto the deck. He looked over the railing and then yelled. After he yelled, someone else yelled from up above. Then a loud bell rang out. Within moments I could feel the Orizaba slow, then drift to a stop.

There were large floodlights on the side of the ship. They were turned on and the lights began to trace back and forth. There were crew members on all the decks, scanning the water with flashlights. A lifeboat filled with several men was lowered. They rowed away from the ship, back in the direction we had come from.

In the stillness of the night I could see them out there, paddling around, finding nothing. Sometime later, I don't know how long, they rowed back. The ropes were secured to the lifeboat and they were hoisted back up. As they rose I could see their faces and their disappointment. One of them made eye contact with me and, as bad as I felt, his look made me feel ten times worse.

Then I was asked to accompany two officers down the hall. On the way we ran into the white-haired, grim-faced captain, who had been coming to find me. The three of them led me to a nearby sitting area and interrogated me about my encounter with the man.

***

"You say he wasn't with you," one of them asked. "Had you met him before?"

"No," I said. "Like I told you, it was the first and only time I saw him."

"And you're sure the two of you didn't go out there together?" came next.

"What? No. I went out there to have a cigarette. By myself."

"Why didn't you smoke on the main deck?" the captain asked.

"Because ... because I wanted some privacy. Alright?"

"Nobody goes to the quiet deck," he said.

I didn't respond. I felt like I was defending myself. I knew I shouldn't have to.

"Why didn't you yell?" came next.

"I ... I was afraid I would startle him."

"There was a crew member stationed on the deck above. He would have heard you."

"But I ... again, I didn't want to startle the man. I was afraid he would fall, or jump."

They all glared at me, saying nothing. My frustration was building.

"Are you trying to insinuate this is somehow my fault?" I demanded, unable to contain myself.

Then there was a long pause, at the end of which the captain broke the silence and said:

"No, no, of course not. Don't be silly."

Then there was another uncomfortable pause, after which one of the other men asked:

"And he didn't say anything about why he was doing, well, what he did?"

"No," I said. "But I knew that he ..."

I stopped myself before I could finish the sentence. To detail my conversation with the bartender might prompt more questions. Such as, why I didn't report that someone had been beat up? I froze.

"Knew what?" came the follow-up. I fumbled for a response.

"I knew ... I knew that if I kept talking to him, I could stall him until help arrived," I said. "But ... but it was too late. Can I have a cigarette?"

The captain looked to one of the other men and nodded. The underling reached in his shirt packet and pulled out a pack of smokes then fumbled in his pocket for a light. He passed me the smoke and then lit it and I took a much-needed drag.

The three men watched me smoke. Nobody said a word for a full minute. I felt like a mouse being sized up by a gang of alley cats. Finally the captain spoke:

"Tell me again his last words."

"He ... he asked me if I had ever been to New York," I answered. "He told me that ... that I should go to the Carnegie Deli. He said something about the corned beef, it was the best ever. That was it."

The captain leaned back in his chair. He took a deep breath in and looked at the other two men.

"Well ... he's not wrong about that," he said. "Good pastrami, too."

The other two men nodded and chuckled in an agreeable way. It disgusted me.

"Really?" I said, interrupting their corned beef and pastrami moment. "A man jumps to his death and you're talking about ... about ... meats?"

The three of them stopped and they all looked at me with disdain. The captain spoke for them:

"My dear," he began, as if I were a child, "I regret that you had to witness the final moments of that unfortunate man. But it is, I am sorry to say, a not-unheard-of reality of this mode of transportation. There is only so much we can do with people who are intent on writing their own end."

I was sick of this. I glared at them.

"May I please go?" I asked.

"Of course," the captain said. Then, as I was leaving the room he said, swear to God, "Enjoy the rest of your voyage."

***

Doctor Morley had been waiting for me. He had questions as well, but unlike the officers of the Orizaba he knew this wasn't the time to ask them.

He told a bursar to bring water and food to my cabin and then escorted me back into the ship and down the corridor. Once in my room I collapsed in the armchair. Doctor Morley pulled the bed curtain back and sat his small frame down on my small bunk. He took off his glasses, pinched his temple, took a deep breath in and out then looked at me.

"Wendy ... I can't think of any words to that would adequately express to you how very, very sorry I am," he began. "To go through that after ... after all that other madness we went through ... it's not fair. It's not fair at all."

I stared off, lost in my own world, numb to what he was saying. My mind kept thinking of that poor poet. My heart was breaking for him. Without a word, I reached for my half-full flask of Widow Watson's. I took one gulp, then another. I offered the flask to Doctor Morley, who shook his head.

"You must feel like you're cursed," he said, which I did. "But you're not. You're a bright, wonderful, remarkable woman ... who happened to be at the wrong place at the wrong time."

"Twice," I added.

"Yes, twice," he conceded. "But that's not my point. My point is that you—you, Wendy Willoughby—did nothing wrong. Nothing."

I wasn't so sure about that. My interview with the officers had only reinforced my sense that I could have done more. But I didn't want to show weakness to Doctor Morley.

"I know," I fibbed. "I'm fine. Really."

"Really?"

"Really. I'm fine."

Soon after there was a knock on the door. A timid-looking waiter wheeled in a serving cart. He removed the covers to reveal a plate of deviled ham and cucumber sandwiches with the crusts cut off. Then the waiter bowed his head, looking quite sorry about everything, and backed out of the cabin.

I wasn't hungry … and when I told that to Doctor Morley he tore into the little sandwiches like a starved vulture. As he gorged himself I took another belt of my whiskey. Neither of us said anything more about what had happened.

***

After Doctor Morley left I changed into nightclothes, washed my face and tried to sleep. I was exhausted, but I couldn't stop thinking about that poor poet.

I could see him, bobbing in the water, watching the ship sail out of sight, no doubt regretting what he had done.

Then I could see him slipping away, beneath the water, drifting down into the abyss. And I'm floating above him, reaching out, trying to catch him. He has a single arm extended, reaching up to me, his eyes vacant.

And there's nothing I can do. He's too deep. As he sinks he becomes smaller and harder to see. Then, he disappears.

I look up. But now I'm not floating in the water … I'm sitting in an inflatable tube. I look around and all I can see is the black ocean, for miles and miles and miles.

Then, as I scan in desperation, I spy a small rowboat. It is coming toward me. And I'm overjoyed, believing it must be someone coming to rescue me. But then the rowboat comes closer and I can better see its sole occupant.

It is the Dead Writer.

He maneuvers his rowboat next to my inflatable tube. I reach out and touch his boat and it all feels so real. I look at him and he looks real too: the unbuttoned shirt, the moustache and scruff, the scar on his forehead.

Without a word he sets his oars down and reaches down between his legs, as if he is looking for something. Then he raises his hands back up and he is holding two bottles of beer. He flips the caps on both and hands one of the bottles over to me. Then he looks down at the water, looks back to me, smiles and says:

"There once was a poet on a ship ... Who decided to take a cool dip,"

"Stop!" I scream, and it echoes across the empty ocean.

The Dead Writer stares at me. "It's funny. You don't want me to finish?"

"No, I do not," I say to the ghost. "It's most inappropriate."

The Dead Writer shakes his head. He takes a chug from his beer and then turns back to me with a smarmy look on his face and says:

"Hell's bells, Wendy. You're such a goddamn drag these days. Get over it, would ya?"

And then he takes another drink. I look around, to see if there is anyone around to help me. But we are alone on the black ocean, just me and him. In every other direction all I can see is darkness and despair.

***

The following day I didn't leave my cabin until sunset, when Doctor Morley insisted we take a walk. He led me up to the main deck and we had been up there no more than two minutes when I saw a woman talking about me.

She was a short, ugly, shrew-nosed beast. I saw her whispering to her unlucky husband, then looking toward me, then whispering to him again. I turned away and there was someone else looking at me. I knew *they* were talking about me, too.

Later, in Doctor Morley's cabin, I confessed that those encounters had made me feel even worse about things.

"Just ignore them," Doctor Morley advised. "People will talk because they have nothing better to do."

"Everyone blames me."

"Nobody blames you. You tried to help, which is more than anyone else did. Stop beating yourself up over things you can't control."

I closed my eyes and took a deep breath. Internally, I continued to horsewhip myself.

"I sense this episode has tapped into uncomfortable memories," Doctor Morley said.

"You think?" I answered, too numb to control my sarcasm.

I made Doctor Morley escort me downstairs. I had dinner in my cabin, alone, and finished my whiskey.

Then, late at night, I went up to the main deck by myself. It was almost deserted. I pulled out a lounge chair and laid down and looked up at the starry sky and wished I could float up and away.

***

By the next morning I had decided that working would help cure my blues. I knocked on Doctor Morley's door early.

"I'd like your portfolio, please," I asked when he opened the door.

"Nonsense," my boss replied. "Work can wait."

"I'm bored and I don't want to go anywhere on this miserable ship," I replied. "It's something to do."

He relented, as I knew he would. I took his binder full of old maps, photographs and documents back to my cabin. I laid them out on both bunks and went through them one by one.

I wish I could say I did it out of unbridled enthusiasm for my work assignment. But the sad truth is I needed something to take my mind off what happened ... and what happened before that.

***

On our final night on the Orizaba I had salted salmon drowned in caper sauce and did my best to avoid the stares of onlookers. Doctor Morley had what appeared to be petrified beef ... and he had no problem glaring back at the gawkers.

It was a quick and quiet meal. Then my boss marched me out of the dining room, chins held high. Next he marched me around the deck, tipping his pith helmet at every pathetic gossip we passed. Finally, he marched me back down to my cabin and said goodnight.

"I apologize for my curtness," he said. "Thinking about tomorrow, you know. Ready to get rolling."

After he went away I fished out the money Tatiana had given me. I went upstairs to the Gentlemen's Lounge, where women weren't allowed. I marched in anyway.

All the old farts with their stinky cigars stopped talking and stared at me. I didn't make eye contact with any of them. I made a beeline for the bar, slapped some money down and asked to buy a bottle of whatever they would sell me.

Then, and only then, did I encounter the one crew member of the Orizaba with a heart. The older gentleman tending bar recognized me and gave me a free bottle of scotch.

"I'll say a prayer for you," he whispered. It almost made me cry.

It wasn't a big bottle and it wasn't a good scotch … but it was good enough. I went back to my cabin, poured myself a healthy glass and began the nightly numbing process.

5

RAIN IN SPAIN

When we came into the harbor at Cadiz it was as if the Heavens had opened up to cry. It was coming down so hard we weren't even allowed to go onto the decks. I watched the deluge from the porthole in my cabin.

Doctor Morley was in my cabin, too, stressing over the day's arrangements:

"I had hoped we might get to Madrid in time to visit the Museum today. At the very least I wanted to show you around, help you get your bearings. Damn this rain."

I watched out the porthole as the liner neared the pier. There were men waiting on the dock to seize the enormous ropes. They were using their hands to shield their faces from the hard, driving rain. Even from a distance they looked miserable.

With the decks closed, we had to wait in a long hallway to get to the gangplank. They herded us like cattle off the ship, then at the bottom of the gangplank was another line for retrieving luggage. Following that we had to wheel our luggage—by ourselves, due to some goddamn strike—to Customs. We stood and waited at least a half-hour before we reached the front of the line.

The grouchy passport clerk waved us forward. He took Doctor Morley's passport and declarations form, looked them over, stamped Doctor's Morley passport and handed it back to him. Then he took my passport and form and looked them over. Right away his eyebrows went up. He looked to us, said "uno momento," took my passport and walked over to a Customs officer. They talked, then looked over at me, then talked some more. The Customs officer left, reappearing moments later with an older and presumably higher-ranking Customs officer. They all walked back to the desk where Doctor Morley and I were waiting. The older Customs officer was holding my passport in his hand.

"Señora Villow-bees," he said. "Podemos hablar en privado? May we speak with you in private?"

I looked at Doctor Morley. Not again, I thought.

***

They took me to a small room that had a desk and a handful of chairs. One officer sat at the desk and took off his hat. The other stood at attention by the door, to make me feel even more uncomfortable.

The older officer looked at my passport. He flipped to the photo, looked at it, looked at me once more then looked back to the photo. Then he took a pen and wrote my name and passport number on a pad of paper.

"This man, the man that jump off the ship," he said, in workable English. "You had never met him before, no?"

"No," I said. "And I didn't so much meet him as encounter him."

"Qué?"

"Les dije todo. I told all this to the officer on the boat. Do we have to go through it again?"

The answer was yes, we did. I spent more than an hour talking with the Customs officers. They asked me all the same questions and I gave all the same answers. They wanted to know why I didn't yell. As their questions grew more tedious, my impatience grew more pronounced.

"Se suicidó. Comprende? He killed himself, and I just happened to be at the absolute worst place at the absolute worst time. Okay?"

The two officers stared at me. Then they looked at each other. The older one picked up a stamp and maintained eye contact with me as he stamped my passport with disgust. Then he slid it across the table to me.

"Gracias, señora," he said. "Bienvenido a España."

***

After our ridiculous delay at Customs it took Doctor Morley an hour to find our driver. Then it took another half-hour for the driver to wind his motorcar back through the crowd to pick us up. Because of the rain, which had begun to come down harder, the motorcars were backed up trying to exit the terminal. So we had to wait again. By the time we finally pulled away from the terminal I was in a foul, foul mood.

About ten minutes into our drive Doctor Morley began his ill-timed diagnosis:

"Wendy, I'm not very good at these situations … but like I said before, I sense the incident on the boat has made a bad situation worse."

"It's that obvious, huh?"

"Yes. And might I offer a suggestion that has helped me immeasurably," he continued. "The best way to deal with troublesome thoughts is to power through them."

As he said 'power' he swung a fist in front of him, like he was rallying a team.

"Power through, right," I said. "I'll try."

"Trying is not enough," he went on. "You need to make a conscious effort to overpower your bad memories, to try and forget the horrible things you saw. You can't allow them to sap all the joy from your life. You deserve better.

"So take those nasty thoughts and emotions and don't give them any sunlight or air. Treat them like a houseplant you want to get rid of. Leave it alone, try not to think about it, and eventually it will wither away and die. Forcing yourself to forget unpleasant things is the way you move on."

"I'm not sure it is," I said. But I had my chin on my hand as I stared out the motorcar window … that made me mumble and Doctor Morley misheard me.

"Ah, good to hear you agree with me," he said. "Moving forward feels good, doesn't it?"

***

It was an hour before midnight when we came into Madrid. The rains, which I had determined were biblical in nature, were still coming down. The streets of the big city were dark and dreary and everything appeared to be closed. I consoled myself dreaming of a hot meal and stiff drink at the hotel.

Then we arrived at the Palace Hotel, a fancy-looking building overlooking a broad avenue. As Doctor Morley checked us in I scoped the place out. It was old and grand, with tall ceilings and Greco-Roman pillars and black-and-white marble floors. In a place like this there had to be a restaurant still open, I assumed. My tastebuds and boozebuds started salivating.

Alas, even at the Palace Hotel all was closed that night … even the in-room dining service.

A bellhop led us to an elevator, up several floors and down a hallway to our rooms. Doctor Morley's room, it turned out, was directly across the hall from mine … as if we needed to be any closer.

I sat in my room and twiddled my thumbs and about ten minutes later I went back down to the lobby. I asked the desk clerk if any cantinas or restaurants nearby were still open. He said no. Then I asked him if I could buy a bottle of wine or booze from the bar. He said no again … but then he smiled and said he had something better. He went into a back office. Minutes later he and came back out with a pitcher.

I took it, thanked him and took a whiff. Odorless.

"Vodka?" I asked, holding out hope.

He gave me a perplexed look. "Uh … agua?" he said.

My disappointment was complete. I took the pitcher and concluded my first day in Spain alone in my hotel room, wishing I had the requisite powers to turn my agua into wine.

Or, better yet, Widow Watson's Whiskey.

6

EL PRIMER DIA

It had been eight long days since we left Chichen Itza. I was sick and tired of Doctor Morley. I suspect he was sick and tired of me, too.

The rains had stopped and it was a cloudy but pleasant morning. Given that it was our first full day on dry land, it would have been nice to walk the mile to the Museum. But his highness was in a yank to get started, so instead of walking we were in a stuffy taxi.

"Va más despacio," the boss commanded our driver. "Slow down, would you? And turn right up here. Gire a la derecha."

Out my window an ornate building with arches and carved columns came into view. It had a tall iron fence ringing its perimeter. Beyond the fence were broad stone steps, and on those steps were several large statues. Doctor Morley gave the poor driver a break and looked past me out my window and said:

"Ah, now see, this is what I was telling you about. This here is the Library entrance. The Museum entrance is on the other side, even though it's the same damn building! The last time I was here, they made me walk all the way around the block—*outside*—just to go from the Museum to the Library. Ridiculous. Mind you, there are doors *inside* that could make it a thirty-second journey."

It was indeed ridiculous. Ridiculous that he had complained about this blasted door a half-dozen times, that is.

"What are all those statues on the steps?" I asked, in a bid to change the subject.

"Driver, it's this turn. Gire a la derecha, sí," he said. "I'm sorry, what's that, Wendy?"

"The statues. Who are they?"

"Ah. Nice to see your curiosity return. Now, let's see, who's up there ... well, that must be San Isodoro on the left. Not sure who that is next to him ... King Alfonso, perhaps? Alfonso the Wise, that is, not the current one. Insert your own joke there. I can't quite see the others, I know Cervantes is up there somewhere. You'll have to look yourself ... you'll have the opportunity, safe to say. This complex will be our headquarters for the next two weeks."

The motorcar turned off the main avenue and onto a side street. The iron fence and the imposing building continued the entire length of the block.

"Sí, and now take one more right and we're there," Doctor Morley said to the driver. "Pull up by the front gate. La puerta principal, sí."

We slowed and made one last turn and the motorcar came to a stop. Doctor Morley motioned for me to get out while he paid the driver.

I double-checked to make sure I had my shoulder bag and got out of the motorcar. As I waited for Doctor Morley I walked toward the tall iron gates. Above them was a sign, also cast in iron: *Bibliotecca y Museos Nacionales.*

"It says both Library and Museum," I said. "That would imply this is an entrance for both."

Doctor Morley closed the motorcar door behind him. His ridiculous pith helmet was askew and he was clutching his portfolio. He looked up, read the sign and shook his head.

"Like I said, there's a door between the two, but it's locked, or at least it was last time, and they wouldn't open it for me. There's a new Director, let's hope he's seen the light. Now, let's get this project started."

The Museum entrance was not as elegant or well-kept as the Library entrance. Leaves and broken branches lined the walkway to the tall front doors. The shrubbery was overgrown, with vines creeping along the building's lower walls. Two small statues, uncleaned in years, adorned the exterior and the modest steps were guarded by two immense stone sphinx. As I studied them I asked:

"Is there a plural form of sphinx? Or is it still sphinx, even if there's two?"

"Sphinges," the boss answered, without missing a beat.

The sphinges were identical and, I dare say, hermaphroditic. They had the face and arms of David, the breasts of Venus and the ribcage of a starving orphan. Their wings were too small and out of proportion with their bodies.

We came up the steps to the tall iron doors. I paused before I stepped inside. My relief at finally reaching our destination was so strong my mouth couldn't hold back.

"Ho-ly sheep-shit," I declared without a thought. "I never thought we'd get here."

Doctor Morley didn't break stride. As he went up the steps toward the doors he said to me, without looking back,

"Again, watch your tongue, Miss Willoughby. You should think about going to a nunnery for a few months to try and clean up your language."

My boss removed his pith helmet. Together, we walked into the Museum.

***

My first impression of the National Archaeological Museum was that it smelled old. It smelled of old things and old people and old air. It was dark, too: There were electric lights on the ceiling, but a good number of them were not lit.

I saw few signs of life, including from behind the ticket desk, where an old woman sat reading a newspaper. Doctor Morley let out a fake cough. The woman gave us the uno-momento finger, read a bit more and then rolled her eyes up to us.

"Ahem. Yes, buenos días, señora," Doctor Morley said. "Cómo estás?"

His friendly demeanor had no effect on her. The old woman stared at him and seemed to chew her cud.

"Ahem. Yes, well, mi nombre es Morley," the boss continued. "Doctor Sylvanus Morley. Director Melida is expecting me."

The old woman kept staring at him. She was still making an odd chewing motion with her mouth. She started smacking her lips.

"That's Sylvanus Morley. From the *Carnegie Institution*," Doctor Morley went on, pausing to see if the Carnegie name would have an impact, which it did not. "I'm an archaeologist. We've travelled here all the way from Mexico and ..."

The old woman held up a hand to stop him from talking. She cleared the abundant phlegm from her throat and picked up a clipboard. She rolled her purple tongue around in her open mouth and said:

"Mor-Lee?"

"Yes. Doctor Sylvanus Morley."

She traced her stubby finger down the page. She found his name and crossed it off. Then she shifted her gaze to me and nodded, cow-like, in my direction.

"Oh, and this is my assistant," Doctor Morley offered. "Mi ayudante."

"Willoughby," I said, jumping in to speed things up. "Wendy Willoughby."

"Billow-Vee?" the old woman said. She started tracing her finger back down the clipboard again. Then she looked up at us and said, "Lo siento, no Billow-Vee."

"Well, there must be some mistake. She's my ayudante ... comprende?" Doctor Morley said, growing more agitated.

"It's Willoughby, with a 'W'," I said to the old woman, but she was busy watching my near-boiling boss:

"Good lord, let's speed things up, shall we?" he said, rapping his knuckles on the counter. "We certainly didn't sail across this ocean for this. Where is Director Melida? Dónde está el Director?"

"En las reuniones. He in meetings, no can bother," came the ticket seller's reply. Then, looking at me, "Usted necesita un boleto."

"A ticket?" Doctor Morley said. "She doesn't need to buy ticket! Don't you know who I am?"

The unfazed look on the old woman's face suggested that even if she knew who he was, she didn't care. She stared at Doctor Morley, without blinking, then raised her trollish finger up and made a 'one' sign. Doctor Morley huffed and puffed and then reached for his wallet and bought my ticket.

"This purchase is made under protest," he said, snatching my ticket from the old woman's clutch. "Have the Director find me the moment he is available, comprende?"

The old lady kept chewing her cud and smacking her lips and said nothing. Doctor Morley let out a final snort of disgust and turned away. He made for the stairs, walking fast, muttering to himself.

I, on the other hand, was in no rush. I slowed my pace so I could peek into one of the ground floor exhibit rooms. I wasn't expecting much ... so what I saw stunned and delighted me.

It was the Egyptian salon—one of several Egyptian salons, I soon discovered—and it was spectacular.

The walls were the color of an ancient desert tomb. Toward the top of the walls there was a magnificent painted frieze featuring animals and palm trees. Above that, inside the molding, were several well-executed Egyptian hieroglyphics. On the ceiling a series of saluting hawks surrounded a bright central mural, which showed a steely-eyed pharaoh receiving offerings from a parade of well-wishers.

Then my eyes came down from the wonders above to the exhibits below. There, in the center of the room, sat two sarcophagi. I took a step closer, when what to my wondering eyes should appear than a real, live mummy … dead, of course. It was all wrinkled and brown and the poor soul's teeth were jutting out. It was disgusting, yet entrancing.

And all around the room were cabinets filled with all manner of Egyptian antiquities. It looked like there were hundreds of objects on display. There were countless small idols and an abundance of pottery. I spied a third sarcophagi, along with even more Tut-like wonders, in the gallery beyond.

I had grown somewhat weary of the Maya. Diving into the world of the Pharaohs would have been a welcome break. But then I heard my boss's too-familiar call:

"Wendy?" Doctor Morley half-hollered. "I'm here, up the stairs. Chop chop."

I took a lingering look and then left the Egyptian room, vowing to return another time. I went back to the main staircase and started up. I could hear Doctor Morley muttering up ahead. He may have been talking to me, but I wasn't listening.

On the mezzanine I paused to look at a large cat-like statue with oversized eyes, then I paused again to peak into one of the adjacent rooms. It had low cabinets and at first seemed unremarkable. But as I came in, the high walls revealed several giant religious-themed tapestries. I made a point to revisit that room as well.

I jogged up the final flight of stairs. The first exhibit room on my left had a sign outside that read *Antiquedades americanas*. I could see Doctor Morley had already gone in. He was scanning the room, looking as if something was wrong.

And I could tell there was, indeed, something wrong. There were only a handful of cabinets in the room and they were all empty. There were a few crates scattered about, nailed shut, and a dolly leaning up against the wall.

Like the Egyptian room, the walls and ceiling had exquisite designs. The walls here were painted to look like large limestone blocks; those faux blocks then met with a sculpted molding that would have been at home at Chichen Itza or Uxmal.

But the room was exhibit-less. Doctor Morley gazed around, looking bewildered.

"Where the hell did everything go?" he said. "There was a large stone ring from Palenque, right here in the middle. These cabinets were all full with Mayan and Olmec and Aztec artifacts. Every last one of them."

He shook his head and I swear I saw steam come out of his ears. Then he walked past the empty cabinets toward the next room. I followed. He stopped when he got to the open doors.

"Well, some of it is still here, thank goodness," he said. "But where in the blazes did they move the primary exhibits?"

He was standing in the doorway leading to the next room, blocking my view. Then he moved to one side and I could see past him.

It was a tight, rectangular room with a high ceiling and dim lighting. The walls were brownish-red. There were two good-sized stelae set against one wall, which I recognized as Mayan. Between them was some bizarre idol I knew wasn't Mayan, or Aztec, or Mesoamerican at all.

Then my eyes came upon the back wall of the small room. There, suspended on the wall, was an enormous Aztec calendar stone. It was magnificent.

"Is that real?" I asked.

"The sun stone? No, but it's a good replica, isn't it?" he said. Then, as he admired the dominating slab, something in the corner of the room caught his eye. A pleasant smile came across his face and he said:

"Ah, I see my contribution is still in its proper place."

I turned around to see what he was looking at. It was another stelae, around five feet tall and two feet wide. It was carved with the image of a Mayan warrior, weapon raised.

"You know how long it took us to drag this sonofabitch out of Palenque?" Doctor Morley said. "Lordy. It was a six-week project just to extricate the stone ... then we had to figure out how to get it out of the blasted jungle. Good times, good times."

"When was that?"

"At least one lifetime ago, almost two. Before the War, that's for sure," he said. His gaze settled upon the next object, an idol, and he said:

"Now, that piece next to it, that little monkey god, he's from Honduras. He's been here much longer. Much of this came from the old Royal Collection, as I'm sure you're aware."

I was not. I studied Doctor Morley's face as his eyes travelled the room. He had a relaxed air about him, as if he were seeing dear friends he had not seen in some time.

In the very center of the room stood an odd display contraption. It was a collection of picture frames, suspended between two tall posts. There were two rows of picture frames on each side of the posts, and a couple dozen frames per row. The frames were mounted on hinges, so that you could push one frame away to view the next one, like the pages of a book.

Below the hanging frames sat two long, low leather benches.

"That's it, by the way," Doctor Morley remarked.

I looked to him and then back to the hanging frames.

"It's … what?" I said.

"The Codex," he replied.

So here it was: my assignment. The ancient document I had travelled from another continent to view and copy. I walked up to the first frame I saw. It held some fragments of paper that didn't look Mayan at all.

"No, the frames on the other side," Doctor Morley said.

I walked around to the other side of the exhibit and bent down to look at the first frame.

There were four small pages in it, mounted two by two, with two pages on top and two on the bottom. Each individual page was about the same size as a normal-sized page from a normal-sized novel. But it was a primitive type of paper: parchment, or maybe vellum.

I took my shoulder bag off, placed it on the low bench and leaned in for a closer inspection of those first pages.

They showed typical Mayan images. Gods with elaborate headdresses, serpents slithering up from below, that sort of thing. Then scattered all over the pages were Mayan glyphs, dozens of them, most quite small. Some of these glyphs were only half-visible due to the wear and tear around the pages; others had been worn off altogether. There were Mayan numerals crammed into the spaces between the glyphs.

I pushed the first frame out of the way, only to discover the pages had images on both sides. The backsides were similar to the front sides: more gods, more serpents, more glyphs. On one page there were even itty-bitty glyphs crammed into the tail of a serpent. There was more color than I expected, too, including rusty browns and several variations of blue.

I turned and looked at the next frame. It was the same setup: four pages, two over two, with color images on both the front and the back. I flipped to the next frame, then the one after that, then I said, out loud:

"You have got to be frickin' kidding me!"

"What's that?" Doctor Morley said, coming up beside me.

"It's ... it's so *detailed*," I said. "Look at all these glyphs! They're so small! I didn't know they would be this small. And there's so many pages!"

"It's remarkable, isn't it?" Doctor Morley said.

"It's an enormous amount of work, that's what it is!" I shot back. "You want me to make a replica of this entire thing?"

Doctor Morley's stern face told me that yes, he did.

"You *cannot* be serious," I went on. "There has to be a hundred pages here!"

"Nonsense. There's only fifty-six."

"Front and back?" I countered.

"Well, I suppose if you count it that way, yes," he agreed. "So it's a hundred-and-twelve. Is that a problem?"

Was he daft?

"You better believe there's a problem," I said, almost in disbelief. "This is a massive undertaking! It would take me a month! I've got what, two weeks? And … you want it in color?"

"Of course I want it in color," Doctor Morley shot back, testier. "If I didn't need color, I would use photographs."

"Then let's color the photographs!"

"We tried that already and it didn't work. It washed out all the details and nuanced shading."

I started flipping through the frames again, exasperated. "You expect me to copy this with a free hand? Nuanced shading and all?"

"Do it however you need to do it," Doctor Morley said, sounding exasperated himself. "Trace it for all I care. Nuances would be greatly appreciated. And take pride in knowing that your work will result in perhaps the most accurate color reproduction ever of the Madrid Codex."

"Such an honor," I replied, rolling my eyes and then moving on. "It's not in very good shape, that's for sure. What's it made of?"

"Reconstituted pulp, mostly," Doctor Morley replied. "But then they slathered a layer of chalk stucco on top and painted on that."

"How was it bound?"

"Not like a normal book. It folds up like an accordion, like this," he said, making a wide accordion-playing motion with his arms. "We're not sure who cut it into individual pages, though. I believe that happened after the two halves of the codice were reunited. Here, let's pull this bench out for you."

He already had one hand on the low bench and was looking up at me, waiting for assistance. I pondered what he had just said as I bent down. We lifted the bench up and away from the frames so I could sit while looking at the Codex.

"What do you mean by reunited?" I asked as we set the bench down.

Doctor Morley placed his end down, let go, stiffened his back and looked at me with an I-knew-it look.

"Now, Miss Willoughby, are you telling me you neglected to read the Archaeological Digest article I told you to read before this trip?" he said.

He was talking about the papers he had given me and asked me to read. Which I had intended to do, until the incident on the Orizaba foiled my good intentions. Doctor Morley sensed my ignorance and the lecture commenced:

"Well then," he began. "What you see before you is one of only three known Mayan codices, the others being in Paris and, of course, Dresden. Now, as to its genesis, there are some—present company excluded—that contend ...,"

"The short version, please," I interrupted.

Doctor Morley stopped and shot me a nasty look. I had to smile a sweet smile to get out of my jam. It worked.

"You really should have read that article," he said. "But very well. The short version: this came out of the Yucatán. There's some torn shards from a papal bull on one of its pages, we suspect that's the only way it survived the Conquest. Remember, Diego de Landa and his ilk were burning everything they could find ... conducting an Inquisition for the New World, if you will."

"Bull?"

"Dammit, Wendy, put a cork in that smart-ass attitude."

"No ... what's a 'papal bull?'"

"Oh, sorry. A papal bull is a formal decree from the Vatican."

I nodded and he continued.

"But it survived and somehow it made it over the ocean. The Codex came to Spain and then, for reasons unknown, someone split it into two parts. Eventually, years later, one part ended up with an academic in Madrid. Charles Brasseur de Bourbourg—a French ethnographer—heard about it, tracked it down, examined it and identified it as a late Mayan piece. Tried to translate it using de Landa's crude Mayan-to-Spanish alphabet, you can imagine how that went. Brasseur de Bourbourg named those seventy pages the Troano, after the fellow that then owned it.

"The other half ended up right next door, buried in the stacks of the National Library. It sat there undisturbed for generations. Now, Wendy, for one hundred dollars, can you name the researcher that said, 'A-ha! These two codices are one in the same!'"

I wasn't playing.

"That would have been easy money if you had read the paper," Doctor Morley said. "The answer is Leon de Rosny. See? You should listen to me. Anyhoo, Rosny was the one that recognized the two codices were actually parts of one larger codex. He notified the Museum and voila, witness the Codex Cortesianus."

He said his last line with a flourish. I didn't share his enthusiasm.

"Why'd they call it that?"

"The Director here at the time was certain it had been brought back by Cortés himself."

"And ... was it?"

"The jury's still out on that," he answered. "Perhaps you will be the first to find the answer."

I sighed and pitied myself. The full scope of my miserable project had been revealed. It was an Atlas-sized undertaking, something that I could envision taking months to complete. I had two work-weeks.

"I imagine you're overwhelmed by this," Doctor Morley said, a more polite way to say what I was thinking. "If it's any consolation, I'm not looking to decipher the damn thing. Most of the glyphs and numerals illustrate astronomical or agricultural events. Those are of no concern to us. What I need you to do is look for marks or patterns that seem, well, out-of-place."

"Out-of-place?"

"Such as a series of images that looked like it may have been drawn by a different person or at a different time. See if any markings or patterns stand out, or if colors that should match up don't match up," he said. "And always, always keep those maps you looked at in the forefront of your thoughts."

I had to bite my tongue. After all this time, I still didn't know exactly what I was supposed to be looking for. I chose to not ask again. I had work to do, miserable work, which meant I needed Doctor Morley to leave me alone.

"Aren't you going to see if you can find the other Mesoamerican exhibits?" I asked, knowing that would send him spiraling off in another direction.

"Yes, yes, right. Perhaps they've moved some things downstairs. They're always moving things around, you know, based upon what visitors want to see. Can't see why they'd abandon these rooms, what with that wonderful molding and all. But more people would see the Mayan and Aztec exhibits on the first floor. They must be in the process of moving it all down there."

"I'm sure that's the case," I said, doubting very much that it was.

"I'll go downstairs and take a look," my boss said, then added, "And I'm sure you're eager to get started."

I gave him an energetic but fake smile-and-nod. Doctor Morley smile-and-nodded back, pivoted and walked out of the room.

I turned back to the Codex. One hundred and how many pages?

"What have you gotten yourself into, silly girl?" I said to myself.

Then I opened my shoulder bag, pulled out my notebook and drawing kit, and pondered my gargantuan task.

***

I began with a ruler. I measured one of the pages in the first frame, then drew a corresponding rectangle in my notebook. I freehanded the little nicks and cuts around the edges, which Doctor Morley had made a point of telling me to include.

I sketched an outline of the largest image on the page, a king, or maybe a god, brandishing a club-like weapon. Then I tried to copy the cloud-like swirls rising up out of his head and the ornaments dangling around his neck. It didn't look right, so I had to erase much of him and start over. It took me fifteen minutes to draw that one figure.

Then I tried to replicate a line of glyphs. Some were too faded to see. And there were numerals drawn below the glyphs, some quite small, and I wanted to get the spacing between everything correct. That proved to be easier thought than done, and I had to get my ruler out again.

When I got that first page outlined to my satisfaction, I got my colored pencils out. I flipped the case open on the bench and tried to choose the best orange and the best blue.

Then it dawned on me: I was supposed to be looking for patterns. So I took a moment and stared at the Codex and tried to remember inhaling Doctor Morley's maps and photographs. As I looked, all I could think was:

"This is such a crock of crap."

And right after I said that I heard voices getting closer. One of the voices was Doctor Morley's. He was in the next room, the empty gallery that had once been the primary American Antiquities room.

"I mean, look at this ceiling!" he said, his voice growing louder. "Look at that! Does that look 'Far East' to you? Does it? No! Of course not! Mesoamerican! The collection belongs here!"

A Spanish voice, much calmer than the American one, responded. I couldn't hear the exact words that person said, but I heard Doctor Morley's response.

"*Paint* it? Why the hell would you paint it?"

Once again I couldn't make out what the other person was saying … then Doctor Morley grew louder:

"A Chinese temple! A Mayan frieze, painted to look like a Chinese temple? That's … well, that's preposterous! An abomination! An insult to two cultures! Who could have made such a dim-witted decision?"

And then a proper-looking gentlemen in a dark suit came striding into the room where I sat copying. He was petite and had a moustache the width of his face. Doctor Morley came in just behind him, badgering away:

"Juan, I ask, who decided this?"

The proper-looking gentlemen wheeled around. He had his hands clasped behind his back. He stared at Doctor Morley like a stern schoolmaster and said:

"I did, Señor Morley. As Director of this Museum, it was my decision. I did it for, as you Americans say, the greater good."

"The greater good!" Doctor Morley exclaimed. "I fail to see how burying the Mayans and the Aztecs and the Incas in the hidden recesses of this place is going ...,"

"There is no 'burying in hidden recesses' going on," the Director said, cutting him. "As I told you, all objects that have been on display shall remain on display. Sí?"

"In a back hallway!" Doctor Morley replied. "In a back hallway, where nobody will ever see it."

The Director smiled. His eyes wandered as he thought of the polite thing to say:

"It may pain you to hear this. But it not the Maya, the Aztec or the Inca that visitors come here to see. They come to see ..."

"You don't have to tell me. The damn mummies," Doctor Morley snarled.

The Director nodded and said:

"Sí. The damn mummies, as you call them, are our top draw. The Egyptian salons are our most popular exhibit rooms. And that is precisely why we need more space for Egyptian artifacts."

"Hmph," Doctor Morley snorted. "I think everyone's a bit Egypt-ed out, aren't they?"

"Not yet," the Director said, after which Doctor Morley snarled:

"Your job is to educate the masses, not give them what they want."

Director Melida didn't care for that remark. He leaned in and wagged a finger at Doctor Morley and said:

"Señor Morley … do not tell me how to do my job. I don't tell you how to do yours."

My boss looked about two feet tall. The Director finished him off:

"If a sealed tomb overflowing with gold and silver is ever unearthed in the Americas, we can revisit this topic. Until then, I have more urgent matters to attend to."

The Director pivoted to me and gave a polite, efficient good-bye nod. Then, without another word, he walked past a deflated Doctor Morley and out of the room.

***

After venting his countless frustrations to me, Doctor Morley left for the Library. He was in a rotten mood, which only added to my own rotten mood.

Copying the Codex was going to be boring, tedious, piss-me-off work. I was mad at my boss for offering me this project and I was at myself for accepting it. I was mad at the Mayans for creating the thing in the first place. I was mad at the Spaniards for not burning it when they had a chance. I was mad at all those dolts Doctor Morley had mentioned that found it and brought it here. I was mad at the Archeological Museum for being open, when I would much rather be at the Prado.

I spent the next two hours measuring and tracing and free-handing and coloring. That netted me a grand total of three completed pages. If my eyes passed over any hidden clues or patterns, I missed them … and that didn't bother me one bit.

At lunchtime, I bought a roll and some fresh-cut ham from a street cart. I sat outside to eat and it was delicious, the perfect lunch. Then I went back into the Museum to resume my duties.

When I came into the room housing the Codex there was an odd, skinny man there. He was leaning against the wall, staring at the Aztec calendar stone, stroking his hairless chin. When he turned around he seemed surprised to see me. He looked at me in a peculiar way, almost as if he knew me. That made me uncomfortable, so I turned back around, went to the mezzanine and pretended to look at tapestries. I stayed there until I heard the man go down the stairs, then I went back up to the top floor to resume my work.

By the end of that first shitty day in Madrid I had completed five and one-half pages. I still had over a hundred to go.

7

THE SHE-DEVIL

The next morning, Doctor Morley escorted me into the Museum the moment the doors opened. Then he shared with me his thoughts on my previous day's efforts, which he found lacking and uninspired.

"There's no such thing as an 'inspired' copy. I did my best."

"Try harder. And pick up the pace," he commanded. Then, before I had a chance to stab him with my pencil, he went off to find Director Melida.

The pages of the Codex looked even more imposing and overwhelming than the day before. My first few pages featured an unreal concentration of gods and kings, many of them sporting bizarre headdresses that were hard to replicate. The glyphs were smaller and never, ever in a straight line. The serpents seemed more detailed, with little dots and speckles all over them.

There was a hideous page dominated by a fading image of a Mayan god. He had snake-like tentacles crawling up out of his neck and he was holding what appeared to be a fresh human heart. Worse, he was crouching down so he could crap Mayan numerals out of his backside. As I copied the markings exploding out his ass, I began to reconsider my decision to pursue the arts.

But, as I worked through the pages, my technique and my familiarity with the layout improved. Many pages had bold horizontal lines, which made roughing things out much easier. I also discovered, the hard way, that it was easier to color some sections before sketching the glyphs.

I was on the tenth or eleventh page when I heard someone walking toward the room. I assumed it was another poor soul who had wandered away from one of the Egyptian salons and gotten lost in the hallways of boredom. So I was startled when I turned and saw the skinny, peculiar man I had seen the day before.

He looked surprised to see me as well. He gave me a polite nod and I nodded back. I thought he was about to say something, but then he stopped himself. Out of the corner of my eye I watched him as he walked across the room, toward the Aztec calendar stone.

He was an odd duck. At first glance he looked almost bald … then I saw he had stubble growing in, as if he had recently shaved his head. He had a faint hint of hair on his upper lip, like he was trying and failing to grow a moustache. He was wearing a grey suit that looked to be several sizes too big and hung off his thin frame.

He stopped in front of the giant stone and put a hand to his chin. He pondered the mighty monolith for a short moment then turned back to me and said:

"Señora, puedo usar esto, por favor?"

He motioned to the second bench, on the other side of the frames.

"Um … oh, yes. No es problema," I replied.

Right away he picked up where I was from:

"Ah, an Americano. Good, good. I thank you."

He bent over, lifted up one end of the other long bench and then slid it across the floor toward the Aztec stone. But instead of putting it squarely in front of the stone, which would have been logical, he dragged the bench all the way to the side wall. He looked up at the stone, decided the bench wasn't quite right, reached down and dragged it a foot or so farther back. Then he sat down, with the bench now a good ten feet away from the stone and at an odd angle. He crossed his legs, then his arms. Finally, he reached up and stroked his bare chin and contemplated the relic.

He was weird. I don't care for weirdos, so I took a break for lunch … and went to find Doctor Morley to see if he wanted to join me.

***

I proceeded down the stairs, out the Museum doors, through the gates, around the corner and down the block to the Library. Then I passed through the Library gates, pausing to inventory the statues on the steps.

In the front sat Alfonso the Wise, crown on head and sword in hand. Next to him was San Isidoro, turning a thick stone page in his stone Bible. Behind them on the back steps stood Nebrija, Luis Vives and Lope de Vega … three men I knew absolutely nothing about. I did, however, know a bit about the last statue. It showed Miguel de Cervantes, his opus in one hand and a feather pen in the other.

I paused again to admire the intricate ironwork around the Library doors, then passed through. It was cool inside, a much more pleasant temperature than the Museum. It smelled better, too.

After the front desks I came through a wide arch and into the main reading room. It was jaw-dropping. The room was a hundred feet tall and on the ceiling were a dozen or more sun-windows. Below those windows rose glorious arches and columns; between those columns were catwalks and bookcases and thousands upon thousands of books. The floor of the great room was covered with long tables and chairs, most of which sat empty. A bored librarian sat at a central, u-shaped desk and I asked him to point me in the right direction.

I wound up and into the stacks. A few minutes later I found Doctor Morley. He was sitting at a small table that was crammed between two tall bookcases. There were piles of books and documents in front of him. His pith helmet was perched on top of one of the piles. I startled him when I spoke.

"Mercy! That *is* a long walk," was all I said, but it was enough to make the former spy jump out of his shoes.

"Dammitall! Don't sneak up on me like that!" he hissed, trying not to yell even though he wanted to.

"I'm sorry. But I see what you mean … it's a pain in the-you-know-what to go all the way around."

"Right? It's ridiculous. The door from the hallway beyond your Mesoamerican room opens up right over there, into that corridor. It could be a back-and-forth thing for us if they would unlock it," Doctor Morley said. "I'm starting to think the Director is keeping it closed just to piss me off."

"And is it working?" I said, trying to be funny.

"Ah. Ha-ha-ha. There's that wit again," my boss said, leaning back in his chair. "Now, to what do I owe the pleasure?"

"I'm going for lunch. I thought you might want to join me."

"I don't have time for lunch. Neither do you, to be quite honest," he said, semi-serious.

"Oh, fiddlesticks. We both have to eat."

"I'll eat tonight," the martyr said. "I'm too busy now."

I didn't push the subject, but wanted to be on good terms with him.

"Any luck with the … hunt?" I asked.

Doctor Morley let out a great sigh and looked at the books and papers in front of him.

"I was able to track down some of Brasseur de Bourbourg's materials, including a notebook. Can't say there's much in here that's original. He had quite an imagination, that man. I found some references to 'Mu' in here, that was his term for Atlantis," he said.

As if on cue I wheeled around and started to walk away. He called after me:

"What the hay? Where are you going?"

I turned back and said:

"If *any* of this involves Atlantis, count me out," I declared. "I'll be at the Prado, then the bar."

He chuckled, even though I was being quite truthful.

"Oh, we're not looking for Atlantis, my dear," he said, now with a fatherly smile. "Unless you want to, of course."

My eyes delivered my answer.

"Very well. Now come back over here, look at what else I found."

He pushed some papers aside and pulled out a small, yellowed page. It was a map.

"Look familiar?" he asked.

It did. It was Frederick Catherwood's map of Kabah. I had never been to Kabah, a Mayan site south of Santa Elena. But I knew a lot about Frederick Catherwood. He was an architect-slash-artist who explored Central America in the 1800s, one of the first white-skinned men to see the lost cities of the New World. I recognized his cartography in an instant.

"Wonderful," I remarked. "Is that what we're looking for? Are we done?"

"If only it were that easy," Doctor Morley said. "Alas, it is but a copy ... probably torn from one of Stephens' lesser-known works. Still, I have to wonder why it's in here with Brasseur's junk. Anyway, I thought you would find that interesting, I know you're a Catherwood fan. Now, how's it going with you?"

"Alright," I replied. "Better."

"Better. How many pages?"

"Ten, I think."

"Ten!"

"I meant twelve. Now on to thirteen," I fibbed.

"You're moving too slow."

"It's slow work. Plus, you told me you want me to look for patterns and all that."

"Well, yes, that's your primary objective. You just need to do it much, much faster."

"I'll do my best. It's so detailed," I said. "But I'll eat fast and get back on it. Which reminds me … do we have dinner plans? I was hoping to visit the Prado before it closes."

Doctor Morley looked at me like I was a moron and said:

"Well, of course we have dinner plans. We're meeting Veronica at eight. We discussed that this morning."

No, we had not discussed anything like that.

"Dinner? With … Veronica?" I said. "Oh no, you *definitely* didn't tell me that."

Doctor Morley gave me a knowing grin and said:

"Then this must be your lucky day. I'll meet you in the lobby a bit before eight, okay?"

I shuddered, dreading dinner with that wretched she-devil.

***

After another delicioso lunch from Dulcinea's, the aromatic little cart outside the Library gates, I got back to business. I ignored all distractions and ignored my aching wrist. By the end of the day I had completed the fourteenth page of the Codex and outlined the fifteenth. Then, in my mind, a workman's whistle went off and I quit for the day.

I loaded my pencils and notebook in my shoulder bag, slid the bench back under the frames and started down the stairs. One of the guards was standing on the mezzanine. I had caught him checking me out the day before. When he saw me he gave a goofy grin.

"Ah, señorita, the day … it is done, no?"

"Almost," I said. He looked like he wanted attention, so I gave him a nice smile and tried to walk past him. It didn't work.

"The day, it is done … but the night, she has not yet started," he said, and maneuvered into my path. "I am Lothario."

"Yes, well, hola Lothario," I replied. I tried to move past him a second time, but that made him turn and start to walk alongside me.

"You are the Vendy, no?" he said. "You are here with the American arqueólogo?"

I didn't want to engage with him but had no choice.

"Yes," I said. "And it's pronounced Wendy."

"Ah, Wuh-endy," he said, struggling with the 'w' sound. "Like with the Peter Pan."

"Exactly, sí."

He gave me his goofiest look yet and then said:

"And you, Vendy, you enjoy Spain so far, ah?"

"I haven't seen much of it," I admitted. "But that's about to change … I'm going to the Prado right now, before they close. You'll have to pardon me."

I kept moving down the stairs, but my escort paused. From in back of me, he said:

"Umm ... señorita, you do know the Prado … that she is closed. Ah?"

"No, they're open until seven today," I informed him, which I knew was true because I had read it on a pamphlet at the hotel.

The guard didn't respond at first. He had one of those I've-got-some-bad-news looks on his face. He said:

"Umm ... you see, it is the floors of the Prado. They are being, how you say, making the surfaces new again?"

"The floors?" I said, trying to piece his clues together. "You mean ... they're ... refinishing the floors?"

"Yes, sí, 'refinishing,' that is the word."

"And the Prado is ... *closed?*"

"Sí."

"For ... for how long?"

The guard seemed frightened to deliver the news. He gulped and said:

"Ummm ... it is closed for two weeks. Maybe three."

I couldn't believe it. My rage wouldn't allow me to believe it.

I stormed out of the Museum, looked for a taxi, couldn't find one, marched down the side street to the Library and found an available driver.

"Llevame al El Prado!" I barked. "Rapido!"

I was sweating and flustered, so the driver must have thought I had robbed a bank or something. He squealed his tires pulling out, then yanked a hard turn onto the side street ... almost tipping our car over. Then he dodged horse-carts and yelling pedestrians and a handful of police officers. At the final intersection he didn't even stop, he just raced through. He came within inches of hitting several other motorcars and then literally scared the shit out of some poor mule. Finally, he cranked hard on the wheel and the car spun around so hard I was thrown across the back seat to the other door. We stopped. I looked out my window and there it was: the Prado. I fumbled for a shirt button and started to pull my money belt over.

"No, no, fue un placer," the driver said, an exhilarated smile on his face. "It was truly my pleasure."

I got out and marched up the steps to the entrance of the one damn place I wanted to visit on this damn trip. As I climbed I could feel my anger rising. Then I saw the doors. There was a sign that said *CERRADO*.

Closed. The goddamn Prado was closed.

My heart broke, metaphorically. I fell to my knees, raised my arms, shook my fists at the Heavens and cried out:

"You have go to be frickin' kidding me!"

***

Not long after, I rode on a river of fury through the lobby and into the dining room of the Palace Hotel.

I was, in spite of my foul mood, in spectacular surroundings. The dining room had a stunning stained-glass dome, dominated by an enormous chandelier. The chandelier must have had ten thousand crystals. Lining the perimeter of the room were double Roman columns; above the columns a delicate swirling facade ran all the way around, like the decorative lip of a bowl. I lost myself in the majesty of the room for a moment, trying to calm myself down.

"Wendy!" came a too-loud and much-too-familiar voice.

Doctor Morley was at a nearby table, waving his napkin in the air. He looked like a fool. But he was alone, which was a relief. I sat down and shared the bad news.

"Would you believe the Prado is *closed?*" was all I could say. "For two weeks!"

"Yes, I just overheard some people talking about that," he said. "I guess the fumes had been making people sick and they had to close the doors to visitors."

"They should *not* be able to do that," I insisted. "What about people that are only here a few days?"

"Well, you're lucky to have a whole other Museum to spend time in," he replied, trying to sound clever and only pissing me off.

Then his eyes drifted up over my shoulder and he said: "Oh, good, here she is."

Doctor Morley stood to greet her. I looked up and there was the Ice Queen herself: Veronica Shetty.

She was wearing one of those Japanese-style dresses. It was black, with red-and-pink embroidered vines climbing up that showed off her curves. It was too bad that she was such a horrible person, because she had wonderful fashion sense.

Veronica strutted across the room like a regal cat. All the men in the room were craning their necks for a better look. She sashayed her way over to our table and said:

"Sylvanus, so good to finally see you in person again," kissing him on both cheeks. "Off to a good start, I hope? Excellent, excellent."

Then she turned to me and looked me up and down.

"Ah, yes. And Wendy. How lovely to see you," she said, in that too-perfect English voice of hers.

"Veronica. Yes. How lovely," I replied.

It was not lovely for either of us. She didn't lean in to give me one of those dopey two-cheek kisses like she had Doctor Morley. Instead, we eyed each other for a second and then she remarked:

"That's such an *interesting* dress. I haven't seen that style in years."

It was so her. I gave her a death stare, along with a gentle nod of my head to thank her for staying true to form.

"Ooh, I know that look," she said with a shit-eating grin. "Apologies. I didn't mean for that to come off the wrong way."

"It's all good," I lied, and she came back with:

"You *are* as angry as they say, aren't you?"

I was at a loss for words. I dug down deep for a cutting comeback but my well was dry. Veronica sensed it and looked away to Doctor Morley, who motioned her to a chair. She sat, and I stood there dazed for a moment. Seething, I sat back down, too ... but my companions ignored me and started jabbering.

"How are the rooms here?" she asked.

"Quite nice," Doctor Morley said. "Nice bed. Food is alright. And you're staying where?"

"Over at the Benengeli. It's down the Gran Via. It's new, you know. Most lovely."

"Expensive?"

"I suppose," Veronica said in a snotty of-course-its-expensive way.

"And is Thatcher staying there too?" Doctor Morley asked.

Veronica cocked her head and said:

"Why, Sylvanus, didn't you get the message?"

Doctor Morley's look indicated he had not gotten the message. Veronica delivered it:

"Thatcher's not coming."

"Not coming!" Doctor Morley said, mouth agape. "What ... why ...?"

"Long story," Veronica replied. "Let's just say it was decided he wasn't the appropriate person for the job."

"Not the ... *appropriate person?*" my boss said, displeased. "Jim is one of the most experienced researchers I know!"

"Again, it's a long story, Sylvanus ... and I'm not at liberty to discuss all the details. Rest assured you'll get all the support you need while you're here."

"Now, see here: I find it preposterous that I wasn't informed of this earlier. No Thatcher? You couldn't have sent a telegram to that effect? Hell, I could have brought another hand from Chichen Itza. I could have brought Blom, for that matter."

"Again, you'll be well-supported," Veronica said.

"Hmph. Who? Joyce? Hunter? Redruth?"

"Howard."

At that name Doctor Morley clenched his jaw and glared at Veronica. His face became a new shade of crimson. Through his teeth he seethed:

"*Howard?*"

"He'll be here tomorrow," was Veronica's reply.

"And is he ...," Doctor Morley began.

"Is he staying at the Benengeli?" Veronica asked, in a teasing tone. "Yes."

"Cute. My question was ... is he still a goddamn drunk?"

"Oh, hush, you and your judgements," Veronica shot back. "He's everything you need."

"He's a pickled blowhard. A useless one, at that," Doctor Morley growled.

"Look at you, you're as mad as she is," Veronica said, with a dismissive nod toward me.

"And how the hell are we supposed to be quiet about these matters with Howard's loose lips around?" my boss asked.

Just then a waiter approached and they stopped talking. Veronica asked about the champagne selection, turned her nose up at each one then ordered wine. I told the waiter to bring me a double whiskey; Doctor Morley followed suit and asked for a double Manhattan. Veronica, it seemed, was enough to drive us both to drink.

"You shouldn't be so quick to judge. Howard's a good man," Veronica said as the waiter departed.

"With all due respect, I've known Howard for far longer than you have," Doctor Morley said. "Men his age don't change, they only harden into their habits. Trust me."

"I appreciate the warning," Veronica said. "But it is what it is."

Doctor Morley huffed and shook his head. I felt like I was being ignored, so I said:

"Who's Howard?"

But they paid no attention to me. Doctor Morley kept going.

"And pardon me for saying it, but ... I doubt he has the physical where-with-all to be of any assistance."

"Again so judgmental, Sylvanus!" Veronica shot back.

"Um ... who's Howard?" I said again and was again ignored.

"Well, pardon me for being upset," Doctor Morley seethed. "It's not like I don't have good reason. Oh, and speaking of being upset, where's the headdress?"

"Don't ask questions you know the answer too," Veronica said. "The headdress is still in Vienna."

Now I held up a hand and said:

"Wait ... you mean, my headdress? The one Oliver and I found?"

It was as if I was invisible and mute. They kept arguing. Doctor Morley folded his arms and said:

"Vienna! That artifact has as much business being in Vienna as ... as ... a snowball in the desert!"

Veronica gave him a sympathetic look, as if she felt sorry he couldn't come up with a wittier comeback. Doctor Morley leaned in a bit, darted his eyes both ways, and said:

"You get my point. That relic holds enormous cultural importance. It doesn't belong in Vienna, it belongs in Mexico."

"And someday it will be returned," Veronica said. "But for now, it's in safe hands."

"Utter bullshit," Doctor Morley continued. "Moctezuma wasn't a goddamn Austrian. And just you wait, those ninnies in Vienna will come up with some excuse not to give it back."

"Oh, give it a rest," Veronica said.

"Watch, they'll say it's too fragile to send it back. Mark my words."

"Enough, Sylvanus."

The waiter came back with our drinks and they stopped talking. I was grateful for both occurrences. We all sipped our booze in peace, then Veronica asked for an update on our efforts.

Doctor Morley then went into a long spiel about everything we had done in Madrid, with a strong emphasis on his efforts and not mine. He went on and on about what he found, or didn't find, in the Library. He dropped historical names that meant nothing to me but may have meant something to Veronica. He rattled on about missing records, and complained it was all too much for one man. Lastly, he said:

"The one bright spot has been Wendy's work. Her reproduction of the Codex will be wonderful."

Without giving me as much as a look Veronica replied:

"We're looking for clues, not a copy, Sylvanus."

"Yes, but the only way to find those clues is to break the Codex down into component parts," Doctor Morley said. "That's what she's doing."

"And is that the best use of her time?"

"I believe so, yes."

I let out a fake cough to remind them I was at the table, too.

"Maybe she should be working with you, instead of being by herself all day." Veronica continued.

"Don't tell me how to manage my people," Doctor Morley snipped.

"Umm ... I'm *right here*," I interjected.

Veronica and Doctor Morley glared at each other for a moment more. Then the she-devil turned her gaze to me. I swear she licked her lips.

"Ah, yes, here you are," she said to me. "I'm sorry, we've been ignoring you, haven't we? Now ... how go your battles, dearie?"

Dearie. Battles. She was a piece of work.

"Better," I offered.

"Better," she repeated. "Mm-hm. All over things?"

With that she arched an eyebrow and I couldn't hold back.

"Must you be such a bitch?" I said.

Doctor Morley gagged. He went for his drink and took a big gulp. Veronica squinted her serpentine eyes at me and went for the kill:

"Oh, stop projecting your nastiness onto others," she said. "I'll remind you that *you're* the one that shot Charles Lindbergh, not me."

Doctor Morley spit-sprayed half his drink over the table. I gasped and couldn't breathe. I think my heart stopped for a moment.

I could not believe this evil woman had just said what she had just said.

Veronica was staring at me, a shit-eating grin on her face. Doctor Morley jerked around to scan behind him and make sure nobody had overheard her words. I was stunned and shocked. I struggled to find the right words to fire back at her. I wasn't finding any … and Veronica knew it.

"Ouch," she said. "I suppose I shouldn't have brought that up. Apologies again."

Then she leaned back in her chair and pulled her itty-bitty evening bag onto her lap. She opened it and pulled out a small silver case. She opened the case and pulled out a thinner-than-normal cigarette and then a fancy silver cigarette holder. She screwed the cigarette into the holder. Out of nowhere some handsome chap swooped in, lit her fancy smoke and then swooped away again.

As I watched her my mind swirled. I didn't dare say anything that might confirm her horrid accusation. But I had a strong suspicion that she already knew more about what transpired in the jungle than she should have. Someone had told her what really happened. My mind and gaze shifted to the most obvious suspect.

"I have no idea what you're talking about," I seethed to Veronica, my glare fixed on Doctor Morley.

"Oh, come now," Veronica said. "You can't truly believe that juicy little detail would remain secret, did you?"

My tongue was still tied. My stomach was in knots. The witch continued to torture me.

"I think it's rather exciting. You're a strong person, being able to keep a red-hot secret like that. The entire world thinks 'Lucky Lindy' was in a crash and beat the odds to survive. If I was the person that pumped a couple of shotgun rounds into him, I'm not sure I'd be able to stay quiet about it."

"Stop it," Doctor Morley said under his breath. "That's enough of such talk."

Veronica kept grinning at me. I had to come up with something.

"Bad things happened out there," was all I could come up with.

"Mm-hm, bad things," Veronica said. "My understanding is that you've been so wrapped up in those 'bad things' that you've become quite the grump."

"Stop attacking me," I protested.

"Oh, I'm not attacking you. I'm simply encouraging you to get over yourself ... and to stop playing the victim. The role doesn't suit you," she said.

I didn't take the bait. She kept at it, leaning forward, cigarette in hand, a wicked smile on her lips:

"You know, there's a question I've been wanting to ask you: Have you ever stopped to consider what Charles Lindbergh must think of you?"

She said it in a low voice but it was enough to make Doctor Morley squirm in his seat. He scanned the room again to make sure no one was listening in.

I was staring at Veronica. I wanted to deliver my response using my fists. I wanted to lunge at her and shove her stupid silver cigarette holder down her smarmy little throat to shut her up. She kept going.

"Think about it. There he was, the most famous man in the world, had the world at his fingertips. Then his path crossed with ... *you*," she said, taking great delight in my suffering. "I saw a picture of him in a newspaper yesterday. He's still in the wheelchair, you know. Can't walk. All because of you."

She took a break and took a drag.

"I'm afraid someone has provided you with bad information," was the best response I could come up with.

"Oh, please. I'm afraid *you're* avoiding the truth, Wendy," she shot back. "You can't be a reliable narrator of your story if you're not being fully honest with yourself, can you? That's what my literature professors would have said."

I continued trying to kill her with my eyes.

"Wendy, I think you need a cold dose of reality here. There are people besides us that know what really happened out there. It's only a matter of time before the true story reveals itself."

I could only glare. I wanted her to vanish in a puff of smoke or fly off on a broom or however it was witches disappeared.

"Again ... I have no idea what you're talking about," I snarled.

She looked at me and grinned and shook her head and took another drag off her cigarette. The monster's feeding was complete.

"I guess denial is more than just a river in Egypt," she said. "Old joke, sorry. Now, Sylvanus, let's discuss more pressing concerns."

8

THE MADNESS OF DOCTOR MORLEY

The following day was overcast and gloomy, matching my mood.

We left the hotel by nine. We took a taxi, which had to turn around on the boulevard to take us to the Museum. As the motorcar made its turn I could see the Prado out my window. It looked cold and grey and closed. It was farther away than ever.

Doctor Morley was yammering away next to me. I'm not sure if he was talking to himself or to me, but I hoped it was the former because I wasn't paying a lick of attention.

While stopped at an intersection, I noticed two men arguing in front of a white government-looking building. Their voices were loud enough for me to hear through the car window.

"España! Tradicion! Monarquía!" one of them chanted, over and over

"Primo de Rivera es un dictador! Un dictador!" the other one yelled back.

Just then the taxi started to move again and Doctor Morley said:

"Well? What do you think?"

And he was waiting for me to respond to whatever the hell it was he had just asked me.

"Um ... sorry, bit of wax in my ear," I said. "Could you repeat that?"

"Hmph," he said. "Ear wax. Right. I asked was how far you expect to get today."

"On the Codex?"

"Of course on the Codex. Goodness, are you still asleep inside?"

"I'm just tired," I replied. "I suppose I'll get up to the ... mid-20s?"

"The mid-20s!" he exclaimed.

"I meant the mid-30s."

"I'm sure you did. Well, I know it's hard, but try to up the pace, okay?" he said. "We've much to do, much to do. I regret not bringing along another set of hands to help us. The Library is overwhelming. I've lost count of how many books and documents I've requested that turn out to be either misfiled or shipped off to Escorial. Maddening. And we're leaving for Seville in what, ten days?"

"I'll be able to finish by then," I offered.

"Oh, you'll need to finish long before that. I'm going to need assistance over at the Library soon enough. Damn, I can't believe I ended up with Howard instead of Jim Thatcher. What a miserable, miserable situation. Double damn. And the Expo! I should have finalized my remarks by now, instead here I am pulling out my remaining hairs on this ... *quest.*"

"Calling it a quest makes it sound like an adventure," I said. "This is more like ... schoolwork."

"Ha, yes, I suppose you're right about that," Doctor Morley said. "Except there's no teachers, and nobody to tell us whether we're getting it right or wrong."

***

After Doctor Morley paid the driver, he walked me through the Museum gates. There was a guard sitting on one of the benches on the walkway, his legs stretched out and his head slumped down. He looked like he was about to take an afternoon nap, though the day had only begun.

Then it was up between the twin sphinges, through the tall iron doors and to the ticket booth. There, the cud-chewing ticket lady farted as she scanned 'ze leest' for our names. It was as if she didn't know us; Doctor Morley didn't care for that and he let her know it.

After that ordeal Doctor Morley spotted the Director in the Egyptian salon.

"Ah, there's my prey right there," he said. "I'll swoop over and catch him now. See you upstairs in a bit."

I started for the stairs. I had only taken two steps when a guard approached me. It was the one I had met the previous day:

"Hola, Vendy! Buenos días! Cómo estás?"

Before I could answer he started walking alongside me toward the stairs.

"Buenos días ...," I began, then I forgot his name.

"Lothario," he replied, with gusto.

"Right, sí, Lothario. I'm well. And you?"

"Oh-ho-ho, it is beautiful day, Vendy, beautiful day," he proclaimed.

"I thought it was rather grey."

"Qué?"

"Grey. You know, cloudy."

"Ah. Cloudy, sí. But the world, she still spins. No?"

"I suppose," I said, surrendering to the fact he was going to walk me all the way up the stairs.

"And Vendy, I do thinking. I say you must come see new play with me. Very good. Very funny."

"I don't have time for plays, Lothario. I'm quite overwhelmed."

"Qué?"

"Overwhelmed. Too much work," I offered. "So if you'll excuse me I ...,"

"Ah, but how it goes, all vork and no play makes Vendy … a bad day. No?"

"Something like that."

"So I take you out. For dinner, then the play. Or play, then dinner. Sí?"

"I'm sorry, I don't ...,"

"No dinner, the lunch. Sí?"

We were rounding the mezzanine. I wished he would walk off into the currency rooms and leave me alone. I was too tired for this.

"Well, I like to go to the cart on the corner and ...,"

"Ah, Dulcinea's! Muy delicioso. We go together?"

"Um, I ... I usually have to eat with my boss. Working lunches, you know," I lied. "But maybe if there's ...,"

"Oh-ho, oh-ho, it is the date then!" Lothario exclaimed. "If not today, tomorrow, sí?"

"We'll see. Now, lo siento, Lothario … its work time for me."

We were at the top of the stairs. I gave him a polite I'm-leaving-now nod and turned. He scampered after me like a devoted puppy.

"Ah, I assist move bench for you, no?" Lothario said, then he ran ahead into the next room. By the time I arrived at my position by the Codex, he had pulled the leather bench out for me. He ceremoniously dusted it off with his hand and then looked at me with a goofy, determined smile.

He was harmless. I smiled and took my seat. Lothario slid the bench in for me and I said good-bye to him yet again. He said good-bye to me several more times before he finally left.

I shook my head and blinked my eyes to try and perk myself up. Then I opened my shoulder bag, took out my supplies and got to work.

***

Again I lost myself in the dense mix of glyphs, gods and Mayan numerals. I outlined first, made the black markings next and then finished with the colors. There was a lot of blue, as Tatiana had warned.

If there were any clues between pages fifteen and eighteen they would remain hidden. My personal quest was to get done as much as I could, as fast as I could. I was sloppy, yes, because I was tired. But I was productive, in a close-enough-is-fine sort of way. My glyphs were good, not perfect. My reptiles and slithering serpents were alright, though I had done better. My take on the disemboweled turtle on page eighteen looked like it belonged in the funny pages, not in a museum.

I had begun outlining page nineteen when it occurred to me that perhaps I should give a shit about this project, and not take it so lightly. I paused, thought about it some more and concluded that I definitely did not give a shit. Just then a fuming Doctor Morley marched in, startling me.

"To hell with this place," the boss snarled. "I've never seen such disorganization. Unbelievable."

He had both hands on his hips. His face was red. He kept going.

"You'd think that someone of the Director's supposed intellect would know a Codex belongs in the Museum, not the Library."

"But ... it *is* here," I said, gesturing to the Mayan artifact in front of my face.

"No, no, no, not that Codex ... the Duran Codex. The Aztec one."

I had no idea what he was talking about.

"Do you have any idea what I'm even talking about? The Duran Codex? Jose Ramirez? Found here?"

I struggled to think up a response and failed. Doctor Morley said:

"Hellcakes on the Hudson. I thought you had a greater appreciation for these historical matters."

What a prick, I thought. The angry archaeologist turned away in disgust. He walked away without another discernible word, though I did hear him muttering to himself as he exited the room. Then he encountered the other guard coming up the stairs and I overheard this exchange:

"Ah, bueno, perfect timing," came Doctor Morley's voice. "Now, what's your name? Qué? Anselmo? Ah, very well, Anselmo ... now, I need you to unlock the interior door to the Library for me. La puerta a la biblioteca, por favor."

"Ah, um ... no permitido," replied the guard.

"Not permitted? Come now, it's a solid quarter-mile to go out and around to the Library entrance," Doctor Morley said. "Unlocking that door would save me a great deal of time ... and you know I'm not stealing anything,"

"Ah, sí, sí," Anselmo said, followed by, "Pero ... no esta permitido."

Then there was silence. I imagined Doctor Morley was turning red again. Then he popped his top and I heard him rattle off a stunning string of English, Spanish and even French swear words. His profanity trailed off as he went down the stairs.

***

I worked for the next two hours undisturbed, pausing only to stretch my aching hands. By the time my tummy growled, demanding food, I had completed page twenty-three. Proud of my efforts—even if it didn't produce any hidden treasure—I got up to go to the Library. I was sure Doctor Morley could use a break as well.

As I came around the Codex frames I was adjusting my shoulder bag and not looking up.

"Woah! Perdón!" came a voice.

I looked up and right in front of me was the skinny man I had seen twice before. He was walking into the room as I was walking out.

"Oh. Lo siento, I'm sorry," I said.

I moved to step around him, and once again I observed he was giving me a peculiar look. I broke eye contact but then he said:

"Señora, I must ask … have you ever been to Paris?"

It was my kind of question.

"Um, no," I replied. "But someday, hopefully."

The skinny man's eyes were brown and intense. He wore a slight grin. He nodded and then said:

"You may think me loco for saying this … but you look very much like someone I know," he said. His accent was thick, but his English was good.

"Oh," was all I could say. "Fascinating. Well, pardon me, I must be going. Lo siento."

I moved around him, and as I did he said:

"*Fano.*"

I didn't know what that word meant, so against my better judgment I asked him.

"Fano?"

"Sí. Fano Messan?" he said. "It is remarkable. The face, the hair. It is all same. You and Fano, you are almost twins!"

He said it with such excited certainty that I didn't know what to say. I dug deep for an old standby:

"If we're related, it's through Adam and Eve," I said, then I walked away from him and into the next room.

The skinny man barked out a single sharp laugh. He didn't seem offended that I was walking away, and I felt good for ending the awkward little exchange on a funny note. Being funny wasn't something I was known for, at least not recently.

***

I came down the stairs, past the Egyptian salon and out the Museum doors. As I walked I couldn't help but dream about my supposed twin in Paris. By the time I reached the sidewalk I had come to the conclusion that perhaps I should swap roles with her. I would go to Paris and live her life; she could go to the Yucatán and live mine.

It was a delicious, Dickensian idea. But by the time I made it down the block and around the corner to the Library entrance, I had popped my own balloon. This Fano person, my twin, wouldn't want to step into my miserable life.

On my way into the Library I said hola to the statues of King Alfonso and San Isidoro. I proceeded inside, made my way through the reading room, wound my way through the bookcases and then into the stacks. I took a set of spiral stairs to the far back corner of the Library, where the dust on the bookshelves looked older than me.

I heard Doctor Morley complaining before I saw him.

"A bumbling blowhard!" I heard him yell. "A washed-up, pie-eyed, fat-assed bumbling blowhard, that's what he is."

"Come now, Sylvanus, be professional about this," came Veronica's voice.

I came around the corner. Doctor Morley was at his little desk, the stacks of books and papers in front of him larger than the day before. Veronica was nearby, leaning against a bookcase, scowling down at him. She saw me and scowled at me, too, for good measure.

Doctor Morley gave me the briefest of glances then continued his bitching:

"Howard should be working on his book. Better yet, he should retire ... because nobody wants to read his damn book. He needs to fade into history."

"Why must you throw around these personal insults? He can help," Veronica replied.

"Bushwa," Doctor Morley said. "He's only going to slow us down. I mean that quite literally. He must have doubled his weight since Egypt."

And then Veronica said something back to him, but I didn't hear it because I was piecing one and one together.

"Wait," I said. "Are you saying that Howard is ...,"

They kept at it and ignored me.

"You could learn a lot from his systems, Sylvanus," Veronica said. "Checklists, grid systems, organization, delegation ... diplomacy,"

"Oh, cut the crap," Doctor Morley snapped. "I don't need any lessons, thank you very much. And tell me, how the hell am I supposed to delegate things when you change the team on me at the last instant?"

"Howard ... *Carter*?" I said, louder this time.

They both stopped talking and looked at me like I was an idiot.

"Is there a problem?" Doctor Morley said.

"You mean the Howard … the Howard you've been talking about is … *Howard Carter?*" I repeated.

"Yes. Why?" Doctor Morley asked, in a pissy tone.

"You mean like … the man that found Tut's tomb, *that* Howard Carter?"

"He used to be that man … but he's not anymore," the boss said. "Now, can I help you with something? As you can see Miss Shetty and I are rather busy."

"I … I wanted to see if you wanted to go with me to Dulcinea's. For lunch."

"Dulcinea's. What's that?"

"It's the little cart out by the circle. They have bread and that good Spanish ham and it's all …,"

"I have time for neither bread nor meat," he said with a dismissive wave. "And since you're on another break, I assume you're making forward progress over there?"

"It's going alright," I responded. Then, seeing that was a poor answer, I said, "Actually, moving along much, much faster. I've started to …,"

As I spoke Veronica straightened out her slinky body, gave me a frustrated look and took her bag up off the floor. Doctor Morley watched her and wasn't listening to me. He said to her:

"What, you're leaving already? You've been here all of ten minutes!"

"I've got to get back to my hotel to meet Howard," she said without making eye contact. "You said you prefer to work alone … and quite frankly, I can't deal with you right now."

"So helpful," Doctor Morley said, which made Veronica spin back around.

"This isn't going to be easy if you insist on being a dink," she scolded. "I suggest you recalibrate your attitude before dinner tonight. I'm sure Howard will be curious about your progress, or lack thereof."

Doctor Morley took a deep breath and said, "I'm sure he will … and I apologize for my snippiness. Stressful times."

Veronica nodded at him and then turned to me. She gave me a patronizing look, sighed and said:

"Tom Sawyer."

"Pardon?" I replied.

"Your hair," the witch said. "That's what it reminds me off. Tom Sawyer."

My jaw fell open. This woman had no shame.

"I'm sure I don't know what you mean," I replied, trying to stay cool.

"Tom Sawyer is an American book. Haven't you heard of it?"

"I know the book, thank you … but you have a problem with my … my *hair*?"

"You might think about shaping it a bit more, my dear," she said. "This isn't the Yucatán, you know."

Then, without another word, she turned and walked away. I stood speechless, paralyzed by her rudeness. As she slithered into the stacks I turned to Doctor Morley. He looked at me with arched eyebrows and said:

"If it's any consolation, I've always considered you to be more of a Huck Finn type."

"Oh, hardy-har-har," I grumbled. "That woman is a *monster.*"

"Sí," my boss replied.

"She can't talk to me like that. She can't talk to you like that, either."

"Yet she does. That's her personality. Deal with it," Doctor Morley said.

"Deal with it? She's lucky I didn't slug her."

"Slugging would not help the cause," he replied. "Remember what I told you: take angry feelings like that and push, push, push them deep down inside you. Now, sit here, tell me what you've found."

He patted a chair next to him. I sat down. I hadn't found anything useful in the Codex. Suddenly I felt like a schoolgirl about to get busted for half-assing her homework.

"So ... good progress?"

"I've made it to page twenty-three. Hoping to get to thirty by the end of the day."

"Anything ... interesting?"

"No."

"I worry you're not looking close enough."

"Well ... I must say I'm not quite sure what I'm looking for."

At that he took a breath in and then nodded.

"I'm starting to feel the same way," he sighed.

Then he looked over the books and papers spread out on his table. He picked up a pencil and tapped it twice on a book.

"On a positive note I did find some of the notes I was seeking earlier. Not the Ramirez files, I'm still on the hunt for those ... but I found a nice cache from Brasseur."

"Mister Atlantis," I murmured.

"Oh, stop it. He plays a big role in the history of your Codex, remember that."

"*My* Codex?"

"Well, your Codex as compared to the Duran Codex. You know what I mean. But these notes here are quite engaging. Putting aside the Atlantis stuff—he called it 'Mu,' by the way—Brasseur was quite the detective. He knew he was on the trail of something big, he just didn't know what it was."

"And we do?"

That kind of popped out and I regretted saying it, so I immediately tried to change the subject:

"What's Howard Carter like?" I asked.

Doctor Morley chortled to himself. Then he looked at me and said:

"Howard? Let's just say he's ... larger than life."

9

GOYA USED TO WORK HERE

That evening I bathed, put on my long-sleeved burgundy dress and combed down my Tom Sawyer hair.

As I gussied myself up I had to laugh thinking about the term 'Mister Carter,' a tongue-in-cheek title-of-honor back at Chichen Itza. Whenever something mysterious was dug up, the teasing about 'Mister Carter' would commence.

"Can you see anything, Mister Carter?" someone would ask, to which the finder would *always* reply:

"Yes, yes, wonderful things!" just like Howard Carter said when he stuck that first candle into Tut's tomb.

As I rode the elevator down, it occurred to me that my colleagues were all going to be quite jealous of me getting to work with the *real* Mister Carter. I debated whether I should ask him for an autograph and decided that would be awkward. Co-workers don't ask each other for autographs.

I came off the lift and walked down the hallway and past the front desks. I looked for my boss and, not seeing him, took a seat on a bench to wait.

The bench was near the Lobby Bar. I couldn't see most of the people in the bar, on account of an enormous fern next to the bench, but I could hear them. Everyone was having a grand time, laughing too loud and talking too loud. Glasses were clinking all over.

I craved a drink and, with Doctor Morley late, there was no time like the present. I stood up and paused to pluck a few pesetas out of my money-belt before walking into the bar. I turned my body toward the fern so nobody would see me, undid a button on my shirt, fished around for the opening and found my secret stash. I took out a bill and, as I did, a sharp laugh exploded nearby.

I froze. The laugh sounded strangely familiar … and I immediately put a face to it. But the face I assigned to that laugh was the face of a man I had seen die half a world away!

I shook my head and told myself I was being ridiculous. I was about to make my move toward the bar when this hidden man, whom I had only heard laugh, spoke:

"... So the old bastard's got this damn baby goat slung over his shoulders and as he walks away I turn to the carabineer and I say 'What will he do?' and the carabineer says 'He'll just wade across the stream' and I say 'No shit! He just walks across the border? Aren't you gonna go after him?' and the carabineer says 'He'll be back by sunset. He *hates* the French.'"

And then this faceless but familiar voice barked out another familiar laugh. My heart jumped. My jaw fell. My eyes must have been big as plates. It sounded just like ...

"Ah, there you are," Doctor Morley said, startling me. "I've been looking everywhere for you. Come, come, let's go."

I was frozen in place. He noticed.

"What's the matter? Chop chop."

The voice behind the fern had stopped talking. I turned to face Doctor Morley.

"Did you hear that?" I asked.

"Hear what?"

"That voice."

"Whose voice?"

I moved past him and around the fern. There was a table there, with several empty glasses on it, but no people.

"What's gotten into you?" Doctor Morley said.

"I swear I heard ... someone."

"Someone?"

"Someone ... whose voice I shouldn't be hearing," I said.

Doctor Morley lowered his chin and looked at me over his glasses. His eyes were getting narrow. He said:

"Goodness gracious, not *this* again."

He was useless. I turned around and scanned the bar. I tried to look at the faces of the men to see if I could see the person I thought I had heard. I didn't. I came to the conclusion that I had let my fertile imagination get the better of me.

***

In the taxi on the way to the restaurant I made three mistakes.

My first mistake was to ask my grumpy boss about our schedule and when I might have some free time.

"Free time? You eat lunch outside every day!" was his reply.

My second mistake occurred when I mentioned how excited I was to meet Mister Carter. That set Doctor Morley off. He went on a long diatribe about some long-ago colleague who had run afoul of Mister Carter on some long-ago dig.

"He always thinks there's only one correct way to do something ... and of course that's always his way. Assumes he's the smartest person in whatever room he's in, you know the type."

"Mm-hm, I do."

"His head is as swollen as his belly ... and that's saying something," Doctor Morley continued. "You know, the only reason Tut hasn't reached beyond the grave to take Carter is because the gods don't want to put up with him."

"That's not a very nice thing to say about a cursed person," I remarked.

"His only curse is having to live with himself," Doctor Morley growled. "Plus ... he's a thief."

"Oh, come on," I said, growing tired of his griping.

"Don't tell me you never heard that," Doctor Morley grumbled. "All those theatrics with him unsealing the tomb for the first time in front of the authorities? Bushwa, one-hundred-percent. He and Carnavon had already snuck in and broken the seal and taken a look around. Everyone at Carnegie knows Carter's a crook, that's why the Institution won't work with him. Why the Met and the Brits still contract with him is beyond me. He's got contraband idols from his glorious find lined up all around his bed, I hear."

"Let those without sin cast the first stone," I said and instantly regretted it.

There had been an incident with Doctor Morley's predecessor back at Chichen Itza ... he had smuggled artifacts out with the diplomatic mail. It was one of those never-bring-it-up topics and I had inadvertently brought it up, even though my quote was technically biblical. There was a long, awkward pause. When I had the courage to look over at Doctor Morley, he was peering at me over his glasses. He had a stern look.

"My, you're not afraid to deliver a swift kick below the belt, are you?" he said. "They must have had one hell of a debate team in East Bittyville."

At that I laughed and told him the honest truth:

"You're not going to believe this, but ... they kicked me off."

Doctor Morley burst out laughing. It was, I have to believe, the happiest point of his day.

***

The taxi slowed and turned off the Gran Via. We wound down a narrow street and stopped. The driver got out and opened the door for us and we stepped out onto the cobblestones.

The restaurant was in an old building with wood paneling on the outside. It didn't look very big. The sign above the wood paneling read *Restaurante Sobrino de Botín* and advertised their wood-burning oven. A pleasant old doorman held the door and waved us in.

The interior looked even older than the exterior: there were brick walls accented with red paneling, red shelving and an impressive red booze cabinet. There was a sprinkling of electric lights and an abundance of candles and lanterns. All the tables had white tablecloths and everyone seemed to be enjoying themselves. This lovely scene was ruined by Veronica, coming forward to greet us:

"Ah, it's America's favorite red-headed scamp," were her very first words.

Before I could muster a comeback, she said:

"I'm sorry, I'm a terrible tease. I *am* kidding, you know."

I squinted at her, and she squinted right back, and I said:

"But of course, Miss … Shetty."

"Good evening, Sylvanus," the she-devil said to my boss. "Heavens, you look tired."

"Thank you for noticing. Yes, I am tired," he replied.

"It's because you take on too much yourself," she said. "Now, come one, Howard's been waiting."

There was a white-shirted host standing in back of her, he pivoted and led us through the restaurant. There were countless paintings on the walls and several small alcoves filled with lanterns and, in one case, a religious bust. Near one wall there was a man carving ham off the leg of a black-footed pig; he looked up when Veronica strutted by and I'm pretty sure he cut himself.

The host led us around a corner to a set of stairs. A sign with an arrow pointing down read *Bodega*. We came down the creaky stairs into a narrow, tubular room that resembled an undersized section of rail tunnel. There were little candles on the tables and punch-holed lanterns hanging from the ceiling. Only a handful of the tables down here were occupied, none of them by anyone that looked famous.

In the rearmost part of this cavern-like space was an alcove, separate and distinct from the main dining area. The host waved us in that direction. At this point I could see one side of a large table in the alcove, but not the other side. I took a deep breath and prepared myself to meet the one and only Howard Carter.

We came into the alcove and seated on the other side of the table was a humongous man with a moustache. He didn't look like the Howard Carter I remembered from newspapers. I thought no-way-this-is-him … but I looked at his face again and yes, it was.

The great archaeologist pushed himself to his feet, wheezing as he did so. As his giant belly was revealed I may have gasped: He was much wider and much heavier than the man I had expected to see. He had to be well over three hundred pounds.

"Ah yes. Right on time. Greetings, Sylvanus … good to see you again," the big man said.

Howard Carter reached out his hand to Doctor Morley. They gripped and started shaking and I could see they were both gripping and shaking too hard.

"Looks like you've held up well," Doctor Morley said when they let go.

"That damned curse will get me yet … but I've evaded it so far," Howard Carter said, his dialect as precise and British as they come. Then he turned his jowly face to me. "And this is?"

"Right. Howard, this is my assistant, Wendy Willoughby," Doctor Morley said.

Howard Carter looked at me, smiled, then took my hand and kissed it. I couldn't believe it.

"Madame Willoughby, it's an honor," he said. "Sylvanus failed to mention you're such a looker."

I blushed, ignoring the inappropriateness of his comment.

"Call me Wendy, please," I said.

"And call me Howard, please," he replied.

He let go off my hand and waved his arm toward the table. Doctor Morley sat on one side of Mister Carter, Veronica sat on his other side and I sat across from him. As I unfolded my napkin I peeked up and studied Mister Carter's face again. The extra weight had made his face much puffier than it used to be. I wondered if anyone had recognized him when he walked into the restaurant and decided that no, they probably didn't.

As soon as we were seated Carter started talking:

"I was just talking to one of the owners. That staircase, it's much too narrow for the modern man, don't you think? They're reluctant to make changes, as you would expect. You know, Goya used to be a waiter here. It's the oldest restaurant in the world, according to the man I spoke with. That mark over on the wall says 1726, they say 1725. Only one oven in all those years. Have you been here, Sylvanus?"

"No," Doctor Morley replied.

"No? Have you, Miss Willoughby?" Mister Carter said, turning my way.

"No, I haven't."

"The suckling pig. That's what they're known for. Last time I was here—when was that, eight years ago? Before the find, that's for certain—well, anyway, we ordered three of them. Three entire piglets! You think that's a lot, but it wasn't enough ... all three were gone in an hour."

On both 'three entire pigs' and 'an hour' Mister Carter slapped his hand on the table so hard our silverware and plates rattled. Seconds later a smiling waiter appeared and went into a too-long monologue about the restaurant's historic oven. Then he told us the specials and only then got around to our drink order, which he should have done first. Veronica jumped in and asked about wines and the poor waiter had to rattle them all off ... then she chose the first one he had said, Rioja Alta.

"Wine, shmine. I'll have a double scotch," Mister Carter said.

"That sounds wonderful. Me too," I said to the waiter, which prompted Doctor Morley to give me an evil eye.

The waiter left us. Mister Carter lowered his voice and leaned his bulky frame forward. As if on cue the rest of us leaned forward, too.

"Now, Sylvanus, tell me where we're at. Any luck with the Codex?"

Doctor Morley sighed and shook his head.

"Nothing. At least, nothing yet. We're still analyzing it."

"We?" Carter said.

"Wendy and I," Doctor Morley said, glancing at me.

Saying I was 'analyzing' anything was a stretch, but I kept my mouth shut.

"And you are comparing those drawings with your maps . . . how?" Mister Carter asked next.

"How? With my eyes," Doctor Morley answered.

"Not that, Sylvanus. What's your process? Are you using a grid?"

"A grid? No. I compare the pages to the maps and the site plans and look for similarities and differences," Doctor Morley said. He was starting to clench his jaw and his lower lip was turning white.

"Similarities and differences?" Mister Carter said. "You need to be more methodical. That's how I found the tomb, you know."

"Yes. You've shared that story before," Doctor Morley said with an arched eyebrow.

"Grid by grid, inch by inch, that's the way to narrow it down, Sylvanus. You should know that by now."

"Stop calling me Sylvanus."

Howard Carter guffawed to himself and leaned back in his chair. He stared at Doctor Morley for a moment in contemplative silence. My boss wasn't even looking him in the eye.

"And Escorial?" Howard Carter went on. "Have you been to see the ecclesiastical records?"

Doctor Morley shook his head and spoke, his eyes still on our table.

"No. No, Howard, I haven't been to Escorial," he said. "We just got here a few days ago. We've been tied up in the Library and the Museum."

"You won't find anything of Diego de Landa's at the Library, Sylvanus."

That was it. Doctor Morley slammed a hand on the table. Then he whipped his red face up toward Howard Carter.

"For the last goddamn time, *don't* call me Sylvanus!"

Howard Carter didn't seem phased. "Calm yourself down, man," he chortled.

The waiter returned. He poured wine for Veronica and Doctor Morley and placed hearty scotches in front of Mister Carter and myself. There was no toast, everyone just shut up and drank for a miracle moment. Then Doctor Morley resumed the fight:

"With all due respect, Howard, your focus on de Landa is unwarranted. I think the Bishop, despite his many faults, is but a bit player in this drama. He's not a central character."

"Well, I respectfully disagree with you on that," Mister Carter said. "That mark you found in the cave, the cross of the Inquisition ... who else would have used such a symbol?"

"So you've fingered the culprit already?" Doctor Morley responded.

"Not at all. But nothing could have been hidden in or spirited out of the Yucatán during that period without de Landa's knowledge," Mister Carter retorted.

"Perhaps it never made it to the Yucatán," Doctor Morley sniffed.

"I think your colleagues have already established that it did," Mister Carter said, shaking his head.

"I think my colleagues are wise enough to know that they don't have all the answers," Doctor Morley jabbed.

"And I think, again, that you're coming at this from the wrong direction," Mister Carter responded. "Think, man, think about who would have had the means and motive to move that treasure out of Mexico …,"

As he said the word 'treasure' the waiter reappeared. Everyone clammed up. The waiter bragged about the oven again and listed the specials. Mister Carter insisted on ordering for everyone, then requested enough food for a small army. The waiter departed again and Veronica Shitty, who had been silent since we sat down, decided this would be a good time to add fuel to the fire:

"Sylvanus, I can't see how you can possibly go to Seville when you have so much unfinished work here in Madrid."

She said it like it was a given fact, not a question to be debated. Doctor Morley turned his red face to her.

"Don't give me that crap, Veronica," my boss snarled. "The Exposition is and always has been my top priority for this trip. I'm going. Period."

"I'll remind you that you have obligations to us that must be kept," Veronica shot back.

Then something unexpected happened. Doctor Morley and Veronica were sharing a death-stare and I glanced over at Mister Carter. I watched him pick up a spoon from the table and slip it into his pocket. He didn't see me watching him. Then he rejoined the conversation:

"I'd say at a minimum we need to get to Escorial," the big man insisted. "Sooner rather than later. Let's see what's there and then determine the most appropriate course of action."

"The most appropriate course of action, Howard, is for me to continue what I've been doing the past several days," Doctor Morley responded. "I can't be flailing around in different directions."

"Hmph. 'Flailing' seems to be exactly what's happening, Sylvanus."

"Goddammit!" Doctor Morley snapped. "Don't. Call. Me. *Sylvanus!*"

***

Over the course of that memorable evening I learned many things.

I learned that the suckling pig at Sobrino de Botín is indeed excellent. The presentation of the dish makes it look like a brave little piglet tried to fly but failed, landing face-down in a pile of potatoes. It was a bit odd to look at, but it was crispy on the outside and tender on the inside. The Iberico ham and the various cheeses and the pickled vegetables were all delicious, too.

I learned—rather, it was reinforced to me—that Doctor Morley doesn't care much for Mister Carter. My boss spent most of the evening with a flushed face and a forked tongue. He lashed out at Mister Carter over pretty much every idea the more-famous archaeologist came up with.

I learned that the great Howard Carter enjoys his scotch … and enjoys having someone to drink his scotch with, that someone being me. He did come off as somewhat bossy and stubborn, but the points he articulated seemed like good ones. And the more I drank, the more I came to appreciate the oversized Egyptologist.

Mister Carter was also, to my surprise, an unrepentant kleptomaniac. During the course of the evening I saw him pocketing two spoons, a knife and a glass salt bowl. When the waiter brought us steamed napkins on a silver tray after the meal, the Egyptologist distracted us and somehow pocketed that, too. Just as surprising was that Mister Carter caught me watching him take the tray ... and didn't seem fazed by it. He simply gave me a mischievous grin and a wink, then went right on with his pilfering.

That night I also learned that Veronica Shitty—pardon me, Shetty—was every bit the miserable demon-spawn I thought she was. She sided with Mister Carter on every issue and did nothing to help the dueling archaeologists find middle ground. She treated Doctor Morley like a naughty child who needed adult supervision. She was nasty to the staff at the restaurant, too: She snarled at our waiter and later snapped at a busboy, which made Mister Carter say:

"Careful now ... remember Goya used to be a busboy here."

To which Doctor Morley responded:

"Enough, Howard ... earlier you said Goya was a waiter."

"No, no, he was a busboy," Mister Carter said. "Such a fascinating figure. Read something on him recently. Did you know he was hauled in front of the Inquisition two separate times?"

I had stayed quiet most of the meal, but talk of a great painter piqued my interest.

"Goya? Really? I never would have expected that," I said.

"Neither would I, Miss Willoughby, neither would I," Mister Carter responded. "Then again … nobody expects the Spanish Inquisition."

And then he looked at me with raised eyebrows, as if he had made a joke and I had missed it.

10
THE AMERICAN NEWSPAPER

The following day began with our daily ritual, the angry taxi ride, during which Doctor Morley went on and on and on about Mister Carter. He called him a "drunken, bloated, washed-up blowhard." He said Mister Carter knew nothing of the Maya and had only a passing familiarity with the Spanish. He made several nasty, unnecessary comments about the Egyptologist's girth.

I was tempted to tell Doctor Morley about Mister Carter's swiping of cutlery and such from the restaurant. But now I thought better of it, not wanting to give my boss any more ammunition.

We got out of the motorcar in front of the Library. Doctor Morley paid the driver and mumbled a good-bye to me. Then, without another word, he walked up the steps, past the statues and inside.

I took my time wandering around the corner to the Museum. I didn't feel like working. I considered what would happen if I ditched my responsibilities and took the day off. It was a nice morning, after all, and a day off would do me good. But then I imagined how Doctor Morley would react to such a move. Not well, I assumed.

So I made my way down the block and into the Museum and past the grumpy ticket lady and upstairs to my bench. I pulled my pencils and my notebook out of my shoulder bag. I positioned myself in front of the Codex and flipped the frames to display pages twenty-nine to thirty-two.

I worked better that day. I suppose I had grown used to the kings and warriors and animals that filled the pages. Many of the images were repetitive and I was able to draw those with increasing efficiency. I had figured out how to better replicate the ancient colors, too, particularly the blues and the rusty browns.

I was on page thirty-three when Lothario came in. He flirted with me, again, then asked me to dinner, again. And I smiled and said no, again. He was pleasant and harmless enough—and I *was* in need of some company—but he didn't come close to fitting the bill.

My morning session was quiet. A few museum-goers filtered through, but there weren't many of them and they didn't stay in my room very long. By one-o'clock I had finished page forty and I was starving.

***

"Lunch? Again?" Doctor Morley said.

"Well, yes, again," I explained. "It is a new day, you know."

"Another day behind, that's what it is," he grumbled.

He was sitting at his usual table in the stacks of the Library. There were books and papers and maps in front of him. A tattered cardboard box sat on the floor, next to his chair.

"You need a break," I said. "C'mon, let's get some food and some fresh air."

"I need a break and can't afford to take one," he said. "Can't see how you can, either, but do as you must."

He was pouting and grouchy. I didn't want to engage with him. I said nothing and turned to leave and he said:

"Wait, wait," he said.

I stopped and thought he might apologize, which was an absurd thing to think. Then he said:

"Let me see your notebook."

"Why?"

"Because I pay you, that's why."

I shot him a pissy look and then pulled my shoulder bag over and took out my sketchbook. I tossed it down in front of him. He gave me a pissy look of his own, then looked down and opened the sketchbook. He opened it to a random page, which I recognized as thirty-five because I knew that damn Codex better than he did. And then he had the nerve to say:

"Alright, so *this* page. Any thoughts? Does it match up with anything?"

I paused, then said:

"Not that I know of."

And at that he slapped a hand down on the table.

"See, that's *exactly* what I mean. You're half-assing this whole thing. You're just copying when you should be looking!"

My jaw fell open and I feigned shock.

"Wh-what? A copy is what you told me to produce!" I said, dismayed. "I'm doing *exactly* as you asked."

"I'm sure."

"I am. And I haven't seen anything. And I shouldn't be blamed for that. And … and I don't appreciate your attitude."

We glared at each other for a moment, both of us holding our breaths. Then Doctor Morley surrendered.

"Okay, let's simmer down a bit," he said, looking back to my copy. "It's, um, safe to say you're back on track, right? At least in terms of completing the damn thing?"

"I think so," I replied, my blood pressure lowering. "But if I don't eat, I'll starve. If I starve, I'll be dead. If I'm dead, I'm of no use to you."

Doctor Morley smirked, shook his head and rolled his eyes all at the same time.

"You better eat then," he relented. "I wouldn't be much of an employer if I allowed my employees to perish like that."

He sighed and turned back to his clutter. His stress hung over him like a storm cloud.

"How's it coming with you?" I asked.

At that he pursed his lips and took an exasperated breath in and out.

"It's overwhelming, frankly," he said. "I found a few items from Jose Ramirez, nothing interesting though. They've probably got boxes from him stashed somewhere, I suspect. But they've changed their damn filing system so many times I might as well be looking for the Holy Grail."

"Maybe we should look for that instead."

"I don't have the coconuts for that search," Doctor Morley deadpanned. "As for Ramirez, there's a semi-competent librarian that comes in on the afternoon shift.

I'll talk to him and bypass the boneheads and see what he can track down for me. Oh, I did find one thing that you may find interesting ... come take a look at this."

With my growling stomach pulling me in the opposite direction, I approached his cluttered desk. He had some old book open. He slid it toward me.

"Now, right here, tell me what you read."

I peered at the book. It was all in an old-style Spanish font with overly-cursive letters. It was hard to read. I focused on some sentences that had been underlined.

"No, no, here ... in the margin," Doctor Morley corrected me.

He pointed to the lower part of the left page. There, in a tiny circle, was the word 'chi', followed by a question mark. I knew 'chi' was a Greek letter ... or maybe an Italian one.

"Now, disregard the word itself for a moment," Doctor Morley said. "Focus on the handwriting. Tell me, does *that* handwriting look the same as *this* handwriting?"

He was holding a piece of paper in his hand. A letter, I thought at first, but it turned out to be someone's notes. I took the paper and looked at the writing and then placed it down next to the book. The writing in the book was, indeed, quite similar to the writing on the piece of paper.

"It does," I said. "Whose is it?"

"Well, I think its Brasseur's!" Doctor Morley responded, now seeming quite pleased with himself. "Remarkable what you can discover when you stay alert, eh?"

I assumed that was a dig at me. I ignored it. I asked:

"So what's 'chi?'"

"Well, 'chi' is many things in many different languages," he said. "But in this context I believe it isn't a what ... but a who."

"A who?"

"Yes ... as in Gaspar Chi. You've heard of him, right?"

I had no idea who Gaspar Chi was. I wanted lunch. Doctor Morley kept talking.

"That was the Spanish name given to him, Gaspar Antonio Chi. But he was a Mayan. De Landa made him into one of his scribes. The Bishop was obsessed with eradicating the ancient belief systems. He used his team of Mayan scribes—including Chi—to help him effectuate that."

"And so this little note in the margins tells you ... what, exactly?" I asked.

Doctor Morley looked at me with a most dramatic look and said:

"It proves that Charles Brasseur de Bourbourg looked at this book."

Then he smirked.

"So yes, that's my big accomplishment for the day," he said. "I know, I know, that's why the Institution pays me the big bucks."

"I'm sure," I said. "What's the book?"

He flipped the book I had been inspecting over. It had a faded red leather cover and any words on it had been either worn off or rubbed off. He flipped the cover open to reveal the title page. It was a crowded coat of arms, held up by some heinous two-headed black bird. There was a line of three crowns hovering above the image. At the bottom there was more old-style swirling Spanish script, which I was struggling to decipher.

"*Historia General de las Indias,*" Doctor Morley said. "Francisco de Gómora's love letter to Cortés. Surprised to find it here. It was banned by Phillip the Second, you know."

I did not know that and did not care. But my boss kept talking, so I stood there and waited for him to stop so I could go.

"Gómora never even went to New World," he went on. "But he was a kiss-ass of the first order and sucked up to Hernán and his sons and came up with this hunk of garbage. It's all puffery, of course ... more fiction than fact. It was published to portray Cortés in the most favorable light, as he wasn't a particularly popular man at the moment. That's neither here nor there, I suppose. But this note, this 'Chi' here ... I wonder what that means. Curious, it is. Very curious."

***

After lunch I made my way back to the third floor. As I came into the Mesoamerican Room, I was surprised to find the thin man I had encountered on previous days.

He was standing dead-center in front of the great Aztec calendar stone. He had his arms crossed and seemed deep in thought and I startled him when I walked in.

"Oops, sorry. Perdóname," I said.

"No es problema," he said.

He was standing too close to my bench and he realized that without me saying anything. He moved a few steps forward, his eyes locked on the ancient monolith.

"You must really like that piece," I remarked as I took my seat.

"Sí, sí," he replied. "It is my queso."

He said 'queso' with a smile then returned his gaze to the great stone. I pulled my bench out, wondering what cheese had to do with the Aztecs, then he said:

"*Fromage.*"

And he said 'fromage' with a great flourish, sounding like a bad Spanish actor trying to speak bad French. I had to stifle a laugh, which he heard. He turned and said:

"It is absurd, sí. That is what makes it true art."

I had no idea what he was talking about. I didn't ask for clarification. I began to take my supplies out of my shoulder bag.

"You work hard, no?" the strange man said.

I looked up and he was looking at me.

"Too hard," I replied. "Not much fun."

"Art is not always about the fun."

"This isn't art," I replied. "This is work."

"All we do as work is art, no?" he said without missing a beat.

"Certainly doesn't feel that way," I sighed as I opened my book.

I could feel him looking over my shoulder. Then he said:

"That, what you do, that is art, is it not?"

"More like copying," I replied.

"If it not be the perfect copy, then it must be art," he declared.

I considered that statement. There was some truth to it. Then, since it had been gnawing at me, I had to ask:

"So … what does cheese have to do with the Aztecs?"

The skinny man looked back to the ancient calendar stone. He studied it for a moment and then he spread both arms wide in the air and said.

"You see, the stone, it shows the time passing on the *arrogancia* of empire," he said. "The, how you say … hubree?"

"Hubris," I corrected him.

"Ah, sí, the hubris," he said.

He made little sense but he spoke like someone very sure of himself. I was still confused, though.

"But … cheese?"

And he turned and he said.

"Sí, sí, like a manchego, semi-curado. It hangs down, no?"

My face must have displayed my ignorance.

"The young cheese, is very soft, no?" he went on. "So we make the stone out of cheese … and then, *ploompf*, it go down."

And with that he made a motion with his fingers and I said:

"You mean melting?"

"Ah, sí. Melting."

"So the calendar stone is melting away, and that represents ... time melting away?"

The man looked at me with a puzzled expression.

"No, no ... it about *empire*, it fade away," he said. "Time?"

"Sorry, I misunderstood," I said.

He shook his head, then went back to staring at the old stone. I got busy again with my copy. He got up not long after that and put his stool away. As he was leaving, he said:

"Señora, sometimes what I see in head, it does not make into the good words, sí?"

"Sí. I know that feeling all too well."

"You been to Prado, no? See the art by El Greco ... y Velázquez?"

I didn't like that question because the answer was an unpleasant one.

"No," I groused. "The Prado is closed. The entire time I'm here."

He looked surprised at first.

"Cerrado?"

"Yes. They're refinishing the floors."

"Oh, sí, the floors ... I remember hearing of this," he said. He lost himself in thought for a moment, then looked up to me and said:

"I know people can get you in. Sí?"

Just like that the odd man became infinitely more interesting.

"Get me in ... to see the Prado?"

He nodded.

"Sí, yes, that would be wonderful!"

"There is, um, una condición."

As he said that he seemed to be studying my face a bit too closely. I wanted to see the Prado … but not *that* bad.

"A condition," I said. "Like what?"

"You see, señora, I am artist, like you," he said, which was not a surprise to me. "My Gala, she has returned to Paris. I have been doing much work on a painting—much, much work—and to finish I need female. To model, sí?"

"Uh-huh," I said, now even more suspicious. "What kind of painting?"

Now the skinny man's face lit up. He smiled broadly, chuckled and said:

"Oh-ho! I sense you worry. Do not. Only the face."

"Right. What kind of painting?"

"I show you at studio. But we have the deal, no?"

"I … I suppose so," I said. "Museum first?"

"Of course, señora, of course."

"When?"

"I talk to my friend, the guard, tonight. We find time very soon. Sí?"

"Sí, absolutely. That would be excelente."

He said good-bye and left the room. As he walked out I felt a bit silly in that I couldn't remember his name, or if he had ever given it to me. I made a point to ask him the next time I saw him.

But the arrangement with the skinny man put me in a much better mood. I would get to see the Prado after all. With that comforting thought inside me, I was able to sail through the rest of the afternoon. I made it all the way to page forty-four and it was, I'm proud to say, damn good work.

***

The evening was mine to do with as I pleased. I wouldn't have to put up with any scatter-brained archaeologists or sharp-tongued she-devils. My priorities were, in order: a nap, a drink, perhaps dinner and then more drinks.

I had crossed the first item off my list and was readying myself for my night out. My hotel room was a mess. It was a very nice room, but I hadn't treated it very well. My clean clothes were scattered over the furniture and hanging from doorknobs. My dirty clothes littered the floor. I promised myself I would clean it all up, tomorrow, maybe.

I put on a clean skirt and a dirty-but-acceptable shirt and smoothed everything out and started on my hair. Just then there was a knock on the door.

"Wendy?" came Doctor Morley's voice from the hallway.

I opened the door but the chain was still on. I peeked out:

"Is there a problem?" I asked, with an attitude that should have reminded him this was my night off.

"Well, no … not really, I mean," Doctor Morley replied. "But … I need to show you something."

"What is it?"

"Can I come in?"

I wondered what he would say if I said 'no' but I went ahead and let him in. As he entered I saw he was carrying a folded newspaper in one hand. Within two seconds he said:

"Goodness gracious, are you alright?"

"I'm fine, why?"

"It looks like a tornado tore through here!"

He waited for me to take the bait. I didn't. He kept going.

"If this is what your room looks like after just a few days I'm terrified about what it will look like by next week …,"

I left the door ajar, determined to keep this short.

"I wasn't expecting the room inspector," I replied. "To what do I owe the pleasure?"

"I'm sorry, am I holding you up?"

"Not yet."

"Yes, well, I see you're in your typical fine mood," he said. "That won't make this any more pleasant. Wendy, this …,"

His voice halted, and for an instant I thought I was being canned or something. Then he took his newspaper out and held it up. It was still folded.

"… This is the New York paper from a few days ago. I found it in the lobby," he explained. "I thought it best to show it to you myself, lest you stumble across it."

I took the newspaper from him. Doctor Morley took an obvious step away from me. My eyes went to the front page.

It was the *New York Herald*. There was a bunch of hooey about President Hoover splashed across the top of the times.

"Turn it over," Doctor Morley said. "Below the fold."

I looked at him and then flipped the paper over to see the bottom half of the front page.

The words jumped off the page and strangled me.

LUCKY LINDY RETURNS TO THANK HIS RESCUERS screamed the headline.

Just below that there was a photograph of the famous flyer. In the photograph Lindbergh was in his wheelchair, surrounded by men in dark uniforms and crisp white caps. I read the caption out loud:

"Colonel Charles A. Lindbergh poses with grateful colleagues at the new Miami headquarters of Pan American Airways. This was Lucky Lindy's first public outing since his remarkable survival following a horrific crash in Central America that killed four."

I looked up to Doctor Morley. He took another step backward.

"His remarkable survival?" I growled. "My frickin' God, this is *unbelievable*. The man's a killer, a cold-blooded killer!"

"Well," Doctor Morley began. "I think we must remem …,"

"Bullshit," I said, cutting him off. "Whatever you're about to say, don't say it. The man is a murderer, nothing more."

My volcano of emotion was beginning to erupt. I kept at it:

"What happened in the jungle was bad enough. But this ... this preposterous cover story is too much. Remarkable survival, my ass."

"Yes, and ...," Doctor Morley tried to say.

"Am I wrong?"

"Well, no, I was going to say that ...,"

"Am I wrong?"

"Let me speak, dammit!" Doctor Morley demanded. Then he waited for me to simmer down, which I didn't want to do.

"This is bullshit, I agree. One-hundred-percent," he said. "We know the truth about what happened. But right now the truth is hiding itself. In that sense, remember what Jesus said: 'it is what it is.'"

"I guarantee you Jesus never said that," I remarked, squinting at him.

"What I'm trying to say is that the truth will percolate up over time," my boss said. "For now, let us recognize this as a time when we must prioritize our own well-being. Let the universe render judgment on others, not us."

Now I went from a squint to looking at him with simmering rage. I rendered my judgment of him and he knew it and that shut him up. I looked back down at the newspaper. I couldn't bring myself to read all the words in the article ... but I couldn't resist looking at the picture.

Lindbergh was smack dab in the middle. His hair was mostly shaved off. His face looked puffier than it had in the jungle, like he had gained weight. But it was hard to tell. He was wearing a big jacket and then there was a blanket over his legs.

I scanned the other men in the photograph. Standing next to Lindbergh's wheelchair was a face I recognized. It was the other pilot who had found us. Eddie, I think.

Then I pulled the newspaper closer and there, in back of everyone, barely visible, was Moses.

I could only see his head. He wasn't smiling, unlike his co-workers, who all wore great big grins. It made me think that maybe Moses knew enough to not participate in the charade.

"Hmph. I'm surprised the great and powerful Mister Trippe isn't here," I growled.

"Um, there's ... there's a picture of him and Lindbergh on the next page," Doctor Morley said.

I didn't turn the page to look. I folded the newspaper back up and handed it back to Doctor Morley.

"To hell with them," I declared. "To hell with Lindbergh and to hell with Juan Trippe and to hell with Pan Am. To hell with them all."

"Are you finished?"

"No. I hope all their airplanes crash and I hope Pan Am goes belly-up and I hope Lindbergh stays in that damn wheelchair the rest of his life. Send them all to the dung heap of history, where they belong."

Doctor Morley didn't respond and I realized he was waiting for me to finish my eruption. But I was done, at least for now. My boss adjusted his glasses and said:

"Well, now you can see why I thought it best to show you this newspaper in private. Your reaction wouldn't go over very well in the lobby."

"That wouldn't bother me one bit."

"I'm sure. Now, as your employer, I'm not in the habit of encouraging you to drink. But you should go get yourself a stiff drink, perhaps several."

Now we were speaking the same language.

"And I know it's not easy, but ... forget about Lindbergh. Forget about Pan American. Pack it all away. Force yourself to forget what happened ... if only for one night."

Then he left and I stood there, alone, stewing.

I had gone several days without dwelling on my awful memories. I had, in fact, made a conscious effort to *not* think about Lindbergh, or the incident in the cave, or the Dead Writer. But now it was flooding into my brain again, trying to drown me in my own misery.

I cursed Doctor Morley for showing me that newspaper. It had made me so goddamn mad. I was mad at him, mad at myself, mad at the situation and mad at the world.

I didn't bother finishing my stupid hair. The Tom Sawyer look would have to do ... and to hell with anyone that didn't like it. I stuffed a few extra pesetas for a few extra drinks into my money belt. I grabbed my key off the bureau and marched out of my room and made for the elevator.

I needed a drink and I needed it now.

11

THE DEAD WRITER RISES

The Lobby Bar was located a few steps past the dining room. There was quite a crowd. The merriment had spilled out of the bar and happy drunks were beginning to occupy the dining area.

I wormed my way through an obstacle course of good-looking people, some speaking Spanish, others English, a few in French. A wave of my-god-I-need-new-clothes washed over me as I made my way up to the bar. Some smarmy socialite shot me a dirty look. I shot it right back at her and she stepped aside.

The center of the bar was congested and there were no stools available. I made my way toward the very end and found an open seat, a step removed from the action.

As I waited for the bartender I debated what to drink. My thoughts drifted back to that damn newspaper. It was going to be a whiskey night, once again.

Then I had to wait for someone to pay attention to me. I could only see one bartender and he seemed overwhelmed. I gave him my best pathetic please-sir-just-one-drink. He gave me a nod and an uno-momento finger.

I scanned the crowd. There were lots of men over-smiling and over-laughing at a lesser number of over-dressed women. Everyone looked to be drinking hard. I studied two men toasting and then discussing their mint-green booze, which I assumed was absinthe. From behind me a British woman was chattering away about her social life:

"Oh, you have to come to La Venencia with us! It's charming, absolutely charming. We're going to have a wicked party, too. The first weekend we're there. Isn't that right, darling? Oh, really, you shouldn't miss it. It's going to be *insanely* fun."

I had no idea where La Venencia and I could have used some insane fun ... but I would settle for a drink. I cast another hopeful look to the bartender, who was now struggling with a corkscrew. He caught my eye again and looked sorry and then turned and yelled:

"Frederico! Apúrate!"

From around the corner came a handsome young man with short, dark hair and a handlebar moustache. He was wiping his hands on his apron. The bartender barked at him:

"You say you want more work, Frederico ... and then we busy, where you at? Huh?" the bartender said, popping a cork as he spoke. "Rapido, rapido!"

The new bartender nodded to his boss and came down my way. He was sweating.

"Lo siento, señora, I so sorry," he said.

"Está bien," I replied. "It's busy here."

Frederico looked over the crowd and nodded.

"Sí, sí. The Exposition, you know," he said. "Everyone, they come to Madrid. Have good time, then to Barcelona. You?"

"Well, in a way," I replied. "I'm going to the other Expo. In Seville. The one showcasing all the former Spanish colonies."

"Ah, sí, yes … the King's Expo. Now, señora, you wanna vino, sí?"

I hadn't heard that expression before—'the King's Expo'—and it caught me off guard.

"Señora?"

"Um, oh, I'm sorry," I said. "No, I'll have a whiskey, please. American whiskey."

"American whiskey."

"Sí. Widow Watson's, if you have it."

Frederico went to his wall of bottles and scanned it. Then he walked to the well and scanned there, too. He came back empty-handed and said:

"Señora, so sorry, the whiskey, it gone," he said. "Big wedding down hall, they take all."

"*All* of your whiskey?"

He nodded. I tried to think of something else. I scanned the bar again and my eyes returned to the two men who had been drinking the lime-green booze. They looked very, very happy.

"Absinthe," I said on a whim. Then I looked at Frederico and repeated it, just to make sure we were both clear. "Absinthe. Yes, I think it's time I try absinthe."

He gave me a well-well-well nod and walked away. He returned with a bottle of green liquid. He took up a rocks glass and didn't put any rocks in it and filled it halfway with the booze. It was a darker green than I expected. The bartender walked away and as he did I took up the glass and sniffed. It smelled like anise. I lifted it up to my lips to take a drink. As I did, a hand reached out and stopped my drinking arm.

"Heavens, darling! You're not going to drink that straight up, are you?"

It was the British woman I had overheard earlier. She kept her hand on my arm and looked at me like I was about to commit a serious faux pas.

"Really, now, you need to drink that properly," she said. "It's quite wretched any other way."

I looked at my drink. It looked fine to me. But the woman sounded like she knew what she was talking about.

"Properly?" I asked.

"Ooh, an American. That explains it," she said. "You've all forgotten how to drink, at least that's what the Count says. Now, let's get you outfitted so you can do this the right way."

She leaned over the bar. She was lovely. She had high cheekbones and a perfect chin. Her hair was cut short, like mine. Well, her hair was cut much nicer than mine … but it was short, like mine. She called out to the young bartender:

"Ah, here he comes. Hola, Frederico!"

Frederico the bartender was carrying an elaborate glass water cooler with two hands. He grunted as he lifted it up. Once he put it down on the bar he gave my new friend a big smile.

"Ah, the Queen Bee, she has returned!" he said. "Cómo estás?"

"Excelente, Frederico, excelente," she said. "You're feeling better today I hope?"

"Ay, caramba," he said with a comical roll of his eyes. "That Pernod, it is too much for me."

"There's no such thing as too much Pernod! In fact, that's what I'll have: a Pernod. Oh, and fetch us the sugar for the absinthe, would you darling? She's a virgin," she said, then turned and whispered to me. "I don't mean you're a real virgin, dear. I just mean with the absinthe."

As she was talking the bartender rotated the big glass water cooler around to reveal two tiny spigots.

"Muy bueno, Frederico, muy bueno," she said to him, then again she did an aside to me. "Freddy was in an awful mood yesterday. He quit his job as a postal clerk to work here full-time, but the manager only schedules him part-time. Poor dear. Now, tell me darling, what's your name?"

"Wendy."

"Wendy! Lovely, makes me think of Wendy from the *Peter Pan* stories."

"People ask me that all the time. It's actually how I got my name."

"From ... *Peter Pan?*"

"Yes," I confirmed. It was the truth.

"Outrageous! How fun!" she said. "Well, Wendy ... welcome to Neverland. Get ready for your first flying lesson."

I liked my new friend already. She turned to face the water cooler.

"Now, this is what's called a fountain," she said. "Ice water, nothing more. And so what you do is this ...,"

At that precise moment, Frederico returned with a small tray. On the tray were two strange slotted spoons and a small bowl filled with sugar cubes. Our bartender put the tray down. My new friend took up a single sugar cube and placed it on one of the slotted spoons and lifted up the spoon and said:

"Fact of the day: sugar won't dissolve in cold water. Alright, let's see that booze."

I was still holding my glass of absinthe. She took it from me and positioned it under one of the fountain's spigots. Then she balanced the spoon on top of the glass, so the sugar cube was suspended over the booze.

"Now, this next part is a wee delicate," she said.

She turned one of the spigots ever-so-slightly. A drop of water began to form and when it was heavy enough it fell and splashed onto the sugar cube. She adjusted the spigot a touch. Another drop formed, then fell. I could see the sugar crystals begin to dissolve.

"Watch the color of the booze change," she said.

I peered down at my glass. As the cold water hit the liquor it made hypnotizing swirls.

"Mint-green is the goal," she said as we watched. "If it's grass-green it will taste too bitter."

"Got it," I said.

Then my new friend straightened up and looked at me.

"Let's give that thirty seconds ... which is enough to for me to guess your story," she said, then she did just that. "I'll guess that you're here from New York with ... well, I'll bet it's a wealthy soon-to-be fiancée. And you two lovebirds are going to travel the continent ... one last hurrah before settling down into domestic bliss and multiple children."

I raised an eyebrow.

"Parts of that sound appealing ... but it's all wrong," I said. "I'm here for work ... and no fiancée, only a boss."

"They're the same thing, if you ask me. But I got the travel-the-continent part correct, didn't I?"

"I wish. Just Spain. Only Madrid and Seville, actually."

"What?" she said, a look of social shock on her face. "You're not even going to the Exposition?"

"The Exposition? Well, I am ... I mean we are. But not the one in Barcelona, the one in Seville."

She looked at me with a surprised look.

"Oh, yes, I heard something about that. That's the one they're trotting the king out for, isn't it? Well, I'm sure it will be ... outstanding. We're hoping to make it to Barcelona ourselves. It should be quite a party. Do you think Seville will be a party like Barcelona is going to be?"

"I'm not sure."

"Honestly, I'm not sure my body can take much more partying. We just came from Pamplona, it was madness up there, pure madness. Okay, now, look."

She was chattering a mile a minute and now she reached out and turned the little water spigot off. There was a tiny bit of sugar left on the spoon but most had dissolved. She dunked the rest of the sugar in and stirred the absinthe with the spoon. In an instant it was all a uniform milky-green color.

"Some people like two sugar cubes," she remarked as she passed me the glass. "But that makes it too sweet, if you ask me. Now, be careful, this is strong stuff."

I had no fear. I lifted the cup and smelled it. The smell of anise had become less pungent. I took a sip; it was bitter and had a strong herbal taste. I swallowed and licked my lips and thought about the flavor. Before I could decide whether I liked the taste, my head started to spin.

"It's good, right?" the woman said.

It was. I took a much larger gulp. My spinning head seemed to rotate even faster as the licorice-y syrup oozed down my throat. I smiled at my drinking instructor, then took another sip of the remarkable, fast-working tonic.

As I did, my new friend turned around to speak with a man in back of her. His back was toward me and I couldn't see his face.

"Love, come meet my new amigo," she said to him. "It's her first time trying absinthe. Look, I think she likes it."

"You've hooked another one, eh?" the man replied.

When I heard his voice I had just taken another drink. My muscles froze in place. I didn't even swallow my mouthful of booze. It was that same all-too-familiar voice I had heard the evening before.

And then the man turned around ... and all the absinthe exploded out of my mouth.

Before me stood the Dead Writer.

The massive mist of lime-green liquor seemed to linger in the air for a second. Then most of it came to rest on the face and clothes of a man I had seen die a half-world away.

He didn't say anything at first. I certainly didn't say anything; I was shocked speechless. He looked down at what was once his clean white shirt, now speckled green with absinthe. He looked back up at me and said:

"That may be the strangest form of greeting I've ever encountered."

And with that he let out a giant laugh. The British woman laughed too. Then, with me still in utter disbelief, the woman handed the Dead Writer a bar towel and he began to wipe his face.

It was him. It was his face, his hair, his moustache, his all-American voice. Was he a ghost? Was I asleep? I stammered, struggling to speak:

"You ... you're ... but you ... Ernie?"

He was dabbing his shirt.

"Bernie?" he asked. "No, no, my name is ...,"

The British woman cut him off.

"Heavens, Wendy ... are you alright?" she said. "You're pale as milk."

"I ... I'm fine, I think," I said, my eyes locked on the ghost. He was now dabbing spots on his striped tie.

"Goodness. I've heard of hallucinations coming on fast, but you take the cake," the woman said. "Maybe absinthe isn't right for you."

I couldn't stop staring at this man, this dead man, in front of me. But he wasn't dead ... he was very much alive. Right here. In the flesh.

"Perhaps you might like some water, darling?" the woman said to me.

"Scotch," I said.

"Scotch?" she replied. "That's the spirit. But come now, let's get you a glass of ...,"

"Scotch. Now," I demanded, my resolve strong. The Dead Writer started talking as he dabbed:

"You know, this reminds me of an incident a few weeks ago. That trip up to Burguete. Bill and I ended up on this bus full of Basques and everyone started sharing their wineskins."

As he spoke I couldn't believe my eyes, or my ears. His mannerisms, his way of speaking, it was all the same. It was him ... yet somehow it wasn't. He carried on:

"Burguete is a nice town and the Basques are good people. They like to drink wine and the wine they make is a very good wine. So we passed the wineskins back and forth on the bus and by the time we got off that deathtrap we were half-pickled. When we left the bus and walked into the station the stationmaster looked down at Bill's shirt. His shirt was stained red with wine, from his neck to his crotch. Bill can't handle wine to save his life, I should add. Well, the stationmaster took pity on him, thinking he was sick, and I said: 'Hell, he's not sick. He's just got a drinking problem ... meaning he can't hold his vino!'"

And then The Dead Writer barked out another big, loud laugh. The woman, my new friend, laughed along with him. My jaw was still on the floor but I managed to force a half-smile, still not believing who I was seeing.

A second later a glass of scotch was handed it to me. I took one gulp and looked up. The Dead Writer was still there. I chugged the rest and looked up at him again. He watched me put the empty glass back on the bar and said:

"My goodness. You're my type of woman."

"Do you … have a twin brother?" I asked.

"No," he replied. "But based on your drinking talents, I suspect you and the Queen Bee may have been separated at birth."

At that the woman snickered. She made another aside to me and said:

"I've had so many goddamn names and titles, I thought it best to go ahead and make myself a queen."

"And long live the Queen, may she reign forever!" the Dead Writer proclaimed. "You know what, I'm going to dart up to the room and put on a clean shirt. We're still here, why not."

"Yes, why don't you do that," the Queen Bee replied. "Wendy will keep me company … won't you, Wendy? Good, good. Oh, darling, while you're up in the room, grab my sweater, would you? I don't want to be cold later."

"The white one?" the Dead Writer asked.

"It's after five, darling. The black one," was the Queen Bee's blunt answer.

"Understood," he said. "As someone once said, I shall return."

"Don't you leave without a kiss," she said.

So the Dead Writer leaned in and planted a big, wet, sloppy kiss on the Queen Bee. It was quite passionate. When he was done he gave her an arched eyebrow and said:

"God, I want you."

And she replied:

"I want you more."

And then the Dead Writer turned and started through the crowd. I watched him go. Still unsure if this entire scene was real or not, I turned back to the Queen Bee. She sure seemed real. She was watching her partner walk away.

"He has such a cute butt, doesn't he?" she said, then sighed. "Good looks and good in bed. The perfect man."

***

The Queen Bee pulled up a stool and sat next to me.

"Frederico!" she called to the bartender. "Another Pernod, amigo, por favor y gracias."

Then she turned to me.

"You still look like you're in utter shock, sweetie," she said. "Don't worry, he's been doused in booze before. It happens more often than you would think."

My mind was still swirling. I knew I must be coming off as an addled goof.

"I'm ... I'm sorry," I said. "He just reminds me of someone."

"It happens," the Queen Bee replied. "Truth be told, I was sitting here thinking that you look like a gal I've seen around Paris."

"Someone else said something similar to me."

"Did they? I wonder if we're thinking of the same person. Fetching girl, she's got short hair too. Rail thin, though. Oh, goodie, here's my drink ... gracias, Frederico. Now, Wendy, a toast. To us."

She raised her fresh Pernod to my scotch and we drank. The hard liquor burned my throat, which was just fine. As I was recovering the Queen Bee reached in her handbag and pulled out a case of cigarettes.

"Smoke?" she asked.

I nodded.

She lit one and handed it to me and then lit another for herself. The one that she gave me tasted like her lipstick, which tasted better than mine. She took a deep drag and then exhaled and through the smoke she said:

"Watch this, two lovely lasses by themselves, we won't be alone for long," she said. "Don't you hate that? God, I hate that. It's alright for men to go out and get drunk and do what they want, but heaven forbid women do the same. They all assume we came here to mate. Right?"

I nodded. She spoke fast and her words were precise.

"My partner in crime, he and his friends sit around the cafés of Montmartre day after day. They drink coffee and talk about all the glorious books they aren't writing. Then they go home and nap and later they go back out and drink again and talk about their invisible novels."

My heart was calming down. I tried to not think about the dead man I had just seen, instead focusing on the conversation at hand.

"It sounds ... terribly counterproductive," I offered.

"Woah, no adverbs, no adverbs allowed," she said. "If you use an adverb, you have to drink."

"Why?"

"Don't question the rules, my dear."

She looked at me like I was obligated to take a drink, so I did.

"Excellent," she said. "So yes, the men drink every time they use an adverb. They hate their adverbs, you know. Then they drink again if a sentence is too long. And they drink twice if you don't use the least complicated words at hand."

She paused for a brief moment then:

"Simplest. Simplest words, is that right? No, it should be 'the most simple words'. See, I must owe a couple drinks for that," she said, taking them. "Damn, I love Pernod. So, Wendy-from-Peter-Pan … tell me about this 'work' you're doing."

"Well, I'm … an artist."

"An artist!" she exclaimed. "Wonderful. What do you do … modern stuff, or more traditional? Oils or watercolor?"

"No, none of that. I work for an archaeologist."

"An … archaeologist? Like in Egypt?"'

"Funny you should say that, but no. I'm here from Mexico."

"You don't look Mexican."

"No, the archaeological camp is in Mexico. In the Yucatán," I said. "I'm from Vermont."

"That's the place your country's last president was from, right?"

"Precisely," I said.

"Drink for that adverb, my dear."

I did. My new friend was a delight and I found myself loosening up, despite the shock from earlier. I was about to get her real name, but just as I was about to ask two men approached.

"Hey-hey, hola, chicas," one of them said. "Qué pasa?"

Both men had over-styled hair and over-sized egos. They had that silly little shake to them that men get when they are trying to be suave.

"Hey-hey yourself, caballeros," the Queen Bee said. She had a smirk on her face as she looked them up and down. "Noche de fiesta, huh?"

"Sí, sí, that is right," the first man said. "But my friend and I, we need company. We going to fine restaurant, but our friends, they can no come. You two, you should come. Sí?"

As he talked he moved in and started to put a hand on her shoulder. She grabbed it before he could and guided it away with a polite smile.

"Oh, gracias, amigo," she said. "But you see, my friend and I are lovers. Ella es mi amor. And we are both very anti-man. What's the term, Wendy? Odiamos a los hombres? I think that's right. We hate men. Sorry."

Then she made a smooching motion, as if she was giving me an invisible kiss. The two interlopers looked at us with wide eyes and open mouths. They slinked away and the Queen Bee toasted me again.

We finished that round of drinks and discussed having another. I wanted to try absinthe again and she agreed to join me. Frederico pulled the elaborate set-up out again and we lined up our glasses and watched the water drip over our sugar cubes. When the booze was a perfect storm of milky green we turned the spigots off, pulled the glasses and toasted. I took one sip and it was still bitter but it wasn't an altogether bad taste. I took another sip and swished it in my mouth, which enhanced its herbal flavor. Before I could swallow:

"Boo!"

It was the Dead Writer. My mouthful of absinthe sprayed out. This time the green mist fell upon poor Frederico, the bartender.

***

For the next hour or so I sat at the bar with the two of them.

The Dead Writer wasn't dead. Of that I was certain: a dead man couldn't drink or talk that much.

And boy, could he talk. He talked about Paris and Pamplona and Kansas City. Then he talked about fishing and hunting. Then he talked about sitting in cafes all day. And the Queen Bee was right about adverbs, too … he didn't use many of them. Whenever he let one slip, he would penalize himself and take a drink.

At some point I asked him again if he had a twin, or a look-alike brother. He did not. I asked if he had ever been to Key West or Florida. He had not.

Then he asked me why I was asking so many strange questions.

"She says you remind her of someone," the Queen Bee offered.

"Me?" the Dead Writer said. "Huh. Living or dead?"

I had to think about that one. I looked at him, looked at her, thought about it a second longer and said:

"Living."

They were both staring at me.

"Gosh, that was dramatic," the Dead Writer said. "Who?"

"Just ... someone I fell out of touch with," I lied, then changed the subject. "Tell me again about Bayonne."

"Ah, Bayonne," he said, snapping back into talking mode. "Bayonne is a good town. It is a good and nice town on the river and the people of Bayonne are friendly and welcoming. It can get hot in the summer but the cooler air blows down off the mountains then rushes up through the river valley. You can stand on the bridge and feel the fresh air coming up from the valley. It is a splendid way to cool down on a hot day. Yes, Bayonne is a good town."

12

El Escorial

"I think you're drinking too much and sleeping too little," Doctor Morley said.

We were waiting for our motorcar to Escorial and I had just told him all about my encounter the previous evening. About seeing the Dead Writer, or at least someone who looked and talked and acted exactly like him.

"It wasn't a dream," I said to him, frustrated. "Come to the bar with me tonight and you'll see. He's real."

"Mm-hm."

"Scoff all you want. I speak the truth. I'm gonna drag you out, you can meet him yourself."

"Well, I certainly can't pass up a chance to meet your imaginary friends," he said. "Maybe I'll get to fly on an imaginary unicorn, too."

He was being an absolute asshole. I fumed in silence as we waited, not bothering to engage with him anymore.

Minutes later, a somewhat-fancy black motorcar pulled toward the curb. I saw Mister Carter through the window, sitting in the front passenger seat. When the motorcar stopped, a big man got out of the driver's side. He was tall, with thick arms and a thick neck and dark skin. He came around the vehicle and looked at Doctor Morley and myself. He nodded but said nothing, then opened the rear door. The odor of overpriced perfume spilled out, alerting me to the presence of Veronica Shitty in the back seat.

"You'll have to sit in the middle," Doctor Morley said from behind me.

I turned and gave him a stare that could have killed an elephant.

"And how long a trip will this be?" I seethed, keeping my voice low.

"A little over an hour," my boss replied.

"You'll pay for this in the afterlife," I said. Then I took a deep breath, got in the motorcar and slid over next to the she-devil.

***

Not long into our journey, Veronica pulled out her cigarette case. Without rolling her window down, she lit up.

I faked a cough. She didn't bite, so I reached in my bag for one of my Campeones. I put it in my mouth, fumbled with the lighter and fired my smoke. Then I asked Doctor Morley to roll down his window a tad. Which he did, but he didn't look very happy about it. He coughed.

"Lord, that stank," Veronica said. "What the hell are you smoking?"

I took a slow drag before answering.

"It's a Campeone."

"Spanish?" Veronica asked.

"Mexican. I brought them over."

"Have one of mine. They're French."

"I don't need a French cigarette. I like mine."

"They smell like wet dog."

I took another drag, maintaining eye contact with her as I did, but when I exhaled I tried to blow it the other way. Doctor Morley coughed again and said:

"Dammit, it's like a ten-cent saloon in here. Driver, tu ventanilla ... can you roll down your window, please? Gracias, gracias. Howard, you too, roll your window down."

"I don't care for the wind," Mister Carter replied and did nothing, even though he was sweating.

Doctor Morley huffed and rolled his own window down the rest of the way.

"Well then, Howard, since I'm losing a day of work in Madrid you might as well provide me with some direction," he said. "Can't see what you expect to find here that we can't find at the National Library."

"The royal repository, my good man," Mister Carter said. "Anything that came to or from Charles or Phillip, it's at Escorial."

"Ah, of course, history's greatest father-and-son conquering duo," Doctor Morley said in a condescending tone.

"Yes, yes," Mister Carter said, oblivious to the sarcasm. "And I believe many of the records from the diocese of the New World are here, too. Some are in Seville, too. But of course I'm sure you knew that."

"Of course I knew that," Doctor Morley said. "What I still fail to understand is how you think we're going to find clues about something in Mexico at a monastery in Spain."

"It's more than a monastery," Veronica added.

"Much, much more than a monastery," Mister Carter chimed in. "You see, Sylvanus, you need to fight this inclination to believe that you, or we, are the first to search for all this. You're not."

"Don't patronize me," my boss grumbled.

"And don't take everything so personally," Mister Carter shot back. "We need to build upon the efforts of others who have sought the same."

I realized they were being careful with their words. I assumed that was because of the driver, but I don't think he was paying them any heed.

"That's what I've been doing, Howard. That's what Frans Blom has been doing, too, and the Thompsons," Doctor Morley said.

"Ah!" Mister Carter said, holding an index finger up for dramatic effect. "But riddle me this: who would have had the most motivation to look for what we're looking for?"

Doctor Morley didn't answer. But I felt like I knew, so I did.

"The king," I offered.

I could feel Doctor Morley giving me his own death stare. Mister Carter said:

"Correct. The person most interested in finding it would be, logically, the person it was stolen from," Mister Carter said.

"It was stolen from the Aztecs, not the king of Spain," Doctor Morley grumbled.

Mister Carter took a deep breath in. He looked over toward the driver, then peeked back at us with a scowl.

"We can discuss these details further when we arrive," Mister Carter said. "Now, Miss Willoughby, I'll assume you've never been to El Escorial?"

"No," I said, not correcting him. "This is my first time in Spain."

"Well, you're in for quite a treat," Mister Carter said, now smiling. "It's a fascinating place. Most people think Juan de Herrera did all the design work, but really it was Juan Bautista de Toledo that put together the first plans. Herrera added the flourishes later. The original concept was much more modest, with a focus on the gridiron."

"The gridiron?" I asked.

"Perhaps griddle is the more appropriate term," Mister Carter answered. "Bautista wanted it all to look like the grate that they burned Saint Lawrence on. Fascinating, isn't it? All that magnificence, with such a macabre inspiration."

***

The countryside was brown and dry. Not as dry as the Yucatán, but not lush either. Gnarled trees baking in the hot sun were the only spots of green.

We came onto a long stretch, over a series of small hills, then into a village. The motorcar turned one last corner and before us stood an enormous stone complex. It was much, much bigger than I expected it to be.

"Ah, there she is," Mister Carter said. "The former center of the universe."

He chuckled as his own wittiness. I kept staring at the massive edifice unveiling itself before me. There were towers jutting up on the corners and within the walls I could see more spires and an enormous dome. I had never been to the Vatican, but that's what it reminded me off.

At the top of the hill Mister Carter directed the driver to take a turn at a long barracks-like building. The Egyptologist said:

"Now, there's four of these four-story buildings around the perimeter, for monks and soldiers and whatnot. Those four four-story buildings form a perfect square around the inner complex. It provided a degree of separation between the kings and his subjects."

Mister Carter told the driver where to park the motorcar; soon we stopped and I was able to get out. I took a deep breath of fresh air and tried to clear Veronica's powerful perfume out of my lungs.

Escorial was massive. It looked like it had been built to withstand barbarians and the like. The walls were high and too tall to scale; the windows were all covered with iron grates. The long, boring facade was broken up by a somewhat-ornate entrance. There were several large Doric columns around the main door, above them two smaller columns framing a statue and a coat of arms.

"That statue is Saint Lawrence, in case you were wondering," Mister Carter said as we made our way toward the entrance. "I had a disagreement some time back with a writer who swore this design was based on Solomon's temple. Poppycock, I told him, there's a statue of San Lorenzo right over the damn door. And he's holding a griddle! I'll tell you, give a writer a dash of historical fact, he'll whip it into a stew of falsehoods in no time."

Mister Carter was in front, acting like our tour guide. Doctor Morley was trailing me. I turned back to check on the whereabouts of the she-devil and spotted her talking with the driver. I found that odd.

"Now, Miss Willoughby, see here," Mister Carter said as he approached the entrance. "Look at all these metal studs on the door. Remarkable, isn't it?"

"Oh, come now, Howard, are you really trying to make this into a sightseeing tour?" Doctor Morley grumbled.

"The glory of Escorial? How can you pass it up?" Mister Carter said. "I think you would find this interesting, Sylvanus."

"*Don't* ... call me Sylvanus"

"Hmph," Mister Carter said with an arched eyebrow. "Very well."

And then Mister Carter turned and went on with his tour-giving.

"Ah, the Patio of the Kings," he said. "Miss Willoughby, you'll note the same Doric columns repeat here, over the vestibule of the church. As we proceed inward, you'll find a blend of Doric, Ionic and Corinthian ...,"

As Mister Carter carried on, I swear I heard a blood vessel in Doctor Morley's brain burst.

"Now, by way of orientation, the seminary is over on this side," Mister Carter said, pointing. "And over on the opposite side is the monastery. The Library is back there, over the entrance ... we'll see that soon enough ... but I can't pass up a peek inside."

"Howard, remember why we're here," Doctor Morley pleaded.

"I'd like to see the inside," came Veronica's voice from behind me.

Doctor Morley growled.

"So would I," I agreed.

"Ridiculous," Doctor Morley snarled.

"Marvelous!" Mister Carter exclaimed.

And the Egyptologist pivoted his great girth around and lumbered toward the steps of the Basilica. He began to speak louder. There were a couple of white-skinned tourists nearby; they gave him a second look. For a brief moment I thought they had recognized him, but they shook their heads and wandered away. The unrecognizable Howard Carter continued walking and talking:

"There are two palaces. One toward the rear corner for the Bourbons, the other in back of the Basilica. That second one was for Phillip and his family. So it all flows around the Basilica, as you can see. An emblem, if you will, of the confluence of the crown and God."

Veronica followed behind him. I started, then turned back to find Doctor Morley standing with his arms crossed.

"Aren't you coming?" I asked.

"If anyone feels the inclination to actually *work*, I'll be in the library," he huffed.

He was giving me a look that said you-better-come-with-me, but it wasn't persuasive enough.

"Right-o," I said. "We'll find you later."

That made him pucker his lips in anger. I smiled at him, then returned to the tour.

***

"... And the completion of Escorial marked both the apex of the Spanish Empire and the beginning of its inevitable decline. Phillip didn't know that at the time, of course ...,"

Mister Carter was a very informative guide. He liked to talk about history, to the point that he over-talked and then had to catch his breath. But even when he was gasping for breath it was interesting:

"... So it all came together as this, a manifestation of his divine right. His family's divine right, I should say. Hooboy, let's stop here for a moment ... yes, thank you. And here, at his fingertips, he would have all that he needed to rule his global empire: the church, his palace, the monastery, the library, the armory ...,"

The Basilica was enormous. There was a splendid dome over the altar and sunlight was pouring in from its' windows. The altar screen was tall as a house and contained paintings by Tibaldi and Zuccaro. It was spectacular.

"... And this is the modest little bedchamber that Phillip slept in. Close to the altar, as you can see, in case any urgent dialogue between king and creator was required. Alright, let's turn around here, there's a staircase down to the crypt just past the altar. Wooh, go on, go on, give me a moment catch my breath."

As I followed Veronica out of the small bedchamber, I looked back to Mister Carter. He was fondling a tassel on King Phillip's four-poster bed. When he saw me looking, he stopped and smiled. Then I looked away and as I did I heard the *pop* as he tore the tassel off. As he walked by me, I could see him stuffing something in his pocket. Sure enough, when I glanced back at the King's bed, the tassel was gone. I said nothing.

Next Mister Carter led us downstairs to the Pantheon of Kings and showed us the tombs of the departed monarchs, all in matching black caskets.

"Interesting fact: after Charles died, he was mummified," our tour guide explained. "But everyone missed Carlos ... so from time-to-time they'd haul his mummy out to check up on him. I heard a story that they pulled him out one time just to see how his face looked compared to Titian's paintings."

"A mummy? That's gruesome," Veronica commented. "Can we move on?"

"Some of us have to think about mummies all the time," Mister Carter said, and for a moment he seemed lost in thought. "But very well. Come here, I'll show you the Pantheon of Infants."

After seeing the depressing tomb for all the poor little princes who didn't make it, we decided to make our way back toward the library. Mister Carter led us back toward the front of the complex and we passed through several art-filled chambers. Then, when he got to the next set of open doors, he stopped.

"Well, well, what do we have here?" he said.

I came up beside him and looked into the next room.

It was an enormous room filled to the walls with every type of old weaponry you could think of. In every direction there were suits of armor, spears, lances ... and more swords than I could count.

"My goodness, I don't recall the armory being this crowded," Mister Carter said.

Veronica had wandered ahead of us. She reached down and ran a hand down a long piece of armor that ran down the fake snout of a fake horse.

"Magnificent!" she declared. "This is the royal collection?"

"Can't say I'm sure," Mister Carter said. "I didn't expect to see this here. There's an armory at the Royal Palace in Madrid. Perhaps they've moved it out of the city for safekeeping."

"Much like the king himself," Veronica deadpanned.

"Ah, witty," Mister Carter said. "My word, look at this. Some of this must go back to the Crusades. Look here, armor for a teenaged Charles! Ooh, look there, that matte-black shield … stunning, simply stunning."

The three of us took different paths through the Armory. I was pretending to peruse the collection, but I was really keeping an eye on Mister Carter. I had a strong suspicion that being around all these shiny objects might make the Egyptologist come down with a case of sticky fingers.

I was right. I saw him bend down to look at a knife tucked into the belt of a suit of chainmail. Then he began to run his fingers over the handle, like he was going to seize hold of it. I let out a loud fake cough:

"Ahem!"

He looked up. Our eyes met. He pursed his lips a bit then gave me a puzzled look.

"Yes. Yes, you're right … we should be going," he said.

He started to walk again. And again, something caught his eye.

"Oh my, a Wheellock gun," he said. "That's a rare sight."

I came up beside him. He was looking at an odd contraption housed in a glass case.

It was a gun unlike any I had ever seen or imagined. It was decorated with finely engraved gold, with an ornate swirling handle and a pair of exposed trigger mechanisms on the side. It looked like the kind of gun Captain Nemo would carry.

"A Wheelock gun?" I asked, thinking of my friend Oliver, lost in the Yucatán somewhere.

"Wheel-lock," Mister Carter replied in a professorial tone. "See here, I wonder if this case lifts off somehow. Help me out, would you?"

"Help you do ... what? No, Mister Carter, I ...,"

"It will only take a moment. I need to see something."

"Really, I don't think that's a good idea, and we really should be ...,"

"Oh, stop stammering and help me," he said. "I just want to see how it works."

He had moved to one side of the wood-and-glass case and was trying to lift it off its pedestal. For some reason, perhaps the sheer force of his will power, I felt compelled to amuse him. I reached down to take hold of the other side.

"Gently now, lift up," Mister Carter said, and I lifted my side of the box. It didn't move. "It must be secured underneath. See if there's a latch on your side."

I knelt down to look underneath the small pedestal. As I bent over, my rear bumped up against a suit of armor.

I didn't bump it hard … but it was hard enough. I looked over and saw the suit of armor—one of the fancy ones, of course—begin to tip. I reached out and caught the legs, at which point the top-half of the armor popped off and fell into the next one, which began to fall as well. Armor began to clatter off the floor. At first I bent over to pick it up but then I realized there was one last suit of armor teetering. I sprung to my feet and caught it below the armpits, seconds before it fell.

I froze. I looked at Mister Carter and he had a great smile on his face.

"Marvelous catch," he said.

"What the hell!" Veronica yell-whispered from across the room.

"It was an accident!" I yell-whispered back.

"Ah, here's the latch," Mister Carter said, still a fumbling with the case of the wheel-lock gun. "Now, Wendy, come back over here and …,"

"No!" I declared. "Stop touching that. You're going to get us all into trouble."

"Me? You're the one knocking into things," he replied.

"Cuál es el problema?" someone hollered from the door. I looked up to see a guard, peering past the armament at us.

"Uh … no problema, no problema," I replied. "Just a … a little accident."

"Accidente?" the guard called back.

"No, no, no accidente!" I called back. I motioned with my eyes to Mister Carter, giving him the lets-go look. He was still transfixed by the wondrous firearm:

"I recently read a fascinating book that said Leonardo designed a wheel-lock gun. I think that would be a few generations before this one. Goodness, I wonder if it still fires?"

He was exhausting. I grabbed him by the arm and pulled—or tried to pull—him along. He was, just like my boss said, a very large man and he proved difficult to move.

***

The library at El Escorial was, without exception, the most remarkable book-space I had ever been in.

The room was much longer than it was wide. There were a series of windows that provided a view back over the Patio of the Kings to the Basilica. The ceiling had barrel-vaults adorned with brilliant, exquisite frescoes.

"Tibaldi again," Mister Carter said as he admired the frescoes with me.

"They're gorgeous," I murmured.

"Each of the liberal arts has a fresco," he went on. "That's astronomy right up there, obviously. Then that's grammar, arithmetic, geometry ... that one is music. I forget the others."

"And what's this?" Veronica asked.

She was standing by a large iron structure near the center of the room. It looked somewhat like a naked globe, but it had knobs and levers for adjusting a multitude of gears housed inside.

"Ah, an armillery sphere," Mister Carter said. "A must for any respectable man hoping to rule the world. I wonder if this belonged to Charles or Phillip?"

Just then a door in the back wall opened. A bald, sleepy-eyed librarian came out wearing a frown. He gave us an exhausted look. Behind him came Doctor Morley.

"Perfect, here they are now," my boss remarked to the librarian. "My colleague will be able to provide you with a more complete rundown of our requests. But we can start with those records from Izamel and Mani. Oh, and any correspondence you might have between the king—either Charles or Phillip—and Cortés."

Now the librarian stopped walking and looked at Doctor Morley.

"Cortés? Hernando Cortés?"

"Yes, Hernán Cortés. Not all of it, just a certain time period."

"Sevilla," the librarian replied. "All that in Sevilla. We here, we just have copies."

"Seville!" Doctor Morley exclaimed, too loud.

"Sí. Los Archivos de las Indias, Sevilla."

Doctor Morley looked like he couldn't believe it. He turned to Mister Carter.

"Howard, were you aware of this?"

"Yes, I suspected that might be the case," Mister Carter replied.

"You *suspected* this?" Doctor Morley said. "Thanks for cluing me in."

"You doth protest too much, Sylvanus," Mister Carter said, then he strode toward the librarian.

"Hola, my good man. English? Very good, very good," Mister Carter began. "First, my apologies for interrupting you ... and second apologies for my colleague's impatience."

Doctor Morley's mouth flung open. The librarian looked happier.

"Now, as he stated, we're interested in some rather particular areas of interest ... but we don't want to take up too much of your time. Now, good man, might we be able to start with a look at whatever files you have on Bishop Diego de Landa? Ignore that request about Cortés, por favor."

The librarian let a half-smile escape then nodded to Mister Carter.

"I will see what I have," he replied. "But Cortés, the conquistadors ... you would not find that here."

"Of course. Understood," Mister Carter said.

Then the librarian cocked his head and said:

"You ... I know you."

Mister Carter beamed. "Yes, well, I ...,"

"You, you finda the tomb of Tut, no?"

Mister Carter beamed even more.

"Sí! Sí!" the librarian said, appearing awe-struck. "Howard Hughes!"

"Carter," the Egyptologist corrected him. "It's Howard Carter."

"Ah, sí, sí, Howard Hughes Carter! My brother, he wants to go find lost treasure because of you," the librarian said.

"Hmph," Mister Carter said. "Well, let him know I already found the last available one."

They both laughed. Then the librarian turned and left us. Mister Carter looked down at Doctor Morley and said:

"We'd be more likely to find an elephant in here than anything marked 'Cortés.' Remember, the crown didn't care for Hernán's methods … or his ambitions."

"I know that," Doctor Morley snapped. "Not everyone needs a history lesson, Howard."

"Call me Mister Hughes, please," Mister Carter said.

He said it with a straight face and maintained it. I laughed. Doctor Morley didn't.

***

Soon the librarian returned with an assistant in tow. The assistant, a monk of some sort, was holding an old oak filing box. He carried it over to a long table at the far end of the room and thunked it down. The librarian undid the latch and opened the top. A stench of dank, musty oldness wafted up. The librarian looked to Mister Carter:

"Arquidiócesis de Yucatán," he said. "There are two more boxes, I carry them up for you."

I caught the poor monk rolling his eyes at that comment. He knew the librarian would be doing no such carrying. Mister Carter was eyeing a label on the box.

"Fifteen-sixty-one to fifteen-seventy-one," he said. "The others are older I hope?"

"No, señor."

"Damn. Well, bring them up anyways. And you said you have an index to correspondence from that period too? Excelente, excelente. Bring that up too, gracias."

The librarian and the poor monk marched away.

"Why only the Yucatán archdiocese?" Doctor Morley asked.

"Because it had enormous territorial jurisdiction, Sylvanus," Mister Carter answered. "And if what we are looking for was at one point in the Tabasco region, I would think the bishop of Yucatán knew of it."

"But the fall of Tenochtitlan predates that archdiocese by decades," Doctor Morley scoffed. "Or didn't you know that?"

"I knew that ... but I can't allow knowledge to overwhelm a good hunch," Mister Carter said.

Veronica was already thumbing through the ancient box. "These look like ordinary tax records, Howard."

"Marvelous, marvelous," Mister Carter replied. "I love all records ... but tax records are my favorite."

The rest of us did not share Mister Carter's enthusiasm. It was just page after page of repetitive records counting the members of various tribes throughout the Yucatán. The writing on the page was Spanish, but the numerals were done in Mayan.

"Gaspar Antonio Chi was the lead on this project, if I'm not mistaken," Doctor Morley commented. "His name came up the other day … but I'm having a senior moment and can't quite remember where."

"You found 'chi' written in a book," I offered.

"Ah, that's right. He was de Landa's right-hand man for a healthy period. The Bishop didn't trust many people but it would appear he trusted Chi," he said, flipping the page. "Now, see here, what's this?"

Doctor Morley had come upon a piece of paper that didn't look like the other pages we had been inspecting. This looked to be a page torn from a book. He took it up and inspected it. It had writing on both sides. I was looking over his shoulder and could see that it was Spanish.

"This doesn't appear to be original, but it's a copy of a letter Cortés sent to the king."

"Cortés!" Mister Carter exclaimed, coming over to look. "So there is something here."

"Again, a copy … don't get too worked up. I remember this. It's one of a handful of updates he sent back to Spain, trying to explain himself. This is the one where he talks about his haul from Tenochtitlan …,"

"That's what we're after!" Veronica said, crowding in to look.

"… Now, is it my eyes? Or am I seeing marks above some of these?" Doctor Morley said, leaning in and squinting. "Perhaps I'm seeing spots."

I looked where he was pointing. He was not seeing spots. There were what appeared to be little hatch-marks above some of the words.

"It's not your eyes," I said. "It looks like someone was checking things off."

"Checking things off!" Mister Carter exclaimed. "Like what?"

"Well, let's see," Doctor Morley said. "*A gold necklace composed of seven pieces, with 185 small emeralds set in it, and 232 gems, like rubies, from which hung 27 small bells of gold, and some pearls ...,*"

Doctor Morley paused, arched his eyebrows and said:

"... There's a check-mark above that."

"Great Scott, man," Mister Carter said. "What else is checked?"

Doctor Morley ran a finger down the page then turned the page over and scanned that page, too.

"Most of them. Not all, but most," Doctor Morley said, then he kept reading: "*Two wheels, one of gold representing the sun, the other of silver bearing the image of the moon ... a gold bracelet ... twenty-four curious and beautiful golden shields, decorated with feathers and small pearls ... several head-dresses, and crowns of feathers and gold, ornamented with pearls and gems.* That sounds like the head-dress you shipped off to Vienna, Veronica."

That was a good burn. Veronica seethed but Doctor Morley kept going:

"*... There were several Mexican books, written in hieroglyphics, on their paper, which was about the consistency of light pasteboard ...,*"

"The Codex!" I said.

"And that is checked as well," Doctor Morley said. "Good Heavens. It's an inventory."

"Good Heavens indeed. We need that piece of paper," Mister Carter declared.

"It's not an original, Howard. We can take notes."

"Hogwash," Mister Carter said, and then he reached out and snatched the page right out of Doctor Morley's hand. He looked at the page, took a guilty-looking scan around the room then stuffed the page inside his jacket.

"Put. That. Back," Doctor Morley growled through clenched teeth.

"You said yourself it's only a copy," Mister Carter replied.

"Put it back or we're done here," Doctor Morley seethed.

And Mister Carter backed down. Without a word he reached back into his jacket, pulled out the page and handed it back to my boss. Doctor Morley eyed Mister Carter and then said to me:

"Wendy. Take notes," so I pulled out my notebook and started to do just that.

Then, a few minutes later, Doctor Morley came upon another interesting find:

"It's a map," he said, which made us all rush to his side. "I've seen this before, too, or one like it. It was done as part of a land treaty. See, this is Mani in the middle, with the big cathedral … then over here is Tekit, up here is Teabo."

"You say you've seen this before?" Veronica asked.

"I have," Doctor Morley said. "The original is at the library at Tulane. This one appears to be either a hand-drawn copy or a draft."

Now Doctor Morley was looking closer at the old, yellowed map.

"Spanish parchment. European ink," he said. "But the writing ...,"

"... Is the same writing as the tax records," I added, finishing his sentence.

Doctor Morley looked at me, I looked at him, and at the same time we both said:

"Chi!"

And as we said it Mister Carter reached down and snatched the map right out of Doctor Morley's fingers. This time the big man put it in his jacket pocket without delay. Then he sniffed, the kind of sniff that says I-don't-have-to-explain-myself, and said:

"Now, Sylvanus, let's see what else we can find in here."

***

During the remainder of that afternoon we didn't find anything that rivaled the letter from Cortés or the land treaty map. By the time we scanned the last folder of tax records, Mister Carter had concluded that the Archive in Seville would provide us with more information than Escorial could.

"Then why the hell did we come here?" Doctor Morley asked.

"Because we must turn over a thousand shovelfuls of dirt before we find the steps we seek," Mister Carter answered.

"Hmph. That saying comes off as a bit self-aggrandizing," Doctor Morley complained.

"Ah, yes ... I forgot that saying was about *me*," the Egyptologist replied.

As we were gathering our things to depart there was yet another dispute between Doctor Morley and Mister Carter. My boss insisted that Mister Carter could not take the land treaty map he had pilfered, to the point that the Mayanologist threatened to quit. Mister Carter, seeming to back down, agreed and took the map out. The Egyptologist made a show of re-opening the document box to put it back inside.

But he never did, in fact, put it back. He waited until Doctor Morley had turned around to leave, then he snatched the ancient map back up. He looked at me with a peculiar look and then, without warning, he opened the flap on my shoulder bag. He slid the map in, lowered the flap and gave me a little nod.

The great Howard Carter was making me an accomplice to crime. I knew Doctor Morley would be furious when he found out. But now we were moving. Any chance I had to say "no" had come and gone.

Doctor Morley walked out first, then Veronica. I stuck next to Mister Carter, ready to blame him if I got nabbed. As we exited the grand room I noticed a sign above the door, in Latin. I asked Mister Carter about it, so as to look cool and calm during the getaway.

"Oh-ho, that sign there?" Mister Carter said. "It says anyone removing items from this library without checking them out will be excommunicated from the church."

Then, after we had passed through that door without incident, he added:

"I hope you're not Catholic."

13

THE DANCE OF THE QUEEN BEE

"A kleptomaniac, that's what he is."

"Mm-hm."

"I can't believe he took it. Pilfering the goods … there's no worse habit for an archaeologist," Doctor Morley went on. "You can see why everyone refuses to work with him."

"Mm-hm."

"You know, Howard wanted me to ask Director Melida about doing a presentation at the Museum," he went on.

"Mm-hm. And did you?"

"I did and the answer was a resounding 'no'. The Director had some choice words about Howard, too."

"Oh, stop. You're projecting."

"I speak the truth. The man's name is mud in the archaeological community."

"I rather like him."

"Well, don't grow too attached," Doctor Morley cautioned. "He's cursed, you know."

As he said that the taxi stopped in front of the Museum. I got out, Doctor Morley paid the driver and then he issued his instructions:

"Our sightseeing at Escorial has left us a day behind. Do your best to make up for lost time, alright? Remember to watch out for patterns and unusual markings."

"Got it."

"And don't waste so much time with the little smudges and nicks. Focus on the images."

"But you said make it an exact copy. To make it exact, I need to include the smudges and nicks."

He looked at me and exhaled.

"I have to pick my battles today, so I'll relent on that one," he said. "Just don't let them slow you down. I'll be in the Library with Howard and Veronica, why don't you come by sometime mid-day."

"I'll be there with bells on," I said.

"Mm-hm," Doctor Morley replied.

***

Perhaps it was pent-up energy. Perhaps it was some inner compulsion telling me to produce the finest copy of the Madrid Codex known to man. Perhaps it was the simple fact that I was nearing the half-way mark.

Whatever the reason, I was on fire.

My lines were crisp. My colors were bold. My eye was sharp.

When the clock struck eleven I was already on page fifty.

"Hey-hey, hola, Vendy!" Lothario the guard said at one point.

I held the palm of my hand up to him—a universal stop sign—and didn't engage. He got the hint and slinked away. I stayed glued to my work and by noon I was halfway done with page fifty-five.

I considered checking in on my motley crew at the Library, but decided my day would be more pleasant if I didn't. So I bought lunch from Dulcinea's ham-cart again, and again I sat and ate on a bench by the Museum steps. I was back at work fifteen minutes later. I finished page fifty-four and worked my way through fifty-five, an ochre-heavy panel highlighted by an impaled enemy. I flipped the hinged frame to reveal the next set of pages.

And at first I thought the page on the top-left was blank ... but then I peered in closer. There was writing down toward the bottom of the page. Latin writing, it appeared ... but the words were backward. The backward writing was contained within a narrow area, roughly one inch wide by three inches long. This small area also had a lighter color than the rest of the Codex, as if it had been done on a different material.

My heart jumped. I studied the image for a few moments, to make sure I was seeing what I thought I was seeing. Then I threw my notebook and supplies back in my shoulder bag, darted down the stairs and made for the Library. By the time I made it all the way through the reading room and into the stacks I was out of breath.

Doctor Morley and Veronica were huddled over his crowded desk. I ran up and declared:

"I've found something!"

And they both stood and it was all very exciting and I started describing it:

"On the bottom ... on the bottom of page fifty-six ... there's a part that looks like it's been torn off," I said, panting from my run. "Or maybe it's been pasted over ...

and there are words … Latin words. It's … it's in an old cursive script but … but the writing, it's reversed, like mirror writing."

Doctor Morley's eyes became little slits. The she-devil sighed.

"You mean the patch?" Doctor Morley inquired. "On page fifty-six? Come now, Wendy … if you had read that Archaeological Digest article you would know that's nothing."

"Nothing?"

"Nothing. It's the remnants of a papal bull, pasted on the Codex to make sure it didn't get tossed in de Landa's fires. Didn't we discuss this?"

"Um … it's ringing a bell," I said.

"You ran all the way over here to tell us that?" he asked, and I nodded. "Well, I'll give you points for enthusiasm."

Veronica gave me a snotty look. The two of them then returned to whatever book or document they had been looking over when I arrived. I felt about two feet tall.

"Where's Mister Carter?" I asked.

"Hungover at the hotel," Doctor Morley answered before Veronica could.

I slunk away and walked back to the Museum.

When I returned to my post I took a closer look at the 'patch' on page fifty-six. I could make out only a few of the backward words; most of the others had been cropped off. But I could make out *Pape* and the beginning of *Archdiocese*.

Next I crooked my head and tried to read another small series of Latin words. They had been written over the first set of backward Latin words in crosswise fashion. I couldn't make heads or tails of them.

Doctor Morley had said it was all nothing and I had no reason to doubt him. But for posterity's sake, I decided to copy the strange writing and markings on page fifty-six. After all … this was to be the greatest color reproduction ever made of the Madrid Codex, wasn't it?

That day I finished page fifty-nine. I was more than halfway done.

***

Later that afternoon, as I came into the hotel after work, a little voice awoke in my head. It told me I should stop at the Lobby Bar and have a drink. While I had planned on a nap before my evening explorations, I knew ignoring one's inner voice would only bring pain and misfortune.

There was a decent-sized crowd at the bar. I scanned to see if my new friends were there but didn't see them. I found an empty stool at the bar and sat down. Within seconds, Frederico had laid a cocktail napkin in front of me.

"Buenas tardes, señora," he said. "Welcome, welcome."

"Gracias, Frederico. Cómo estás?"

"Bien. What can I get for you?"

"I think I'll try the absinthe again."

He gave me that forced, polite smile that bartenders make when you order something that's a pain in the ass.

"You want I put azúcar y agua in for you?"

"No, I'd prefer to do that myself."

He forced another half-smile, went away and came back with the absinthe and a glass. He filled the glass up halfway with booze then left to fetch the awkward fountain of ice water. He placed the fountain down, then left once more to fetch the sugar bowl and the slotted spoon.

"All good?" he said once I had everything.

"All good," I replied. "Gracias, Frederico."

I positioned my absinthe under one of the spouts, took out a sugar cube and placed it on the spoon. I balanced the spoon over my booze and gently turned the tiny spigot on the fountain. A drop fell onto the sugar cube. After a few more drops, I turned the spigot off and removed the spoon and took a taste. It was just right. I held it in my mouth for a second.

"You're getting good at that!" came a voice behind me.

She surprised me. I gagged and nearly choked.

"Goodness gracious! That's what I call a drinking problem, dearie," the Queen Bee said.

Without a word I looked around to see if the Dead Writer was with her. I didn't see him. I must have looked shocked.

"Ooh, I did catch you off-guard, didn't I?" she continued. "I'm wicked like that, sorry. But so glad to see you here! Dying for a drinkie-poo, I am. Ah, Frederico! Amigo! So good to see you. A Pernod, por favor? Gracias, gracias."

Then she turned to me and said:

"Now, tell me about Wendy's day."

She remembered my name, which was delightful until I remembered I didn't know hers.

"It was ... work," I said. "Boring."

"Work is boring by definition … that's why I avoid it at all costs," she said. Frederico brought her a Pernod and she toasted me.

"You don't work?" I asked.

"No … I just marry men who do."

She said that with a straight face. It seemed cold at first, but then she flashed her perfect-in-every-way smile.

"That's a joke," she said with a mischievous wink. "And how goes your great treasure hunt?"

I froze. "My ... what?"

"You said you worked for an archaeologist. Aren't all archaeologists looking for fabled lost treasure?"

"It's ... it's not like that at all," I replied. "It's more like ... research."

"Research," the Queen Bee mimicked.

I nodded.

"You're sure you're not holding out on me, are you?" she said with a devilish wink.

My mind swirled. Did she know something about why I was here? I fumbled for an answer … but it didn't matter because suddenly her face lit up and she changed the topic:

"Oh! The *party!*"

"The what?" I asked.

"I never told you about the party!" she said. "Oh, yes-yes-yes ... you have to come with. It's going to be epic!"

"When?"

"Tonight, dearie! You must come, you simply must. It's at some grand old mansion over by the Royal Palace. The

Cerralbo place, I think it's called. Poopsie says the rich old fart that owned it died and his executor is throwing a big bash before the joint gets sold off."

"Poopsie?" I repeated, hoping she would let her partner's name slip.

"My lesser half. He's out carousing, but we're meeting down here in the Lobby at nine. That's early for these Spaniards but late for me, don't you agree?"

I could only nod. She talked so fast it was hard to get a word in.

"Wonderful, wonderful. It will be a blast, I promise. We heard about it from some Paris friends that we ran into on the Gran Via. Thank goodness we did, would have hated to miss it! There's nothing worse than missing a good party, wouldn't you agree? Right, right, cheers to that," she said, and toasted me. "Goodness, that Pernod is good. Better than water, if you ask me."

Then she laughed. She was delightful and I couldn't help but laugh, too. We sat and chattered away and had more drinks and then agreed we both needed a siesta before the party. When she got up to leave she kissed me on both cheeks, which I had always found pretentious. But with her it seemed very natural. I liked the Queen Bee very much.

As she walked away I looked around. Every single man in the place was watching her sashay away. Quite a few women, too. Who could blame them? She was mesmerizing.

Then I turned back to interrogate my bartender:

"Frederico, I need to know that woman's name."

"She is the Queen Bee, señora."

"I mean her *real* name."

"Lo siento … I know, but I cannot tell you," Frederico said.

"Why? Is there some *law* that says you can't tell me her name?" I said, pressing him.

"Uh … no law, señora," the bartender replied. "Just hotel policy."

***

In my room I tried to nap, but I couldn't sleep. I was delighted to have an invitation to a party … though my excitement was somewhat tempered by the fact I would be attending the party with a person that might be a ghost.

So as I lay there I concocted a series of questions in my mind for the Dead Writer. Surely, he must be directly related to the man I saw die. I had asked him twice if he had a twin and he had said no. Perhaps he had distant cousins who looked like him?

By and by I gave up on my dreams of a siesta and started to think about what I would wear. I had packed one decent dress, the long-sleeved burgundy one that Tatiana had warned me about. I immediately regretted not taking her advice and bringing something fancier.

I bathed, did my hair several times, put on a touch of makeup then rubbed it off. After a good half-hour of labor in the mirror I felt better about myself.

On my way back to the lobby I made a detour to Doctor Morley's room and knocked on his door. I knew he was at dinner with Veronica, but I hoped I might get lucky and find him. I wanted him to come with me, so he could see the Dead Writer with his own eyes.

I wanted him to tell me I wasn't being crazy … but he wasn't around to do so.

***

I walked alone into the Lobby Bar a little before nine. There was a big group of hard-drinking men at the bar and a few of them drunk-goggled me as I looked for my friends.

"Huh-huh, hola bebe," one of them said. I ignored him. Then came a shout from a nearby table.

"Yoo-hoo, Wendy! Over here!"

The crowd seemed to part and there was the Queen Bee, waving to me from her seat. The Dead Writer was sitting across from her and he turned and gave me a smile. Perhaps he was a mirage? But no … he stood up as I approached and said:

"Ah, greetings, Madame Willoughby. You look lovely this evening, so glad you could join us."

And he pulled out a chair for me and waited for me to sit. A ghost wouldn't be that polite, I thought. Then, as he pushed me in, I could smell his musky scent. A ghost wouldn't smell that nice, I thought.

After he pushed me in, he sat down. I had him on one side of me and the Queen Bee on the other.

"That dress! I love it!" she said. "Burgundy is the new black, you know."

"Thanks," I replied. "I wasn't sure what to wear. I like yours, too."

I did. She was wearing a stunning red dress. It was sleeveless and had a cascade of ruffles running along the bottom. I would describe it as part Flamenco dress, part evening dress … and perfect for a night out in Spain.

"You're just in time, dear," she said. "We were debating what to drink. I'm considering having some of that absinthe you're so keen on."

"I'm keen on whiskey, too," I offered.

"I feel like you need a funny hat and a horse to drink whiskey," she said. "It's too cowboy and too harsh on my throat. Scotch is the same. But that absinthe, it makes one hallucinate, doesn't it? Hallucinating is always a good thing."

"You're confusing hallucinating with being drunk," the Dead Writer interjected.

"I am not. The hallucinogenic properties of absinthe are well-documented," the Queen Bee replied. "And I do believe I'm overdue for a hallucinogenic experience. You should join us, poopsie."

"Absinthe isn't masculine enough for me," he said. "I prefer tough, no-nonsense, get-to-the-point drinking. Oh, speaking of which, there's our booze-boy now. Flag him down."

There was a young man taking drink orders at the next table. The Queen Bee cast a single glance his way and he came trotting over with a smile. That smile disappeared when she ordered absinthe.

"See, absinthe is a pain in the-you-know-what. You've got to learn to keep it simple," the Dead Writer opined. He turned to the waiter and said:

"Jerez, por favor."

"Sherry? Oh, yes … that's *much* more masculine," the Queen Bee teased.

The Dead Writer smirked at her and then corrected his order:

"Make that a brandy instead. A double. Straight up."

The waiter left and the two of them giggled. They were peas in a pod.

"Alright, Wendy, first things first," the Queen Bee said, laying a hand on my forearm. "It's going to be an absurd night. So tell us … are you a good drunk or a bad drunk?"

"Pardon?"

"We've got some friends that are good, fun drunks … and we've got other friends that are nasty, miserable drunks," she explained.

"I'm a wonderful drunk, by the way," the Dead Writer offered.

"He's wonderful unless he has gin," the Queen Bee shot back, and they both laughed. "But it's a bit like the good-witch, bad-witch thing. So which are you?"

I thought about it and spoke the truth:

"I suppose it depends on the circumstances and the company."

And at that the Dead Writer let out a sharp laugh and slapped the table. I didn't think what I said was particularly funny, but he did.

"The circumstances and the company. Classic," he said. "I've got to remember that one."

"But it's not an answer!" the Queen Bee protested, smiling. "It's one or the other, Wendy. Good or bad. There is no in-between."

"Well, I'm ... I'm good, I suppose."

"Ding-ding, correct answer," she said. "Now, second question, do you ...,"

"... Do you have any family in the United States?" I blurted out, looking right at the Dead Writer.

He looked stunned. "Eh?"

"I'm sorry," I said, realizing I had said out loud what was going through my head. "I ... I ... you just look very familiar to me. Do you have any cousins, maybe?"

"Um ... no?"

I felt like an idiot. The Queen Bee rescued me:

"What a peculiar question!" she said. "I'll tell you, it's refreshing to have someone new to talk to ... isn't it, butterbuns?"

"Don't call me that in public," the Dead Writer said. "Now, Wendy, you really think I look familiar? Maybe you're confusing me with Valentino ...,"

"Oh, please," the Queen Bee groaned.

"What? We've got the same jawline, same eyes," the Dead Writer said, squinting his eyes and trying to look like a movie star.

"Dream on, brother, dream on," the Queen Bee said. "Oh, poopsie, I never told you that Wendy ate at Botín's."

"You did!" the Dead Writer said, seeming excited about it. "You had the suckling pig, I hope."

"I did. It was incredible," I replied.

"Isn't it? Best dish in town, that's what I say," he said.

"You two and your baby pigs," the Queen Bee said.

"It's a suckling pig, not a baby pig. There's a difference," he said.

"Nonsense. It's a cute little baby piglet," she countered.

"Well, it's an extraordinarily delicious little baby piglet," the Dead Writer replied, drinking for his adverb. "They've been serving that dish for hundreds of years, my love, so they must be doing something right."

Then he turned to me and said:

"You know, El Greco used to work there."

"I believe it was Goya, actually," I said.

"No, no," the Dead Writer replied, shaking his head. "It was El Greco. He was a cook, I believe."

***

An hour later we were shit-faced in a taxi on our way to the party. The more the Dead Writer drank, the more he talked:

"Most of the good places are in the Quarter. There's the Dingo, of course, but too many damn people go there these days. And Mickey's. Oh, and there's this new joint, The Select."

"I *love* The Select. Such a dive," the Queen Bee added.

She was on one side of me, he the other. I turned to her and said:

"A dive?"

"That means it's good, sweetie."

"Yes, yes, dive bars are good bars," the Dead Writer explained. "Not enough of them in Paris these days, if you ask me. Oh, and there's plenty of establishments up around Montmartre ... but those are more like cafés, not bars."

"It all sounds wonderful," I said, struggling to get a word in.

"Oh, Wendy ... it's such a shame you missed Pamplona," the Queen Bee said.

"Yes, yes, Pamplona. Damned fine fiesta, damned fine. Nothing like it," the Dead Writer agreed. "Bulls in the street and cock-eyed drunks all over town. But I should add that some of the locals take it very, very seriously. It is a religious festival, after all. It's a sign of one's devotion to slap a bull on the street."

"Ooh, tell her about the bull that knocked you down in the ring," the Queen Bee said.

"Ha! Yes, yes, quite a day that was. It wasn't one of the nasty bulls in the street, mind you. It was in the Plaza de Toros. See, the bulls that run through the streets are ultimately making their way to the bullring ...,"

"Adverb. You owe another drink," the Queen Bee ordered.

"Ouch, my mistake," he said and drank his penalty. "So, those bulls will be the stars of the afternoon show. And when they get the big ones corralled they let out older, slower bulls with tape over their horns. Now, those bulls chase us brave warriors around and ...,"

"Brave warriors!" the Queen Bee mocked.

"Stop it, would you? Let me finish. So, they let those older bulls out and ...,"

As he talked I looked at him and tried to listen to what he was saying. But my mind was drifting back to Yaxchilan. I was thinking of that time—after the crash, but before the nastiness truly began—when we sat around the fire and talked. The Dead Writer sounded then just like he sounded now. The voice, the affectations, the laugh … everything about him was the same.

As we made our way down the Gran Via he went on and on about Pamplona. Then, somehow, he shifted mid-topic and started talking about Toronto. Then he circled back and told me more about Paris.

He sure liked to talk about places he had been and things he had done. He liked to talk in general, I suppose. Some people are like that.

***

There was a line of motorcars outside the Cerralbo Mansion and we had to wait our turn. Then a handsome chap in a tuxedo opened the door of the taxi for us. He offered me an elbow and escorted me to the front doors. I felt like royalty.

The Dead Writer and the Queen Bee were in back of me, he escorting her.

"What happens here stays here," he said.

"Easy, brave warrior," the Queen Bee sighed.

We came inside. There were several more handsome chaps in tuxedos waiting for us, and one of them with a white bow-tie greeted us. But my eyes were instantly drawn to my surroundings: the room was astounding. I felt like I had walked into Versailles or something.

"Oy vey, look at this place," the Dead Writer said.

"Remarkable," the Queen Bee added.

It was, indeed, a remarkable room. There were marble columns and dark wood and paintings and chandeliers and busts. There was gold trim everywhere. It looked like the kind of place where Vanderbilts or Rockefellers would live.

There were well-dressed people going up the marble stairs in either direction.

"I vote this way," the Dead Writer said, pointing to the right.

"And I vote this way," the Queen Bee countered, pointing to the left. "Why don't you go scout in that direction, sugarplum. Wendy and I will go this way."

"What if we never see each other again?" he asked, eyebrow arched.

"It will be tragic ... but we'll muddle through somehow," she answered.

"It will be hard," he said.

"Yes. I know full well how *hard* it can get," the Queen Bee said, in a mock-serious way. Then she scooped an arm under my elbow and led me away. As we walked she said:

"We're not going to find you a hunky hook-up with my man-anchor around. If it's only the two of us it will be much easier."

"I'm not looking for a hunky hook-up," I said.

"Don't be silly, of course you are," she said. "You're lonely. You need a friend."

I stopped walking and glared at her.

"I'm not *lonely*."

"Okay, wrong words," the Queen Bee said. "I meant you are deserving of attention from the male species."

That was better, and I said so.

"Sorry. Sometimes I say nasty things but I'm not really trying to be nasty. I hope you understand."

"I do the same thing all the time," I replied.

We wound up the stairs and into a corridor filled with more paintings and more statues and more well-dressed people. In the following room we found a well-stocked bar. The Queen Bee got us two glasses of Pernod. The bartender winked at her as he put the glasses down and then he winked at me, too.

We took our drinks and walked toward the next room. I could feel every single male eye following us. It was a new feeling for me, but I suspect a daily if not constant occurrence for the Queen Bee.

In yet another gilded room we found a spot to stop and sip and people-watch. Most of the men wore tuxedos with long tails. A few were in dress military uniform, medals and all. There were fewer women, but they looked gorgeous in their sleeveless gowns and done-up hair. I felt both under-dressed and out-of-style.

"Alright, let's pick a man out for you," the Queen Bee said.

I shot her another look.

"What?" she said with a smirk. "Not a permanent man, just a temporary one."

"Lovely."

"Oh, come on. Look around, this place is swimming with eligible chaps. That tall, dark one over there ... he's cute. Or look to your left ... there's a man over there looking this way. I think he's checking you out."

"I doubt that," I said. My eyes followed hers around the room. The tall, dark one was indeed cute. And there was a purple-suited man with a moustache looking our way too, but he wasn't as cute.

"Or those two blokes by the bar," the Queen Bee went on, motioning with her drink. "One for each of us ... or two for one of us."

I laughed out loud. "I hope your boyfriend didn't hear that."

"Boyfriend?" she said. "Sweetie, when it comes to categorizing, I keep everyone in friend territory ... even him."

When I gave her a puzzled look she continued:

"I suppose I should let you in on my little secret. I'm recently divorced."

"I'm sorry."

"Don't be. It's a cause for celebration."

I didn't know what to say, so I took a sip of my Pernod. The Queen Bee went on:

"I married a rich and stupid man. I was content with that. But then he turned out to be jealous, too. Mad jealous, if you know what I mean."

"Jealous of ...?"

"Other men."

"Ah."

"So ... you and ...," I paused mid-sentence, hoping she would come in with the Dead Writer's name. She didn't. "... and ... he ... are not a couple?"

"A couple? No, no, of course not. At least I don't think so. We're just best friends who love each other and have sex. It's fantastically low-pressure. Here, let's both drink to that adverb."

We did. She kept going:

"You know, I shouldn't be telling you this. And don't tell him, okay? But my best-friend-with-benefits went through some tough times. Injured during the War, right near the end."

"How?"

"Shrapnel. He doesn't like to talk about it. Put some nice puncture holes in his mid-section."

"Poor man."

"That's not the half of it," the Queen Bee said. "Some quack field doctor told him he was so torn up he couldn't, you know ...,"

My face told her I didn't know.

"Screw. Copulate. Play hide the salami," she continued. "But I always sensed that wasn't right. So I sent him to a specialist in Paris. They set him straight. Gave him these wonderful little blue pills."

She paused and polished off her Pernod, then said:

"Now he can poke whiskers with the best of them. God, that Pernod is delicious. Let's get another, shall we?"

***

In the next room there was another surprise: an armory, the second I had seen in as many days.

It wasn't particularly large but it was an impressive collection. There were several full suits of armor and displays of swords and assorted weapons. The Queen Bee and I studied what appeared to be a woman's outfit with a nicely tailored vest.

"So the men get armor, the women get street clothes?" she said.

"It must have been for an assistant or something," I replied.

"No, I think they made the women go out on the battlefield like this. Here, we'll ask this man. Señor, do you know anything about this?"

She was speaking to someone in back of me. I turned around and there was the man with the purple suit and moustache that had been eyeing us earlier. I hadn't noticed him standing near us.

"Perdón?"

"This outfit," the Queen Bee said. "Who is it for?"

The man looked at her, then at me, then moved past us to the outfit. He was using a walking stick, which seemed odd because he didn't look particularly old. He studied the outfit for a moment then turned to us:

"This is for the escudero," he said, his English good but his accent thick. "One who carries the shield."

"Like a squire?" I asked.

"Sí, señorita," he answered.

"See, I'm right," I declared.

"That you are," the Queen Bee replied in a mischievous tone. "And what's your name, amigo?"

The man with the moustache turned to her. He jutted out his chin and answered:

"I am Benito. Benito Barataria."

The Queen Bee gave me an arched eyebrow.

"Goodness, such a regal name! Well, Benito Bara-whatever … this is Wendy. She's single."

My jaw fell again. I was speechless. The man laughed.

"That is … good to know," he said.

"Excuse us for one moment, please," I said and took the Queen Bee by the arm. She hollered over her shoulder to the man and told him we would be back. I led her into the next room, which was another armory … for horses.

"You're ridiculous," I said when we were out of sight and earshot of the man. "I don't need your help with men, alright?"

"Oops," she smirked. "Old habits die hard. Oh, look, perfect, there's another bar! Should we keep up with the Pernod or switch to something else? I know, let's do a shot of something wicked and then have more Pernod. Good? Good."

As we moved toward the bar I glanced back toward the armory. The man in purple was watching us go, an odd smile on his face.

***

The rest of the night was a blur. A riotous, exhilarating, drunken blur.

We finally made it to the grand ballroom and reunited with the Dead Writer. There was music by two wonderful guitarists—siblings, I learned—and they were followed by a big band that had everyone on their feet. We drank and laughed and danced like there was no tomorrow. The Queen Bee flirted with every man she saw and kept introducing me to the better-looking ones.

It was, without a doubt, the most epic party I had ever been too. At one point everyone in the ballroom was dancing around with their hands up in the air, just like Tatiana had joked about. I made a mental note to tell her about it, knowing full well I was probably too wasted to remember any of it.

I have no idea what time we left. It was very, very late and we were very, very drunk. Then, in the taxi on the way back, we joked and laughed more. Then it got quiet when the Dead Writer and the Queen Bee started smooching.

By the time we arrived back at the hotel their smooching had turned into lustful pawing. They kept at it as we stumbled to the lift. Then, on the ride up, they were all over each other. I looked away but couldn't help but listen:

"You are my Zeus," she purred, and I knew damn well that wasn't his name.

"That's right, kitten. I'm your Zeus. And my lightning bolts are ready for you."

It was awful. She replied:

"Mm-hm, yes, cast your mighty bolts into my dark, dark underworld."

"Oh yes, you shall witness my ..."

"*Please.* Please stop," I pleaded.

By luck, at that moment the lift stopped at their floor. The lovebirds untangled themselves somewhat. They both looked at me and then returned to looking at each other.

"Good night, Wendy," the Queen Bee said, then, "Take me to Olympus, Zeus."

Without any more words being spoken they exited the lift and walked away, holding hands. The lift doors closed. I rode up to my floor, fumbled in my money belt for my key and unlocked my room.

I kicked my shoes off and unzipped my pathetic dress. I promised myself I would buy something new before I went out like that again. I wanted to fit in, which meant I needed nicer clothes.

And yes, maybe the Queen Bee had been correct. Maybe I needed a friend. I *was* deserving of attention from the male species, wasn't I?

The sun was already rising. I pulled the curtains tight and collapsed onto my bed, hoping for a few hours of sleep.

14

FRUSTRATIONS, FRUSTRATIONS

"I saw the Dead Writer again last night."

"That would be a good first sentence for a novel," Doctor Morley replied, without looking up.

"I'm not joking. I saw him. He took me to a party."

"Oh, a party. Mm-hm. Did you dance?"

"Well ... yes, yes we did."

"Mm-hm, splendid," he said, still not looking at me, his face buried in some papers. But I saw his eyebrows move up in a my-assistant-is-bonkers sort of way.

"You're not very supportive," I seethed, turning away and looking out the taxi window.

"I'm trying to be."

"But you don't believe me."

"I didn't say that," Doctor Morley replied, now deigning to look me in the eye. "And I'll remind you that I have more realistic concerns to attend to."

"Hmph!"

"Oh, please, enough with the snootiness," he said. "Tell you what: next time you see this dead man, give him this."

Doctor Morley reached inside his suit coat and pulled out a small white card and handed it to me. It read: Sylvanus G. Morley, Carnegie Institution ... and then gave his address in Merida.

"Perfect. He can look you up in the Yucatán."

"Ha ha. No, just give him that card. Tell him I'd like to buy him a drink at the hotel," he said. "Or dinner, whichever he would prefer. Breakfast, even."

I wasn't sure if he was making fun of me. I squinted at him.

"Promise?" I said.

"Promise," Doctor Morley said.

We didn't discuss the matter any further. We rode in silence up the Paseo del Prado and through the big circle with the big, white government building. The taxi slowed as we approached the Library.

"Can I ride around to the Museum entrance?" I asked as Doctor Morley got out.

"No, no, come with me. I need you to be on the same page as me," he said. Then he stared at me with an odd look and said, "On the same page. That's a joke."

"It's not a very good one."

"I'm too educated to be funny," Doctor Morley said.

He paid the driver and we went up the steps and past the grand statues and into the Library. He was babbling away about something as we made our way up through the glorious reading room. I, on the other hand, was admiring the leaded-glass sun-roofs in the ceiling. It occurred to me that the two libraries I had visited while in Spain were the nicest libraries I had ever seen.

"Are you even listening to me?" Doctor Morley asked.

"Of course," I lied.

He kept talking about something. We wound up a spiral staircase, into the stacks and to the same desk Doctor

Morley had been using since we started. He plopped his bag down on the table, then he stooped down, reached under the desk and pulled out a box. He lifted it up and put it on the table next to his bag.

"Every good spy has a secret hiding place," he said. He opened the box and started to pull out the stash of books he had collected since we had arrived. He walked me through some of it, including a tattered book that contained images of the Duran Codex.

"That's the one that was found here?" I asked.

"Exactly. They've got the original stashed somewhere, under lock and key. They've promised me they'll find it for me. But I'm still waiting, as you can see."

The images in the Duran Codex looked like they had been painted by a young child. Yet there was an artistic flourish to them that gave them life, or, in some instances, death. There were scenes of sacrifice. There were scenes of battle. Then I flipped to a page that showed a large image of an Aztec overlooking what appeared to be a shooting star.

"Moctezuma," Doctor Morley said from behind me. "This is when he saw the comet that foretold the downfall of his civilization."

"I thought you said that story was bullshit."

"Indeed. Rational men don't abide by heavenly omens," he replied.

The next page showed a man in European garb, behind him a horse and an angry mob of armored men holding spears. Moctezuma, looking much like he did on the previous page, was presenting the conquistador with a necklace.

"The man of the hour," I said.

"Indeed," Doctor Morley agreed. "Cortés and Moctezuma. A meeting that would change the course of many civilizations … for better or worse."

I kept turning pages. I knew how the story ended, but it was still hard to see the images. Here were the Aztecs, dressed in bright plumage and holding ancient weapons, overpowered by men with full-body armor and guns. The next page showed Moctezuma's dead body being thrown over a wall by the Spaniards. The page after showed the fire at Tenochtitlan. The images were uncomfortable, but I couldn't look away.

Just then I heard footsteps coming toward us, along with Mister Carter's heavy breathing.

"*Huff-puff-wooh*," he panted as they came closer. "Is this it? Ah, yes, there's Sylvanus right there. Good morning, Sylvanus."

"Good morning. Don't call me that. Glad you could join us."

"Mm-hm. My good man, why are you hidden in the hinterlands like this? You should spread out in the reading room, at a larger table, don't you think?"

"No. I prefer privacy."

"But it's quite crowded for all of us here, isn't it?"

"Yes. I'm hopeful you'll all leave soon," Doctor Morley deadpanned.

"Ah, I see the puppies have piddled in your tea again this morning. Lovely," Mister Carter said.

"Enough, you two," Veronica interjected, and the two archaeologists became silent. "Good morning, Wendy."

It wasn't an entirely unpleasant greeting.

"Good morning, Veronica," I said.

"I didn't expect to see you here," she replied.

"Doctor Morley asked me to come."

"He did, did he?" she said, then turned to Doctor Morley with a fake smile. Before my boss could say anything, Mister Carter spied my book and barged between them.

"Ah, the History of the Indies!" he remarked.

"History of the Indies *of New Spain*," Doctor Morley corrected.

"That's what I meant," Mister Carter said. "Of New Spain. By ... Castillo, right?"

"No. Castillo wrote the *True History of the Conquest*," Doctor Morley said. "Diego Duran wrote this one, then Fernando Ramirez found it here in the Library."

"Ramirez?" Mister Carter asked.

"Right. Mexican historian. Surely you've heard of him."

"Can't say I have," Mister Carter sniffed. "So which one did that chap Bartholomew write?"

"Bartolome," Doctor Morley sighed. "Bartolome de las Casas. He's the one that did *History of the Indies*."

"... *of New Spain*," Mister Carter added.

"No, dammit, that's this one," Doctor Morley said.

"I thought this was the Duran Codex," I interjected, not knowing enough to stay quiet. Doctor Morley wheeled to me and said:

"It's got two names, alright! Duran Codex is shorthand. You should know that."

"It's all quite confusing, Sylvanus," Mister Carter added. "What's the one by Gómora?"

Now Doctor Morley wheeled around to him.

"That's *General History of the Indies. Historia General de las Indias*," he said, frustrated. "It's not confusing at all if you know what you're talking about."

But it was confusing. Very confusing. And when we all sat down and Doctor Morley walked us through some of his thoughts, the rest of us remained perplexed. And I could see in his eyes that he was furious that we couldn't understand what he was talking about.

"Dammit all," Doctor Morley grumbled at one point. "Frustrations, frustrations, frustrations …,"

It went on like this for some time. Doctor Morley would pull something out of his box or out of his portfolio. He would then explain what it was, but fail to explain why he considered it to be important. Then, Mister Carter would ask an off-point question and that would make Doctor Morley mad. Next, Veronica would make some catty remark about how they both needed to work together. Then, within minutes, they would all be bickering again. I could only marvel in suffering silence at their inability to agree on anything. Eventually, Doctor Morley pulled out a book by Augustus Le Plongeon and things went from bad to worse.

"Le Plongeon?" Mister Carter said, half-offended. "He was a crackpot, man!"

"Even a blind squirrel can find a nut every now and then," Doctor Morley responded.

"My understanding is the Le Plongeon squirrel was deaf and dumb as well as blind. Wasn't he looking for Atlantis?" Mister Carter said.

"In his defense, I think that part of his curriculum vitae is overstated," Doctor Morley said. "And it was 'Mu', not Atlantis."

"Mu!" Mister Carter declared, then turned to both Veronica and I to show his amusement. "Ho-ho, that's right. Mu! Well, if we don't find what we're looking for, maybe we'll find a lost continent."

Again I felt a rush to head for the door, if that's the direction this was all taking.

"Hardy-har," Doctor Morley sniffed. "I'll remind you that he built off Bourbourg's work, so we can't say that ...,"

"Bourbourg!" Mister Carter exclaimed. "Another crackpot."

"You seem to think they're all crackpots, Howard."

"Come now, Sylvanus. The fact that Bourbourg believed mankind began on the wrong side of the world is prima facie evidence of crackpottery."

"The *wrong side* of the world?" Doctor Morley shot back. "It's not an absurd proposition, Howie."

"Don't call me Howie."

"Don't call me Sylvanus! And if you don't see that as a very real possibility in the development of the human species then ... then ... well, we'll have to agree to disagree."

And at that Doctor Morley began to flip through the Le Plongeon book, using an unnecessarily-angry page-turning motion.

"Don't speak for a moment, alright?" he said to Mister Carter without looking at him. "Now, here, look ... here's Le Plongeon's analysis of De Landa's notes."

"De Landa again?" Veronica asked.

"Right. Le Plongeon found Diego de Landa's attempted translation of the Mayan writing system here in the Library. He used that to try to identify anything in the Codex that seemed out of place. And then, look here ...,"

He held the book up to Mister Carter, who adjusted his glasses and stooped his big frame down.

"A hatchmark?" he asked.

"What? No, no, not a hatchmark ... is says 'chi'," Doctor Morley answered.

"And that is ... who again?" Mister Carter asked.

"Chi!" Doctor Morley seethed. "Gaspar Chi. The scribe. De Landa's scribe."

"Ah, yes ... the Mayan," Mister Carter said, still peering at the book. "I do think that's a hatchmark, though."

"Don't be obtuse. It says 'chi'."

"I'm not sure it does. But what if it did?"

"It would be further evidence that Chi helped Diego de Landa develop his Mayan Rosetta Stone ... and that it wasn't created by de Landa out of thin air."

Then Veronica jumped in:

"And what, pray tell, does that have to do with what we're looking for?"

Doctor Morley rolled his head to her and squinted over his glasses and said:

"Nothing. Not a single frickin' thing, Veronica. How about that?"

And she glared right back at him and the air went out of the room. I felt a chill on my neck. Veronica stood up, put her hands on her hips and looked down at Doctor Morley. I thought she might beat him.

"My patience is wearing thin, Morley," she said. "And your prickly attitude is doing little to move this along. I suggest you take stock of your situation and make changes accordingly."

Doctor Morley's face was white. His lips were pursed in silence. The she-devil lit into him:

"Now, I'm going to take a nice goddamn walk over to the goddamn Museum to see the goddamn Codex. Wendy, you're coming with me. Howard, you're staying here … and I expect you to talk some goddamn sense into our colleague here. When I come back, I expect there to be a goddamn plan to reach our goddamn goal."

And with that she walked away. We were all stunned. Then she yelled back:

"Wendy! Come!"

I scrambled to my feet, grabbed my shoulder bag and scurried after her. The she-devil had worked some kind of magic on me and I was powerless to resist.

***

Veronica was fuming mad. I followed her through the stacks.

"Stubborn ass," she muttered. "Where the hell are we? Which way to the Museum?"

"You have to go outside and go around the block," I answered.

"Outside and around the block? But it's the same damn building!"

"Yes, it's very frustrating."

At that very moment some poor sap pushing a book cart came into her view.

"Ah, there's someone. Hola! Come here, come here," she hollered, waving the man over. "There's a door over to the Museum, is there not?"

The man seemed stunned as well. He didn't speak English. She kept going:

"La puerta. Open-it-up-o. The door-o to the Museum-o."

Somehow that last part he understood. "Ees locked, señora," he said, shrugging his shoulders.

"Don't be ridiculous. Unlock it," Veronica said.

"I no have key, señora."

Veronica huffed like the big bad wolf and turned down the spiral staircase. We worked our way back through the stacks, me trailing her, then through the reading room. She marched in silence past the long tables and then out the main door to the front steps. By the statue of San Isidoro she wheeled around to me. I could see the frustration on her well-kept face.

"Your employer is a superb Mayanologist. But he's a royal pain-in-the-butt."

"Yes, he is," I agreed.

"He's out of his element. He doesn't understand Spain, and that's his biggest weakness," she said. "It's so goddamn frustrating."

"I wish I could help," I said.

"Me too," she answered. Then she turned away and went down the rest of the steps and I followed her out to the sidewalk. We were about halfway down the block, going toward the Museum, when she turned to me and said:

"Wendy, I know we may have had some ... minor disagreements in the past. But I have an obligation to keep this project on track and ... and, well, you asked me back there if you could help in any way. The answer is yes, there is."

She walked and talked:

"I've decided to bring on a new partner in this venture. Your boss is not going to like it. He doesn't like anyone getting in his way ... be it Howard or me or anyone else."

I couldn't disagree with that.

"And the favor I'm asking of you is to be receptive to his involvement, and to encourage your boss to be receptive as well."

"He doesn't like it when I tell him what to do, either," I offered.

"That doesn't surprise me. Stubborn ass."

She came with me into the Museum. The old hag at the ticket window scowled at me; Veronica gave her an I'll-just-be-a-minute finger and walked right through with no problem. Then it was through the lobby, past the entrance to the Egyptian Salon and up the stairs. Lothario was waiting with eager eyes on the mezzanine; as we passed Veronica cast some sort of paralyzing spell over him, rendering him unable to blink or breathe. We proceeded all the way to the top floor and turned into the Mesoamerican room. It was here that she stopped, turned to me and said:

"Wendy, while we have a moment ... I want to apologize to you for the other evening. I'm sorry I said those mean things about you ... and, well, shooting Colonel Lindbergh and all that."

It seemed sincere. I nodded.

"Thank you," I said. "I appreciate that."

"They've changed these rooms around some, haven't they? I seem to remember more stuff."

"Long story," I said. "They're moving things around. Some of it is in the back corridor."

"It's hard for the Mayans and Aztecs to compete with Egyptians, I suppose."

"Precisely."

Veronica looked over to the Codex in the middle of the room. She sighed.

"I hope we're not wasting your time," she said, then she turned to look me in the eye. "Between you and me, I'm less and less of a believer in the Codex theory."

"Pardon?"

"Perhaps I shouldn't have said that. I know your boss still believes in it, at least I think he does. But we can't put all of our eggs in one basket now, can we?"

"Are you saying ... I should stop?"

"Heavens no. Sylvanus would be furious."

And with that Veronica helped me slide out the bench. She sat next to me and we compared my reproduction with the pages of the real Codex. She commended me on my system and my steady hand. Then she perused the Mesoamerican collection a bit before departing, leaving me alone with my thoughts.

I had always feared I was wasting my time with my Codex copy. After hearing someone verbalize that depressing possibility, I was tempted to half-ass my way to the finish line. But I knew if I did so, there would be a price to pay.

So I worked hard and did my best and lost myself in the ancient manuscript again. By the time Lothario told me the Museum was closing, I was halfway done with page seventy-eight.

15
A USEFUL MAN

Back at the Hotel, a bellboy chased me down and handed me a message. It was from the Queen Bee:

"Hola darling, hope this note finds you and finds you well! We had the ducky idea to go to Toledo. Going to drink and watch the swordmakers! Back in Madrid in a couple of days. Don't work too hard ... and find a friend!"

Instead of signing the bottom—which would have enlightened me as to her name—she had drawn a small happy face. The happy face had one eye x-ed out and a tongue lurching out of its mouth, like a drunk.

"Frick," I said. Then I saw the bellboy was still there and had heard me. I went through the mechanics of opening my money belt and tipping him a few coins, in effect paying for bad news.

With my evening plans shot, I went to my room and sulked. I tried to read a little bit, then sulked some more and finally decided it was late enough to start drinking.

I had no plans to leave the hotel so I didn't put much thought or preparation into my appearance. I chose a plain white shirt and a plain tan skirt and made my way down to the lobby.

It was a bit early for the partiers and the bar was mostly empty. I made my way to a center stool and plopped myself down. Frederico was the only one working.

"Hola, señora, cómo estás?"

"Ha sido un largo dia," I replied. It had, indeed, been a long day. "Whiskey, por favor."

He nodded and turned and scanned and went to the other side and came back empty handed. He shrugged his shoulders.

"Still out?" I grumbled. "Then a Pernod, por favor."

"Sí, señora."

"And a shot of scotch to go with it. Bring that first, actually ... and make it a double. Un doble."

"Sí, señora."

As he fetched my drinks and I fumbled under my shirt for my money belt. I had to turn away when someone approached the bar and ordered:

"Sangria, por favor."

The voice was deep and Spanish. It sounded like a man I had met at the party. I yanked out a few pesetas, buttoned up and rotated back in my stool. Sure enough, it was him ... and sure enough, he was looking right at me.

"Ah!" he said. "I know you!"

It was the man that had been wearing a purple suit. Now we was wearing a striped blazer with a purple flower on the lapel. He looked nice. His hair wasn't as slicked back and it was longer than I remembered. His facial hair seemed fuller; now he had some scruff to go with his groomed moustache.

"Yes. Good evening, señor ...,"

"Barataria," he replied. "But please ... call me Benito."

"Benito. Does anyone call you Benny?"

"They would not dare. And it is ... Vendy, no?"

"Wendy."

"Ah, sí. May I sit?" he said, motioning to the stool next to mine.

I nodded. As he sat I noticed again that he carried a walking stick. He propped it up against the bar as he settled into his seat. One of his legs appeared to be very stiff. I wanted to ask him about it, but didn't want to be rude.

"You are staying at this hotel, ah?" he asked.

"Sí. You?"

"No, I stay nearby. But where I stay, the bar and restaurant, they are closed. So I come here."

Just then Frederico returned and placed our drinks down. I snatched up my scotch first. I glanced over and Benito was looking down at his glass of wine. There were little chunks of fruit in it. He leered up at the bartender.

"Una cuchara," he said, in a not-entirely-pleasant voice. "A spoon, por favor."

"Señor?" Frederico queried.

"To take the silly fruit out," Benito said. "I want sangria, eh? Not a … fruit cup."

Frederico stared at him for a brief second, then darted to fetch a spoon, then took the Spaniard's drink and plucked the fruit out. When all was clear he handed the sangria back. Benito took it up and took a swig. His face puckered.

"They serve better wine in prisons," he informed Frederico, then turned to me. "Vendy … I toast to you and to your ancestors."

I raised my scotch to his lousy sangria and we tinked glasses. As we did, I noticed he was missing most of his middle finger. I tried not to stare at the little stump that remained.

"So ... what brings you to Madrid?" Benito asked. His accent was thick but his English was near-perfect.

"My job," I replied. "I work for an archaeologist."

"Ah! You are an archaeologist?"

"No, I only work for one," I said. "I do his artwork. He assigns me things to draw and I draw them."

"And ... you like?" he asked.

"Somedays I do," I answered. "And you?"

"I am but an old soldier."

"You certainly don't look very old," I said. "And didn't Spain stay neutral in the War?"

"Not that war. In Morocco. I was in the Army of Africa, in the war against the Berbers, under Colonel Franco."

I thought it best to not display any more of my ignorance about Spanish history, so out of my mouth came:

"Is it hard not having a middle finger?"

He looked at me like I was nuts and I instantly regretted letting those dumb words pass my lips. But Benito smiled, looked at the little stump and said:

"I still have nine others," and like an idiot I followed with:

"But don't you miss being able to give people the middle finger with that hand?"

It was such a stupid thing to say. I waited for him to laugh. Instead he looked a bit offended.

"That is not a matter to joke about, señorita."

"I'm sorry. Words fly out of my mouth sometimes. I didn't mean to joke about your finger."

"You can joke about my finger all you wish. But the sign of the middle finger, that is no laughing matter."

"The sign of the middle finger?" I said, and without thinking I flicked one of mine up and looked at it.

"Madre mía!" he said. "Put that down!"

I did as he asked. He seemed quite serious.

"You find middle fingers *that* offensive?"

"Sí!" he exclaimed. "It is a dirty and offensive sign. Very dirty, very offensive."

And then he stopped and took a drink of his fruitless sangria. I could see in his face that he had not been joking.

"Well, I'm sorry. Lo siento."

"It is alright. I am told I have to, as they say, 'get over it'," he said.

"People tell me the same thing."

After that uncomfortable start, the conversation became much more interesting. He was an engaging fellow, strong in his opinions. He had a certain charm and politeness about him. He complimented me several times, first on my thoughts and then on my looks.

We also drank so much that I dared mention politics:

"Everyone seems so angry in Madrid," I said. "Do you support Diego de Rivera?"

"The Prime Minister? Sí, I support him … as long as he supports the monarchy."

"So you support King Alfonso."

"I support any king, as long as they are strong. It is when España has a strong king that we are at our best."

"I sense that's not a popular view."

"Because many people are stupid. They do not see that when men like Carlos and Felipe were in control, España grew and prospered. You know of Carlos and Felipe? Charles and Phillip?"

"All too well."

"They were strong men. The father and son, they create an empire on which the sun never sets. But then, over time, as España loses its traditions and its heritage … the empire, that is lost as well."

"Maybe you should have a president."

"Presidente!" he exclaimed, looking shocked. "No, no. Lo siento, Vendy … but that is worse than a prime minister."

"But shouldn't everyone have a vote … so they have a voice?"

He looked at me like I was crazy.

"Ah, you Americans … still so idealistic," he replied. "No, Vendy … to encourage that would be to encourage more collapse. That cannot be allowed to happen."

"Hmph. Sounds like you think certain people shouldn't vote."

"Sí."

He said it with such certainty I was taken aback.

"Really! And who is it that you think shouldn't be able to vote?"

He paused and thought about and said:

"Well, the Jews, of course ... and the Franciscans ... and the Freemasons ...,"

"What?" I exclaimed. "I hope you're joking!"

"... And the Bolsheviks. And any leftist, even the Spanish ones," he kept on. "Really, anyone that seeks to destroy Christian civilization in España."

When he said it he seemed so serious. But now he started to smile, which made me smile ... and it dawned on me he was play-acting. I clinked his drink.

"My, you're quite the troublemaker," I said.

"You have no idea," Benito replied.

And as the evening progressed I found myself looking more and more into his eyes. There was a mysterious elegance about him.

Perhaps, I thought, I should take the Queen Bee's advice and make a new friend.

***

Two drinks later, I asked him up to my room. He seemed quite excited at the invitation.

We finished our drinks and got up to leave. As he got out of his stool he took up his walking cane. The handle was carved to resemble a bird's head.

"That's quite elegant," I remarked. "Is that supposed to be an eagle?"

"An eagle?" he said, showing me the carved head. "'Tis a parrot, mi señora."

He gave me an elbow and I hooked my hand under his arm. We made for the lift and, once inside, he planted his first clumsy kiss on me.

'Clumsy' would, to my great disappointment, turn out to be the theme of the night.

I would soon discover that Benito used a cane and limped because he only had one good leg: his other was lopped off at the knee. He walked using an artificial leg that was secured to his leg-stump with belts. It took him a good five minutes to get that damn fake leg off. By the time he did, much of the magic was gone.

He got into the bed with me and positioned himself between my legs. Then he started thrusting about, always in the wrong place, so I reached down to help him find his target. As I grabbed hold of him, he got a funny look on his face … and then I felt a warm sensation on my upper thigh.

Then he collapsed onto the other side of the bed, a smile of orgasmic bliss on his face. He was asleep in minutes. I got up and toweled myself off, then crawled back into the bed and snuggled up to him.

It felt good to be in a warm bed with a warm man … even if this particular man wasn't as useful as he could have been.

16
MUTUAL INTERESTS

I awoke unsatisfied.

It was raining outside, I still hadn't seen the Prado and my encounter with the one-legged man had been a dud. I debated staying inside under the covers all day, then dragged my disappointed butt out of bed and got dressed.

I met Doctor Morley in the Lobby. He was in a lousy mood. We got a taxi and as we were pulling away from the Hotel I could see the Prado through the mist, beckoning me.

"I forgot to tell you that a man I met has offered to take me to the Prado," I said.

"I thought they were refinishing the floors," Doctor Morley replied.

"He knows someone that can get us in. I believe we're going in the next couple of days."

"During the daytime?"

"I would assume so."

"I'm not sure we can afford to have you gone during working hours."

I almost blurted out what Veronica had said about my work, that it might be a waste of time. But I didn't want to add fuel to his fire, so I tried another angle.

"I think seeing the Prado will help me with my work on the Codex."

"Bushwa. You want a day off."

"Bushwa yourself. I only want a few hours to see it."

"You shouldn't cuss at your employer like that."

"Bushwa isn't a cuss word … and you said it first."

After that he said nothing. I took the silence as indication that my request for a few hours off had been approved. Now I just had to stay on his good side, lest he cancel it.

***

Despite a minor hangover I once again made excellent progress on my Codex copy. By the time I broke for lunch I was on page eighty-five. I wanted this damn project done and I knew the end wasn't that far off.

I didn't have an umbrella and the rain was still coming down hard. I asked Lothario if he had an umbrella I could borrow. That, of course, led to him carrying his umbrella for me while escorting me down the block to the front of the Library. At Dulcinea's I ordered my usual; they loaded it all into a brown paper bag for me and then Lothario escorted me back to the Museum. We paused at the entrance.

"I cannot tell a lie … I was going to smuggle my food in. It's too wet to eat outside," I confided to the guard.

"Mm. And where you plan eat?" Lothario asked.

"The Arab Courtyard or the Roman Patio."

"You can go Courtyard but tell nobody, sí? It be our little secret," he said, then he winked.

I worried I had bitten off more than I could chew. Lothario escorted me all the way up to the Mezzanine then into the Arab Courtyard, one of the Museum's two atriums. It had a splendid glass-and-iron ceiling, an impressive collection of middle-eastern arches and a lovely but non-working fountain.

As I sat on a bench and ate, Lothario pointed out a lamp that came from Alhambra. He informed me that the fountain, which had small stone lions encircling it, was a replica but a very good one. He asked me out several times; I invented several excuses to explain my constant unavailability. Eventually he decided to give up on me and get back to his work. It was time for me to do the same.

Lunch had renewed my energy. I sailed through that afternoon and only quit because my right hand was cramping. I had finished page ninety-one and felt so pleased with myself that I felt compelled to review my work.

I went back to page one and, using my left hand, improved my shading along the edges of the pages. I went so far as to make crosshatches in several spots, then smudged them with a wet finger, to make the paper look aged. I even spent some time on my page fifty-six, which was the mostly-blank page that contained the curious backward writing.

Truth be told, by this point I had given up looking for clues. The Codex project had become, for me at least, an opportunity to hone my artistic skills. I was beginning to think of life beyond the treasure hunt, of life beyond

Chichen Itza. My Codex copy would be my artistic farewell to the Carnegie Institution ... and the entire Mayan culture.

When the clock struck four I packed up and went downstairs. The rain had stopped and I told Lothario that no, he didn't need to escort me again. I walked down the block and up into the Library and through the reading room to find my boss.

I had just come into the stacks when I came upon Veronica. She was coming down the spiral staircase that I was about to go up.

"Ah, here she is," Veronica said to me. "How goes it?"

"Good. Very good, in fact."

"Did you find something?"

"Well, not *that* good," I said. "How's he doing?"

"He's ... typical," Veronica replied. "By the way, thank you again for our little chat yesterday about our new partner. I just spoke with Sylvanus about it. I hope we're still on the same page?"

I wasn't used to such directness. I could only nod, to which Veronica said:

"Excellent, excellent. I knew I could count on you."

***

I approached Doctor Morley's desk with caution, lest I provoke the ill-tempered beast. I was surprised to find him looking relaxed. He was leaning back in his chair, hands clasped behind his head, glasses perched on his forehead, staring at the ceiling.

I faked a cough to get his attention. His head snapped down and his glasses dropped and landed crooked on his nose.

"Oh, sorry ... daydreaming," he said.

"Nothing to apologize for. Dreaming about what?"

"About the Exposition. My speech."

"That's work, not daydreaming."

"I'll take what I can get. And how are you doing?"

"Fantástico," I replied. "I finished ninety-one. I should be able to wrap it up in the next day or two."

I pulled my notebook out of my shoulder bag and handed it to him. He flipped through the pages, pausing here and there to give me compliments. That made me feel good.

"It's really coming along, Wendy," he said. "We'll have to get it properly photographed once you're finished. I'll bet most people won't be able to tell yours from the real thing. So ... spot anything unusual today?"

"No," I said. "Nothing. Sorry."

Doctor Morley sighed and said:

"Don't apologize. I'm starting to worry we're looking for something that isn't there."

"Whatever do you mean?" I asked.

He sighed again and didn't answer right away, then:

"Veronica has come into contact with a gentleman here in Madrid. He has ... mutual interests. He's looking for the same thing ... and he's got her thinking our team is going about everything the wrong way."

"Oh," I said, playing stupid. "And what do you think of that?"

"I'm not sure what to think. I'm not keen on bringing in an outsider; Howard's complicated my efforts already. I can't deal with another all-talk, no-work blowhard. But …,"

"But?"

"But we've come up empty-handed so far. I've found things that intrigue me, but nothing that would lead to concrete action steps."

"And who is this person?"

"She says he was a captain in the Spanish Legion. That's all I know."

"Are you going to meet him?"

"I think we all are, soon. Veronica has gone to speak with Howard now."

"Interesting. Why does this person think you're on the wrong path?"

"I'm still trying to understand that," Doctor Morley replied. "It has something to do with a sword."

***

Once again I had the evening to do as I pleased. I was freshening up for a trip to the Lobby Bar when there was a knock on the door. I feared Doctor Morley had cancelled his plans and had come to ruin my evening. Through the closed door I asked who it was.

"Just us, back from the dead," came the Dead Writer's voice, followed by the Queen Bee's giggle.

I unlatched the door and opened it.

"Surprise, surprise!" the Queen Bee proclaimed, marching right in. "We're baaack!"

The Dead Writer strolled in behind her, a book tucked his arm. My room was an absolute mess and I was horrified anyone was seeing it, especially them.

"That was a quick trip," I remarked.

"Quick and thorough," the Queen Bee replied. "Toledo is quite a place but it's not all that big. Very dramatic, though. It rises up on a hill and it's very picturesque."

"Did you have fun?"

"We always have fun! We drank and then saw the Cathedral, then we drank some more and watched the swordmakers. A successful adventure, am I right, darling?"

Her darling was looking out my window and now he glanced around at my messy, embarrassing room.

"Another fine hotel room destroyed by its female occupant," the Dead Writer said. "I ask again, is it nature ... or nurture?"

"Human nature," the Queen Bee answered. "Deal with it. So, Wendy, how goes it? You survived without us?"

"Somehow," I said, grabbing a wrinkled shirt off my bed and tossing it behind a chair.

The Dead Writer was still inspecting my room. As he did he sniffed the air and said:

"It smells like sex in here."

"It does! I was thinking the same thing!" the Queen Bee agreed. "Anything you need to tell us about, Wendy?"

"It does not smell like *sex* in here!" I protested.

"Mm-hm, mm-hm," she said with a smirk. "Don't worry, we won't pry. I'm not fit to judge."

"No, you're definitely not," the Dead Writer said.

"Hush, you," came the retort. "So, Wendy, we're going to hit the town later. Much later. There's this little place called La Venencia. It's adorable and we heard there's some fun music coming tonight. Come with?"

"Really?"

"Of course really! A tricycle only works with three wheels, right? We need you!"

That made me smile, which was all the confirmation the Queen Bee needed:

"Ah, see, I knew she was in. We didn't even have to ask. Alright, let's say ten o'clock in the Lobby Bar. The plan is made."

It felt good to be needed, if only for partying. But then, in a sudden panic, my thoughts jumped to my pathetic wardrobe and my ugly burgundy dress. The Queen Bee must have sensed something was amiss, for out-of-the-blue she said:

"Oh, and would you like that red dress I wore the other night? I think it would fit you like a glove."

I fumbled for an appropriate response. I didn't want to admit I didn't have any other going-out clothes ... but I wanted that dress.

"The red one? I ... I don't want to impose, but I suppose if I could borrow it then ...,"

"It's not imposing at all, dear. And not only can you borrow it, you can have it. It's on loan from someone I'm no longer friends with, so I don't need it back."

"I couldn't possibly …,"

"… You couldn't possibly say no, right?"

"Right," I said. "Thank you."

We talked a bit more about Toledo and then we discussed my work. I told them that I was going to see the Prado and they were excited for me. Then, as they got up to leave, I asked a question that had been nagging at me.

"How did you find my room?" I inquired. "The clerks refuse to tell me anything."

"The powers of flirtation can overcome any hotel privacy policy," the Queen Bee said with a wink.

After they left I stood in my room and a thought occurred to me. On the previous times I had seen the Dead Writer I had been drinking … but this time I had been one-hundred-percent undrunk.

Therefore, he must be real. Maybe.

***

A bit later there was another knock. It was an attendant holding a long garment bag. I snatched it from him and rushed to open it up and try the dress on.

It was beautiful and far more daring than anything I owned. It was sleeveless, with a v-shaped drop in the back, a lesser drop in the front and a glorious frilly bottom. The chest was a bit loose, but overall it was a wonderful fit. Even better, it was long enough that nobody would notice my shoes, which didn't match the dress.

Then I met the Queen Bee and the Dead Writer in the Lobby Bar. They both greeted me with hugs and kisses on the cheeks. They went on and on about how lovely I looked in the red dress. They were, I was beginning to think, the best friends I had had in a long time ... and I still didn't know their real names.

We had another round and laughed and talked more, then the three of us stumbled out of the hotel. I thought we would fetch a taxi but instead the Dead Writer announced:

"The Metro! To the Metro!"

And without thinking I laughed and turned to the Queen Bee and seconded the motion:

"The Dead Writer has spoken! To the Metro!"

And the moment I said it I caught myself. She looked at me funny and asked:

"The *Dead Writer*? Where'd that come from?"

"I ... I don't know."

"The last thing that narcissist needs is another nickname. But I like that one," she said, then yelled up to our leader. "Dead Writer, lead on!"

He turned around with a great smile.

"I'm not dead yet, you vultures!"

The Queen Bee and I hooked arms and we followed the Dead Writer away from the hotel. We paraded our way down the Paseo del Prado, laughing about everything and nothing at the same time. At the next big circle, we came to the Athocha Metro station. We went down the stairs and the Dead Writer bought our tickets.

I had only been on this type of underground train once before, in Boston. I remember those trains being dreadfully slow and I was disappointed to find the Madrid trains were no faster. We were creeping along the tracks and I knew that we could walk faster on the sidewalk … but it was fun nevertheless.

We rode the slow, plodding train all the way to the Sol station. Then we got out and decided we wanted to ride some more, so we transferred to the other line and rode it for several stops. Then we got off at the Retiro stop and turned back around. We took the train back two stops, laughed our way up to the sidewalk and then giggled arm-in-arm to La Vanencia.

The bar was, to use their term, a dive. But it was a glorious dive, full of life and energy and people I would never otherwise associate with. There was row after row of dusty bottles rising high on the wall and dusty men gathered around the bar. There were large casks of wine, spigoted, around which were gathered rowdy shit-faced patrons.

At first we all sat together, but then the Dead Writer got to chatting with some angry man about Primo Rivera. They moved to a different table.

"I think we've landed in a hotbed of the resistance, I'm sure that will be an interesting conversation," the Queen Bee remarked. "Snoogums worries that this business about kings and loyalists is going to lead to a bad place."

"Tensions do seem high."

"Yes, yes," the Queen Bee said. "But never mind the serious stuff … let's talk about your romantic encounter."

I feigned shock. She smiled.

"Nice try, sister," she said. "You can't put one over on me."

"I have no idea what you're talking about!"

She gave me an oh-please look. I didn't like to discuss such matters, but I relented.

"There was nothing romantic about it," I whispered.

"Aha! Confirmation!" she said, far too loud.

"Shh!"

"Nothing to be shy about, dear. Good work. A good man?"

"A ... useful man, I suppose."

"Ouch. Not so good, huh?"

"Nothing to write home about."

"Damn. American? English?"

"Spanish, actually."

"Ooh, interesante! Why was the sex bad?"

"I didn't say that!"

"Yes you did, with your eyes."

"It was ... short."

"Short! Him?"

"Well, yes. Him ... and what he did. Short."

"Oh my."

"Yes. And he had a fake leg."

At that the Queen Been spit-sprayed half of her drink out. When she composed herself she said:

"He *didn't*. Tell me he didn't."

"He did. He had to take it off so we could do our thing."

"Oh my. How ... *memorable*!"

"Mm-hm."

"We'll get you a better equipped one for tonight."

"I think its best I take a breather, thank you," I said.

"But you're wearing the red dress. That's a lucky dress, you know."

"Well, the next time I'm looking to get lucky I'll be sure to wear it."

The rest of the evening was every bit as pleasant as my previous outing with them. There was joking and laughing and teasing. Then there was dancing and eating and more drinking and much more laughing.

And as we drank the Dead Writer talked and talked and talked. His stories seemed limitless. He went on and on about bullfighting and the 'art' of it and why Spaniards take so much pride in it.

But I didn't want to hear about Pamplona, or anywhere in Spain for that matter. I asked him to tell me more about Paris. I wanted to know more about Montmartre and the Quarter. As he talked, I wanted to visit every single café and restaurant he rattled off.

Then, during our drunken taxi ride back to the Hotel a tantalizing thought popped into my mind: *I should quit my job and move to Paris.*

17

THE DAMN PRADO

By the next morning, the thought of starting over in a new place had taken on a life of its own.

My new plan was to finish my work in Madrid and then be done with it. Doctor Morley didn't need me in Seville, at least I didn't think so. Therefore I would tell him here in Madrid, perhaps tonight at the hotel. I was leaving my job with the Institution. I wouldn't be going back to Chichen Itza. I was going to take what little money I had, go to Paris and make the best of it.

But completing my work on the Codex was imperative. I didn't want to insult Doctor Morley by leaving without having finished it. I would be a professional and I would complete my assignment.

Both Lothario and Anselmo wandered through as I was working but I didn't acknowledge either. I wanted to finish. The last twenty or so pages contained mostly glyphs—which I had become quite adept at copying—and very little color.

On page one-hundred I let out a little celebratory hurrah. From behind me came a voice:

"Ah! She is here and she is energized!"

I turned around. It was my skinny artist friend. He said:

"So lucky to find you here. I just speak with mi amigo … today is our day, sí?"

"Today? I … I'm sorry, I've got work to finish."

"Qué? He works only today, so we must go today."

I looked at him then looked back to the Codex. I had raised expectations with Doctor Morley that I would finish today.

"Can we go later?" I pleaded. "I have to get this done before I go."

The skinny man walked around the frames and stood near my bench. He looked over my shoulder and asked:

"How many more pages you have to do?"

I did the calculation and told him. He looked down at my notebook and then sighed.

"Very well," he said. "I shall help you. Then, we shall see the Prado."

He made it sound like an offer that could not be refused. Before I could say a word, he sat down next to me. He looked over at the page I had been working on.

"Just one notebook?"

"Yes, just this one," I confirmed.

"Let us work fast, no?" he said. "You do outline. I do the rest."

It didn't sound like much of a plan. But I did as instructed: I spent several minutes tracing and free-handing the basic shapes of the next page. Then I passed the notebook to him. He looked at it, looked up at the original and then picked up a pencil.

He took the pencil and touched up my first glyph; the result looked just like the real thing. Then he picked up an orange pencil and used the side of the tip to do some shading, which was perfect. Next he touched up the orange with some red, which replicated the colors of the Codex exactly.

It took him all of three minutes to do what would have taken me a half-hour. He handed the notebook back to me.

"Faster," he said, but there was no way I could operate at his speed. He was ten times quicker than me … and a hundred times better.

Despite the mismatch in artistic talent, we made it work. I traced and outlined, he finalized and colored. We passed the notebook back and forth, which allowed one of us to work while the other rested their hand.

And that was how I completed my sure-to-be-legendary, full-color reproduction of the Madrid Codex: with the help of a man I barely knew, because he had offered to get me into the Prado.

I didn't tell Doctor Morley I was leaving. As the saying goes, it would be easier to ask for forgiveness than permission.

***

The skinny man escorted me down the stairs and out the doors. As we were coming down the steps I stopped by one of the flying sphinges.

"I need a smoke," I said. "Want one?"

He did. I fished my Campeones out of my shoulder bag. Then, to look sophisticated, I lit two cigarettes at once and handed one to him. He smiled, took it from me and inhaled a deep drag. As he exhaled he was looking past me, back toward the Museum.

"The moustache of Velázquez … is dramatic, no?" he said.

I turned around to see what he was looking at. On the steps there was a statue of the painter Diego Velázquez. He had lovely flowing locks and a well-groomed moustache that was curled up at the tips.

"It looks hard to maintain," I offered.

"I think it would look good on me," he said.

"I'm not trying to be mean, but … I don't think you have enough hair up there to pull it off."

He reached up and ran two fingers along the sparse stubble under his nose. He knew I was right.

"There's another statue of Velázquez over on the Library steps," I went on. "You Spaniards must sure like him."

"We do, we do," the skinny man agreed. "Velázquez, he takes us to places we could not otherwise go. You shall soon see."

He was smirking as he said that. At first I didn't understand what he meant.

***

But I got his little joke when we arrived at our destination: the 'Velázquez entrance' to the Prado.

There was yet another statue of the artist there. In this likeness he was seated, stone paintbrush and stone palette in hand, ready to paint. The moustache on this version was even more pronounced and gravity-defying than the one at the Archaeological Museum. My guide walked closer and studied it.

"I can use the moustache wax, no?" he said.

"Perhaps," I relented. "But it will take a long time to grow yours out to that length."

"Then I shall start today!" he declared.

"In which case I'm honored to be here for such a momentous occasion," I said.

He liked that remark and laughed. Then we walked up to the doors of the museum together. He knocked on it three times, waited a few seconds, knocked two more times, waited again, then gave it one last knock. Sure enough, someone inside responded to his code and I could hear the lock being undone.

The heavy door swung open. A tall, uniformed guard stood in front of us. For a second I worried that this was not the man that my friend had expected. But the guard smiled broadly and said:

"Ah, Salvador! Cómo estás?"

"Bien, Alejandro, bien," my guide replied.

The guard waved us in and shut the door behind us. And just like that, I was finally inside the Prado.

There were electric lights overhead and only a few of them were on. They cast enough light for me to see what we had walked into: a broad gallery, lined with magnificent paintings. Tall arches led into even more galleries. I couldn't wait to get started, but I was polite as my friend introduced me to the guard and we exchanged pleasantries. He told us of a few places we couldn't go because of the floor refinishing and warned us we would get sick if we tried. When the guard left us, I was so excited I ran up to the first painting I saw.

It was, fittingly, by Velázquez. It was the head of a deer and it was very nice. The next painting was by Velázquez, too, and showed the crucifixion. The three after that were also *all* by Velázquez. They showed Queen Isabel riding a horse, Queen Margerita riding a horse and some duke riding a horse. I turned to Salvador and said:

"Am I to assume everything here is by Velázquez?"

"In this wing, sí," my guide replied.

I didn't mind. Salvador showed me two he was particular for: one displaying Apollo arriving in Vulcan's forge; the other displaying a hunky and horny Roman god. Then we came to a large, tall painting that showed a young girl being dressed by servants. I recognized it but couldn't put a name to it.

"*Las Meninas*," Salvador said without me asking. "My favorite. See, look at the mirror in the background … you can see the King and Queen, the girl's parents, watching. Then here you can see Velázquez painted himself into the scene, too. So you are left with the conclusion that you are seeing the royal toddler not from the artist's perspective, but from the King's."

"That's quite clever," I said.

"Clever? Señora, it is *beyond* clever. The true artist knows that a small change in one's perspective can reveal things that have long been hidden."

"Do you always talk in such mysterious terms?" I asked.

"Sí," he conceded. "It is, how you say, a bad habit."

From there it was into a gallery dominated by Goyas. I was struck by the contrast in themes from painting to painting: one frame would show men being shot, the next a picnic, the one after that a street riot. Salvador told me a bit about the master's style; in return I told him that Goya had worked in some capacity at Sobrino de Botín. He didn't believe it.

There were more masterpieces in the next gallery: A colorful cardinal—the religious kind—done by Raphael; a series of stoic portraits by El Greco; Saint George battling a dragon by Rubens; a homely, overdressed woman by Rembrandt.

By and by, we came into a narrow hallway lined with small frames. I got close to inspect one of them and was surprised by what I saw.

It was a crude colored drawing, a far cry from the oil-painted canvases we had been viewing. It showed a conquistador being presented with gifts from a robed king.

"Cortés," I whispered.

"And Montezuma," Salvador said. "Actually, in Mexico they say 'Moctezuma'."

"Yes, they do."

"Cortés, his legacy is a bit … muddled, no?"

"So I hear," I replied.

The two of us looked at the series of pictures together. There was Cortés riding his horse into Tenochtitlan, the Aztecs parading out to greet him. Then there was Moctezuma showing Cortés his throne room. One scene showed Cortés and Moctezuma dining under a tent, while a Spanish galleon burns in the background; I explained to

Sal how Cortés had scuttled his own ships to prevent his men from deserting.

Toward the end of the corridor there were two frames showing the disintegration of the relationship. In one, Cortés and his men have come upon a sacrificial slaughter. In the next Moctezuma is on a balcony, pleading for peace … with Spanish soldiers behind him and angry Aztecs on the streets below.

"This is where the people killed their king," Salvador remarked, and I insisted the jury was still out on that.

There was a larger oil painting featuring Cortés in the next room. It showed Cortés ordering his men to put Moctezuma in shackles. The great king looks agitated. Between Cortés and Moctezuma stood a well-dressed, darker-skinned woman: Doña Marina, the conquistador's wife and translator.

And as I was discussing her, my eyes came to rest on an object in the painting I hadn't noticed before. Attached to his belt Cortés had a sword, a long one, with an ornate, swirling handle. It looked a bit like the sword that the Dead Writer had discovered at Yaxchilan. That got my mind throbbing and I asked if we could move along. Salvador asked why.

"I'm just … a bit sick of Hernán Cortés," I said.

From there we wandered down a long hallway and then into a blue room with a tall ceiling. Dominating one wall was a monstrous painting of the Spanish Inquisition. It showed hundreds of black-clad men observing a religious ritual. Around the perimeter were other men with swords and spears, rounding wrongdoers up and forcing them into the ceremony.

"This happened at the Plaza Mayor, not far from here," my guide said. "These outfits, the sanbenito ... they show what sins the accused have committed, no? Then they were judged here in the middle by the bishops. Some would be whipped and tortured, others would be burned alive."

"It looks brutal. These men here on the outside look surprised to be there."

"Sí. Of course, nobody expects the Spanish Inquisition."

I contemplated the uncomfortable scene before me and said:

"I can't understand how this place is capable of such beauty, yet such cruelty."

"This place. You mean España?" Salvador asked, and I nodded.

"And you're from ... the United States? Careful, señora ... the sands of time run fast and hungry," he explained. "They run fast and hungry and each new generation devours the last. It is all well and good to judge ... but it is inevitable that judgment will someday fall on us, as well."

"Um ... okay. Are there any happy paintings we could see?"

"No. There are no happy paintings at the Prado."

He smirked at me after he said that, then he led me to a more uplifting gallery. There were some Impressionist paintings in one room and he told me he knew some of the artists. He even said he knew Pablo Picasso, which I only half-believed. But I asked him about Paris and he went on and on about his friends and some movie he was making. He said I could see some of it when I posed for him.

As we neared the end of our tour, I asked him if there were any art schools in Paris. He told me there were, but they were all a waste of time. When I pried, he coughed up to the fact that he had been kicked out of some fancy art school for being a disruptor. I confided that I was a disruptor too, and told him about getting kicked off the debate team back in high school. He laughed so loud it echoed through the empty corridors of the Prado.

"The world needs more anarquía, señora. Much more."

"Anarchy leads to chaos," I replied.

"Sí," Salvador said. "But it is only by destroying the old that you can create the new."

18

THE SONS OF CORTES

Doctor Morley and I were in the Lobby, waiting for a motorcar to pick us up. I was telling him about the sword I had seen in the painting of Cortés while at the Prado:

"I'm telling you, it was just like that one from Yaxchilan."

"Swords were a mass-produced item. Toledo alone had dozens of swordmakers."

"Well, it looked identical," I said.

"Mm-hm."

"Jeezum crow … must you dismiss everything I say? You told me if I see something I should say something, but every time I say something you think I'm crazy."

"That's not true. From time to time you say things that aren't crazy," he deadpanned.

"Oh, aren't you a clever cricket," I sneered, and Doctor Morley looked proud of himself for his little dig.

A horn beeped; it was our motorcar honking at a mule-drawn fruit cart. After the ass passed, the motorcar pulled forward. The door opened and a scrawny driver got out and opened the rear door for us. Doctor Morley and I climbed in and came upon an argument in progress:

"He could have met us here," Mister Carter was saying. "I'm sure they have a perfectly fine breakfast at this hotel.

Do they, Sylvanus? Do they have a breakfast here, a proper English breakfast?"

"Hmph. Good morning, Howard, I'd remind you to please not call me …,"

"It's not about breakfast, Howard," Veronica interjected. "It's about having a secure place out of public view. You should appreciate that more than anyone."

She was sitting in the back; Mister Carter was up front next to the driver. Doctor Morley and I squeezed in the back with Veronica. The driver closed the door and then we were off and the argument resumed:

"It's all a tad uncomfortable, like we're going off to some hidden lair," Mister Carter said. "And it would be nice to have food available."

"You already ate," Veronica sighed.

"It was unsatisfactory," Mister Carter sniffed.

Veronica ignored him, turning to us and shaking her head.

"Good news: Wendy finished her work on the Codex," Doctor Morley said to her. "It came out excellent. Very detailed and easy on the eyes."

"Oh, yes, that is good news," Veronica replied. "And … anything?"

"I'm still examining it against my portfolio," Doctor Morley said. "It's not easy when you don't quite know what you're looking for."

"I can imagine," Veronica said in a suspicious tone. "Well, I'm sure you'll be interested in what our new friend has to say about all this."

And then she turned and looked out the window. I sensed the she-devil was up to something.

We rode down the Paseo del Prado and then turned onto the Gran Via. Then we took a turn onto a broad avenue and from there each succeeding street was narrower than the last. We drove for a good fifteen minutes, passing from the nice part of town, through the so-so part of town and into the bad part of town. The driver slowed, looked down at the scrap of paper with the address and then stopped. We were at the head of what can only be described as a dark alley.

"What?" Mister Carter said. "This can't be right."

"Treinta y cuatro, calle Flintos."

"This is it. Get out," Veronica said.

"Hmph. I suggest we make this quick," Mister Carter said, opening his door and stepping out.

HONNNNNK!

A truck barreled past, coming so close to Mister Carter it blew his hat off. The rest of us, still in the motorcar, looked at him with mouths agape. The Egyptologist had escaped death by no more than a few inches. Mister Carter straightened up, his enormous belly jiggling, and said:

"Just the pubescent Pharaoh acting up again. Come on, let's get this over with."

***

The four of us walked into the dark alley. It smelled like pee and I had to pull a sliver of shirt up to cover my nose. Veronica led us down the cobblestones and past several run-down, boarded-up buildings. She stopped at a low, worn door that had a thirty-four painted on it.

She knocked. We waited. She knocked again.

"This can't be it," Mister Carter said.

"I know this is it," Veronica replied … and at that same moment I heard sounds from inside.

A bump. Someone fiddling with the door. The sound of an old lock being slid back.

Then the door opened. Out of the darkness stepped a tall, broad, dark-skinned man … and he wacked his head into the door frame. Hard.

The enormous man staggered back and shook the daze out of his head. It was only then that I realized why he looked familiar: this man had been the driver for our trip to Escorial.

Doctor Morley recognized him, too. He turned to Veronica and said:

"Well, well. I see you started playing games earlier than I expected."

Veronica gave my boss an oh-please look. Then she looked back to the giant who had opened the door:

"Buenas tardes, Musa," she said to him.

"Ungh. Buenas tardes, Señora Shitty," the big man replied.

I tried to stifle my laugh but didn't succeed. The she-devil shot me a nasty glare.

Whereas the big man had been dressed unremarkably during our drive to Escorial, today he was wearing long, flowing robes. His skin tone suggested exotic heritage, his clothing confirmed it. He grunted, motioning us in.

Each of us had to walk past the towering hulk as we entered. I would estimate he was at least two feet taller than me and two hundred pounds heavier. I gave him a little smile as I passed but didn't receive one in return.

Once we were all jammed inside, he came to our front and led us down a corridor. We passed through an abandoned pantry and an abandoned kitchen, then came through a swinging door and into a long, rectangular room. There were a few tables and chairs scattered about. It was clear the space had been, at some point in history, a restaurant.

"Jils," our enormous escort mumbled.

"He wants us to sit," Mister Carter said. "He's speaking Arabic, or at least trying to."

And at that the big man swung around and gave Mister Carter an angry glare.

Veronica looked down at a chair. She brushed a hand over the seat and a cloud of dust came off.

"I'll stand, thank you," she said.

Mister Carter took out a handkerchief and made a big production of dusting a seat off. He then offered the chair to me, a charming gesture, and proceeded to clean a second seat off for himself. He then held out his dusty handkerchief to Doctor Morley, who shook his head and chose to stand.

"Well then, I sure hope this has been worth the trouble," my boss said. "Let's get on with it."

The big man had a blank expression on his face. At that same moment, I heard the footsteps of someone coming in from another room. Only then did it dawn on me that the man who had answered the door, our one-time driver, was not the man we were there to see.

And then I picked up on something. There was something not-quite-right about the approaching footsteps. Like one foot was not moving in-time with its partner. Then I realized there was a third click that fell in-between the thump of two feet ... as if the person was using a cane.

Before I even heard his voice I had deduced who it was:

"Ah, estupendo, you are all here!"

It was Benito, the Spaniard from the Lobby Bar. My 'friend.'

I couldn't believe it ... but I didn't want the others to know that I knew him. I stayed silent, which was easy as I had stopped breathing.

He was wearing a baggy black suit with a purple tie. He strode up to Mister Carter and extended his hand.

"Finally, the great Howard Carter!" he said. "I am Benito Barataria. It is an honor to meet you. I am, as they say, your numero-uno fan."

"Oh! Well, that's refreshing to hear. The pleasure is mine, sir," Mister Carter said with a deferential bow.

"And this must be the one and only Sylvanus Morley," Benito said next. "Allow me to shake the hand of the great Mayanologist."

They shook and Benito kept at it:

"I am familiar with the work you have done at Palenque, Tulum and Copan. I also read your recent article on Mayan linguistics. I found it fascinating."

Doctor Morley looked surprised and pleased by the unexpected plaudits. I, on the other hand, didn't believe for a single second this was all on the up-and-up.

Benito came to Veronica and they seemed to share a wicked, wordless moment. Then Benito proceeded until he was right in front of me. I waited to see what kind of bullshit greeting I was about to get; I expected him to pretend like he didn't know me.

Instead he stepped forward and looked into my eyes. He brought both hands up to pull my face toward him. Then … he kissed me. *On the lips.*

And he held it for a second before he disengaged. I was shocked and humiliated and angry. Out of instinct, I brought my hand up and smacked him—hard—across the face. I heard my companions gasp.

Benito stepped back, felt his slapped cheek and smiled at me.

"And it is good to see you too, Vendy," he said, then he winked.

"You know each other?" Doctor Morley asked.

"Apparently not," I muttered.

"Sí, Señor Morley, we do," Benito said. "She and I, we are lovers."

"What? We're nothing of the sort!" I exclaimed.

Benito grinned at me then turned back to Doctor Morley.

"She is so feisty, no?" he said, and before I could charge him he moved on. "And I believe you have already met my Moorish man-servant, Musa, no? He doesn't speak much, but that's probably for the best. Musa, fetch us some vino."

Doctor Morley squinted at Benito.

"*Man-servant?* Isn't that term—and job description—a bit out-of-date?"

"Good service never goes out of style," Benito declared, then he clapped his hands twice.

At the clapping Musa bowed to Benito and left the room. Our host smacked the seat of a chair twice, making the dust rise up, then he sat down and faced us. He smiled and placed his walking stick across his lap.

"So …," he began. "How goes it?"

There was an awkward silence. I looked over at Doctor Morley, who was looking at Mister Carter, who was looking at Veronica. The she-devil spoke.

"They've found nothing useful," she said.

"That's not true," Doctor Morley interjected. "You don't speak for me."

"Well, it's the truth, isn't it? The Codex has been a dead end," Veronica shot back.

"We don't know that yet. And may I remind you coming back to go through the Codex again was your idea?" Doctor Morley responded.

"Quiet, you two," Mister Carter scolded. "I'd say our host should be the one answering questions, not us," which sounded sensible. "He can begin by telling us what this is all about."

"You are indeed a wise man, Señor Carter," Benito said. "And I am indeed rude for not starting there. My colleague has not told you of my efforts, correct?"

He motioned to Veronica and the rest of us stared at her.

"Your ... *colleague?*" Doctor Morley said, more to her than to him.

"Decisions had to be made, Sylvanus," the she-devil said, ice-cold.

Benito gritted his teeth in an almost comical way.

"Oopsie," he said. "I guess I am more aware of your work than you are of mine, no?"

"Yes ... it would appear so," Mister Carter grumbled, with an angry eye on Veronica.

"Aha. Sí," Benito said. "Well, yes, I know of your work with the Codex ... and with de Landa's records at Escorial ...,"

"Veronica!" Doctor Morley seethed. "You've been giving this man updates?"

The she-devil gave my boss another cold stare.

"... And I am afraid to say that the answer you seek does not lie in either place," Benito concluded.

"You have no way of knowing such things," Mister Carter said.

Just then Musa returned carrying a jug of wine and a stack of plain drinking glasses. He put the glasses down and served us as if he was a waiter. He poured Benito's first. Our host took a sip and smacked his lips and said:

"Now ... if this were a play, this would be the scene where a character appears and reveals many long-hidden secrets, no? Allow me to play that role myself ...," he began.

Doctor Morley let out a sarcastic laugh.

"It may seem funny, Señor Morley, but hear me out. I think you'll find my story quite remarkable," he said. "And rest assured I know of what I speak. You see, I have sought the lost treasure of Cortés for many years."

"Of ... Cortés?" my boss inquired.

"Sí, I am aware you call it by another name. To me it goes by the name of the honorable family it was taken from."

"Pshaw. It was taken from the Aztecs," Doctor Morley grumbled.

"No, no ... it was *given* by the Aztecs to Hernán Cortés ... and then it was *stolen* from Cortés," Benito shot back, pounding a fist into the table.

At that Doctor Morley crossed his arms and shook his head as if to say this-is-nonsense. Benito watched him, took a moment to gather his thoughts and then asked:

"Tell me, Señor Morley ... have you ever heard of the Sword of the Spaniard?"

"The ... *Sword of the Spaniard?*" Doctor Morley answered with a snort. "Never."

"Ah. Then this is a conversation that is long overdue," our host said. "For without the sword, you will be unable to obtain that which you seek."

"Ridiculous," Doctor Morley muttered.

"Let's hear him out, Sylvanus," Mister Carter said.

"Don't call me Sylvanus, Howard."

"Then allow him to speak," Mister Carter scolded.

"I am … but my time is short," Doctor Morley hissed back.

"Yes, yes, I'm sure you want to get back to the Library so you can dig more useless holes," Mister Carter snapped.

"You're the useless hole, Howard."

"Don't take your frustrations out on me, Sylvanus."

"Don't call me Sylvanus!"

Benito had been observing this little exchange between Mister Carter and Doctor Morley in silence. Now he spoke up:

"Tell me, Señor Carter, you are a British citizen, sí? And Señor Morley, you are an American, sí?"

Then he glanced at both Veronica and myself.

"… And over here an Englishwoman and another American," he said. "Shocked, shocked I am that this remarkable team cannot find a treasure given by the Aztecs to a Spaniard and lost in Mexico."

"Spare us your humor," Doctor Morley said. "And we can't even be sure it's in Mexico."

"Oh, but it is," Benito declared. "Of that I am positive."

"Hmph. And what makes you so sure?" Doctor Morley queried.

Benito smiled. "Because I know the story of the sons of Cortés … and the swords their father gave them. Would you like to hear that story?"

"No," Doctor Morley grumbled.

But the rest of us wanted to hear the story. So Musa topped off our wine and Benito began:

***

"The great conquistador had, as you know, several children by several different women. Most were daughters, but there were a handful of male heirs … most notably the two Martíns and their brother Luis."

"*Two* Martíns?" Mister Carter asked.

"Sí," Benito answered. "The first Martín was the son of Cortés and Doña Marina, a slave that became his interpreter and then his lover …,"

"… La Malinche," I interjected. "And their child was El Mestizo."

"Sí. Martín the Bastard," Benito replied, stressing the last word. "This first Martín Cortés was followed by Luis. He, of course, was a bastard too."

"I don't think those terms are necessary," Doctor Morley said.

"Ah, but in those days one's lineage determined one's destiny, no?" Benito continued. "A decade later, Cortés married Doña Juana de Zúñiga and they produced another son, another Martín. But *this* Martín, as the legitimate offspring of his father and a noblewoman, was able to inherit his father's title. The second Martín—Don Martín, if you will—would become, like his father, the Marquis of the Valley of Oaxaca.

"The conquistador kept all of his sons close. As they grew, they were able to join their father on expeditions in the Americas and in Spain. As Cortés was viewed with suspicion by the king and the court, his sons would also become his closest confidantes.

"You will recall that the conquistador returned to Spain from the New World twice," Benito went on. "The first was in 1528 to face a tribunal over his insubordination to King Carlos. His second return was in 1541. By then, he was a shadow of the great warrior he once was. He was an old, bitter man with a lifetime of enemies … not the least of which was the Holy Roman Emperor himself."

"I wasn't expecting a history lesson," Doctor Morley interrupted.

"And here, Señor Morley, is what you will not read in the history books. In 1545, two years before he died, Cortés summoned his three sons to his home outside Seville. There, he presented each of his sons with a sword … replicas of the very sword he himself had carried to the New World."

As he spoke those words my heart skipped a beat. The sword I had seen in the painting of Cortés at the Prado had looked almost identical to the sword we had found at Yaxchilan. I had even told Doctor Morley about it. I glanced over at Doctor Morley. Sure enough, he was looking at me, a puzzled expression on his face. Benito kept talking:

"… And on that same day, the conquistador revealed to his sons a secret … one he had been too embarrassed to disclose. The riches he had collected in the New World, which he had hidden away, had been *stolen*."

"Stolen!" Mister Carter exclaimed.

"Sí, Señor Carter. So the father, he entrusted his three sons to find and reclaim all that rightfully belonged to the Cortés family," Benito went on. "And to impress upon them the importance of working together—these were brothers from other mothers, no?—he presented his three sons with three swords. Now, Señor Morley, you must be familiar with the Encomenderos Conspiracy, no?"

Doctor Morley nodded. "I am. The Cortés brothers returned to Mexico and flexed their muscle. They wanted to preserve the encomienda system—slavery, really— which the crown had outlawed. Martín Cortés wanted to overthrow Spanish rule and reap the benefits for himself. They were charged with treason and conspiracy. The brothers were lucky to escape with their heads."

"Sí," Benito said. "And ... you know *why* they returned to Mexico?"

"Indeed. They shared their father's belief that the Cortés family—and not the king of Spain—was the new royal bloodline of Mexico," Doctor Morley replied.

I studied Doctor Morley's face. He had stopped objecting to everything and I sensed the wheels in his mind were spinning fast. Benito took a dramatic pause, sipped his wine, smacked his lips and said:

"A popular belief, Señor Morley ... but incorrect," Benito said, with great flair. "The brothers Cortés had returned to the New World on a quest to find their father's lost treasure. And on that quest, each of the brothers carried a sword—gifts from their father—symbolizing their family's destiny. Martín the Bastard wielded what became known as the Sword of the Mestizo. Luis carried the Sword of the Second-Born. And the elder Martín, his father's heir, carried what Gómora called the Sword of the Spaniard …,"

"Gómora?" Doctor Morley interjected. "What does he have to do with this?"

"Why, Señor Morley … you have not heard of Lopez de Gómora?"

"Of course I have. He was Cortés' biographer and propagandist. I've read his writings and I've never heard of any swords or some hidden motive behind the brothers' return to Mexico."

"Pardon me, which book did Gómora do?" Mister Carter whispered to Doctor Morley.

"Dammit, Howard, it's *Historia General de Las Indias*," my boss grumbled. "There's an original copy at the Library."

"Ah, yes, that's what I thought," Mister Carter said.

"Señor Morley, I would invite you to revisit that book again … and you will see that it is in fact dedicated to Martín Cortés, not his father …," Benito went on. "And much of my information, though not all, comes from the historian's diary. Gómora tells the story of Luis, who had his sword destroyed during a battle near Veracruz, no? Then the sword of Martín the Bastard was lost in battle, at the place where their father had first hidden the treasure. Only Martín—the second Martín, that is—retained his.

"That single remaining sword would take on an importance far beyond the symbolic. For the three brothers agreed they would use that one sword to hide their *own* secrets … that being their progress in finding their father's lost treasure."

Now Doctor Morley scrunched his face up. "Hold on, I was with you there for a moment … but now you're saying they hid clues about their search on … a sword?"

"In the sword, Señor Morley," Benito said, but then, "Or maybe on the sword … of that I am not sure."

Doctor Morley peered over his glasses at Benito, looking skeptical.

"I know much of this is hard to believe," our host said. "But my belief in Gómora's writings is very strong. There are clues, Señor Morley, in or on that sword. To find what we are looking for, we must have it."

"Have it?" Mister Carter said. "Well … where is the blasted thing?"

"The Sword of the Spaniard, Señor Carter, is stored at the Archivo de las Indias."

"Ho!" Mister Carter said. "We were discussing going there to review some records. That's in Seville, yes?"

"Sí. It is among many weapons of the conquistadors kept there."

"Okay, hold on, that doesn't make sense," Doctor Morley said. "Martín Cortés wasn't a conquistador himself … he's just a footnote in history. Why would a museum want his stuff?"

"Gómora says that Martín presented the sword to the Archive and explained it was his father's."

"Why would he do that?" Mister Carter asked.

"To keep it safe," Benito responded.

"Fine. We'll go to the Archive and take a look at it, then," Doctor Morley said. "Though I'll add I find this a bit far-fetched."

"History takes many twists and turns, Señor Morley," Benito said. "And I wish it were as simple as going to Sevilla and asking to see it. I have tried to do just that. But all such objects are kept locked in the Archive and are not available for viewing."

"Well, what do you expect us to do ... break in?" Doctor Morley asked.

"I am hoping that is not necessary," Benito replied.

"What do you mean by that?" my boss shot back.

"Señor Morley, I know that you are scheduled to attend the Exposition in Sevilla," Benito said. "During the Exposition, there will be a ceremony commemorating the conquistadors. At this ceremony will be the sword of Pizzaro, the sword of Ponce de León, the sword of de Soto ... and the sword of Cortés."

"Which isn't the sword of Hernán Cortés ... but of his son, the second Martín Cortés, correct?" Mister Carter interjected.

"Sí."

"And you think that sword will somehow help us?" Doctor Morley inquired, sounding skeptical.

"Sí, I know it will," Benito responded. "Only with the sword will we find that which we seek."

Doctor Morley had his arms crossed. He was shaking his head.

"Ridiculous. A sword? Count me out," he said. "I'll have nothing to do with this. I came here with a mission and I'm going to complete that and be done with it."

"Your mission is to see things through to the end, Sylvanus," Veronica hissed.

"And I'll do that, I'll see my current project through to the end. Anything beyond that is not happening and is not open to negotiation," Doctor Morley said. "Now then ... I think I've heard enough of all this. Howard, Wendy, shall we?"

My boss turned to go back the way we had come in. I turned to go, too. Musa, the giant, was standing between us and the door. Benito spoke:

"And I cannot stop you," he said, despite appearances. "But tell me this, Doctor Morley ... what would your fellow archaeologists make of your secret intelligence background?"

Doctor Morley spun around. "Pardon me?"

"Using your professional credentials to conduct covert operations on behalf of your government," Benito went on, not blinking. "I would think even your colleagues at the Carnegie Institution would frown on such a misrepresentation, no?"

Doctor Morley looked like a deer in the headlights.

"What ... what the hell is this?" he stammered. "Are you trying to blackmail me? Is that what this is?"

"Of course not. I am simply using certain information to my advantage," Benito replied.

"That's blackmail!" Doctor Morley declared.

"You will thank me when we have the sword," Benito said. "Then you will understand."

"That's blackmail in furtherance of a criminal act. Absurd," my boss said before turning away in anger.

"Absurd, indeed," Mister Carter seconded. "You're nothing but a wild-eyed profiteer, man. We had them all over Luxor, as prevalent as mosquitoes and about as useful. Count me out, too … and Miss Shetty, may I have a word with you outside?"

Veronica stayed put. Her eyes were on Benito. He, in turn, had both hands clasped behind his back and was smiling at Mister Carter.

"Luxor, sí," Benito said. "Tell me, Mister Carter … how are things going in Egypt?"

Mister Carter had just pushed himself out of the seat. He turned and squinted at Benito and said:

"Egypt? Well, I … I have no idea. I pulled out of the Valley of the Kings years ago."

"Yes. Left with full pockets, so I hear," Benito said, arching his eyebrows.

"If you're going to blackmail him for pilfering Tut's tomb you're wasting your time," Doctor Morley heckled. "Everyone knows."

Mister Carter's jaw fell open. "Wh-what? Pilfering the tomb? Me?"

"Oh, stop it, Howard. The entire world knows," Doctor Morley said.

Mister Carter was speechless. His attention, and ours, turned back to Benito.

"Sí, lo siento, everyone knows of your midnight break-in," our host said, making Mister Carter gasp again. "I do not think they are aware of your *current* activities in Egypt, though."

There was another awkward pause, then Mister Carter said:

"Again, my work in the Valley is over. If you've heard otherwise, you've been provided with bad information, amigo."

"I speak not of the Valley of the Kings ... amigo," Benito said. "But I think many, many people would be interested in your current work in the desert outside Alexandria."

Now Mister Carter made a visible jump and looked over at the rest of us again. He was sweating.

"I ... I have no idea what you're talking about," he stammered.

"Come now, Mister Carter. The Egyptian government has granted excavation rights to a British company of which you are the primary investor. Sí?"

"Nonsense," the Egyptologist replied.

"No? Compania Ret-Rac? That is not you?" Benito pressed.

"Um ... no," Mister Carter insisted.

"And ... are you not listed as both the head officer and registered agent of Compania Ret-Rac?" Benito went on. "And is not Ret-Rac your last name, spelled backward?"

Mister Carter ran a finger inside his shirt collar to release some heat.

"Alexandria?" Doctor Morley asked out loud. "What's in Alexandria?"

Mister Carter wasn't going to answer, so Benito did:

"A tomb, Señor Morley. But in a way it is much more than that ... sí, Señor Carter? It is, one would say, the final chapter of legendary love story. You see, Señor Carter seeks the lost tomb of Cleopatra and Marc Antony."

The words coming out of his mouth seemed unreal. Mister Carter said nothing at first. Then, the great Egyptologist downed the remainder of his wine and confessed:

"Dammit, man! If word gets out about my license, speculators will swarm the desert."

Benito nodded. "Your secret will remain safe with me, Señor Carter."

"If I help you get your sword, right?" Mister Carter said.

"It is not my sword and it will benefit all of us. You shall see," Benito replied.

I waited for Mister Carter to tell him off. Instead came this:

"Only if there's something in it for me."

Benito grinned from ear-to-ear.

***

So our frustrated little team became joined at the hip with a detestable wretch, one that I had accidentally slept with. And our quest, already confusing and disjointed, was about to become even more so.

At some point during Benito's presentation I decided I had to confront him. He was good at spinning manure into magic … but I wanted him to know I was on to him.

When Musa led us out I lingered, so I could be the last to talk with Benito.

"I have every reason to disbelieve every word you say," I told him when we were alone. "You were watching me at the party. You came to the hotel to track me down. You're nothing but a liar and I'm on to you."

"Mmm, sí … I like it when you get angry."

"Don't look at me that way. You're a fraud."

"And you … are beautiful," he said, with smoldering eyes. "How I wish we could make love again."

That comment literally took my ability to speak away. After I composed myself I said:

"That was not 'making love' … that was a drunken mistake. One I'll never make again, that's for sure."

"Mm-hm," Benito said. "You American girls … you like the 'bad boy,' no?"

He was still smiling. But then, instead of engaging him verbally, I gave him the middle finger.

The color rushed out of his face. He furrowed his brow and flared his nostrils.

"Put. That. Away. You sweating dog, you," he snarled.

I raised my middle digit higher in open defiance. His face grew scarlet as his temperature rose. Feeling I had tortured him enough, I lowered my one-finger salute. We glared at each other for a long, nasty moment and then I turned to go. As I walked out I said, over my shoulder:

"Don't think I haven't figured you out, Benito. You're nothing but a pirate."

19

FOUR BLIND MICE

The awkward partnership began in earnest the next morning.

We were gathered in Doctor Morley's room at the Palace Hotel. The contents of his portfolio—letters, photographs and whatnot—littered the top of the bed. Various maps filled the little table by the window. The notebook containing my reproduction of the Codex was open on the bureau.

Veronica was sitting in an armchair next to the little table. She had two maps in her hand and she was comparing them. From time to time she would sigh, shake her head and then look around with her patented I'm-smart-you're-stupid glare.

Doctor Morley and Mister Carter were hovering over the bed, arguing about something or other. They had been bickering ever since Mister Carter arrived late and hungover. My boss dropped some not-so-subtle hints about the Egyptologist's boozy odor. In return, Mister Carter castigated Doctor Morley for his shitty attitude.

Benito Barataria was pacing the room, his hands clasped behind his back. From time to time he would snarl and ask a question then roll his eyes at the answer. His pacing was making me uncomfortable. I still couldn't get over the fact that I had brought him back to my room that night. It had been a very, very poor decision on my part. I vowed to never drink alcohol again.

Musa—Benito's 'man-servant'—was sitting next to me on the loveseat. He took up a good two-thirds of it. He wasn't paying attention to the tiresome never-ending chatter of our motley little crew. Instead he was reading, or at least trying to. He had found a magazine in the lobby … but he seemed to linger only on pages with pictures.

The current state of disagreement was as follows:

Doctor Morley believed his current path was not only correct, it had been half-blazed by others. He argued we all should be back at the Library, where he might find some nugget of information left by Brasseur or Ramirez. He insisted that those two researchers were one-hundred-percent certain there was a map hidden within the Codex … they just couldn't find it.

Mister Carter was skeptical about such claims. He advised Doctor Morley not to spend too much more time in the Library or on the Codex. Both of those wells had come up dry, he opined, and it was time to move on. He felt we should leave Madrid and get to Seville, where the records of the Spanish missionaries were kept. It was the same argument he had made several times before: the early Dominican friars—and later the bishops—saw all and knew all.

Benito believed they were both wrong. He was adamant that they needed to travel to Seville, but for a wholly separate reason: to see the sword of Martín Cortés. The second Martín, that is. He listened with varying degrees of patience to Doctor Morley and Mister Carter's theories but he didn't budge in his beliefs. The answer, he kept saying, was in the sword.

"What does that mean, *'in'* the sword?" Doctor Morley asked. "Like, hidden inside?"

"I believe so," Benito answered. "Or perhaps engraved onto the blade."

"If you don't know what it is, how can you be positive something is there?" was Doctor Morley's follow-up.

"I could ask you the same question, no?" Benito said. "Not to be rude, Señor Morley ... but where does your belief that there is a map in the Codex come from?"

He said it politely but Doctor Morley's face puckered up.

"Haven't we addressed this? It comes from Brasseur and Ramirez," my boss said. "They both wrote of disaffected conquistadors who didn't like that Cortés was taking what belonged to the crown. They had to send a message back to Spain ... but that message had to be hidden, otherwise Cortés or his minions would discover it. Thus, someone hid a clue about where the treasure was located in one of the Mayan artifacts sent back to the king. It was the only way of alerting him without alerting Cortés."

"And they believe that artifact was ... the Codex?" Benito inquired, and Doctor Morley nodded his head.

"Disaffected conquistadors," Benito mused. "Interesante, interesante. But ... it might not be in the Codex, and instead be hidden somewhere else?"

Doctor Morley gave an awkward nod.

"Aha. And so far you have ... nothing?"

It was a rhetorical question that Benito didn't need an answer to. Doctor Morley glared at him.

"Then ... might it not make sense to go to Seville immediately?" Benito suggested, one eye on Mister Carter. "Your colleague here wants to go to the Archive, no? We can always return to Madrid after."

"Excellent idea, Benito," Mister Carter said. "I think it would be extremely useful to see de Landa's records, Sylvanus. And it would seem logical to kill two birds with one stone and ask to view the sword as well."

"The sword is unavailable for public viewing," Benito said without hesitation. "The Archive will not permit it. Again, that is why we must go to the sword ceremony at the Exposition."

"Come now, I'm sure they'll let *me* see it," Mister Carter said. "I've still got some weight I can throw around."

Doctor Morley glanced at me and we shared a silent, unspoken joke. But Benito looked serious. He said:

"No. It is impossible. Do not even ask."

"Come now, it can't hurt to make a request to inspect the thing," Mister Carter said. "It's not exactly Excalibur."

"No, Señor Carter. If we must take more aggressive steps to secure the sword, we cannot inquire about it first."

"*Aggressive steps?*" my boss jumped in. "What do you mean by that?"

"I believe you know what that means, Señor Morley."

Doctor Morley gave Benito a dirty look. He turned to Veronica.

"Well, Miss Shetty … is that what you've signed us all up for? A criminal conspiracy?"

The she-devil was smoking. She took a drag before answering then said:

"I'll do whatever it takes to accomplish the mission. Remember, Sylvanus … there's a big pot of fame and glory at the end of our rainbow."

***

The team of rivals worked through the afternoon. I spent over an hour going through my copy of the Codex with Mister Carter, hoping to see something I had missed. We didn't find anything, but the Egyptologist did tell I had done an excellent job.

At one point I excused myself and went to the Lobby to buy a cup of American coffee. They only served it at the restaurant and I had to wait while they made it, so I sat. Not more than two seconds later the Queen Bee strode by.

"Ooh, what a lovely surprise!" she said. "Are we having a drink?"

"American coffee," I said. "I'm stuck upstairs. Working."

"Ugh," the Queen Bee said. "That's no fun. Partying later?"

"Believe it or not, I've got plans," I said. "I have to go over to my friend's studio. He's the one that got me into the Prado. Posing for him is the price of the tour."

"Pose! Naked, I hope?"

"No!" I exclaimed, then thought about it. "At least … I hope not."

"Pity. Rest assured getting naked is quite acceptable if the artist is charming and hunky. Is he?"

"No, not in a traditional sense," I said. "But I'll be okay. Where's your other half?"

"Oh, he's gone over to the consulate to see if he can use one of their typewriters. His broke and he's working on a piece for one of the Paris papers. It's due soon and he's a getting a bit bonkers about it."

"Can we all get together again soon?" I said.

"Of course," the Queen Bee replied. "You're Wendy, I'm Tinkerbell and you-know-who is Peter Pan. The story doesn't work without all three of us!"

20

THE GREAT MASTURBATOR

My evening at Salvador's studio had arrived.

Feeling brave, I decided to take the Metro. I used the station across the boulevard from the hotel and rode it three stops to the end of the line. Again, I was struck by the absurd slowness of the supposedly modern people-mover.

Up on the sidewalk, I consulted my map and then wound through a nice—but not that nice—part of Madrid. Twice I had to ignore cat-calls and whistles. I carried on and found Sal's address without getting lost.

It was a typical city apartment building, three stories high. I went in through the front door and up the common flight of stairs. He hadn't given me an apartment number, but had told me I would know it when I saw it. Sure enough, one of the doors stood out: It had been painted in a bright purple hue. The letters *D-A-L-I* were stenciled over the purple door in a bright pink. I knocked. There were footsteps and Salvador opened the door.

He was wearing a tie and had his shirtsleeves rolled up. In one hand he held a glass of red wine.

"Buenas noches, señorita ... cómo estás?" he asked, waving me in.

"Fantástico," I answered as I entered.

In the narrow entryway there were several small paintings. I wanted to look at each of them, but he waved me along. The entryway opened up into a surprisingly large studio space. There were paintings all over the walls, two easels set up in the back and a velvet couch in the middle. It was what I had always imagined a real artist's studio would look like.

"It's a nice space," I told him, and he agreed with me.

"Vino?" he asked.

I gave him a look that said he shouldn't have to ask. He chuckled and walked to a cabinet to fetch my beverage. As he did, I decided to check out Sal's work.

The first painting I focused on was bizarre beyond words.

At the center of the painting was a fleshy-colored blob. Parts of the blob looked somewhat ... anatomical. There was a big grasshopper—with ants covering its belly—attached to the blob's underside. In the upper-right corner a woman's head emerged from the blob ... her eyes closed, her hair flowing. Pressing onto the woman's nose was a man-mound, bulging out from the undershorts of some headless chap standing next to her. It was all very, very strange.

Sal returned with my wine and handed me my glass.

"*Visage du Grand Masturbateur,*" he said. "*Face of the Great Masturbator.* You like?"

"I'm trying to understand it all. Is this supposed to be a horse?" I asked, pointing to the blob and then sipping my wine.

"Horse?" Sal replied. "No, no, is a female ... here is vagina."

I spit a cloud of wine out of my mouth in shock. He kept talking:

"And here you have the birth canal, no? And these bugs around here, they show the foulness, the shame, the putridness of copulation, si?"

I didn't know what to say. I pointed to the blob.

"So ... this isn't her leg?"

"No, that is her ass."

"And who is this man?"

"He is just a man."

"Having her face so close to his ... unit ... is very suggestive," I remarked, sipping my wine again.

"Ah, but her eyes are closed, see? She is sad, but she accepts the fact that he has been castrated."

This time I choked on my wine instead of blowing it out.

"He has castrated *himself*, to be precise," the artist clarified. "That is why there is the blood running down his leg, no?"

"Oh. Of course," I said. "And ... what's this little fishhook thingy sticking out of her ... her posterior exit?"

"Oh, that. My centering on this picture was not so good. I do that just for balance, you know?"

"And the ants?"

"Eh," he shrugged. "I do the ants to screw with people's minds."

He proceeded to walk me through more of the paintings and sketches on his wall. Many of them suggested Salvador had some pretty big sexual hang-ups, but I stayed mum on that.

We came to one that was half-finished. The part of the canvas that had been worked on showed a phallic-looking silo.

"Is that supposed to be …," I started.

"Sí. The silo is the shaft of the erect penis. These bales of hay in the foreground, those are the balls. Then you see the tree in back of silo, ah? That is the pubic hair—my pubic hair, if you will—when viewed from underneath the balls. And here on top, this little white flag erupting from the silo, that's …,"

"Enough," I interjected. "I get it. It's quite … unique."

"I am so glad you like! This is what I need you for, ah?"

"Me?"

I turned to look at the dick-like silo again.

"This? Me?"

"Sí, señora. I will put you over here, in profile."

"I don't understand."

"A profile is side view of face, no?"

"I know what a profile is. I don't understand the painting. What's it mean?"

"To be honest … this one, it means nothing," he answered. "Sometimes, as saying goes, a penis is just a penis."

I decided to stop asking questions.

I was blown away by the diverseness of his portfolio. For every crazy modern-looking piece there seemed to be an equally amazing traditional work. He had one portrait that looked like it could have been done by Goya himself. Next to that several sketches had been tacked to the wall. They were studies of a tall man in armor, posing and expressing himself. In some of the sketches there were also rough images of a shorter, fatter man on a horse. Then one sheet showed the two characters together and it dawned on me it was Don Quixote and Sancho Panza.

"You like the sketches, no?" Salvador asked.

"I like," I replied. "Their tale hits close to home."

"Qué?"

"Long story, never mind," I said.

On another wall there was an oversized canvas. It had not been painted on but there were pencil marks all over it. It showed a desolate desert landscape dotted with leafless trees. Hanging from several of the branches—melting off, I deduced—were funny-looking blobs with scribbling in them. I peered in closer at one of the blogs and recognized the inspiration.

The blobs were little Aztec calendar stones. This was the painting he had been coming to the Museum to research, day after day. I studied it for a moment, concluded it made no sense and told him so.

"I just don't think the empire-melting-away theme works," I said. "I'm up to my eyeballs in that damn world and your message escaped even me. It needs a different theme. How about, instead of an empire melting away, time melts away?"

"Time?" Salvador replied. "This painting, it is not about time. It is about empire."

"But it's confusing. What about making them little clocks, instead of little calendar stones?"

He didn't say anything at first. He looked at the canvas, shook his said and said:

"Clocks? No. I try to show millennia, not hours. I call it … *La Impersistencia del Imperio.*"

I thought *The Impersistence of Empire* was a crummy name, but I kept my opinion to myself.

***

And then I modeled for his penis-silo picture.

He had me sit in a chair under a single electric light. I had to look up toward the light, keeping my eyes closed. He stood in front of me with a draft pad and sketched me once. Then he walked over to my side and sketched me from there. Finally, he went over to the opposite side and did a third sketch.

He showed me when he was done. All three were remarkable. In less than forty-five minutes he had created an evocative, compelling image of me far superior to any photograph I had ever been in. He made my hair and lips look fantastic.

"Now, Vendy … are you ready for the film?" he asked after.

"What film?"

"My film. You see Fano, sí?"

Fano. It took me a second to realize he was referring to my supposed doppelganger in Paris.

"Sí," I replied. "Let's see how my long-lost twin has held up."

Salvador then went to a cabinet and pulled out a bag. He brought it to the table and out of the bag he pulled a film tin.

"My projector, is not so fancy, sí? But it works."

It was a hand-cranked projector, an Edison, screwed to a long board. He clamped his film roll onto an arm of the projector then spent several minutes threading the film through to the receiving reel. When he was ready he asked me to flick off his overhead light. He turned the bulb of the projector on and started to turn the crank.

A title image appeared on the wall in front of us: *Un Chien Andalou.*

The film opens with a man sharpening a razor. Then the man decides he would rather sharpen his razor on the balcony. It is daytime, but when he looks up the sky is dark and he can see the moon. Then we see a woman's face. She is looking into the camera. The man with the razor is now holding her eye open, we see the moon again, then … *the razor cuts into the woman's eyeball.*

"Oh my god!" I screamed, turning away as goo oozed out. "That's disgusting! What kind of film is this?"

"Patience, patience," Salvador said.

If I had the patience of Job and the wisdom of Solomon I still wouldn't have understood it. The next scene had a man in a nun's habit riding a bicycle, while some worried woman flutters about her apartment. She looks out her window to see the man dressed as a nun has, inexplicably, died on the sidewalk below. Then the woman turns around and there is a man in her apartment, staring at his hand. She joins him and they see there are ants crawling out of a hole in his palm.

"I don't get it," I whispered.

"The ants are freaky, no? Shh … here she comes."

There was a random shot of a hairy armpit, which I hoped wasn't hers. That was followed by an overhead shot of a short-haired woman. We can't see her face but we see she has a stick. She's using the stick to poke a dismembered hand laying in the street. A crowd gathers around to watch her. The camera angle changes and we can see more of the woman's face as policemen push the onlookers away. Then we cut to a close shot of the woman.

I gasped. She *did* look like me.

Her hair was brushed to the other side but that was the biggest difference. Her face looked strikingly similar to mine, right down to the tiny nose and too-narrow lips. She was wearing a coat but appeared to be skinny and unencumbered by her bosom … again, just like me.

"Her hair … you cannot see here, but it is red like yours," Salvador noted.

With me as the star, the movie became much more interesting. In it, my doppelganger continues to poke the dismembered hand with a stick. The police push the crowd back. I am fascinated by the hand, using the stick to roll it over again and again. A policeman reaches down and picks up the hand and puts in in a striped box. He hands the box to me and I clutch it to my chest. The policeman pushes the crowd away and the onlookers disperse. I am alone in the street with the boxed-up hand. Motorcars start to drive by, but I don't budge.

Then … I get run over by a car. My lifeless body lies in the street, my beloved dismembered hand next to me. I whispered again to Sal:

"Do I come back to life?"

"No," he replied. "Lo siento."

From there it went from weird to downright unsettling. A minute later we are back in the apartment and there are two decaying donkeys stuffed into two grand pianos. Then we see the man with the spider-hand is using ropes to drag the pianos somewhere. Attached to his ropes are also the Ten Commandment tablets and two funny-looking priests, one of them played by Salvador. Then we are back inside the apartment with the woman. She is looking at a butterfly. Suddenly, she is on the beach. Salvador appears again, not a priest this time, and the two walk off hand-in-hand. On the beach they find the box that the dismembered hand— the one that meant so much to me—had been in. The end, I hoped, but no: the final shot was of the woman and Salvador, both buried up to their chests in the sand. They both looked dead.

Salvador stopped cranking the projector. He looked at me with a big smile.

"Bueno, no?" he said, appearing quite pleased with it. "Is it … too political?"

"Political? No, not at all. It's … unforgettable," I said, an honest assessment.

"If you come to Paris someday I put you in film, no? Maybe you and Fano together, no? The twin trouble-makers of Montmartre, ah?"

"That sounds wonderful," I said. "I've actually been thinking about Paris. A lot."

"You would do well there, señora."

That led to a longer conversation about Paris. Salvador had his own studio there. He said he always needed help. He name-dropped Picasso again and told me good studio assistants were very hard to come by.

"I am going back in a few days … you could join, no?" he asked out of the blue.

I was floored. Alas, I was—for the moment, at least—still employed.

"I wish I could. I have to finish my work … and we're leaving for Seville in a couple of days."

The thought hit me that I could quit my job and not go to Seville at all. Reading my mind, Salvador said:

"Vendy, why do you not bid adieu to your job … and come to Paris instead?"

My inner voice was now in perfect synchronization with outside suggestions. The idea seemed surreal: *living in Paris.*

A cascade of dreams washed over me: working for Salvador, meeting other artists, partying with the Queen Bee and the Dead Writer. Meeting my twin. Visiting the Louvre. Seeing Montmartre. Getting drunk in the Latin Quarter.

Paris. That's where I would start fresh.

21

MAPS OF MANI

The following morning I accompanied Doctor Morley to the Library.

He had compiled a list of illustrations that he wanted me to copy. As I was working through them, I came across a map that looked somewhat similar to a map I had studied on the Orizaba. I pointed it out to Doctor Morley.

"By Jove, Wendy … I hadn't noticed that," he said. "Good eye. See, I knew that homework would pay off."

Which wasn't true. This was the first and only time I made a connection between Doctor Morley's portfolio and anything we had seen in Spain. But who was I to tell my boss not to be happy with me?

After a couple hours at the Library, we walked out and around the block to the Museum. There, Doctor Morley had me make an etching of a piece of Mayan pottery, which was easy. Next, he had me do a color illustration of an Aztec necklace, a tougher challenge due to the Museum's poor lighting. Before I had finished the necklace, he decided I should sketch some Mayan earrings he had spotted.

At mid-day my boss ignored my desperate pleas for lunch. Instead, he stuffed me into a taxi and the two of us drove off toward Benito's to meet the others.

"Do you think he and Musa sleep at that old place?" I asked Doctor Morley during the ride.

"What a peculiar question," my boss answered. "I suppose so. Seems like a full-service hideout, what with the kitchen and all."

"I'd rather be going to Paris than some hideout," I sighed, saying out loud what I meant to say in my head.

"Paris?" Doctor Morley said. "You'll have to do that some other trip, I'm afraid."

I kept my thoughts to myself. I was still struggling with whether to quit before we left for Seville.

***

At Benito's hideout, Musa escorted us inside and into the dining room. There we found Veronica and Mister Carter, sitting at a table, huddled over a book.

"Ah, here he is right here … Glad you could make it, Sylvanus," Mister Carter said. "We've been having quite the discussion about a man you know better than I."

"Don't call me Sylvanus. Who?"

"Diego de Landa."

"De Landa again?"

"Yes, the Bishop. Him and that wicked fire. You know quite a bit about that event, don't you?"

"I do," Doctor Morley answered, approaching the table. "For accuracy's sake, he wasn't bishop when he ordered the auto da fé at Mani. He was only a friar then … he didn't become bishop until much later. But even as a friar, he was one of the most powerful men in the Yucatán."

"And a wicked one, it would seem," Mister Carter said.

"It depends on your perspective. De Landa burned thousands of years of Mayan history and culture in a single day ... so yes, there was a wicked side," Doctor Morley opined. "But as an archaeologist, I have to give partial credit where credit is due. His early translations of the Mayan language were an important building block for us."

"And his reputation in the church?" Mister Carter asked.

"To borrow a phrase, it's complicated," Doctor Morley answered.

The boss and I sat. Mister Carter gave me a little nod. Veronica failed to acknowledge my presence or existence. She fingered a passage in the book and asked Doctor Morley:

"This Chi fellow, the scribe ... when did he work with de Landa?"

"I can't say I'm sure."

"Was he with de Landa at Mani, when the fire happened?"

"In 1562? Again, I'm not sure. What prompts these questions?"

"I've been digging through this book by James Churchward ...," Mister Carter began.

"Churchward!" Doctor Morley exclaimed. "Howard, I don't think ...,"

"Yes, yes, he's a ding-dong, I'm well aware of that," Mister Carter said. "Lots more references to 'Mu' in here, by the way, if you'd rather search for Atlantis. Ha! Just joking, of course. Miss Willoughby, do sit back down. Now, Sylvanus, look here ...,"

My boss didn't bother making the obligatory correction about his name. He took the book that Mister Carter was sliding toward him and turned it over to look at the spine. He read the title out loud:

"Conspiracies and Conquistadors: Untold Tales of the New World."

"Gripping title, no? Now, on the page I had open, read the bottom paragraph," Mister Carter said.

"I don't like when people play games with history, Howard."

"Then you shouldn't be here. Go on, read it."

Doctor Morley exhaled and began to read aloud from the book:

"In the absence of an on-site strongman like Cortés, the Spanish missionaries of the Yucatán took on greater importance. Whereas the conquest of the Aztecs was achieved with swords and horses, the conquest of the Maya would be accomplished with bibles and book burnings. One of the earliest missionaries, Diego de Landa, oversaw a diocese that included hundreds of thousands of Mayans. He was a powerful administrator and a ruthless enforcer of his Inquisitorial mandate. His overzealous methods led to tensions with both the crown and colonial governors. As de Landa's isolation rose, rumors of his double-dealing became commonplace, leading …,"

Doctor Morley paused. I could see he was reading the rest of the sentence to himself. Now he read it out loud:

"… Leading many to believe his notorious auto-de-fé at Mani wasn't about destroying Mayan artifacts. Rather, it was to destroy evidence of his less-than-holy ways."

Doctor Morley flipped to the next page, then the next. He said:

"Well. That's a hell of an unsupported allegation to make. Is there anything else about de Landa in here?"

"Not that I've found," Mister Carter said. "But that's a promising lead, is it not?"

"I've never heard such rumors before," Doctor Morley replied. "And I've been in and around the Yucatán for decades."

"Well, I think it's an interesting development," Mister Carter went on. "Churchward lives in London, I believe. I'm half-tempted to send him a telegram and ask for his sources on that."

"You'll do nothing of the sort, Howard. Loose lips sink ships," Veronica warned, then turned to me. "Speaking of loose lips … how are you, Wendy?"

She had a wicked smile.

"What's that supposed to mean?" I asked.

"Well, a little bird told me that you've been having quite the time in Madrid."

"It's been better than expected, thank you."

"Mm-hm," the she-devil replied. "Careful, heartbreaker."

I was loading my response into the chamber when Benito strode in from the other room. He was carrying a newspaper.

"The King is coming to the Exposition!" he announced.

"Well, I would expect that," Doctor Morley replied, not impressed. "The reunion wouldn't be complete without him."

"He is coming, Señor Morley, on the *same day* as the ceremony of the swords ...," Benito shot back, through clenched teeth.

"The same day?" Veronica chimed in. "That will mean more security."

"Sí. It will be harder to obtain the sword," Benito argued.

"Woah, woah ...," Doctor Morley said. "Again the presumption here seems to be that we need to steal something. Are we not even going to ask to see it first?"

"That's exactly what I've been saying, Sylvanus," Mister Carter agreed.

"We have discussed this, amigos. They will not let anyone view it. Therefore, we must find ... an alternative method," Benito said.

"An alternative method. Right. You're going to steal it in front of the monarch himself?" my boss teased.

Benito took a deep, frustrated inhale and then said:

"No, Señor Morley. But we will use the ceremony to observe the sword and its handler, so we are prepared to take action when the time comes. Sí?"

"A sword," Doctor Morley scoffed, looking away. "This is ridiculous."

"Bite your tongue," Benito growled. "What is ridiculous is you, jumping around, looking for something here and then something there. You have no idea what you are even looking for!"

"Don't snap at me," Doctor Morley snapped. "You simply lack the intellect to see what I'm seeing ... which is a nice, bright path that will lead us in the right direction. If you stay out of my goddamn way, that is!"

Benito stepped toward my boss, one hand on his walking stick, as if he might club him. But the Spaniard stopped, curled his lip and turned away. He glared at Veronica then shook his head at me. Finally he turned to Mister Carter, who had been ignoring them and studying maps:

"I do say, Mister Barataria … you might want to review what we've found. We've uncovered lots of arrows pointing toward de Landa, which would suggest Mani is a key place for …,"

"Gómora did not discuss de Landa. Gómora did not discuss Mani," Benito shot back. "Both of you are on the wrong path … but each in your own way."

"So go find the damn thing yourself!" Doctor Morley suggested.

"Perhaps I will," Benito replied.

"Fine," Doctor Morley huffed.

"Fine!" I jumped in, as I thought Benito leaving us was a wonderful idea.

"Stay out of this, Wendy," Doctor Morley snapped. "Nobody asked you."

I retreated back into the wallpaper. My opinions were not welcome here, which only hardened my resolve.

22

PARISIAN DREAMS

It was the day before we were to leave for Seville.

In the morning, I rode to the Library with Doctor Morley and did a few last-minute tasks for him. Then, not knowing if we would return to Madrid, I went to the Museum for my farewell tour.

I started on the third floor, making a few final improvements to my Codex copy. Then I said adiós to the damned thing, hoping to never see it again. Next I saluted the Aztec calendar stone and gave a farewell to the Mayan pottery. My time in the Mesoamerican salon had come to a much-appreciated end.

On the way out, I took a moment to peruse the skulls and bones kept on the other side of the top floor. Then I went down to the mezzanine for one last walk past the tapestries and the currency cabinets. I strolled through the Roman Patio and admired the broken statues, then came into the Arab Courtyard, the most relaxing spot in the Museum.

I was coming down to the ground floor when Lothario spotted me.

"Ah, Vendy!" he said. "I was afraid you had left, no?"

"Still here, Lothario. Last day though. We're off to the Exposition tomorrow."

"Ah, Barcelona!"

"No. Seville."

"Oh, sí. So ... you view exhibits, ah?"

"Yes. I've spent so much time upstairs with the Codex I missed most everything else. Doing a little catching up."

"Sí, then I walk with you."

That wasn't what I wanted but with Lothario it was no use objecting. He strolled with me down the stairs, yakking away, then we wandered into the first Egyptian salon. He kept blabbering as I admired the two sarcophagi and didn't stop as I moved on to the cabinets. Ancient Egypt fascinated me and I didn't get to see much of it, so this was a treat ... so much so that I was able to shut out the gabbing guard:

"... And living with mi madre, she cooks every night, sí?"

"Mm-hm," I replied, my focus locked on four exquisite bronze idols.

"... She say I should get married. But I say no, not Lothario ...,"

"Uh-huh," I offered, looking up and around at the tomb-inspired artwork on the ceiling and walls.

Lothario continued to enlighten me on all aspects of his personal life as we moved into the Far East salon. I marveled at the craftsmanship of the Chinese carved furniture as he told me about his favorite foods. I ran my hand along an exquisite Japanese vase as he told me about his favorite vacation spots. Next it was on to more pottery and more vases in the Roman and Greek rooms, where I learned his favorite color.

He kept at it as we came through the Greek salon and into the Iberian rooms. By the time we came to the

Christian exhibits, dominated by a massive iron gate from some monastery, I thought he might ask me to marry him, right then and there.

But I avoided the ring and escaped with a simple good-bye hug. Anselmo, the other guard, got a handshake. The cud-chewing ticket lady only got a nod.

With a final good-bye to the twin sphinges, I left the Museum ... assuming I would never return.

***

In the afternoon I braved the Metro again and travelled to Salvador's studio. I knocked, heard an uno-momento holler and waited. He answered the door wearing a suit and tie. The cuffs of his coat and his shirt were rolled up onto his forearms. His hands were speckled with pain.

"You wear a suit to paint?" was my first question.

"Sí, of course. What else would I wear?" he answered.

He had begun work on my likeness in the penis painting. He had made my hair much longer but it was a lovely profile view of my face. I thanked him for having my face pointed away from the phallic silo, not toward it.

We sat down for wine and I told him my plan:

"I can't work up the nerve to do it ... yet," I confided. "My boss is preparing for a speech, I don't want to add to his stress. I'll tell him in Seville, then make my way to Paris."

"I think it is a wise decision, señora," he said. "You can stay with me for as long as you need."

"I'm going to have to send for my things and get them sent from Mexico."

"Why bother? You will be in a city, no? Buy new things."

"You're a smart man," I told him. "Thank you for encouraging me."

"De nada," he replied. "And remember, mi casa es su casa, in Madrid or in Paris."

I thanked him. Before I left, he showed me the spare key to his apartment, hidden in the hallway.

***

In the early evening I dove into the tornadic disaster that was my hotel room. I laid out my clothes and folded them nice so they would be wearable in Seville. Doctor Morley stopped by twice, to update me about the next day's travel plans and to complain about Mister Carter.

After I was all organized, I cleaned up and made for the Lobby Bar. I wanted to see the Queen Bee and the Dead Writer again and that was my best bet for finding them. Sure enough, I was only on my second drink when the Queen Bee appeared out of nowhere and saddled up to me.

"Hello, old friend!" she exclaimed. "You have no idea how glad I am to see you … you're leaving soon, right? And what's that you're drinking?"

"It's just wine, the rioja," I said. "And yes, we leave tomorrow morning."

"Ooh, I'll have wine too. We can both be winos! Frederico, una rioja, por favor … gracias, thank you."

"Where's your ... other half?" I inquired.

"Who, my dead writer? Ha! Don't think I don't remember that. His typewriter problems got to be too much, he went back to Paris early. Oh goodie, here's my wine ... here's to us, darling."

She raised her glass up to toast me. The words she had said—*he went back to Paris early*—started to register in my brain. The Queen Bee smiled at me, clinked my glass and ... something peculiar happened.

My lips started to tremble. My cheeks began to shake. My eyes were becoming moist.

And then I burst into tears.

"*Bwaah-huh-huh! Bwaah-huh-huh!*"

I don't like to cry but suddenly I was crying, hard. The Queen Bee looked at me with sad, surprised eyes. Her sympathetic look made me cry more.

"*Bwaah-huh-huh!* I ... I'm sorry, I ... *Bwaah-huh-huh!*"

"Oh my goodness!" the Queen Bee said. "Wendy, darling, what's the matter?"

"*Bwah-huh-huh-huh,*" I carried on, unable to stop.

"Did I say something wrong?"

"*Hoo-huh-huh* ... *sniff* ... no, no," I said, embarrassed to be seen like this.

"Señora, here," came a voice. It was Frederico giving me a napkin to wipe my tears, which triggered another round.

"*Bwaah-huh-huh-huh,*" I continued, inconsolable.

And then the Queen Bee got up out of her stool, wrapped her arms around me and hugged.

I don't know how long she hugged me. But it was a long time, because I couldn't let go. She held me and rubbed my back and I cried and cried into her shoulder. At some point I saw through my waterworks that others in the bar were watching this sorry spectacle. She told me to ignore them and held me until I stopped. Then she settled back into her stool, clinked her glass to mine and we both drank. After a minute she said:

"My goodness. You needed that."

"Yes," I said, still sniffling. "I'm sorry."

"Don't be," she said. "But you have to tell me why."

"I'm just … I'm just sad I won't see … your companion again."

"My companion? *He's* what you're upset about?"

"I … I just didn't get a chance to say good-bye."

"He'll be thrilled to know he made such an impression," the Queen Bee said. "I've never had anyone be jealous of him before."

"I'm not *jealous*, I'm sorry, this is all coming off wrong," I said. "It's … hard to explain. I told you he reminded me of someone, right?"

She nodded sympathetically.

"Well, I … I didn't get a chance to say good-bye to that person either," I said. "So hearing he had left dredged up some bad memories."

My friend placed an understanding hand on top of mine. She looked me in the eyes and said:

"We don't always get a chance to say good-bye, Wendy."

23

THE EXPOSITION

At dawn we left the Palace Hotel and took a taxi to the central station. There were special trains running daily to the Expositions in Barcelona and Seville. The platform servicing Barcelona was far more crowded than the platform for Seville. For a moment, I debated ditching my group and joining the partygoers headed north to the fun Expo.

We found Mister Carter and Veronica waiting for us on the platform. Behind them was a porter, looking bored while standing watch over their luggage. Doctor Morley motioned to the porter, who took our belongings and put them on his cart.

Doctor Morley asked to have a word with Mister Carter and the two of them walked down the platform and out of sight. Veronica watched them like a hawk and seemed perturbed that she wasn't involved. She reached into her bag for one of her silly little cigarettes. She lit it and only after she took a puff did she offer me one.

"No thanks," I said. "I brought my own."

I reached into my shoulder bag and pulled out a pack of Corafinas. I ripped open the pack and took a smoke out and put it to my lips. As I struck the match Veronica said:

"Corafina. Can't say I've ever heard of those."

"Really?" I replied, the unlit cigarette still dangling from my mouth. "They're quite the rage. Very expensive."

Of course, I had never tried Corafinas before. They weren't expensive and I assume they weren't the rage anywhere. But I played it cool and lit my smoke. I could feel the she-devil judging me in silence. I returned the favor and judged the wench right back. Then the two of us stood there, not speaking, smoking our respective cigarettes. The entire episode was emblematic of our relationship.

Soon after, the train arrived. Benito was still nowhere to be seen; there was some panic and Doctor Morley became quite flustered and blew his top at the porter. Seconds later, Benito and Musa appeared from around the corner. Doctor Morley didn't apologize to the porter, so I did on his behalf.

And then we were off. We had been assigned to separate cabins, and within minutes after leaving the station Benito was in ours. That didn't sit well with Doctor Morley:

"See here, I've got to spend some time on my remarks," he told Benito.

"A word alone, por favor?" was Benito's reply.

"Anything you can say to me, you can say to her," my boss said, nodding to me.

"Not this," Benito replied.

Doctor Morley frowned and took a deep breath in. Without another word I got up, giving Benito an evil glare as I squeezed past him. He glared right back and, as soon as I was in the corridor, the door closed and I heard the deadbolt slide into place.

Musa was the only one in the corridor with me. I gave him an uncomfortable smile and then watched the outskirts of Madrid go by.

"Have you ever been to Seville?" I asked Musa at some point, trying to be polite.

"Uh-huh, sí, once," he grunted. "With Señor Benito."

Those were the most words I had heard him speak at once.

"And … how did you come to work for Señor Benito?"

Musa stared at me and did not answer.

"I mean … where did you two meet?" I clarified.

Again he did not answer. He looked to me, then looked back out to the passing scenery and said:

"You try make Musa amigo."

"I'm only trying to be friendly."

Still looking out the train window, the giant man looked at me out the corner of one eye:

"Musa need no amigo. Musa need no friend."

And at that he walked away in the other direction, toward the far end and exit of the train car. He didn't come back for some time.

I wasn't sure if I had made him mad, or sad.

***

At the station in Seville we transferred our bags to a taxi, then motored through crowded streets to the small inn where we were staying. Our rooms weren't ready yet, so we left our bags at the front desk and made for the Exposition.

The doorman directed us down a main thoroughfare to get to the main entrance. But Benito insisted that we take a back way:

"We must familiarize ourselves with the less-travelled routes, no?" he explained.

The less-travelled route took us through what seemed like a different world. While the main avenues were clean, with lovely decorative arches marking the path to the Expo, the side streets were just the opposite. Here, a quarter-mile from the Expo, we saw unwashed children playing in muddy puddles. We saw angry-looking men with nothing to do ... and women who looked like they had given up hope. Several times we were asked for money; I was the only one who saw fit to give.

"The not-so-hidden side of Spain," Mister Carter commented.

My nose and my heartstrings were grateful to emerge from the squalidness. We made our way to the entrance, then waited twenty minutes while Doctor Morley's name was cleared. Once we had our tickets we made our way through the gates. We followed the crowd to the area called the Plaza de España, the hub of the Expo.

The Plaza was dominated by a long horseshoe-shaped building that hugged an open area containing a fountain, a winding moat and several small bridges. There were ceramic alcoves celebrating each of the Spanish provinces, with benches for tired Expo-goers.

Beyond the Plaza, floating in the river, was a full-sized replica of an old Spanish galleon. It had a tall mast in the middle and shorter masts on the fore and aft. The larger sails had enormous red Spanish crosses painted on them.

"Well, that could be the Niña or the Pinta ... but judging from the length that's Cristobal Colon's flagship, the Santa María," Mister Carter said. "How nice of the Spanish to celebrate Portugal's most famous son."

"Columbus was Italian, not Portugese," Doctor Morley corrected.

"Nonsense. He was Catalonian," Benito declared.

"I thought he was a Greek," Veronica opined.

I didn't give a crap one way or the other. I found myself struck by how different the climate was in Seville compared to Madrid. Here there were towering palms, warm winds and a brighter sun. The air was filled with the smell of flowers. It was lovely.

We took a turn off the main path—a wrong turn, in my opinion—and found ourselves immersed in industrial displays. There were exhibits from mining companies and metallurgy outfits and tool manufacturers. There were all kinds of machines on display and it was boring as hell.

Next we passed by a series of small buildings with signs in front indicating they were 'art palaces.' I wanted to go in and was told I had to do so on my own time. Instead, Doctor Morley dragged us to the United States pavilion. He introduced himself and handed out cards with his name. He acted interested as he admired our homeland's lame display of refrigerators and sewing machines.

Then it was on to the various exhibits from the former Spanish colonies. The Peruvian exhibit had some decent pre-Columbian artifacts, along with a room filled with stuffed llamas and alpacas. The Columbian Pavilion had an impressive collection of emeralds and a little café for coffee. There was another coffee café in the Brazilian Pavilion, along with a demonstration of coffee-cultivating techniques. Chile was showing off mining equipment, which didn't excite me much. Guatemala's building was small and mostly empty and it appeared they put in even less effort than the Americans. The Cubans, bless them, focused on sugar and tobacco … two of my favorite things.

Only then did we reach the best part: the Carnival.

I'm sure it was designed for children, but the Carnival area was overflowing with adults. And who could blame them? There were two carousels, a whirly-go-round and even a roller coaster. There were games where you throw darts and games where you toss hoops over bottles. Everyone was walking around with fried food and ice cream and tremendous smiles.

"My God, look at these animals. It's like hell on earth," Veronica remarked, true to form. I took that to mean the she-devil despised not just the adults having fun, but the happy children too.

I, on the other hand, thought the Carnival was the most delightful part of the Expo. But then, as we moved on toward the Mexico pavilion, we came upon something even more remarkable and astounding: a miniature train.

It wasn't a toy train, either. It really ran, with an undersized locomotive pulling a series of undersized passenger cars over narrow tracks. The passenger cars each carried a half-dozen people and every seat was filled.

"I am *not* leaving here without riding that," I said.

"Don't be silly. Let's see how the Mexican Pavilion turned out," my boss said.

I had already made my decision. I walked away without a word and got in line. A second later Musa joined me.

"Oh, now you want to be friends, huh?" I teased.

He almost broke a smile at that. Almost.

The rest of our grumpy companions went ahead and then Musa and I rode the delightful little train. Other than the party at the mansion, it was the most fun I had experienced since arriving in Spain. The train went faster than we thought it would, looped around and climbed up into a series of faux mountains. Then there was a curvy little dip coming out of the faux mountains; everyone screamed with joy as they came down. Even Musa was grinning and giggling.

After, the happy goon escorted me toward the Mexican Pavilion. We stopped to admire the reflecting pool in front of one of the art palaces, sniffed the flowers at the well-manicured Royal Garden and admired the statues at the Don Quixote roundabout.

And then I laid eyes on the Mexican Pavilion for the first time. It was, in a word, revolutionary.

It was a three-tiered structure that resembled a Mesoamerican pyramid, complete with a temple on top. It was painted with just the right mix of yellow and orange, making it appear older than it was. From an architectural standpoint it had to be Mayan-inspired, perhaps with some Toltec influences.

Admiring it, I was struck by the thought that I had seen hundreds of Spanish buildings back in the Yucatán, particularly in Merida. This, however, was the first Mexican building I had seen in Spain.

I was blown away by the endless little tributes sprinkled around the façade. There were chac-mool statues lounging on the roof, detailed stelae above the *Mexico* sign and a coat of arms I did not recognize. Framing the doors to the pavilion were two carved serpent heads—snakes of Quetzalcoaltl—not unlike the stone heads at the base of El Castillo.

Musa and I made our way to the steps, which rose in temple-like fashion to the entrance. Coming in, I noticed two stelae set into alcoves just inside the door. I recognized one as an Aztec warrior. On the opposite side, facing him, was a sword-bearing conquistador in full armor.

We came into the Pavilion's central courtyard. Above, the ceiling rose high and there was stained glass throughout. Colorful woven rugs hung down between the arches and above the arches were more carved reliefs. There was so much to look at, it was hard to take in.

Musa walked away to find Benito. Just then Doctor Morley found me:

"Wendy, there you are, good you finally made it," he said. "Well … what do you think?"

"It's astounding," I replied. "I can't get over how much detail there is. You must be proud."

"I haven't made it past this area yet … but what I've seen so far is, well, it's alright."

"Just alright?"

"I'm a bit surprised to see Cortés depicted in here … quite surprised, really," he said. "But the architecture is astounding, isn't it? It's based on Sadil. Have you been to Sadil? No? Well, it's worth the trip when we get back."

I nodded. He spotted someone.

"Oh, Wendy, here's a man I want you to meet. Luis, por favor, come meet someone."

A short, wild-haired Mexican man came up.

"Wendy, this is Luis Urbina, the poet," my boss said.

"Oh, sí, Señor Urbina, I've heard of you," I said, like a moron. "I'm Wendy."

"Luis is here as part of the main delegation. Mexico has done a fine job, haven't they? They've sent artists and poets here, not just political muckety-mucks," Doctor Morley explained, then spied someone else. "Oh, look! There's Grangerford, I didn't know he was coming. I'll say hello. I'll be right back, pardon me."

And then I found myself standing alone with a poet I barely knew. I hoped it would go better than the last time.

"So, Vendy ... the Pavilion, you like?" Señor Urbina asked me.

"Sí, I do. It's much better than the other ones, at least that's my impression. What do you think?"

"I worry the Spanish, they will storm the temple and take our gold," he said with a straight face.

I wasn't sure whether I should laugh or not ... but then he did, so I did too.

"Doctor Morley, he tell me you here to make copy of Codex, sí?" the poet asked.

"Um, sí," I answered, surprised my boss had told anyone that.

"Muy bueno. The Codex, it is important for story of Mexico. Too many people, they do not know our history."

"Well, I'm glad I can ... play a part in that story, I suppose. Even though I'm American, of course."

"No es un problema," Señor Urbina replied. "Most stories about Mexico, they do not have many Mexicans in them."

Again I wasn't sure what to do. Was that a joke?

"Eso es una broma, señorita," the poet said, confirming it was. "It is okay to laugh sometimes."

**

A bit later I walked with Doctor Morley into one of the ground floor galleries. There we found Mister Carter and Veronica. Together, the four of us explored the Pavilion.

On the first level there was a collection of murals featuring farmers throughout the ages. There were bins with Mexican agricultural crops. A woman in traditional Mayan dress was rolling out a tortilla on a stone; Doctor Morley said hello to her in her native tongue and discovered she was not Mayan but Brazilian.

We took the stairs to the second floor. There we found a series of gorgeous, evocative murals by Diego Rivera, an artist I admired. It showed people going about their daily lives, working in the fields and practicing their faiths. There was a good representation of El Castillo, which Doctor Morley felt was "cartoonish." Another room had cabinet after cabinet filled with Mesoamerican objects; the room after that was showing a film about the Mexican economy. We finished our rounds and agreed to go back downstairs, to the first floor. Only then did the lot of us notice, for the first time, the four reliefs carved into the wall above the stairs.

The first relief showed a cross carrying priest. The next one showed a smiling Moctezuma, recognizable from his head-dress. The third relief showed a woman and a young boy. The final showed Cortés, with his familiar facial hair.

"I see we have several of our main characters on stage, eh?" Mister Carter said, then pointed them out. "De Landa, Moctezuma, Doña Marina—La Malinche, if you will—with the little Mestizo, the first Martín Cortés. And then the star of the show, the great conquistador himself …,"

"Stop that," came an angry growl.

It was Doctor Morley. He was studying the reliefs and didn't look happy.

"This isn't funny, Howard. I'm not sure if that's supposed to be de Landa or some random friar … but I do know the tone of this entire place is a bit off. Don't you agree?"

"I'm not sure I'm on the same boat," Mister Carter replied.

"This is, what, the fourth representation of Cortés I've seen in here?" Doctor Morley explained. "And there's a relief of one of his foot soldiers by the door, staring down an unarmed Aztec. It's not right."

"It's a hard balance, Sylvanus."

"Don't call me that, Howard. And it's not a hard balance if you're approaching it objectively. That's *not* what they're doing here. They're saying that there existed uncivilized Aztecs and Mayans and Toltecs. And then

Cortés arrived ... met La Malinche ... and the literal product of that union is a new goddamn race."

"Come on, man. They're just historical decorations," Mister Carter chided.

"Hmph. Well, sometimes bullshit is revealed in the most unexpected places."

24

THE BISHOP OF YUCATAN

I overslept and missed breakfast. Doctor Morley knocked on my door, hollered that they were leaving without me and then stomped away. I jumped out of bed, threw on some clothes and grabbed my shoulder bag.

I had to hustle to catch up with the group. When I found them, Mister Carter was lagging Benito and the others by a half-block. I felt a need to slow down and walk with him. Mister Carter was, like me, a good but misunderstood soul.

The Archive was housed in an imposing two-story building with pointed spires at each end. The windows had iron gates that looked impenetrable. It looked ready to withstand an attack.

"Remind you of anywhere?" Mister Carter asked.

"Escorial," I answered.

"Very good. Juan de Herrera designed this as well, about a decade after he finished the ... *huff, hoo* ... Escorial job," Mister Carter said, winded. "Let's rest here for a moment, shall we?"

We stopped. He caught his breath and remarked on the heat and wiped his brow. When we got going again he continued:

"That would have been under Philip the Second, of course."

"Of course."

". . . And at that time Seville's merchants needed a headquarters. They had quite the racket going on, you know."

"Mm-hm."

". . . It really is remarkable, you know … wooh, this heat! We should have taken a taxi," Mister Carter continued. "So … as I was saying … it really is remarkable how in these great empires, it's usually … let's slow down a bit … it's usually just one or two great leaders who . . . get it done."

I slowed down, not wanting to witness a heart attack. He kept at it:

"So here in Spain, it would be Charles and Phillip. In Egypt, it's Ramesses the Great. In France, love them or hate them, it's … *huff, puff* … in France it has to be Louis the Fourteenth and Napoleon. In Rome, it was …,"

As he babbled on I wondered how this fascinating, razor-sharp man could have let himself go like this. He was drenched in sweat. His face was raspberry-red. His breathing was short and out of rhythm. It occurred to me that if the curse of King Tut didn't get him, the curse of his gut certainly would.

We all huddled at the front door of the Archive before we went in.

"Again, do *not* mention the sword while we are here," Benito said. "To do so would only raise suspicions after the fact."

"Hmph. I still think we should ask to see it," Mister Carter declared.

"Me too," Doctor Morley seconded.

"No. If we do, they will piece one and one together and find us," Benito explained.

"But what if they let us view it?" Mister Carter said. "Then we won't have to steal anything."

"Shh! No talk like that," Benito implored.

"Perhaps it can't hurt to ask," Veronica chimed in.

"All of you, hush," Benito said. "We cannot have our future options limited. We stick to the plan."

I watched as Doctor Morley and Mister Carter exchanged a frustrated look. Then we opened the tall, heavy iron door and entered the Archive.

***

The first floor was rather plain and assuming, but the second floor of the Archive of the Indies was spectacular.

There were large rooms with unique vaulted ceilings, as nice as any I had seen. The designs painted inside the vaults used perspective tricks, making the ceiling seem higher. On the walls of every corridor and wall there were massive mahogany bookcases. Many of the books had been turned inward, revealing gilded pages.

"Now, this building originally housed the Commodities Exchange," Mister Carter began, without prompting. "Enabling merchants trading with the New World to …,"

"No. Stop with the history lessons, Howard," Doctor Morley. "Let's do our business here and be done with it. I've things to do."

"Chill, Sylvanus. Stop and smell the roses."

"I'm allergic to roses," Doctor Morley replied, which I think was truthful.

Benito had taken lead and walked us around to the back side of the top floor. There, in yet another gloriously-vaulted room, was an old guard sitting at a desk. He saw us the second we came around the corner and there was no avoiding him.

Benito slunk back, allowing Doctor Morley and Mister Carter to move forward. Then, in turn, Doctor Morley slunk back, leaving only Mister Carter.

The Egyptologist approached the desk:

"Hola, my good man. Might there be a librarian about? We have some older items we'd like to view."

The old guard nodded.

"Sí, I help."

"Ah, yes, that would be much appreciated. Now then … we understand you have a sword here that was wielded by Hernán Cortés …,"

There was an audible gasp amongst our little group.

"… We'd like to inspect it, por favor. As you're fetching that, we'll compile a list of other materials we're on the hunt for. Gracias, my good man."

Then Mister Carter smiled at the guard, who remained expressionless. The Egyptologist then pivoted around to face us, looking pleased with himself.

Benito appeared to be in the midst of a stroke. Veronica reminded me of a stunned cobra. Musa looked confused. Doctor Morley, on the other hand, was smiling.

"Heh-heh. Oh, that was rich," my boss chuckled.

"Señor," the guard said to Mister Carter. "Las armas de los conquistadores, they are unavailable for public viewing."

"Come now, amigo ... we only want to take a quick look."

"Lo siento."

"Please go ask your boss about that, would you? Tell him Howard Carter is asking."

The name meant nothing to the guard, that much I could tell. But the old man dutifully got up, dusted himself off and meandered away to find his supervisor.

When the old man was gone Benito unloaded on Mister Carter:

"*What* have you done? You were not to ask for or even speak of the sword!"

"You didn't tell me that," Mister Carter replied.

"I told you several times! Don't. Ask. For. It! Now you have only made our job harder."

"I asked, he said no," the Egyptologist explained. "I fail to see the problem."

Benito could only glare, then I caught him exchanging an evil look with Veronica.

"And who knows, perhaps we'll get lucky and his manager will say yes," Mister Carter went on. "Now ... let's write down what we're in the market for. Besides the sword, of course. I'm thinking we should start with those ecclesiastical records, starting with de Landa's records from Mani. Sylvanus, what do you think of that?"

Doctor Morley wasn't paying attention to Mister Carter. He remained focused on Benito. Benito, in turn, was looking all around the room, studying the place.

"Señor Barataria, tell me … what is your plan regarding this piece of Cortés cutlery?" my boss asked. "Is it your intent to … overpower a guard and take it?"

"Of course not," Benito said without making eye contact. "If we do it my way, they'll never even know it's missing."

Then there was a sound. We turned, and the old guard was walking back toward us.

"Lo siento," he said. "I ask my supervisor, he say no. We have swords that go to ceremony tomorrow at Expo. Sí?"

"Yes, of course, thank you for checking my good man," Mister Carter said. "Now then, you also serve as the de facto librarian for this section?"

The old guard shrugged his shoulders.

"We're on the hunt for whatever you may have here from, or about, Diego de Landa."

"Quién es ese?"

"A New World friar," Mister Carter explained. "The diocese of Mani, in the Yucatán."

The old guard had no idea what he was talking about. Doctor Morley had to step in, speaking in Spanish and directing the guard to the files on the Izamel diocese, not Mani. Now the guard nodded and went away again.

"I must see the other hallway," Benito announced. He, Musa and Veronica then walked around the corner to scope out the other upstairs corridors.

"And I must take a rest," Mister Carter said, plopping his extensive fanny into the nearest chair.

Doctor Morley and I looked at each other. The thought occurred to me that there was no perfect time for me to quit, but this was as good a time as any. I started to open my mouth, but just as I did he put a finger to his lips:

"Shhh," he whispered. "Let's walk this way."

He turned and walked back the way we had come in. I followed and came up beside him. We rounded the corner and were alone. I started to open my mouth again ... and then Doctor Morley said:

"Wendy, I've always lived under the belief that when you start a project you should see it through to the end ...,"

At this point I had not said a word about leaving.

"... But there come times when one's inner compass must take priority over owns' professional obligations ...,"

Had he read my mind? Did he know I was going to quit all along?

"Wendy ... I have been growing increasingly uncomfortable with the work we're doing and who we're doing it with ...,"

No, he had not read my mind. He continued:

"... My professional reputation is too valuable to be sucked through this looking glass. I can no longer be associated with Benito, or Veronica for that matter. I'm going to tell them that my involvement in these matters will soon be ending."

"You mean ... you're going to *quit*?" I asked.

"I hate that word, but yes, I'm quitting," he explained. "I'm not sure when. I'm somewhat curious what we're going to find here. But today or tomorrow, I'm going to inform them. Then you and I can enjoy the rest of the trip."

"But … won't Veronica be mad?"

"Yes. And there will be repercussions. I've been going through those in my head. I'm sure once the Institute understands the extent of what I was asked to do, they'll see I had no choice."

My inner self was debating whether I should go ahead and do my own quitting, right now. Then, out of my mouth, sprang:

"Why don't you do it right now?" which was a question for me, not my boss.

"You're right, Wendy. I should do it right now," he answered. "But, like I said, I'm a wee bit curious about what records are here … and what this blasted sword is all about."

***

Soon the guard returned and our group reunited to see what he had found.

He pulled out a list he had made of boxes that might be of interest; Doctor Morley indicated which two of them we wanted to see. Then we gathered around a long table and again dove into old clerical documents.

The first thing of interest we found was a floor plan for some temple.

"Well, well. I think this may be the lost plans for the San Francisco temple in Campeche," Doctor Morley said. "And here, this writing style ... once again, I suspect Chi did this."

"The scribe did architectural drawings too?" Mister Carter asked.

"He did whatever de Landa asked of him," my boss answered.

Next, in a large file labelled *Evidencia*, we found letters from de Landa's inquest:

"This one goes back to his early days, coming upon a Mayan boy about to be sacrificed," Doctor Morley said, reading one of the letters. "He argued the practice was widespread. The more idols and skulls he found, the angrier he became."

"Well, human sacrifice isn't very Christian, is it?" Mister Carter said.

"And here, it talks about the Inquisition at Mani and the auto de fé," Doctor Morley went on. "This letter says de Landa would have those that failed to repent hung from a garrucha ... that's a type of hoist. They would tie heavy rocks to their feet, whip them and then throw hot wax on their bloodied bodies."

"That's isn't very Christian either," Mister Carter repeated.

"Didn't the Church punish de Landa for his actions?" I asked.

"No. They sent him back to Mexico, named him Bishop of Yucatán," Doctor Morley answered. "Here's a lovely description from the firestarter himself: *We found a large number of books and, as they contained nothing but superstition and lies of the devil, we burned them all, which the Maya regretted to an amazing degree, and which caused them much affliction.*

"And listen to this fellow's description: *With the suspicion of this idolatry, they collected all the books and ancient writings, which the Indians had and in order to erase all the danger and memory of the ancient rites, as many as they were able to find were burned publicly on the day of the auto-de-fé and at the same time with this were destroyed the history of their antiquities.*"

Now Benito, who had been listening without much interest, announced:

"This is a waste of time. We have an operation to prepare for," and he and Musa walked away.

Veronica stayed, moving closer to Doctor Morley once Benito had left. It was about one minute after that we came upon an old, stich-bound notebook. My boss began to turn the pages. Suddenly, he grew excited and unable to form a sentence:

"What is this? Is this? It can't be. Can it? The writing, though. Oh! The glyphs! It is!"

"Tell us, man!" Mister Carter commanded.

"I think it's some of de Landa's notes regarding his book, *Relación de las Cosas de Yucatán*! Yes, it is, it is! That's the book that Brasseur found in Madrid, remember? What a find!"

"I thought you hated de Landa," Veronica sneered.

"Oh, I do, I do," Doctor Morley answered. "But his early efforts helped us decipher some of the Mayan glyphs. In that sense, he was both a destroyer of Mayan knowledge and one of the few preservers of it. Here, look … this is a page with Spanish words, along with their corresponding Mayan symbols."

We all huddled over to view the page.

"These glyphs would have been made by one of his scribes, presumably Chi. Again, he was de Landa's 'Boy Friday,' if you will."

Toward the bottom of the page I noticed, toward one corner, a series of sloppy glyphs. Next to them were Spanish words that looked like they had been scrawled in haste, then crossed through. I pointed them out to Doctor Morley, who proceeded to take out his tiny magnifying glass for a closer look:

"Let's see ... again, this looks to be the handiwork of Chi ... the writing is tough, but I know some of it ... it says: *I. Do. Not. Want. To.*"

"Do not want to ... do what?" Mister Carter asked.

"I don't have the foggiest idea. *I do not want to*? What a strange thing to translate."

Then I could hear both Doctor Morley's and Mister Carter's brain mechanisms firing. After a bit my boss looked to the Egyptologist, a curious look on his face, and announced:

"Diego de Landa wanted Chi to do something ... but for whatever reason, the scribe didn't want to do it."

Doctor Morley continued combing through the documents. We found pages of inventories from missions and convents throughout eastern Mexico, from the Yucatán to Chiapas and Tabasco. There were inventories of people, too, organized by village and tribe, much like we had seen at Escorial. There were general updates from

Spanish priests in Mexico to Spanish priests in Spain, along with countless administrative documents. It all became dreadfully dull.

Then, Doctor Morley pulled out one last surprise:

"Well, lookie here … another map of Mani," he said. "Howard, this looks quite similar to the one you pilfered from Escorial, does it not?"

"It does indeed, Sylvanus. Like salt to pepper."

"This one seems incomplete, though … almost as if it were a draft or something," Doctor Morley went on. "It looks like some things have been erased … and this line here was redrawn."

"A preparatory work," Mister Carter declared. "Our man Chi was honing his map-making skills. Here, let me take a closer look. I'm quite familiar with my copy."

"Don't steal this one," Doctor Morley warned.

"I wouldn't think of it," Mister Carter replied.

So Doctor Morley passed this newest map to Mister Carter. But just as the Mayanologist handed the ancient document over, the Egyptologist expressed sudden alarm.

"Great ghosts of Gibraltar, man! Look at the size of that squirrel!" he said, pointing out a nearby window.

And Doctor Morley fell for it. But I didn't, so only I witnessed Mister Carter slipping this latest prize into his pocket.

25

THE KING AND THE CONQUISTADORS

It was the day that King Alfonso and his family were coming to the Expo. The gates were mobbed and security was tight. There was an intimidating line of soldiers before the gates, then once through the gates you had to be patted down by other, meaner soldiers. There were still more soldiers positioned throughout the grounds.

The tight security didn't deter those that still supported their king from coming out. There was an astonishing number of white-haired gentlemen in their Sunday finest. There were little old ladies carrying tiny Spanish flags, holding hands to keep close in the crowd. There were overstimulated children, determined dads and exhausted mothers.

I had never seen a monarch before, at least not a living one. As the massive crowd moved toward the Plaza of the Conquistadors, the excitement began to wash over me, too.

Benito was growing agitated. He wanted us all to push through the crowd to find a better viewing location for the sword ceremony. When Mister Carter said he couldn't and wouldn't do that, Benito got snippy and declared he was going ahead. He insisted someone come with him, but nobody volunteered.

"I'll remind you of our objective. We're not here to watch the show," he snarled before leaving.

The rest of us—including Musa and the she-devil—made our way into the Plaza. We wove through the crowd until we found a workable viewing spot near the central fountain, which had been turned off for the occasion.

I had walked through the Plaza a day earlier but I hadn't taken the time to inspect the various statues that dotted the space. I asked my boss to identify them.

"That big one is Columbus, of course … then over there is Balboa," Doctor Morley said. "That must be Pizarro over there. Not sure what those two over toward the other pavilion are. Oh, and there's Cortés, of course."

I turned to look at the Cortés statue. Even from a distance of a hundred feet or so I could tell it wasn't a good likeness. The conqueror looked bored, with vacant eyes and a nondescript sword.

Veronica pointed out two other statues, both of naked men lounging. "And who are these exhibitionists?" she asked.

Doctor Morley peered over at them. "I'm not sure," he said. "Those look almost Roman or Greek. But you know those Spaniards, never missing an opportunity to cram art, religion and conquest into one place."

At that a man in front of us turned around and gave Doctor Morley a nasty glare.

"I'd suggest you keep your commentary to yourself, Sylvanus," Mister Carter whispered.

The Plaza continued to fill to capacity. Then, the ceremony began.

First the Army marched in, wearing their finest dress uniforms. Following them came a long line of military and government officials, many in funny hats. Then there was a line of mayors, not just from Spain but from Central and South America as well.

Everyone took their places. Trumpets trumpeted then King Alfonso and the Queen entered. There was a ridiculous amount of pomp and circumstance, after which the royal couple was led to a shaded gazebo. There was more pomp and circumstance as a portable altar was carried out. A big procession of religious types came next, led by a bishop. He bowed to the King and Queen and then bowed to the altar. Finally, mass began ... and I thought it would never end. What I had hoped would be a two-minute group prayer was instead a thirty-minute endeavor. Much of it was in Latin. By the end I was indeed praying my hardest ... for the conclusion of mass or death, whichever came first.

After that another honor guard was named which included several of the guest mayors. They were escorted out and, a few minutes later, they returned with their ceremonial offerings.

"Cristobal Colon!" came the announcement. Out came a group of men carrying a flag with a Spanish cross, just like the cross on the Santa María's sails.

"Hernando de Soto!" came next, and out came a group with a triangle-shaped banner.

"Sebastian Elcano!" followed, with his honor guard carrying what looked like an old compass.

Then came a book from Balboa and another flag for Pinzón. We were running out of conquistadors.

"Francisco Pizarro!" was announced. His group came in. The lead man was carrying a sword.

"About time," Veronica muttered.

From our vantage point we could see Benito, who was much closer to the temporary altar. He glanced back at us and I could see the hungry look in his eyes. I watched him as he wound through the crowd to improve his vantage point. Then:

"Hernán Cortés!"

The final honor guard came in. A lone mayor was in front. In his hand this mayor-from-somewhere carried a sword.

Out of the corner of my eye I could see Benito. He was craning his neck to get a better look. I wouldn't have been surprised if he had charged the dais and taken the thing, right there and then.

The different honor guards with their various offerings all lined up in front of the altar, in view of King Alfonso. One by one the respective groups would approach the altar. Some words about each of the famous men were spoken. Then the honor guard would present the gift to the bishop, with heads bowed.

That was all well and good, until we got to the final two conquistadors.

When the honor guard for Pizarro came up the announcer went into a long spiel about Panama and Peru. Then there was an odd explanation about how the delegation needs to make an offering in case anything the conquistador did was sinful. The lead mayor of the group then laid Pizarro's sword in front of the bishop.

"What the hell?" I heard Doctor Morley mutter. "They're apologizing … to the *church?*"

Then came the Cortés delegation. As they approached the altar I scanned the crowd, looking for Benito. He had found his way to the very front, not more than twenty feet from the action.

Once again, the announcer talked about the conquistador's legacy, this time about Mexico and Central America. Then, like Pizarro, there was a big wind-up about why the offering was being made: in case the word of the big guy upstairs had been violated. Doctor Morley was unable to keep his mouth shut at that:

"Hmph. How about they apologize to the cultures they tried to extinguish?"

Which caused the man in front of us to spin around again and deliver another nasty look.

***

When the ceremony ended there was a twenty-minute de-procession. The King and Queen went out first, then all the mayors and politicians, then the priests and the bishops. Then each of the uniformed squads had to do their little spins and kicks.

"He's moving, let's go," Veronica said.

Benito had worked his way around to the outside of the departing waves. He was snaking toward the area where the ceremony participants were gathering.

We moved in the same direction as Benito. Then, reunited, we walked together, all of us keeping an eye on one man: the mayor holding the sword of Cortés.

It was clear the bespectacled mayor didn't know what to do with the ancient weapon. He looked around, being careful to keep the tip down. Then the mayor with the Pizarro sword came up and joined him. They both looked around and shrugged their shoulders.

"Chrissakes! They're searching for someone to give them too," Benito declared. "I'm going in."

And before any of us could say a word, Benito slinked his way past a few military types and headed straight for the two sword-holding mayors. The rest of us held our breath.

"My word. Is he simply going to … ask for it?" Mister Carter asked.

And that appeared to be the case. But just as Benito came within ten feet, a man in uniform approached the mayors, greeted them and took possession of both swords.

Benito froze, turning around to give us a can-you-believe-my-luck look. Had he arrived thirty seconds earlier, he would have had his damn sword.

So then we had to follow this man in uniform, who I dubbed the Army Man. He was carrying one sword in each hand: the sword of Pizarro in his left, the sword of Cortés in his right. He began to walk in the direction of the gates. Onlookers took note of the big blades and pointed and steered clear. A child with a play sword from the souvenir shop made a pretend thrust, which made our Army Man play-scamper away. Then he strutted and smiled and preened as he made his way toward the gates.

Out on the sidewalk the Army Man spotted someone he knew. They stopped and talked, this new man gesturing toward the swords. Then the Army Man handed one of the swords—the Cortés one, I believe—to this new man. In return, the new man pulled out a pack of cigarettes and shook one out for the Army Man. As the Army Man lit his smoke and then enjoyed it, his friend made little jabs and thrusts with the sword on the street.

We were all watching this from about thirty yards away.

"This is torture," Benito snarled. I didn't doubt him.

When the Army Man was done with his smoke he tossed his butt in the street. Then, he wielded the sword of Pizarro and struck a ridiculous fencing pose. His friend then made a similarly stupid pose, then the two of them starting to jig back and forth, play-fighting. At first they tried to not let the blades touch, then they gave up on that.

CLINK! CLINK-CLINK!

A few Expo-goers had stopped to admire the dueling dolts.

CLINK-CLINK! CLINK!

And as we watched the swords of two conquistadors clank, I heard Benito say:

"I want to kill both of these idiots."

When the swordfight of the simpletons ended, the sword of Cortés was handed back to our Army Man. The two knuckleheads said their good-byes, then we followed the Army Man down the next block. He stuck to the main avenue. Once again, folks in front of him steered clear when they saw the two swords he was carrying.

We followed him all the way to the Archive. The Army Man walked up to the closed front doors. Unable to knock because of his weaponry, he kicked one of the doors with his feet. A moment later someone cracked a door for him.

The Army Man disappeared inside, reappearing soon after without either sword.

"Happy?" Mister Carter said to Benito.

"Sí, Señor Carter. I would not have us do what we need to do without knowing the sword was here."

"They don't seem to treat it with much care," Mister Carter observed. "Hell, they don't even have a sheath. Absurd."

"It suggests it will not be missed when we take it," Benito replied.

"It also shows you'll need a blanket or something, lest you find yourself brandishing a sword on the streets of Seville."

"An excellent point, Señor Carter."

At that Doctor Morley cleared his throat. We were still on the sidewalk, but we all turned to face him.

"I think this is as good a time as any," my boss began. "Veronica, Howard, Señor Barataria … the time has come for us to part ways. Seville will mark the end of this expedition for Wendy and myself."

"Part ways?" Veronica responded, in seeming disbelief. "Part ways with … me? Nonsense, Sylvanus. You know you can't do that …,"

"I can, Veronica, and I am," my boss said, holding firm. "I'm fully aware such a move will not meet with your approval. But my decision does not require your consent. I cannot—physically or mentally or logistically—continue on this present course."

"Unacceptable," Veronica growled. "We *need* you."

"No, you need someone that can devote all their time to a project that has no end in sight. That cannot be me, Veronica, you know that," he continued. "Howard, I apologize if this inconveniences you in any way. You'll be a better lead on this, I'm sure."

"A professional decision. No offense taken, Sylvanus," Mister Carter replied, which was nice.

Veronica was having none of it.

"Sylvanus, we have made plans around you. Why, Benito's plan *requires* you. And we need you to inspect the sword," she pleaded.

"The sword is a red herring, Veronica," Doctor Morley said.

"No," Benito jumped in. "The sword is the answer, Señor Morley. And Miss Shetty is correct: my plan requires all of us."

"I told you, I want nothing to do with stealing that sword," my boss repeated.

"Then you shall be a lookout only, while I go in and take it unnoticed," Benito said. "After all is done, you can see it for yourself ... and then you will believe."

"I doubt that. As I said, I'm done. Let's go, Wendy."

"Come on, man, be on lookout," Mister Carter jumped in. "That's all I'm doing. Be a sport, Sylvanus. Help us get this damn thing so we can move on."

Doctor Morley looked over their faces. I was sure he was about to dress them all down. Instead, he sighed and said:

"Well ... I suppose being on lookout is alright. That way I'm not technically stealing anything."

They all smiled at him. But Doctor Morley wasn't smiling.

"But that's going to be it. For now, I'm going back to my room," my boss said, ending the conversation. "My remarks are tomorrow. I'm sure you've all forgotten, but I do have other work to attend to here."

And then he turned heel and walked away, me scurrying after him.

He was upset. Not ugly-crying upset, but silent-brooding upset. I asked him if he wanted to talk, he said no.

I knew he must be upset about deserting the search for the treasure. But I sensed he was also upset by the Expo itself, and what he had seen at the Mexican Pavilion. I had a hunch he might do something bold about that, too.

26

DOCTOR MORLEY'S ANGRY SPEECH

My boss was not a happy man.

He sat at the breakfast table and ignored the plate of food in front of him. He was staring at his notes for his presentation.

I was quiet as a mouse, as I had been for the entire morning. But he was sighing and huffing and shaking his head as he prepared himself. My curiosity was killing me:

"A penny for your thoughts," I said.

He looked over his glasses at me and raised an eyebrow.

"I'm not that cheap," he replied.

"A dime, then."

"American? I don't trust the peseta."

I nodded. He set his pencil down and then took his glasses off. He pinched his temples and then blinked his eyes a few times.

"Frustrated, I suppose," he said. "Not a fan of what's happening here. I suppose you knew that already."

I nodded.

"I wish I could tell our hosts what I honestly think of their Expo," he continued, leaning in and giving me a knowing look. "All that revisionist crap yesterday made me sick to my stomach. It's as if the empire is alive and well."

"Don't say that."

"Why not? That's what they're saying, isn't it?"

"But they're the hosts. You're an invited guest."

"I know, I know," he said. "But someone should say it. It needs to be said. Have you heard anyone in Seville mention the …. the … *massacres* committed by men like Cortés and Pizarro? All in the name of God and kings?"

"Uh … no."

"Have you heard any talk about … about … respecting the self-determination of the peoples they encountered? Or recognition of the revolts and revolutions on their watch?"

"Uh … no again," I replied.

He stabbed at a piece of ham, decided against it and started to play with his eggs.

"How long do you have?" I asked.

"They told me fifteen minutes. I have an hour's worth of materials here."

"That's good, right?"

"I suppose. I'm going to just talk about excavations at Chichen Itza and Uxmal and Palenque and be done with it."

"Perfect," I said, trying to be agreeable. "Will there be questions?"

"Questions? No, not with all those dignitaries there."

"Have you seen any of the others?" I asked.

"You mean our former fellow conspirators? No," he answered. "We'll see them tonight for our little moonlit opera. Then we'll be free of them."

"Any regrets about yesterday?"

"None," he replied. "Felt good to quit."

Oh, how I wanted to tell him right then and there. But his speech was only hours away. I would tell him after.

***

It was busy Saturday morning at the Exposition. The weekend throngs were pouring in. It seemed like every street vendor in Seville had been allowed to set up along the main pathway, which added to the congestion. It took us at least fifteen minutes to get from the gates to the Mexican Pavilion, Doctor Morley's agitation rising correspondingly.

At the entrance to the Pavilion, Doctor Morley was greeted by a tall uniformed Spaniard. That man led him over to a larger group, and everyone shook hands and then they all posed for photographs. They idled about for a bit then the tall uniformed man led them all inside. I followed along. They posed for more pictures in the central courtyard, Doctor Morley front and center. Then they proceeded into the wing that a few days ago had held an agricultural display. The machinery and whatnot had been pushed to the walls and a hundred or more chairs set out, creating an impromptu lecture room.

The dignitaries made for a makeshift dais near the front of the room. Most of the folding chairs were taken, so I found a spot against the back wall where I could stand. The room was more crowded than I expected it to be. As dignitaries made their way through the room to the dais a few people applauded. But they were a minority; it seemed like a serious, reserved audience.

There was some sorting-out of speakers on the dais, then the tall uniformed man kicked things off. He did a lot of thanking and recognizing. He thanked King Alfonso and Primo Rivera and Seville and everyone who made everything possible. He recognized the dignitaries, all of them, and introduced them one-by-one. Following each introduction there was a round of polite applause.

As this was going on, I glanced over and noticed that Benito and Veronica had arrived. They were standing in the rear of the room, like me, but farther off to one side. Veronica saw me and gave me a bitchy nod and I gave her a bitchy nod back. Benito's attention was on the dais. I didn't see Musa anywhere.

The tall uniformed man then turned over the podium to a shorter uniformed man. He, in turn, turned over the podium to an Ambassador. The Ambassador then talked for far too long about topics too numerous to detail.

Finally, it came time for Doctor Morley to speak. I'm not sure if anyone else was excited to hear him, but I sure was.

When he arrived at the podium he paused and looked out over the crowd. He took a sip of water. He looked nervous. He adjusted his glasses, cleared his throat and began:

"Thank you. It's good to be here."

"Gracias. Es bueno estar aqui," came the translation.

Doctor Morley glanced over at his translator and gave him a nervous smile.

"To begin, uh, to begin I'd like to acknowledge all those individuals and entities that have made this Exposition possible. I appreciate how much work this has been."

Then he waited for the translation.

"And, of course, my sincere appreciation to the city of Seville. I'm sure these pavilions will serve as a source of wonder in this community for generations to come."

The translator did his thing.

"Um ... it's been surprisingly difficult for me to decide what to talk about today. At first, I thought I should update you on the Carnegie Institution's work in Central and South America. But there's exhibits here that can fill you in on that ...,"

He waited for the translation again.

"Then I thought, well, perhaps I will talk about the Yucatán. My Yucatán, a place that is very dear to me. I thought I might discuss what the situation is there now, hundreds of years after the first encounters between the Maya and the Spanish. It's different from modern-day Seville, I can tell you that."

He meant the last sentence as a joke and chuckled at it himself. But the joke didn't translate well and nobody else laughed.

"But, uh, but finally I decided that I didn't want to talk about the Yucatán. I don't even want to talk about the Maya, even though the Mayan culture is my expertise. No, today I want to talk about ... the Aztecs."

At that moment I looked back to where Benito and Veronica were standing. They exchanged a curious look.

They were even more surprised when Doctor Morley delivered his next line:

"Specifically … I'd like to talk about Cortés, Moctezuma … and the Night of Sorrows."

Now Benito and Veronica flared their nostrils and shared a shocked look. In unison, they both turned toward the podium and gave Doctor Morley death-stares as he waited for the translation. Doctor Morley, for his part, never cast his eyes in their direction.

"While much is made of the first meeting between Cortés and Moctezuma, it is their last meeting—on the day before that famous, fateful night—that better represents the change that had, by then, occurred.

"A battered Moctezuma—tortured by soldiers, then stoned by his own people—lay dying in his palace. The great Aztec king made Cortés promise that he would look after Moctezuma's daughters. Of course, Cortés would go on to do just that … marrying one of them soon thereafter."

After the translation there were a few giggles from the crowd.

"And then … as hallucinations gripped Moctezuma, making him think his own blood was the water of his daily bath … Cortés leaned down, said good-bye and …,"

There was dramatic pause. He looked out over the crowd and took a breath.

"… *Then your brave Hernán Cortés murdered this already-dying king with his bare hands.*"

And Doctor Morley said the last part of that with a sneer, two hands gripping the podium.

The translator translated ... and by the time he finished there was outrage in the room. From every direction came shouts and even a few boos. My boss kept going:

"And tell me, what respect did they show Moctezuma? How did they treat this man who, in this building at least, is represented as a happy hotelier? I'll tell you: your soldiers tossed his dead body over the walls of his palace and into the street!"

Now there were louder boos. Some people had stood up, others were walking out. It was thrilling. I was beaming from ear-to-ear, so proud of my boss.

"Boo and hiss all you want, my friends ... you know the rest. Cortés and his army loaded up all the gold and silver they had acquired, all the idols and statues they had stolen, anything of value that wasn't nailed down. They loaded their carts and their wagons and made for the causeways, hoping to abscond during the night with the greatest treasure of the New World."

Now I swung around to see if I could see Benito or Veronica. I could not, at first. Then, toward the front, I saw Benito, trying to worm his way closer.

"The story should be taught here as it is taught in Mexico," my boss continued. "At midnight, this supposedly honorable man and his supposedly righteous army tried to sneak out of town. Then, when the Aztecs rowed out to surprise the Spaniards on the causeways, the massacre was on. And it was just that: a massacre!"

"Boo!", "Get off the Stage!", "Apaga el microfono!" came from the crowd.

"The battles beget the fires ... and when Tenochtitlan burned that night, the hopes and dreams of an entire race of people went up in flames," Doctor Morley went on, still angry. "So when I came in here and saw the lies and half-truths and misrepresentations ... it made me want to *vomit.*"

The translator actually translated that last part. Despite the commotion, the speech continued:

"You're all maintaining a myth that the Spanish influence on the peoples of the New World had nothing but positive outcomes. If any of you saw fit to come to the Yucatán, I'd show you that's not the case.

"There was a wondrous, thriving world in Mesoamerica before the arrival of the conquistadors. They had governments, schools, books, road systems, water systems. Their people had a connection to their earth that we, despite our cultured European blood, cannot comprehend.

"That world ended on the Night of Sorrows. What was left behind was not some new race, the product of Cortés and his locally-grown consort. What was left behind was death and destruction, the end of one civilization at the hands of a mightier one."

"Boo!", "Comunista!", "Cortés es un heroe!" came more shouts.

"Hero, my ass," Doctor Morley shot back. "I'll end with this: when Hernán Cortés sat under a tree and cried, watching what was left of Tenochtitlan burn ... who do you think he was crying for? Was it the Aztecs, whose king he had murdered? No. Was it the men of his army that had met their fate in the muck? Perhaps.

"But I believe the great conquistador was crying for *you*," Doctor Morley said, now pointing out over the crowd. "He was crying for a people too blinded by their greatness to see the folly of their ways."

That prompted the strongest outpouring of boos yet. It carried on for a full minute. Oddly enough, during that minute I scanned the crowd and found a few people clapping. I also spied Benito, waiting for Doctor Morley to get off the stage.

My boss didn't mind the outrage. He stood there and took it all in, wearing a curious smile. Then he tapped his notecards on the podium, leaned into the microphone and said:

"Gracias. Thank you for your time and for the invitation."

Then he walked off the dais with his head held high.

***

It was chaos after that. Everyone was upset. Doctor Morley paid it no heed, marching through the crowd and straight out the door. I chased after him. Benito and Veronica were not far behind.

Doctor Morley walked away from the Pavilion and toward a small fountain. There he stopped and took a deep breath. He turned around and saw me.

"I need a cigarette," were his first words. I obeyed.

Then, a few seconds later, Benito came storming toward him:

"La Leyenda Negra!" Benito barked. "How dare you impugn my people with your 'black legend' lies! You should be ashamed of yourself!"

"I'm ashamed of nothing," Doctor Morley replied. "And I didn't impugn your people ... I impugned your ancestors."

"Anti-Iberian propaganda," Benito seethed, red in the face. "The crown and its pursuits were always noble."

"Please. I know more about your crowned shams than you do," Doctor Morley fired back.

"And ... you mention the *treasure*?" Benito went on, quieter. "You play with fire, amigo."

As he said that the Spaniard brought his walking stick up, thrusting its parrot-head handle toward my boss.

"Remove your little bird from my face, please," Doctor Morley deadpanned. "And I'll thank you for not questioning what I do in my primary profession. I said nothing that affects you or your pursuits."

"You insulted an entire nation," Benito snarled. "You Americans ... you throw the stones, sí? But you should look in the mirror. You not without sin, no?"

Doctor Morley took a deep drag in, then blew the smoke right into Benito's face and said:

"That's a topic for a different speech, I guess."

***

Later that afternoon, I quit my job.

It happened at the Inn, in Doctor Morley's room. I asked to speak with him and, before I could even start, I began to mist up.

"I ... I'm sorry," I said between sniffles. "But ... I think it's time for me to make a change. I ... I'm not going back to the Yucatán."

"Not going back?" he said. "You mean you're ... quitting?"

I nodded.

"Whatever are you going to do? Where will you go?"

"I'm going to go to Paris," I replied. "I know people there, suddenly."

"Not imaginary people, I hope?"

"No. Real ones."

"My goodness," Doctor Morley said. "Well ... I can't say I'm all that surprised."

I stopped sniffling. "You're ... you're not?"

"Of course not," he said. "Doesn't take a brain surgeon to see you're not happy with your current path. I can't begrudge you for that, been there myself."

"It's not that I'm unhappy," I explained, though I was. "It's that I feel there's something else calling me."

He nodded. "And ... is this an impulsive decision, or a rational one?"

"A little of both, I expect."

That made him laugh. He leaned back and exhaled. I felt relieved that the hardest part was over.

"You'll probably need a work visa," he said.

"I'm going to check with the consulate when I arrive."

"Do these friends have job leads for you?"

I nodded.

"Well, seems like you've been putting some thought into this," he said. "And … will you be joining me in the last hurrah tonight?"

"I suppose I'm curious enough to participate," I conceded.

"Good. I guess this will be our final appearance in this odd little drama," he said.

"I'm surprised you agreed to go."

"Between you and me, there's a method to my madness," Doctor Morley said with a half-grin.

"I was hoping that was the case. Care to let me in?"

"Well, since you just quit I shouldn't," he teased. "But if there *is* something to that sword, or something to those maps, I need to misdirect them."

"Misdirect them!" I replied, thrilled at his spy-like move.

"Indeed. If the treasure of Tenochtitlan does indeed exist, I'd rather it stay hidden than fall into the wrong hands yet again."

27

LOS LADRONES DE SEVILLA

At a half-hour before midnight, the five conspirators—Doctor Morley and myself included—set out for the Archive of the Indies. Our mission: to steal the sword of the second Martín Cortés.

We left the inn in two separate groups, so as not to draw too much attention. Benito, Doctor Morley and Musa went first. A few minutes later a second group with Mister Carter, Veronica and myself departed.

We did our best to avoid the busier streets and ducked our heads as we passed by cafés and cantinas. We cut through a narrow alleyway and came onto a broader avenue. There, before us, rose the Cathedral of Seville and La Giralda, its iconic bell tower.

The towering minaret overlooked a well-lit square, in the center of which sat the Archive. My group looped around the backside of the Cathedral. In a dark alcove on the north side of the massive church we met up with Benito, Veronica and Musa.

Benito walked us through the plan, yet again:

There were two guards. On the hour, every hour, one of the two guards would come out of the Archive's lone entrance to patrol the perimeter. He would close the door behind him then walk clockwise around the entire building, a journey that took him about four minutes. On a prior night's surveillance Benito had noticed the guard would close the door behind him … but not lock it.

The moment the guard began his patrol, Veronica would spring into action. She would strut her stuff across the square and intercept him on the back side of the building. There, she would flirt shamelessly. She would ask the guard if he wanted to share a cigarette with her. Her assignment was to keep him distracted for as long as possible.

As the she-devil worked her magic, Benito and I would make a run for the door. If it was unlocked, we would walk right in; figuring we could act like drunk tourists if caught. If the door was locked, Benito would spend no more than sixty seconds trying to jimmy it open.

Inside the Archive the plan would be more free-flowing. If we got lucky and the inside guard didn't see us enter, we should be able to wind our way up to the room where the sword was kept. We would go there, jimmy that second lock, take the sword and make our escape.

I asked Benito what would happen if this second guard found us inside:

"That is why, after we go in, you must stay a good distance away from me," he answered. "I will remain hidden. Let him see you, tell him you believed the Archive was still open. Then keep talking for as long as it takes for me to complete the task."

Doctor Morley has been listening and shaking his head.

"A lot could go wrong here," my boss said, then looked to Musa. "What's he doing?"

"My man-servant will position himself along our escape route," Benito said. "He will take care of anyone that comes after us."

"Take care of?" Doctor Morley repeated. "As in … hurt them?"

"No, no, of course not," Benito insisted. "Nobody will be hurt."

Mister Carter was to be on lookout at our present spot near the Cathedral. Doctor Morley would be on lookout on the far side. They were instructed to whistle—then shout—if anyone looked to be approaching.

Everyone scurried to their places. I was nestled in the shadows with Benito, our eyes on the doors. The moon was perfectly framed behind the Cathedral's tower, adding a romantic glow to our treachery.

Then, from across the city, bells began to toll. Midnight had arrived. It was time.

In my mind, a song from a locally-inspired opera began to play.

No, not the one by Bizet. The one by Rossini, about a barber.

***

The door opened triumphantly. Dim light cast out from inside the Archive.

Into this dim light stepped a figure. From his cap I knew it was a guard. He paused in the door frame.

In perfect time to my head-music, the guard stretched his arms high over his head.

Next he did a little back-bend, put his hands to his hips and looked out over the square. He then turned back to the door he had come through and closed it … but only partway. We could still see a sliver of light between the door and frame.

Benito and I shared a look: *the guard had left the door open.*

The guard came down the steps and fumbled in his pocket, pulling something out. Then, a beam shot forth. He had a flashlight. The battery in it must have been loose, as he shook the thing up and down. For a few seconds he was in perfect time, conducting the strings in my head.

He kept fiddling with his flashlight and began to walk, to his right and in the direction of the Cathedral. He shone his light against the first floor of the Archive, then up and across the second floor windows.

The guard neared the first corner. Veronica appeared.

She came from a corner of the Cathedral. She was wearing a black, tight-fitting dress and a black, silly hat. Despite her horrendous headgear she looked gorgeous and instantly available.

The she-devil strutted her slinky fanny toward the Archive, on a path to intercept the guard. She was jiggling her boobs and swinging her hips. She paused, in view of him, spinning around a bit and fluffing her hind-feathers up. She looked like a hen in heat.

And oh, he saw her. The guard directed his flashlight beam in her direction. The she-devil paraded and preened in his spotlight. She smiled seductively, then pantomimed that she needed a cigarette. Without words the guard nodded, reached in his shirt pocket and pulled out a pack of smokes. He offered them to her.

Veronica reached down and plucked out a cigarette. The guard followed suit. He put the pack of smokes back in his pocket and found his matches. Then, with great flourish, he struck the match, lit the she-devil's cigarette and then his own.

At the flame, Benito stood up. My inner orchestra struck a dramatic note. It was our turn.

The guard distracted, Benito and I made our move to cross the open square and reach the door. Veronica saw us moving, positioning herself so as to keep the guard's attention pointed away in the opposite direction. We crept a little, then ran a little, then stopped, then crept a little more. It was all going according to plan.

Until it wasn't. Within twenty feet of us reaching the door, it suddenly swung open, the light again spilling into the square. Now out stepped a second guard. From somewhere, either Mister Carter or Doctor Morley whistled.

In a heartbeat, Benito spun around. I did the same. We walked away from the entrance, turning to go along another side of the Archive.

This second guard would have no reason to suspect we were up to no good. But when we rounded the corner, Benito stopped and, keeping close to the building, looked back. I did the same.

Guard number-two was looking over at guard number-one. Guard number-one continued his mating dance with the she-devil. Guard number-two shook his head, came down the steps … and began to walk in our direction. Unlike the first, this one carried no flashlight and appeared to be out for a stroll, not on patrol.

Benito and I shared a panicked look. Then we turned tail and walked, double-time, toward the backside of the Archive. Benito must have thought there would be a place to hide along the back wall, but there were no alcoves or bushes large enough to conceal us.

We were stuck. If we were to keep going around the building, we would come into view of the first guard. If we were to run away, across the deserted square, we would certainly be seen. Our minds swirled.

Then Benito, most unexpectedly and most inappropriately, grabbed me around the waist with both hands, as if he were going to kiss or embrace me. Which wasn't gonna happen. I pushed him away, even though I knew his goal was theatrical romance, not the real thing. But I had my standards and I wasn't going to share any further embraces with him, fictional or otherwise.

I spun away and could see the frustration on his face. But I had a brilliant idea.

I smoothed my skirt, turned and walked back in the direction we came from. I rounded the corner and came face-to-face with the second guard.

I smiled, trying to look every bit as available and trampy as Veronica. I acted surprised to see him … but very pleased. I played tipsy and gave him a big, flirty smile. Then I put two fingers to my lips, the universal symbol for needing a smoke.

The second guard's eyebrows shot up. He did indeed have a smoke … and he went so far as to light it and then hand it to me. I nodded my gracias then looped my arm under his. The young man looked delighted by his sudden good fortune.

I accompanied my lucky watchman back toward the rear corner of the building. At just the right moment, I used my arm to spin my guard around, an impromptu dance move. Benito, to his credit, saw what I was up to and was able to skip between us and the building, undetected.

Both guards were now occupied, one by Veronica and one by me. I took my guard and led him by the arm along the Archive's back wall. He was saying something to me in Spanish, but I was too distracted to follow so I just laughed. I hoped Benito would work fast.

At that point my guard and I came to the other back corner, opposite the Cathedral. In the shadows I could make out the hulking shadow of Mister Carter. Then, as we followed the sidewall, I spotted Veronica and her guard.

She had her prey wrapped around her finger. They were smoking and giggling and she kept moving to keep his eyes away from the Archive. I laughed louder to my escort, so as to alert the she-devil to our approach.

Sensing the thief inside needed much more time, I stopped. My guard stopped, too. I used a finger to draw him toward me. I grabbed hold of his tie and pulled him in as if I wanted him to kiss me, which I did not. I teased him, turning my head at the last second and playing hard to get.

Veronica had been watching and she did the same, teasing her guard. She snuffed out her smoke then brought both arms up to his shoulders. She plucked his cap off his head and donned it herself. Her guard had the aroused look of a schoolboy who had, at that very second, hit puberty.

A bit of competition then ensued. Veronica continued to tease and tempt her charge; I did the same with mine. We both kept our backs to the Cathedral, to keep the guards looking in the direction we wanted them to.

Soon, though, the two men began to pull away. First to go was Veronica's guard. He took his cap back, bowed to the she-devil and then resumed his patrol. As he passed me and my guard—mine was better-looking, for the record— the two co-workers shared a happy smile. Then, my charge turned away and headed for the front door.

Again I heard whistling, alerting Benito to the guard's approach.

I had to stop him. So I chased after my guard, grabbed him by the elbow and spun him around. As he looked at me, I threw my cigarette to the ground with great gusto. I grabbed his face with both hands and gave him the biggest, wettest kiss of his life.

His arms splayed out in surprise, then came to rest around my waist. Now he was kissing me back and I had no choice but to keep up the ruse. But, out of the corner of my eye, I was watching the entrance. I knew that time was again drawing short: soon the other guard would finish his perimeter patrol.

Then I saw the door of the Archive open, just a touch. A head peeked out to see if the coast was clear, which it was.

Benito Barataria came down the steps. He had the sword swaddled in a blanket and tucked under one arm. At the bottom of the steps, he turned and made for the shadows where we had first hidden.

As he hobbled away, his fake leg never quite in sync with his real one, he tucked his prize further under his arm. At the first decent shadow he stopped and composed himself. I saw him take up his walking stick, which he had been holding but not using. He held the walking stick up to his face, as if he were inspecting it, then he put it down and used it to totter off out of my view.

I untangled myself from my guard. He said something in Spanish about his loins aching for me, but I was done with him. Saying nothing, I gave him one last little peck on the cheek.

I turned and walked away, toward the Cathedral and then down an intersecting street. I could feel the guard watching me go.

The curtain came down on a successful performance. Now, it was time to see what secrets—if any—were hidden in this much-ballyhooed sword.

28

DISAPPOINTMENT AND DISCOVERY

We were certain we had pulled off the clever heist without detection. Nevertheless, we played it safe upon our return, re-entering the inn one-by-one.

I made my way to Benito's room, number twelve, upstairs. I knocked three times. There was a murmur of voices and I heard the door being unlocked. Musa grunted me in.

"Ugh. Bueno," the muscled man grunted to me.

"Thank you. We couldn't have done it without you," I teased, to a blank face.

Veronica and Doctor Morley were already there; Benito was not. A moment after I entered, there was a knock. Mister Carter came in, huffing and puffing.

"He's ... not ... here?" the Egyptologist panted.

We shook our heads. I saw Doctor Morley and Mister Carter exchange a nervous glance. It occurred to me for the first time that perhaps Benito might not join us at all. Instead, maybe he would take his precious cargo and flee. That would have been fine by me ... but soon there was another series of knocks.

Musa opened the door and Benito clumped in. He still had the sword tucked under one arm, rolled up in a dark blanket.

"Come on, come on, let's see it," Mister Carter demanded.

Benito approached the bed and laid down his package, holding the swaddled sword as if it were the baby Jesus. Then he took a deep breath and began to unwrap it. At this point the rest of us were all gathered around the bed, looking down. Doctor Morley was standing next to me.

Benito unwrapped the sword. I caught a glimpse of the handle and then saw the blade and all I could think was:

Holy shit. I had seen this sword before ... or an identical one.

It looked exactly like the sword that we had found at Yaxchilan.

But that wasn't all. This sword also looked very much like the sword I had seen in the portrait of Cortés at the Prado.

I said nothing. But I knew Doctor Morley must have picked up on the striking similarities to the Yaxchilan sword. I cast a nervous look over to my soon-to-be-former boss. He caught my eye and gave me a don't-say-anything look.

Benito picked up the weapon. He had a look of wonder on his face. He pulled the handle close to his face and studied it.

"Come on, man, let us have a look!" Mister Carter said.

"I should be the only one that holds it," Benito replied.

"Don't be an ass. Put it back on the bed," Doctor Morley demanded.

Benito shot my boss a dirty look but took the suggestion and placed the sword back down. Then all of us, Musa included, bent over to get a better look.

The sword was about three feet long. The blade—a straight blade, not curved—was sharp on both sides. I didn't notice any engravings on the metal. Before the handle was a swirling cross-guard, which curved back to help form a knuckle-guard. The grip was all steel, with grooves for a firmer hold. Topping the handle was a grooved iron ball, which held the other end of the knuckle-guard.

"Turn it over," Doctor Morley suggested, and we did. "Ah, look, here's something on the blade."

We all followed his finger. Near the handle, visible through the swirls of the cross-guard, was a mark. Three marks, to be precise. They appeared to be three little crowns.

"The mark of a Toledan swordmaker?" Mister Carter asked.

The rest of us looked to Doctor Morley. Doctor Morley, in turn, looked up to Benito and said:

"Three crowns. That's from the Cortés coat of arms, isn't it?"

"It is, Señor Morley. You do, as the saying goes, know your stuff."

"I saw his coat of arms outside his home in Cuernavaca. Funny how one remembers details like that," Doctor Morley replied. "Alright, I guess that confirms it is indeed from the Cortés family. I don't see any other engravings, though, do you?"

"The handle, Sylvanus," Mister Carter said. "Perhaps that little ball on top screws off."

Doctor Morley lifted the handle up and tried to twist the ball below the hilt. It didn't budge.

"That's solid metal, I think," my boss says. "This all feels like a single expanse of steel, the entire handle all the way to the tip. These guards were welded on, obviously … but the rest seems like one piece."

"Nonsense. Let me see," Benito demanded.

He put his walking stick to the side and took the sword from Doctor Morley. He held it with the tip down, inspecting the little ball near the handle. He picked at it with a fingernail. Then, looking a bit frustrated, he picked at some of the grooves on the grip.

"See? One piece, correct?" Doctor Morley inquired.

Benito didn't answer. He tried to wiggle the knuckle-guard and then the cross-guard. Nothing moved. Then he took the blanket off the bed, wrapped it around the blade so he wouldn't cut himself, and tried to twist the handle. Again, nothing moved.

"Careful, don't break it," Veronica warned.

"Shut your mouth, I won't break anything," Benito barked. "Perhaps the guard slides up or down, no? There must be something in the handle."

"*In* the handle? It's one-hundred-percent steel!" Doctor Morley repeated.

"Sí, that must be the case … here, hold this while I use two hands on the guard," Benito said, sounding more distressed.

He tried pulling up on the cross-guard then pulling out on the knuckle-guard. He tried to wiggle everything once again. Nothing moved.

It was while he was doing this that Doctor Morley noticed something on Benito's sleeve.

"I say … is that blood?"

Benito stopped, glancing down.

"Sí. I cut myself, while retrieving the sword."

"Where?" Doctor Morley asked.

"In the Archive."

"No … where did you cut yourself?"

And at that third question from Doctor Morley, Benito stopped what he was doing and gave my boss a menacing look:

"Under my armpit, señor. I do not appreciate your tone."

"I'm only expressing concern," Doctor Morley went on. "Which armpit?"

Benito, with a look of contempt wrinkling his face, drew a side of his coat back. There was blood staining the side of his shirt.

"Do you need medical attention?" Doctor Morley asked.

"I do not trust doctors," Benito sneered, then returned his gaze to the sword.

During this time Veronica had been somewhat silent. Now, her pacing and dramatic exhales commanded everyone's attention.

"There's nothing here, is there, Benito?" she chided. "There's nothing special about this blade. It's just a Toledan sword stamped with the Cortés crest. That's it."

"Blasphemy. It hold answers that we have yet to uncover," Benito shot back.

"You told me, Benito, that you were *positive* the sword would help us," the she-devil continued. "Instead, it's just another false lead. I swear, none of you men have any idea what you're talking about."

"See here, woman!" Mister Carter jumped in. "Don't drag me down with this. You're the one that brought a team together with no idea how to manage one."

Which made Veronica get right up into Mister Carter's face:

"Well, I never imagined the legendary Howard Carter would need so much goddamn managing."

Then she looked around at each of us with a death stare worthy of Medusa:

"It's over. I've have it with the lot of you," she hissed.

"Hmph. If you're firing us, I'll remind you I already quit," Doctor Morley said. "And so did Wendy."

That was news to the rest of them, I believe ... but nobody gave a hoot. Veronica kept at it:

"Benito, I have a mind to bill you for all our expenses in Seville. Howard, you'll have to find your own way back to London, or Alexandria, or wherever the hell you're going."

"I say, this is all most unprofessional," Mister Carter responded. "And I do think you're being rash about things. Might I suggest we take stock of what we have?"

"We. Have. *Nothing*," Veronica seethed.

"Ah, well, there was a time in the Valley of the Kings when I thought I had nothing," Mister Carter went on. "And Carnarvon and the rest told me to move on, that it was over. But then a worker found ...,"

"Shut the hell up, Howard," the she-devil interjected.

"He's not all wrong, Veronica," Doctor Morley jumped in. "I'll be taking my portfolio with me ... so this is your last chance to view it. This is last call on seeing Wendy's reproduction of the Codex, too."

"Yes, let's get it all out," Mister Carter confirmed. "The maps we found at Escorial and the Archive, too. Perhaps we've missed something."

Veronica sneered but didn't say no. Doctor Morley went to fetch his portfolio. Mister Carter went to fetch his stolen maps. I went to get my notebook, with my copy of the Codex.

Benito, for his part, was still staring at the sword on the bed. He was a stubborn, stubborn man.

***

We reconvened a few minutes later. The sword of the second Martín Cortés was moved off the bed. Doctor Morley began to take items out of his portfolio, including the maps I had 'inhaled' on the Orizaba. As I was thinking back to that fateful voyage, he said:

"Wendy ... you don't have to stay."

I was shocked. "You mean … leave?"

"Yes. I'll take the Codex with me when we're finished. If you want to get on with things, you have my permission to get started."

"You mean … like start a new life?" I said, presuming he was being philosophical.

"No, I meant get a drink or something. Bars and cafés are still open, you know," he went on. "But yes, you can start a new life, too. I'm sure you're ready."

I didn't know what to say. I looked over my once-colleagues. Benito was still fiddling with his precious sword, Musa observing him. Mister Carter had placed his two pilfered land treaty maps next to Doctor Morley's items; he had a serious Sherlock Holmes-like look about him. Then Veronica, smoking by the window, caught me looking at her and gave me a cold glare.

"I'm tempted to go," I told Doctor Morley. "But … I'll stay until you leave."

"Of course," he said. "Thank you."

Then we all gathered around the bed. Benito had his arms crossed in defiance.

"I suppose a good place to start would be the Codex," Doctor Morley said. "This is Wendy's copy. An excellent reproduction … thank you, Wendy. Both she and I have been through my portfolio, page by page, versus the Codex, page by page. Nothing jumped out at us."

My efforts had not been quite that thorough, but nobody needed to hear that.

"I dare say, who was the genesis of this Codex theory?" Mister Carter asked.

"Le Plongeon," Doctor Morley answered. "He's the one that said 'the answer lies within' it."

"Wasn't Le Plongeon amongst your legion of whack-a-doodles?" Mister Carter pressed.

"He was one of them," the Mayanologist said. "Rosny and your man Churchward had similar beliefs."

"And you've combed through the Codex and all your materials?" the Egyptologist went on.

Doctor Morley shook his head. At this point, Mister Carter had hold of the notebook containing my Codex copy; now he handed it to Benito, who still had his arms crossed.

"Would you like to look through this?" Mister Carter asked.

"No," Benito huffed. "It is useless to me."

So Mister Carter took my notebook and tossed it over onto a side table. This damn project—that I had spent weeks on, that had consumed all my free time—had been yanked off the main stage. I knew it would still have value to Doctor Morley, but to see it treated that way felt *wrong*.

"Now, see here, man," Mister Carter went on. "Let's line your older maps up with these land treaty maps of mine. Look for corresponding points or lines."

Benito was growing more frustrated.

"Unless you can find a mark from the Cortés brothers, this is a pointless exercise," he sneered.

"Yes, yes, that would be the three crowns, correct?" Mister Carter said, taking him literally. "That's a good idea. Here, can we get some more light? Let's move that lamp over."

They all huddled even closer around the bed, comparing maps and bickering over things and ignoring me. I stood alone near the back of the room, contemplating. I was debating whether or not it was time for me to make my exit.

"I hate to say it, Howard … but I don't think your maps of Mani are anything, either," Doctor Morley said.

"It pains me to agree with you, Sylvanus … but alas, I'm afraid it's true. Well, they'll look good framed at the house."

Doctor Morley frowned at him. Then Mister Carter took both maps of Mani and reached over to put them on the small table, the same table that held my notebook. He did so, then turned back to the bed. The movement of his massiveness caused a gust of air which sent one of the land treaty maps to the floor.

I bent down and picked it up. I'm not sure if it was the map from Escorial, or the map from the Archive.

I had seen it before, of course. But I had never studied it.

The layout of the map was circular in nature. Inside the circle were small stick-figure churches with little crosses on top. Some of the churches were bigger than others. Lines divided territories up within the circle, with all lines coming to the center and intersecting at one church: Mani.

I stood there, with everyone else ignoring me ... and suddenly I had a thought.

I went to the little table and retrieved my copy of the Codex. I took the notebook over to a bureau and set it down. I flipped it open to the page I was thinking of: page fifty-six, the mostly-blank page with the odd Spanish writing.

I set the land treaty map next to it to compare it to the Codex page. It didn't match up the way I thought it might.

Then, divine inspiration: I turned my notebook a quarter-turn …

And I saw it.

It wasn't the patch with writing, the torn papal bull … no, it was the little scuff marks and doodles on the remainder of the page.

All those stray little marks now seemed to align with the land treaty map. There, near the center of page fifty-six, was a smudge that lined up with Mani. Above that and to the left was what I thought had been a stray scribble … but now I could see it was, to my eye at least, Tipical. Above Mani and to the right was a smudge that had to be Akil. Below, a larger smudge that had to be Dzan or Tikil.

My heart was pounding. I still had not said anything.

"Um … Doctor Morley, could I speak with you?"

He turned around. "Ah, so this is it? Our big farewell?"

"Um … maybe. Could you join me over here?"

He left the other conspirators and came up to the bureau. I had my notebook turned sideways, revealing my page fifty-six, and the land treaty map sitting just below it. I whispered, as low as I could:

"Look here," I said. "If you line up that smudge in the center of the page with Mani on the other map, you'll see that Tipical is here … Akil up here …,"

He saw it right away. "And this is Dzan … and this way over here must be Tekit," he whispered.

He looked up at me with moon-sized eyes. We both swallowed hard, unsure of our next move. It turned out we wouldn't have to think long.

"Why are you whispering?" Benito said, suddenly next to us. "What have you found?"

"Well, we're not sure it's anything," Doctor Morley replied. "We were discussing …,"

"Why is this turned sideways?" Benito went on, pushing me aside. "You found something, no?"

Benito compared my page fifty-six to the map.

"*Santa madre de Cristo,*" he said. "This is … Mani? And this at top, this is Teabo on the land treaty map, no?"

Benito, nostrils flaring, turned to Doctor Morley:

"This is it!" the Spaniard declared. "We need to see the original. Right away."

By now Mister Carter and Veronica had rushed up. They crowded around the bureau and I was, once again, pushed to the cheap seats.

"Remarkable!" Mister Carter said. "To think, everyone dwelled on that Spanish patch up top … but it was hidden in plain sight all along!"

"How accurate is this?" Veronica asked them, then she turned to me. "You did this. How accurate is it?"

"I … I suppose it's pretty good," I said.

"Is it perfect?" she asked.

"Well, nobody's perfect," I answered.

The witch sneered at me and turned back to the others.

"Benito's right. We've got to get back to Madrid," she said.

"The copy's quite adequate, don't you think?" Mister Carter observed.

"She said it's not perfect," Veronica said, to them, not me. "I wonder if there were more lines than she showed. Wendy, were there more lines?"

"I … I don't know."

"She doesn't know," the she-devil repeated to the others. "We can't trust her work."

Despite my pending exit from the story, I didn't appreciate the criticism. Still, I kept mum.

"I agree, Veronica, we have to see the original," Mister Carter said. "Sylvanus, what say you?"

"Me?" Doctor Morley said. "I'm out."

"Out!" Mister Carter repeated, surprised.

Now Doctor Morley made like a worker whose day had ended. He brushed his hands together, then held his palms up … a silent I'm-done-with-this.

"Señor Morley, you cannot leave us now," Benito remarked. "This may be when we need your expertise on the Yucatán the most."

"Oh-ho, Señor Barataria … I thought you considered our old maps to be useless," Doctor Morley teased. "How good that you see paper is often mightier than the sword."

"Is that how that goes?" Mister Carter asked, more to himself.

"Señor Morley, let me repeat: the sword shall prove its importance soon enough. But I must insist you accompany us back to Madrid. Let's view the real thing together, sí?"

"Lo siento, amigo," Doctor Morley said. "Mine and Wendy's involvement in these matters is no more. You seem to have a plan, I suggest you execute it. As for me, I'm going to gather up my portfolio ... and tomorrow I'm going to explore the Exposition. I think it's high time I rode that little train."

I smiled at him. I knew he would enjoy the train, very much.

"But ... you cannot take all of these materials," Benito remarked, looking over the map-strewn bed. "It is ... all we have, no?"

Doctor Morley thought about that. He gave me an apologetic look, then said:

"Very well. Borrow Wendy's copy of the Codex if you must," he said. "Between that and Howard's maps—and your sword, of course—you've got all you need."

I was stunned. He was letting them take *my* work?

The rest of the gang looked at each other.

"I suppose you are right," Benito said. "Gracias. But before you go ... might you walk us through your thoughts on the map's locations?"

"Well ... I suppose that'll be alright," Doctor Morley replied. "Wendy ... are you staying or going?"

"I think it's time for me to go," I said. It was.

"Right-o, go and have a little fun on the town," he said. "We'll meet up sometime tomorrow, alright? Then we can discuss travel plans. Good? Good."

He moved away. Veronica approached.

"Good-byes come sooner than expected," the she-devil said. "Adios, Wendy."

That was it. She turned and walked away. There was no final fight, no me calling her 'Miss Shitty' to her face.

I shook Musa's hand, receiving a grunt in return. Then Benito hobbled forward.

"It seems like only yesterday that we made love," he whispered, seeming serious.

"Again … that wasn't love," I whispered back. "Good luck, Benito."

"And good luck to you," he said, punctuating it with an odd wink before turning away.

Just like that, my participation in the bizarre treasure hunt came to an end.

As I exited the room, it dawned on me that my employment with the Carnegie Institution was also over. I was free to do as I pleased.

Excitement washed over me. I literally jumped for joy in that little hallway. Then I jogged to my room, so I could put on my red dress and hit the town.

29

THE REBELLIOUS BIRD

I put on the Queen Bee's gorgeous dress and fixed my hair back. Unable to wear my money belt due to the low cut of the back of the dress, I fished some pesetas out and hid them in the bosom of the dress. Lord knows, I had the extra space.

I had my first, fast glass of wine at the inn's little bar. Then I had a sangria—with fruit—at a café nearby. Next, a whiskey at some overpriced joint down the street.

A few men flirted with me. None of them excited me very much. I moved on, hoping to find live music. Soon I came upon a small cantina from which emanated a big sound. I could hear speedy guitar music, ferocious clapping and rowdy hoots and hollers.

I made my way inside. It was not as crowded as I would have expected from the level of noise. But it was a lively bunch, about two dozen folks drinking and laughing, mostly men.

I picked a seat by the door. Several of the men turned and looked at me. I knew I was looking happy and sexy; the lusty glares confirmed it. I smiled and waved to the waiter.

It was a young man, skinny and polite:

"Buenas noches, señora," he said. "Tu viniste a bailar?"

"Dance? No, I only came to drink," I answered, like some zozzled rummy.

He sort of laughed but gave me an odd look and said:

"Lo siento mucho. I see the dress, you know, and ...,"

BRRR-ANNNG!

It was one of the guitar players. It was the most confident chord I had ever heard. He played another:

BRRRRR-ANNNG!

And then he started plucking the strings, slow at first but then faster. A few people started to clap.

"Señora?"

The waiter was waiting for me to answer. The music had distracted me. I ordered a sangria, the waiter left and I turned my attention back to the guitar player.

He strummed a few more loud chords, did a little riff of notes and then settled into a rhythm. Then, out of nowhere, a dancer appeared. She breezed past my table and the room's attention shifted to her.

She was tall, elegant and confident. She was wearing a long yellow dress with blue trim. She hiked up the front of her dress a bit as she made her way to the center of the café.

Then *BRRR-ANNNG* the guitar player tore out another strong chord. The woman brought her arms up above her head and struck a pose. I looked up at her smooth, perfect hands and saw that she was wearing cymbals on her fingers. She began to *tink-tink* and *tink-tink* with them, in time with the guitar player's chords. Soon, everyone in the cafe was clapping along.

Then she began to dance.

She danced the flamenco—or something close to it— and it was entrancing. I couldn't take my eyes of her. She spun around and jutted a leg out and swung her arms up. Then, while *tink-tinking* away with her finger cymbals, she brought her hands down by her shoulders. Finally, she thrust her arms forward and brought them back up again and spun around. She was so graceful.

My first sangria went down in less than a minute. I wanted more: more dancing, more sangria, more of this energy. When the dancer stopped we all clapped and I got the waiter's attention and pointed at my empty glass. He nodded. From behind me, a man's voice asked:

"It would seem that you are celebrating."

It was a Spanish voice, but fortunately not one I recognized. I turned and found myself face-to-face with a square-jawed man at the next table. He was handsome, middle-aged, with salt-and-pepper hair. He reminded me of Douglas Fairbanks, the actor from those Zorro movies. In fact, this man would have made a better Zorro than Douglas Fairbanks. I could only stare at him.

"Perdón," he said. "Hablas inglés?"

"No ... no, sorry, I mean yes," I stammered. "Yes, I do."

"Are you sure?" the good-looking man asked. "American?"

"Sí."

"And are you enjoying the Exposition?" he asked.

"I am," I said, which was half-true. "Have you been?"

"No. I am just in from Barcelona and the Exposition there."

"And ... how was Barcelona?"

"It was remarkable, just remarkable."

Then he slid his chair over and was more at my table than his, which was just fine by me. He extended his hand.

"I am Antonio," he said.

We shook and I introduced myself.

"How do you say that last name again? Villa-zee?"

"Willow-bee."

"Ah, sí, yes. When you go back to America?"

"Oh … I'm not going back, actually. I'm moving to Paris."

"To Paris!"

"I still can't believe it. I'm very excited. Today—tonight, really—I ended my job. So, cheers to me."

We clinked glasses.

"Sí, cheers to you," he said. "What was your job?"

"I worked as an assistant … for an archaeologist," I said.

"Ooh! That sounds very exciting, Vendy."

"It had some exciting moments. Glad to be done with it."

"Sí. And in America, where does the assistant to an archeologist work?"

"In Mexico. The Yucatán."

"Oh-ho!" he exclaimed. "Archaeologist from Yucatán? That must be the tiny man that go loco in speech at Expo, no?"

"I don't know what you're talking about," I tried.

"Uh-huh. Your face, it says different, Vendy."

I was too tipsy to lie and didn't see much reason to.

"Sí … that was my boss," I said. "He caused quite a stir."

"Yes, even at my hotel, they talk about it. Many people very upset," he said, though he himself was smiling and chuckling.

"Yep, they were."

"Ha! That is good, for people to be upset. Is healthy," he said.

"How so?"

"Well, it is like you Americans, no? You like ... pardon me, Vendy ... you Americans like the smell of your own shit. We Spanish, we are not that different, sí?"

"I'm not following," I confessed.

"We as people do many great things, no? Many things we proud of. But then when comes to bad things, shitty things, we convince ourselves not so bad, it no stink like shit. Sí?"

"Um ... sure."

"And so it take someone from another place to point that out," he continued. "Like in America, one hundred years ago a man could buy another man, no? And do whatever he wanted with that man, no?"

"Well, yes, but we've made a lot of progress since then and ...,"

"... And so all are equal now?" he interrupted, eyebrows raised.

"Not yet. But I'm sure that over time we ...,"

"So answer is no. I show you that your shit *does* stink, no?" he said, then as an aside, "Not your actual poo, señorita. It is a figure of speech."

"Fine. But at least we didn't burn people at the stake," I countered.

"Did you not burn witches?"

"Okay, forget that example. But I think the good parts of America far outweigh the bad."

"And I feel the same way of my country. I hope I am not offending you."

"No offense taken. But I'll be honest, what I've seen over the past few weeks gives me reason to think Spain's balance may be out of whack," I said. "Historically speaking, of course."

Now his eyes lit up.

"Hoo-hoo-hoo! The fire in you, sí! I love it!"

"Sorry, it's been a long day."

"I understand, Vendy," he said. "And is not unique. Many people, they come here knowing only of conquistadors and kings, no? Then they come and they waste time at museums and palaces and Escorial and think that is all there is to España. Swords and wars, sí?

"But only if you live here do you appreciate what makes up special," he continued. "We have respect for our traditions and our faith, sí? You come to my town, Malaga, during Holy Week. Everyone come out to see the statue of the Virgin Mary be carried up the street. The statue, she very heavy. Men, they get hurt and break bones just try to keep her up.

"Now, are they the holiest or most powerful of men? Are they priests, bishops, rich men, kings? No, they come from all walks of life. The barber, the butcher, the shopkeeper. And it is great honor to carry her, okay? And we do not do it just for the ticket to heaven … though that would be nice. We do it because it is who we are. We try to hold on to the good parts of and get rid of the bad parts, comprendéis?"

"In a way."

"Lo siento, I do not mean to be so serious," he said. "You must be going to dance, no?"

"Oh … I don't know how to do the flamenco."

"But you are wearing the dress of the rebellious bird, no?"

"What's the rebellious bird?"

"*Carmen*," he replied. "The opera. You have heard of it … no?"

"I know some of the songs," I replied. "I can sing a funny song to the tune of *Habanera*."

We laughed and drank and talked some more. I was interested in him romantically, but I sensed he wasn't of the same mind. We had fun, though. He kept encouraging me to dance, so eventually I did.

I didn't dare do the cymbals, which he said was good because it was apparently a controversial new fad. But I got onto the floor, drunk and delighted, and struck a pose with my arms behind my back.

The guitar player ripped out a chord:

BRRR-ANNNG!

And at that I brought up my arms up over my head, like the dancers before me.

BRRR-AANNG! BRRR-ANNNG!

As the guitar player picked up speed, I did too. I sashayed my hips and grooved my belly and kicked my legs. There was no rhyme or reason to it; I just did whatever felt good. I tossed my arms up and down and around and people started to clap along.

And I loved it. As they clapped I spun faster, then I would stop, then I would strike a new pose. I came to realize the guitar player was watching my arms, playing louder as I raised them up. So my big finale had me flailing my limbs all over, spinning around and around, while everyone in the cantina applauded. When I finished, a great cheer went up.

Exhausted, I made my way back to the table. I was surprised to see my new friend, Antonio, had disappeared. He had been there while I was dancing, but now he was gone.

Despite his Irish exit, my night carried on. I drank a bit more, danced a bit more and flirted a bit more. But then the extent of the long day—Doctor Morley's speech, the comedy at the Archive—began to wash over me.

***

When I returned to the inn I was still tipsy, but resolute in my determination to effectuate a great and profound change in my life. The move to Paris was a difficult but necessary first step.

As I passed through the lobby, I overheard the clerks talking excitedly about something. It sounded like there had been some kind of incident at the Expo.

I was curious, but not curious enough to ask what had happened. Sleep was a higher priority. After all, my new life began tomorrow.

30

ABANDONED

And so it was that I woke up in a little Inn in Seville, hungover as hell but at peace with the decisions I had made. Bright beams of sunlight burst through the window, over the bed and onto my tired legs. I took that to be heavenly endorsement of my plan.

I sprung up, figuring every moment I wasted in bed was a moment I wasn't spending on my new path. I washed, dressed and made my way out the door.

I needed breakfast and decided to see if my now-former boss wanted to join me. So I went to Doctor Morley's door and knocked, to no answer.

So I went down to the dining room, which was empty. I considered checking with my former companions, to see if he was with them, but decided against it.

Then I went to the lobby. Doctor Morley wasn't there, nor was he on the sidewalk outside. I came back and in and pondered what to do. As I was thinking, I overheard two men talking:

"Sí, la policía, they have entire street blocked off," one of them said.

"Tan triste, that poor man!"

I assumed someone had been mugged or something. I stepped outside, thought more about my circumstances then decided to ask the desk clerk if there were any messages for me:

"I'm wondering if my companion left anything for me. The name is Willoughby?"

"Vell-oof-bee?" the clerk replied.

"Will-o-bee," I said, but still I had to spell it for him.

And as it turned out he did have something for me. It was an envelope. I took it, thanked him and walked away to open it.

It was a note from Doctor Morley:

Wendy: Agreed to assist our compadres in Madrid. Back tomorrow. Leave when you're ready, your room is paid for. Thanks for all, Sylvanus.

Thanks for all … Sylvanus? I studied the note for a bit. It was his handwriting, of that I was positive. But he wouldn't be back until tomorrow? I hadn't planned to stay a whole other day. Didn't he want to say good-bye to me?

Something wasn't right. Part of my unease came from the fact that the situation just didn't make much sense to me. I couldn't understand why Doctor Morley would go back to Madrid with Benito after all that had happened. He had insisted he was done with them. Had he changed his mind?

I returned to the front desk.

"Can you tell me if Sylvanus Morley checked out?" I asked, wondering if they had kept their rooms.

"Sí, Señora Vell-oof-bee … he and his amigos, they all check out."

"When?"

"Very early. A woman, she come down here and do it all."

"A woman. A tall, bitchy-looking woman?"

He nodded. My mind was spinning. I didn't know what to make of this.

"Will there be anything else, señora?" the clerk asked.

"Um … no, no. Gracias, thank you," I said and started to walk away.

The two men that had been talking about the police had been joined by another man. A horrible thought crossed my mind. I returned a third time to the clerk. I bent down to speak to him in a low voice.

"Lo siento … I couldn't help but overhear those men talking," I said. "Did something bad happen at the Exposition?"

"No, señora … not at the Exposition, but very near … at the Archivo General," he answered.

Every bit of blood rushed out of my head. It's a wonder I didn't faint.

"The … Archive?" I repeated.

"Sí!" he said, eyes wide. "Last night, someone break in … and they steal sword of Hernán Cortés!"

"They did … what? A … sword?" I stammered as my mind spiraled.

"Sí, señora, the sword of the great conquistador, Hernán Cortés," he said. "And whoever did it, they use sword to murder one of the guards!"

"A … a … *murder?* Who?"

"The oldest guard, Señor Rocinante. He had worked there his whole life!"

"No!" I exclaimed, in disbelief.

"Sí, señora," he confirmed. "Un asesinato. A murder! And during the Expo!"

He was quite alarmed by the news and showed it. I was a thousand times more alarmed than he was, but had to maintain my composure.

"How ... how awful," was all I could say.

The clerk agreed. I walked away and—not knowing what else I could do—returned to my room.

My story, it seemed, had taken an unpleasant and unwelcome twist.

***

By the time I made it back to my room, I had concluded I needed to get the hell out of Seville.

Benito had killed someone. It explained the blood on his shirt. He hadn't been wounded at all. Something had gone wrong, he had murdered the guard ... and I was in a prime position to get blamed for it.

At first I thought I should go directly to Paris. But I worried if I got nabbed, such a journey might look suspicious ... like I was trying to flee the country.

No, I would go to Madrid. That's where Doctor Morley was. I had to find him. He needed to know what had happened, as I suspected he had no idea. I would have to steer him away from Benito, then the two of us would get as far away from that killer as possible.

I packed up my suitcase, secured my money belt and threw on my shoulder bag. I used a back stairway and back door to exit the inn. I lugged the suitcase down the block and jumped into the first open taxi I could find. I was doing all I could to, in effect, disappear.

At the train station I plastered myself to the walls and didn't make eye contact. I bought a one-way ticket back to Madrid, then made my way to the far end of the platform. I waited there for the train ... and wondered if my freedom had been short-lived.

31

THE MUSEUM

I spent the entire ride hunkered down in the rear seat of an almost-empty car. But as we got closer to Madrid, more and more people boarded the train.

By the time we reached the outskirts of the city the car was almost full. Some clueless dolt overcame the negative energy I was giving off and sat next to me. He tried to talk to me in Spanish; I played dumb. Then he tried English; I acted like I didn't know that language, either.

At the station in Madrid, I skirted the walls and stuck to the shadows. While I had no reason to believe anyone as after me, recent events had educated me on how quickly things change.

I had decided the Palace Hotel was a logical first stop. I thought maybe, just maybe, I might find Doctor Morley there. Perhaps he would be staying there tonight … so he would have dropped off his bag, right? Perhaps he had already checked in. Perhaps I would even find him having breakfast, as it was early and the Museum wasn't open yet.

An inner voice was telling me to pinch my pesetas and walk to the hotel. But I was eager, so I nabbed another taxi. Within five minutes I was at the entrance.

Inside the main door, I asked a bellhop to watch my suitcase for me. Then, keeping my head and profile low, I went inside and scanned the lobby. Next, I scanned the restaurant. Finally, throwing caution to the wind, I approached the front desk.

"Buenos días," I said, and the clerk replied in English, so I asked:

"Have you seen Doctor Morley this morning? Sylvanus Morley?"

The clerk's face curled up, and he looked down at his book and flipped a few pages.

"I am sorry, but Doctor Morley checked out several days ago."

"I know he did, but ... perhaps he returned and checked back in?"

The clerk did me the favor of looking at his book again.

"No, señora. He did not."

I stood there, not knowing what to do, then asked:

"I wonder if he might have left a message for me. Can you please check to see if you have anything for a Wendy Willoughby?"

"Vell-o-beet?"

"Willoughby," I said, and once again had to spell it.

The clerk went away and into the office behind the desk and then returned.

"I see nothing. Lo siento," he said.

"It's alright," I said. "I think I know where I might find him."

I thanked the clerk and made my way back to the bellhop. I broke my no-spending rule again, reaching into my money-belt for a coin to tip him. I asked him to watch over my suitcase for the afternoon, explaining I would be back later. I would keep my shoulder bag with me, but I had no desire to drag my suitcase all the way to the Museum … which is where I was sure Doctor Morley was.

I dipped into my money-belt one last time and pulled out a peseta for the taxi fare.

***

At the Museum, the twin sphinges welcomed me home. I made my way up the steps and through the open door. My favorite ticket lady was not at her station, so I walked right in.

The place seemed lifeless. The Egyptian salon was empty. I made my way to the stairs and up. At this point, I wanted to find Doctor Morley and only Doctor Morley. I wanted to tell him the horrible news about the murder of the guard in Seville. I did not, however, want to find Benito … the man responsible for the murder itself.

With fingers crossed, I came to the top of the stairs. To my left I could hear voices, my first sign that others were on the top floor. They didn't notice me. I turned and tiptoed through what used to be the first Mesoamerican room.

As I came through the empty gallery I could hear several male voices ahead. I didn't hear Doctor Morley's voice, but I didn't hear Benito's, either. I crept forward to spy in.

I peeked around the corner into the second room. There were seven or eight men in there. A few looked to be police officers. They were all crowded around the Codex case.

The sight of them surprised me. My mind spun then my body panicked. I took a small step backward.

CRRRUNNNCH.

I had stepped on something. I looked down and saw shards of glass on the floor.

Then I looked up. A few of the men were staring directly at me. One by one the rest of them raised their heads, the last being Director Melida.

The Director stared at me for a minute. His face scrunched up, first with surprise and then with anger. He pointed at me and shouted:

"*La ladrona!* That is the thief!"

Now the men on my side of the Codex frame took a step toward me. Director Melida was marching my way.

"What have you done? Where is it?" he demanded.

"I … I haven't done anything!" I stammered. "I'm only … looking for Doctor Morley!"

There were footsteps behind me. I turned and saw Lothario and Anselmo, the Museum guards, encroaching from behind me. Even Lothario looked mad. I wheeled back around, my heart pounding.

"Who has it?" Director Melida barked. "You? Morley?"

"I didn't take anything!"

"*Alto!*" he shouted. "Seize her!"

I heard speedy steps behind me. I darted forward, just missing Anselmo's grab. The big guard wheeled around and started walking toward me again. Then, from the corner of my eye, I saw Lothario positioning himself to block my path.

The police officers that had been with Director Melida were creeping closer.

"There's been a misunderstanding!" I pleaded. "Malentendido! I didn't do anything!"

They weren't listening. My mind raced. I had been set up. I had been set up and I was about to be arrested for stealing something I didn't steal. Worse, I feared that would lead to me being blamed for a murder I didn't commit!

I was scared. Without considering the consequences, I made a run for it.

I bolted toward the stairs. The second I started running, Anselmo tried to charge me, stumbling as I eluded his grasp.

I ran out of the room, toward a shocked Lothario.

"Soy inocente!" I yelled as I charged.

"Alto, Vendy! Alto!" Lothario shouted.

I tried to make a move past him. He lunged at me, snagging a finger on my shoulder bag. But the strap broke on one end, causing my once-admirer to crash to the floor.

As I came to the top of the stairs I turned to look back. The police officers were charging my way, Director Melida scurrying after them. Anselmo had pulled himself up and Lothario was trying to do the same.

I ran down the stairs at top speed, one hand sliding down the railing and one hand clutching the broken strap of my bag. My shoes slipped on the mezzanine, but I remained up and made the turn. I kept running. Ahead of me, reflected off the marble floor, I could see the light from the open door.

Suddenly, that light represented my freedom. I bounded down the stairs, two steps at a time. I sprinted toward the ticket desk, the front door and my escape.

But then, from out of nowhere, a tall uniformed man appeared in the doorway. He saw me and stopped, blocking my exit. I froze then wheeled around. An army of pursuers was coming down the stairs: police officers, Director Melida, Lothario and Anselmo.

I jerked to the left, into the Egyptian Salon. My intent was to get the officer blocking the door to move toward me and, sure enough, he did. So I kept running, past the sarcophagi, around the cabinets and toward a display of idols on the back wall. Then I jerked left again, into Christian Antiquities.

At this point I assumed I might have the high hand. I swerved once more, passing into the narrow hallway under the stairs that led past the Director's office. Then I cut back on the other side of the stairs, thinking I should now have a clean path to the exit.

I sprinted. And then … I saw the front door start to close.

The tall man in uniform must have suspected what I was up to. He shut the door the entire way. Then, looking me in the eye, he turned the lock.

I wheeled around. People were coming at me from all directions. I tried to make one last move, to run into the Iberian section, but someone grabbed me from behind.

It was Lothario. "Lo siento, Vendy," he said. "Please, stop the running."

I struggled, but the rest began to gather around me. Director Melida stepped into the center of my view.

"Where is it?" he demanded.

"I didn't take anything!" I insisted.

The director shook his head and looked to one of the officers.

"Esposas," he snarled. "Put the handcuffs on her."

Handcuffs? From my side, a brawny-looking policeman approached.

"Vendy, I need spin you around this way, sí?" Lothario said.

He did so. He looked sad for me. A big policeman came up beside him, unclasping the handcuffs from his belt. I was about to be arrested.

And at that precise moment a volcano of memories erupted in my mind:

That horrible crash. The water in the plane. Captain Cabrera's dead body. The photographer, torn apart. Lindbergh, frickin' crazy, sticks and leaves in his hair. The cave. The bats. The flash of light. That awful sound.

So, too, I flashed back to my own actions:

Grabbing the shotgun. Following Lindbergh out. Doing what had to be done.

And with those awful thoughts came the awful emotions:

The guilt. The shame. The hurt. Mad at myself. Mad at others. Mad at the world.

It was as if time stood still. All those bad memories, all the anger, all the hurt flowed out of my head, through my heart … and down into my right foot.

"Lo siento, Lothario," I whispered.

The poor guard gave me a puzzled look.

Then I brought my foot up, fast and hard, into Lothario's groin.

The men gasped, every last one of them.

Lothario's eyes were bugged out, his mouth frozen open in shock and pain. He teetered, moaned, grasped his crotch and fell over.

Before the others could react, I swung my half-broken shoulder bag around. It caught the policeman with the handcuffs square in the face. He lost his balance and fell backward. I swung my bag around again, full circle, making the rest take a step back.

Director Melida couldn't believe it. His mouth was agape.

I didn't say a word … I just turned and bolted at top speed for the stairs. Before the officers could react, I had darted between them.

I took two steps at a time, sliding as I rounded the mezzanine. As I sprinted up toward the third floor I glanced down. Several men were running up after me.

At the top, I made a quick decision and turned into the first Mesoamerican room, the empty one. By the time I had made it to the far side of that room, I heard footsteps gaining behind me.

I darted into the second Mesoamerican room, crunching over broken glass from the Codex frame. At the

Aztec calendar stone I exited, jigging into the back corridor. Then, I decided to run through the Arab Courtyard.

By now my pursuers had split up. As I came down the short steps I saw Anselmo, the guard, coming into the Courtyard from a different direction. I swerved around him, my feet slipping on the marble as I rounded the central fountain. I made for the steps leading up and out of the courtyard.

I rushed across the central corridor, past the back of the staircase and then down a few steps into the Roman Patio. I spun around and, sure enough, one of the police officers—a big, strong one—was still after me. Knowing I had only one shot, I slowed and grabbed hold off a small statue, which proved too heavy to lift. Instead, I snatched up the object next to it: an ancient Roman bust.

I ran toward the Roman Patio's far exit. Just then, an unexpected surprise: Anselmo appeared, blocking my path. But I didn't stop … if I had, the officer in back of me would have nabbed me. Instead, I lifted that Roman bust high up over my head and charged toward the guard.

Anselmo seemed confused about what to do. As I came at him he slipped, fell and then looked up at me.

At this point I had the Roman bust held high in both arms. I rushed up and he cowered; I had already kicked his co-worker in the nuts, he must have assumed I was going to bash his skull in. Instead, I jumped over him and ran into the rearmost corridor.

Still running, I raised that old bust as high as I could … and then smashed it into the knob of the door leading from the Museum to the Library.

BAM!

Wood splintered. The bust broke in two. With a kick, I burst through that goddamn door.

And now I was in the stacks of the Library. Familiar with the layout, I darted around several bookcases and then dared to peek back again. Two police officers, including the biggest one, were still after me. I ducked, hoping they hadn't seen me.

"Alto! Alto!" one of them yelled.

There was no way in hell I was stopping. I bolted again into the stacks, winding my way between the bookcases, making my way to the spiral staircase that led to the ground floor. But then one of the officers cut me off, blocking my access. I jerked left, unsure of the path I now found myself on.

This new corridor came to an end at a railing. Beyond it, one floor down, lay the grand expanse of the main reading room.

I looked right and found an unwelcome wall blocking that egress. Then, to the left, I saw the big police officer spot me and start to come my way. I turned around and, sure enough, the smaller one was coming up from behind.

I didn't know what to do. I could jump to the main floor, a plummet of twenty feet or so ... and break my legs on a table. I could charge the men, or fight them ... a dubious proposition. Then I glanced to my right again and noticed a rope cleated to the wall. The other end of the rope went up to the ceiling, connecting to a pulley which then connected to one of four chandeliers.

I had no time to think it through. I seized the rope and began to unwind it from the cleat. My vision was that I would make like a swashbuckler, swinging down into the room, landing on my feet and not breaking stride.

I swung one foot and then the other over the railing. With a final glance at my pursuers, I pulled the rope out of the cleat and jumped.

It did not go as expected.

Instead of swinging forward, the weight of the chandelier pulled me upward ... fast. I soared, a veritable Tinkerbell, rising higher and higher above the reading room and the stunned patrons below. At the same time, the chandelier dropped, making the readers dive for cover.

KER-SMASH!

The chandelier crashed onto floor below ... after which I was left dangling by a rope over the reading room. Everyone was staring up at me. There was much yelling.

I started to swing my legs, like a child on a school swing-set. Little by little the section of rope between me and the pulley began to sway. I kicked higher and higher, trying to swing myself over to an edge ... and then I let go, soaring through the air. I caught hold of a railing with both hands and, somehow, wiggled myself up and over.

I looked back to my pursuers. They looked as surprised by my awkward leap as I was. They both took off toward me, but by now I had a good lead. I turned and starting running again, then spun down the first staircase I found. There, at last, I saw the Library doors.

Before I could breathe a sigh of relief, a Library guard stepped in front of me. Without slowing down, I took up my broken shoulder bag and started to whip it over my head. He ducked once, then twice … but on my third go-round my bag caught him across the face. He staggered back.

I soared the rest of the way to the exit and ran out the door. I came down between the statues, bolted through the gates and onto the sidewalk. I turned toward the main avenue, thinking I would make a run toward the Columbus statue in the middle of the traffic circle. I reconsidered and realized it was better to hide myself.

So I slowed my pace, lowered my head and tried to blend in with the other pedestrians on the sidewalk. As I was panting and sweating and red in the face, I still garnered some stares. Then, a decent distance from the Library entrance, I ducked behind a tall hedge. I took a moment to tie up the broken strap of my shoulder bag.

"What the hell did you just do, Wendy?" I asked myself.

I stayed behind the hedge for a solid minute … then dared to stick my head around, to see if anyone was still chasing me. I looked and, sure enough, saw the Library guard coming my way.

He saw me as well. I began to run again.

I sprinted along the hedge then back out to the sidewalk. The big guard was hot on my heels. I looped back, toward the Library entrance, but stayed outside the fence.

As I came to the corner I looked down the block, toward the Museum. Coming my way was Director Melida, with more police and a limping Lothario. The Director pointed at me, causing the officers with him to charge my way.

I high-tailed it in the last direction I could, the sidewalk that ran around the traffic circle. My legs were killing me, my lungs more so. But I had always been a quick runner, so I took off, as fast as my legs would carry me. I slowed only to look back. One police officer was still keeping pace: the biggest one, of course.

Pedestrians were jumping out of my way, terrified of the crazed Tom Sawyer careening down the sidewalk. A man tried to step in front of me to stop me; I pushed him down. But that little delay caused me precious time. The big policeman was closing in.

I again sprinted, but now each step brought with it soreness and pain. There was only so long I could keep this up.

Then, an opportunity: I spied the steps to a Metro station, dead ahead.

I held my line on the sidewalk, to throw off my pursuer as long as I could. Then, at the last moment, I swerved toward the steps, somehow keeping my balance, descending to the station below.

My feet echoed off the tile floors as I ran. I hopped over the ticket turnstile, ignoring a yell from the ticket taker, then ran down to the platform. It was empty: no people, no train.

I ran to the far end of the platform, wondering if there might be an exit on the far end. There wasn't. Then I heard heavy footsteps approaching. I had nowhere to go.

So I jumped down onto the tracks, falling in the process. I pulled myself up and then bolted for the tunnel, to hide myself in the darkness. But no sooner had I done so then I heard the heavy footsteps again, coming onto the platform.

I ran down the train tracks, through the darkened tunnel. I had no idea how far I would have to run to the next station. But when I found one, I would be able to worm up to the street. Hopefully, my running would be over.

And the moment that thought popped into my head, I spotted a train ahead of me.

It wasn't coming toward me; it was going away from me. And the damn thing was moving slower than I was. But on the back of the train there was a small platform, near the hitch, on which I could ride to safety.

So I sprinted, one final time. I ran until I caught up to the train and then grabbed hold of a railing. I somehow pulled myself up to, then onto, the small platform.

The back of the train had two windows framing a narrow door. I stayed low, so nobody inside the train would see me. But it was for naught: right away, a little girl inside the car saw me. We made eye contact, then she began to turn around to tell someone about me.

"No, shhhh, shhhh," I said, trying to silence her, as if she could hear me through the glass.

And somehow she understood. She remained silent and watched me as I steadied myself on the small platform. I stayed low and looked up to the little girl to thank her with my eyes.

But I saw she wasn't watching me. She was looking past me, down the tracks.

I followed her gaze. There, through the darkness, I could make out a figure. It was the big policeman. He was still after me. I turned back to the little girl:

"Abre la puerta," I mouthed. "Open the door, por favor?"

I looked back. My pursuer was gaining.

Now a mother came and joined the little girl at the window. She looked a tad surprised to see me clinging to the rear of the train. Then a few more passengers came up and looked.

At this point I had nothing to lose:

"Abre la puerta!" I yelled. "Let me in! Let me in!"

I made eye contact again with the little girl. Her eyes got wide. She pointed. I turned.

The big policeman was right there. He reached out and grabbed hold of my ankle; I held the railing tight. Then he got a grip on the railing on the opposite side. He pulled himself up, beside me.

Now the brute brought his left hand up high and swung down, trying to knock my arm loose. I held firm. He turned his body toward mine, using his bulk to smother me.

And for the second time that day I kicked a man in the balls, bringing my knee firmly up into the policeman's groin. But he held on. He shook his head, roared a little then looked at me with eyes of fury.

I sensed I had made a bad, bad mistake.

The policeman reared back. This time he swung with a closed fist, aiming for the face. He grazed me on the first try, but caught me on his second. My head cracked against the train. From inside, I could hear an 'ooh' from our onlookers.

I tried to kick again; he blocked me. He got a hand on my back leg and pushed me against the train. I struggled and fought … but he was too big and too strong. He overpowered me, pulling me into a backward headlock.

Then he took a cheap shot, giving me a blow to my lower back. The spectators 'oohed' again.

But while I was in that headlock I saw something. Hanging from the officer's belt were his handcuffs … the same pair he had tried to put on me at the Museum.

I faked more struggle and, without him knowing, unclasped the handcuffs and plucked them away from him.

As he tried to pin my body against the train with his own body I looked up. His right hand was still grasping the railing. I forced my free hand up.

The handcuffs swung around and locked around the metal.

The big policeman heard the *clank*. He began to rotate his upper body back my way, and as he did I was able to lift my arm higher. I reached up and, before he could figure what was happening, cuffed him to the train.

He saw what I had done. He tried to punch me with his free hand, then he used his legs to pin me in a wrestling hold. So I bit him in the closest spot I could, which was his ass.

He screamed in pain and jerked back. I rolled away, falling off the back of the train.

My body slammed into the tracks. I swallowed the pain and pushed myself up.

The train was rolling away, with the angry policeman handcuffed to it.

In the window, stunned passengers watched with mouths agape. The little girl smiled, then waved good-bye. I think I waved back.

32

ALONE AND AFRAID

I don't remember how I made it to Sal's studio.

I have a vague recollection of coming up out of the Metro somewhere. I was discombobulated and confused and numb from the whole experience.

I think I asked someone for directions. Then, somehow, I travelled undetected until I reached his building. Thank goodness he had showed me where he kept the spare key.

I couldn't sleep, though I was exhausted. I may have closed my eyes during the course of the night, but I guarantee you my mind never let me rest.

When the sun started peeking through the windows, I stayed glued to the purple armchair I had spent the night in. I fidgeted and swore at myself and questioned my judgment from the prior day.

Perhaps I shouldn't have kicked Lothario in the nuts and run away. Perhaps I should have stopped and tried to explain the mix-up. Maybe they would have understood.

But then maybe they would have tossed me in jail. Maybe I would have ended up in some Spanish prison, forgotten, lawyer-less, framed for one crime and perhaps two.

The Embassy was another thought. I could go to the U.S. Embassy and explain everything. I could tell them that Doctor Morley had been abducted and that I had been set-up. I'd tell them I had no idea where the missing page of the Codex was, which was the truth … but I knew damn well who did.

Then, of course, they'd ask about the murder in Seville. Yes, I was there, I'd tell them. But no, I didn't murder anyone. That was the other guy. I was only there to participate in the theft of the sword.

I'm sure the folks at the Embassy would also want to know how Doctor Morley and I got tied up in all this. I'd have to tell them that we'd all been working together. Then they'd ask why a respected archaeologist from the Carnegie Institution was working with a slime-ball like Benito. I certainly couldn't tell them the truth: That it all had to do with funding the excavations at Chichen Itza. Doctor Morley didn't want that news to get out, and I didn't want to put myself in a position where I would blurt it out. So I concluded the Embassy was out of the question.

My next thought was that I should flee Madrid and get the hell out of Spain. I had rejected that idea once before, when I was in Seville, and regretted it. But now, fleeing the country made all the sense in the world: I could take the train straight to Paris and try to alert authorities from there.

I reached down to my money belt, to double-check that I had my passport. I didn't. I remembered it was in my suitcase, which was with the concierge at the Palace Hotel.

Which meant I had to go to the Hotel first … which meant I'd have to disguise myself somehow. Then I'd leave the studio, retrieve my suitcase and then try to make it to a train station. I could slink aboard, buy a ticket from the conductor and be off to Paris.

Ah, but the conductor on the train ... he might be suspicious. I'd be an American on the run and those aren't hard to spot. He'd ask to see my passport ... and by then every cop in Spain would be looking for me. The jig would be up. They'd want to know why I was running if I was innocent. It was a question for which I had no good answer.

On top of all this I still had a million unanswered questions about how I came to such a sorry point. I thought about that silly sword and those damn maps and the damn Codex and Hernán Cortés and his three damn sons. It all made no sense to me.

In fact, the entire situation was absurd. It was as if I had fallen down a rabbit-hole—like Alice— and now I had to find a way out of some bizarre Wonderland.

By the afternoon I had concluded there was only one option: I had to find Benito, so I could find Doctor Morley.

33

TO FIND THE THIEF

I woke up the next morning to a hideous sight.

Before me I saw a woman, her hands and feet and head cut off. From her noggin-less neck sprang little trees. From those trees jumped little stick-figures. Near her was a donkey, decayed and infested with maggots. Next to that sat a dismembered head, male, sliced open to expose the brain. Floating above all of that was a single eyeball and what appeared to be bloody sperm.

It was an awful painting, the worst in Sal's entire studio. It made no sense to have a man's decapitated head but then have the nearby decapitated body be a woman's. And whatever message was being sent by the decaying donkey was beyond me.

Yet I was thankful for the grotesque canvas. It took my mind off more pressing concerns. But soon enough my thoughts returned to my shitty situation. I stared at the ceiling and muttered to myself:

"Damn you, Wendy. How'd you ever get yourself in such a scrape?"

I gave myself a few more minutes of self-pity then pushed myself up. My legs and my back and my shoulders were still aching from the whole Museum incident ... but time was my enemy.

I bent down and peeked under the front door. I saw no one in the hallway, but I did spy a newspaper sitting by a neighbor's door. I unlocked the door, reached out and grabbed the newspaper as fast as I could. Then I locked the door back up, sat on the floor and unfolded the paper.

There was a long headline across the top:

ASESINATO DE SEVILLA; ROBO EN MADRID.

The two events had already been tied together. All air left my lungs. Then, my surprise turned to absolute shock. Below the bold headline there were two pictures, one a photograph and one a sketch.

The first picture, the photograph, showed a smiling older man in uniform. I recognized his face immediately: it was the friendly guard that had helped us at the Archive. I stared at the sweet man's face and as I did the true extent of Benito's viciousness hit me. He was a killer, a cold-blooded killer. Just like Lindbergh.

The other picture wasn't a photograph. It was a drawing. A sketch, like the police release when they're looking for someone.

It was, purportedly, a sketch of me. But it was terrible and looked nothing like me. In the drawing my hair was too dark and my eyes were too far apart. My eyebrows were much too bushy, like a man's. They had given me an ugly, snarling mouth and a bulbous, off-center nose. I looked like Mister Hyde.

"Is that supposed to be ... *me?*" I asked the newspaper, and received no denial.

It was the very definition of bad news and good news. The bad news was that I was apparently being sought for both the theft at the Museum and the murder in Seville.

The good news was that the police sketch was awful. Hopefully, that would make my expedition to find Benito—and Doctor Morley—less challenging than it would otherwise be.

***

I had never known a man that possessed as many items of clothing as Sal. He had a dozen nice suits, a rack full of white shirts, an impressive collection of shoes and a few hats.

His pants, I was pleased to discover, were the same waist size as mine. I had to roll the pant cuffs, but other than that they fit me well. Then I donned the jacket over a white shirt, both of which were three sizes too big.

I selected a manly-looking hat and checked myself in the bathroom mirror. I looked like an amateur theater production. So I used one of Salvador's eyeliners—he had several—to draw a thin moustache over my lip. It looked ridiculous, but the last thing I wanted to look like was an American woman.

My first thought—my only thought—was to go back to the abandoned restaurant where we had first met Benito. While it seemed illogical they would return to such an obvious place, I had no other ideas. I pulled Sal's hat low over my eyes, took a deep breath and left the studio.

Again I stuck to the side streets, avoiding eye contact at all times, keeping my head low. I plucked a few coins out of my money-belt for a pastry and a coffee to stay alive. I tried to add a German accent to my Spanish as I ordered; the accent was as pathetic as my fake moustache.

An hour later I had made it to the alley leading to Benito's lair. I crept up and tried to peer through the papered-over windows, to see if I could spy any people or lights inside. I didn't see anything, but wasn't sure. So I rapped on the door with my knuckles and sprinted out of the alley. I ran across the intersecting street, hiding myself behind a parked truck. I looked back and waited. Nobody appeared.

I made the decision to wait and watch. As I waited, dark clouds turned to storm clouds. I took refuge in the doorway of an abandoned building nearby, crouching down to ease the pain in my legs. The pedestrians walking by must have thought I was tipsy, addled or both. I didn't care, as long as they thought I was male and not the monster from the newspaper.

One hour went by, then two, then three. Motorcars barreling down the wet street splattered my already-soaked man-clothes. I was miserable. As morning turned to afternoon, I began to give up hope that Benito would ever return here. I squeezed my brain for a new idea.

Then, a light bulb over my head: Veronica's hotel.

She had bragged about it at our first dinner in Madrid. I remember it being somewhere on the Gran Via. I searched my memories. It was on the tip of my tongue. The Benny-jelly? The Boon-gooley?

Then it hit me: The Benengeli.

I trod through the rain-soaked streets and made my way to the Gran Via. I stopped on a side street to again to refresh my disguise, checking my reflection in a store window. My pathetic moustache had run off during the rain; to avoid looking like a clown I wiped the rest away. I pulled my hat lower and returned to the main boulevard.

Within a hundred yards I came to a newsstand. That terrible headline—*Murder in Seville; Theft in Madrid*—blared from dozens of newspapers. A few copies were hanging down from a wire, revealing the hideous sketch of me. I cringed, then walked faster.

Eventually I located the Benengeli. It looked small but very fancy. As I had at the hideout, I positioned myself across the street in a shadowy doorway and waited. It was all I could do. I watched the people come and go for an hour or more. I kept an eye on those getting out of taxis, or getting in them. Then, success:

The she-devil herself walked out the Benengeli's doors. She paused under the canopy, talking to the doorman and then lighting a smoke. The doorman flagged a taxi over and opened the door for her.

The minute that taxi door closed, I bolted for another nearby taxi. I splashed through the puddles, opened the door and dove into the back seat.

"Siga ese coche!" I commanded. "Follow that car!"

To which the driver turned around and looked at his strange, soaked passenger. His gaze told me he thought I was a bum. I dug out a peseta and chucked it at him.

"Please," I pleaded. "I can't lose them. Dos pesetas, if you insist."

That worked. He took off, catching up to Veronica's taxi within two blocks.

"Farther back," I instructed. "Más lejos."

He understood, allowing a good distance to build between them and us. The she-devil's taxi led us off the Gran Via and into a neighborhood I had not been to before. Here, the houses were enormous … but most of them looked empty and run-down. It was a once-nice neighborhood that wasn't nice anymore.

I told the driver to fall back even more, worried Veronica might look back. We tailed them for a while longer then finally her taxi stopped. Her driver got out and opened her door, then he pulled out an umbrella and began to walk Veronica to the gates of a house.

I thanked my driver and, when I was sure the she-devil was out of sight, got out. I crept through the rain, sticking close to a shrubbery running along the sidewalk, until I could see through the gates.

There, before me, stood a rundown, boarded-up mansion. Through the mist I could make out light escaping through gaps in the covered windows, on all floors.

This was it. I had no doubt Doctor Morley was inside. Now, I only had to rescue him.

I found a dry spot where I could wait until nightfall.

***

A nearby church had tolled eleven when I made my move.

I emerged from the overhang of a small shed, which had given me shelter from the rain. I set out to loop around the back perimeter of the rundown mansion. While the rain had stopped, the ground and foliage was still quite wet. Within no time I was soaked to the bone again.

In the rear of the property was a carriage-house structure. I pinned myself to the walls and traced around it, then I sprinted to the back corner of the main house. I paused to make sure nobody had seen me, then slinked around the side to find a way to climb up.

As luck would have it, I found a terraced chimney that rose from the ground and up the side of the mansion. I tested the structure, pulling on a few bricks to ensure they were still mortared, then began to climb. Panic struck when, midway through my climb, a single brick wiggled out and fell to the ground. I prepared myself to jump and run, worried someone inside might come out. But I heard no stirs, no angry killers storming my way.

I pulled myself onto the porch roof. I got low and crept forward.

At the first window I didn't see any light emanating from between the boards. There was light coming from the second window, though … but the boards were so tight I was unable to spy inside. So I crept around the corner to the front side of the house, to a different window. Here, there was a gap between two boards, allowing me to peek into the lit room inside:

There I saw Doctor Morley. Sitting, alone, in a ratty armchair. Behind him, a tattered bed.

I spied in from different angles, to ensure he was alone. Then I tap-tap-tapped on the wood. Inside, Doctor Morley didn't budge. I tapped again, a louder shave-and-a-haircut tap. Now he looked up toward the window. I gave him a single tap to say yes, it's me.

He looked around, appearing nervous. Then he got up and tip-toed to the window. He peeked through. I gave him a little wave. I whispered, hoping he could hear me through both wood and glass:

"I'm going to try to take a board off," I said.

I looked through the crack again. Doctor Morley was nervously eyeing the bedroom's door. He turned back to me and nodded.

I straightened up, trying to plant my feet better on the old porch roof. I looked the window up and down and selected the best board to pluck out. Then, I grabbed hold and pulled.

The board gave instantly. I toppled back. The board flew out of my hand. I hit the porch roof, hard.

There was a loud *CRACK*. The section of roof under me gave way, sending me crashing down onto the porch below.

Dazed, I didn't even have time to pull myself up before the front door opened.

It was Musa. He looked down at me, then up at the hole through the porch roof. From behind him, Benito and the she-devil appeared.

"Ah, here she is. I told you she had found us," Veronica sneered.

"Sí, sí, it is about time," Benito said. "Buenas noches, mi amor … we have been expecting you."

34

REUNITED

"You should have run away," Doctor Morley said.

"I *did* run," I explained. "But I decided to come find you."

"Why?"

"Why? To rescue you!"

"Hmph. Very brave, but very foolish. You should have gone to the police and explained it to them."

"Like I said, I didn't think they would believe me."

"You could have gone to the Embassy."

"And tell them what? That I knew about—but wasn't responsible for—a crime? That I was part of a gang looking for lost treasure and things fell apart? I'm sure they'd like that."

"They might have listened."

"No, they wouldn't have!" I insisted. "Stop criticizing my planning. I'm trying my best."

We were both tied to chairs. Doctor Morley had his forearms tied to his tattered armchair; I was secured to a much less comfortable dining chair. My hands were bound behind my back. Unlike my boss, my feet had been tied as well.

"If this is your best, I'd hate to see your worst," Doctor Morley deadpanned.

"Keep your punchlines to yourself," I hissed.

Our room—Doctor Morley's room, before my arrival—was dim and drafty. There was a messy bed, a dusty mahogany dresser, a few end-tables and the two chairs holding us.

"Well, you missed quite a scene at the Museum a few mornings ago," my tied-up boss remarked. "After all these years finding inventory for these places, it felt odd to be taking something out."

"I'm sure," I said. "Who broke the frame?"

"The frame? Oh, that was Benito. He didn't dare let Musa perform such a delicate … hold on, how did *you* know the Codex frame was broken?"

"How? Because I went there."

"You *went* there? To the Museum? Why?"

"To find you."

"Well, that was a questionable decision. They know who you work for … I have to think I'm a person of interest to them."

"Oh, I'm quite sure you're a person of interest to them. I certainly am."

"What's that supposed to mean?"

"Well, I went to find you … I went upstairs and into the Mesoamerican room and there they all were."

"Who?"

"Director Melida, his guards … a few police officers."

"The police! What did you tell them?"

"Uh … there wasn't much talking."

"Oh no. Explain?"

"They accused me and, well, I didn't think being thrown in some Spanish prison was a good idea. So I, you know, ran away."

"Ran away! Did they chase you?"

"They did. It's in all the newspapers."

"The newspapers! They must think you took the Codex page?"

"I suppose I didn't do much to make them think otherwise."

"This is awful, awful," Doctor Morley said. "Did anyone get hurt?"

"Um … there may have been some injuries," I said. "No deaths, though. I may have kicked someone in the groin."

"In the *groin*? Oh … Wendy, Wendy," he moaned.

"Has Benito told you about the guard in Seville yet?" I asked.

"What guard? At the Archive?"

"Yes. The old man upstairs, the one that helped us. I heard about it the day you disappeared."

"What happened to him?"

"Someone killed him," I said. "And we both know who that someone was."

Doctor Morley went silent for a moment, then said:

"My word. And how …?"

"The sword would be my guess."

"Damn. That explains the blood on his sleeve that night."

"He's a killer," I stated. "That's why I came to find you."

Doctor Morley let out a big sigh.

"Murder, theft ... and now we've been kidnapped," he said. "This is what I get for leaving the office."

***

A short time later Benito entered, followed by his man-servant and the she-devil.

"Untie Señor Morley," he commanded Musa.

The big man did as he was told.

"However ... I think it best we leave you restrained for a bit longer, no?" Benito then said to me.

"Why did you kill that guard?" I hissed.

"The guard in Sevilla?" Benito replied. "I did not kill him. He fell and impaled himself."

I didn't dignify his sick humor with a response. I could only glare.

"You had quite the time at the Museum of Archaeology, no? I have read all about it. You have become the star criminal!"

"I'm not a criminal," I growled. "And it's only a matter of time 'til someone catches up with you."

"Ho! But Vendy ... they are not looking for me," he said, then winked. "For that, I thank you for being so ... *predictable*."

I had been set up. I wanted to take a swing at him.

"Ah, sí, I can feel your anger," Benito said. "That is why I leave you tied up, no?"

"She has no value to you," Doctor Morley said, now up and walking. "Let her go."

"Only when she agrees to play nice," Benito replied. "Vendy, are you ready to play nice?"

Death stare.

"Let me say it another way," he said next, coming closer. "I can be done with you at any time, sí? But if you help … and you play nice … I let you live."

I had never had my life threatened before. I didn't like it. Benito saw my unease and spelled out the terms:

"You see, Vendy … you have looked at the maps more than anyone, no? You already show us you have the, what is phrase, the numero-uno eye. So now, no more copies … this time, we look at the real thing. Together."

***

The mansion's kitchen had several electric lights. It was there that page fifty-six of the Codex was laid out on a table, for all to inspect.

It was also in the kitchen that I saw Mister Carter. I had not seen him previously and didn't know he was at the mansion. He did not look well. There were great bags under his eyes. He was testy. I could smell the scotch seeping out of his pores.

"Come on, I can't see it, turn it more my way," the Egyptologist ordered.

"Don't touch it," Benito scolded. "It's delicate."

"Here's your materials, Sylvanus," Veronica said, approaching the table with Doctor Morley's portfolio.

"Yes. How nice. Thank you, Veronica, for giving that back," Doctor Morley sneered at her.

"Get the other maps out," Benito said.

Doctor Morley pulled out his collection of maps from his portfolio. Mister Carter pulled out his two land treaty maps, which he had stashed inside his coat. Doctor Morley placed the land treaty maps on either side of the Codex page. He then lined other several other maps, including a map of the Yucatán, above the three stolen items.

Then Doctor Morley dug in his portfolio for his little magnifying glass. He studied the large mark in the middle of page fifty-six first.

"This is an intentional drawing, not a stray scribble, no doubt about that," Doctor Morley said. "And it's absolutely a church. You can see the cross on top, a door in front and even an arch over here. If it is indeed Mani, that's the door to the main structure … and next to it there's an outdoor chapel, featuring a big arch. Here, Howard, you look."

"Mani. That must be where it is," Benito declared.

"Oh, please. This isn't *Treasure Island* … there's not a big 'X' marking the spot," Doctor Morley said. "These other marks on the page could be something, too."

"Indeed, Sylvanus," Mister Carter said, using the magnifying glass to compare the documents himself. "It's more akin to my second land treaty map than the first, but yes … on all three, it looks similar."

"What's that little mark, just below it?" Veronica said.

"I'm thinking that must be Pencuyut, or perhaps Xaya," Doctor Morley answered.

"And what's this little string of characters, down here?" Veronica asked next.

"You know, I'm not sure. Howard, hand me that magnifier, thank you. Now, let's see … it looks like someone tried to draw a little fence or something. Or is it … yes, yes, I think it is!"

Doctor Morley had grown more excited. We gathered around.

"It's almost like writing … or are those Roman numerals? Here, someone write this down, this is what it looks like: *v-t-v, a-l-i-s, a*. Yes, *v-t-v-a-l-i-s-a*."

"That's not a numeral," Mister Carter sniffed. "A Spanish word, perhaps? Or Latin?"

"Not one that's familiar to me," Doctor Morley answered.

"Those marks are meaningless," Benito jumped in. "Clearly, what we seek is at Mani."

"Calm down, you're getting ahead of yourself," Doctor Morley said. "This other mark up here is clearer. I think that must be Teabo. There's a small chapel there."

"It is not at a small chapel!" Benito snapped back. "You said yourself that de Landa was responsible for the fire at Mani. This man, this 'Chi' … was he not at Mani too?"

"I believe he was, but that's not dispositive," Doctor Morley argued. "What, you think you're going to take your magic sword to Mani and stick it in some magical keyhole and the treasure will be revealed to you?"

Then Doctor Morley let out a giggle and looked to Mister Carter, who likewise chuckled. I watched Benito, who didn't smile one bit. I think that was, indeed, his plan.

***

Benito's thoughts on what we had found did not change one bit that day.

Doctor Morley threw out several other possibilities about how the maps might line up. He even thought we might have page fifty-six oriented upside down, which would have put Teabo where Uxmal was and vice-versa.

But Benito was having none of it. He was adamant that we had found where the treasure was … now we only had to go and retrieve it.

"We should leave tomorrow," he said. "Out of Santander, direct to Havana."

"Based on just this?" Doctor Morley asked. "Preposterous."

"There is no time to lose, señor."

"No time to lose? It's been missing for hundreds of years!" Doctor Morley said back. "Who the hell is gonna find it before we do?"

Now Benito turned to Veronica:

"What is the young man's name again?" he asked.

"Oliver," Veronica answered. "Oliver Wheelock."

I sprang to attention. *Oliver?*

"Oliver?" I interjected. "You mean … Pan Am Oliver? What's he got to do with this?"

Veronica looked over at me with serpentine satisfaction.

"Stop playing dumb, Wendy … we all know what he's up to," she said.

"What he's up to? He's wandering the Yucatán … drinking and partying!" I argued.

"He's gone back to Yaxchilan, Wendy … we figured that out a long time ago," Veronica shot back.

I looked to my boss. Had he told them about Oliver? He looked away.

"Doctor Morley? What did you tell them?" I asked, not wanting to believe it. "Oliver has nothing to do with this!"

"It slipped out, Wendy," my former boss explained. "I'm sorry. I'm sure your friend has given up by now anyway."

***

That unpleasant exchange only reinforced my belief that Doctor Morley and I were in great danger. We needed to get away from Benito and his gang, fast.

We needed to break out, go to the authorities and explain everything. Then I would contact someone with the Institute—Tatiana maybe, or Doctor Blom. I would see if there was any word of a drunk Florida boy wandering the Yucatán.

But getting out of here was my first and foremost concern. So that night, when Musa escorted Doctor Morley and I back upstairs to our shabby accommodations, I kept my eyes out for possible escape routes.

35

MY PERILOUS PLAN

To my surprise and disappointment, Musa walked me to a different bedroom on the second floor. This one was on the opposite side and across the stairway from the room where I had first found Doctor Morley.

There was no electric light inside, but the glow from the hallway revealed a bedroom much like the other one. It had a nasty-looking bed covered with a single frayed blanket, a single dining chair and a sooty fireplace.

"Ungh. You. Here," Musa gestured.

Without objection I entered. The goon closed and locked the door from the outside. I found myself alone in a pitch-black room; I fumbled for the bed, remembered the condition of it, and fumbled for the chair instead.

When my eyes steadied, I scanned my confines. Along one wall were two windows, boarded up. There was another door, which I found to be a closet, but that was it.

I sat and listened to the footsteps and muffled talk going on downstairs. I didn't dare make a move before the others were asleep. But they stayed awake for hours, leading me to lie down on the stained bed, using my near-empty shoulder bag as my pillow.

Somehow, I slept ... and I must have been out for hours. When I awoke I could detect no light emanating from under the door and no noises from downstairs. I remained still as a mouse for a long time, listening for any footsteps. There were none. I got to my feet and tip-toed to the nearest window, moving at a snail's pace to lessen the chances of a floor creak.

There were no latches or locks on the windows. I seized the handles on the lower sash and gave a gentle tug. It slid up with almost no effort. Using one hand to hold the sash up, I then pushed on one of the boards. It fell off, as if it had been waiting generations for someone to do just that.

I held my breath as the board slipped away, thinking it would thunk on the porch roof. Instead I heard it land on foliage, with minimal sound. I maneuvered a second board out and used it to prop the sash open.

Jutting my head out the window, I discovered there was no porch at all on this side. It was a straight drop down, some twenty-five feet or more, into an overgrown hedge. The board I had dropped was visible, lying on top of the shrubbery.

My brilliant plan had been to go out this window and use the porch roof to come around the front. I would then skirt around the hole in the roof and go to the far side of the mansion. There, I would try to enter Doctor Morley's room from a different window. We would then climb out, descend the chimney, run through the shadows to the carriage-house and away to safety.

I would have to make do without the porch roof, somehow. I leaned out the window to scan the mansion's exterior. It was brick, for the most part. But below me I spied a narrow strip of decorative white stone, delineating between the first and second floors. It was a thin outcropping, at most a single inch wide.

That narrow strip of stone was my only option. If I fell, I would fall into the bushes and presumably live. But if I made it, my plan would be back on track.

I retrieved my shoulder bag—my last remaining possession. Then I removed a third board from the window, setting it down inside. I crawled up onto the windowsill and lowered one leg over the side.

The thin protruding of decorative stone was slippery. But I was able to get my toes on, then I found turning my foot sideways against the wall provided greater support. I pushed myself up to lower my second leg ... and as I did I brushed the board propping the window open.

The board fell outward, down to the hedges. The sash fell downward, onto my leg and arm.

"*Motherf...*," I began, then bit my tongue. I endured the blinding pain in silence.

I paused, unsure if the racket had been loud enough to rouse my captors. But there was no turning back. Wiggling my bruised extremities out from under the sash, I lowered my second leg down. With a firm grip on the window frame I began to inch forward.

Hugging the wall, I used my fingernails to dig into the mortar between the bricks. I scooched along, swallowing the pain from my fingers and wrists, and made my way to the corner. There, I found a better grip on some marble accent stones. I pulled myself around to the front of the mansion, feeling great relief as my feet reached the porch roof.

The moonlight revealed the hole through the roof I had created during my first rescue attempt. I moved gingerly around it, again holding tight to the bricks, until I came to the first of Doctor Morley's windows.

The board I had torn off had not been replaced, allowing me to peer inside. It was dark and quiet. I assumed Doctor Morley was in the bed, which was nearer the window that faced the side of the house. So I crept forward at a snail's pace, terrified the porch roof would give way again.

I made it to that next window without incident, only to re-discover the boards on it were placed too tight together. I could not see inside to the bed, which I assumed was very close.

I pulled an edge of one of the boards. It was loose. I pried it out, placed it gently on the roof then proceeded to pull out three more boards.

Now all that separated me from him was the pane of glass. I tapped once, then twice. I tapped using shave-and-a-haircut again, to no response. He was, it appeared, in a deep slumber … which meant I would have to enter the room to wake him up.

I pulled up on the window. It was, to my relief, unlocked. I slid it open and lowered myself into the room, being careful not to let the sash come crashing down on me.

I heard him breathing. He was out.

"Doctor Morley," I whispered. "*Psst* … Doctor Morley …,"

I inched forward. My foot knocked into something: an empty glass bottle. I knew the sound all too well. I froze in place as the bottle rolled and tinkled.

Nearby, Doctor Morley stirred in his bed.

I shuffled my feet forward. Yet again, one of my feet came into contact with a glass bottle … a different one. It rattled louder than the first.

"Doctor Morley!" I whispered, louder this time.

The occupant of the bed jumped, startled awake.

"Who goes there?" came a voice … Mister Carter's voice.

Shit. They had moved Doctor Morley to a different room. The Egyptologist carried on:

"Who's there? Is this a dream?" he said.

I could see his enormous frame sit up in the bed. He kept going:

"Is that you, Tutankhamun? Is it my time?"

"No, no, it's me," I whispered, not thinking to include my name.

"That voice! That youthful voice! Oh, it *is* you, child of Thebes … you have come to carry me home!" Mister Carter babbled, growing louder.

"*Shhh!*"

"I knew, I knew you would come for me!"

"*Shhh!*" I tried again. "It's just me, Wendy!"

I don't know if he was drunk, delirious or hallucinating. But he wouldn't stop.

"Oh, mighty pharaoh ... I was wrong to enter the tomb!" he shouted, loud. "I was wrong, wrong! Forgive me!"

And now I could hear footsteps from the hallway. In seconds, I found myself crawling back out the window and onto the porch roof. Then, as I lowered the window back down, but before I could replace the boards, the door to the room opened. Light streamed in. Benito entered, then Musa. They scanned the room and then saw my face, watching them like a dunce through the window.

"She's out!" Benito shouted.

Musa stormed my way. Benito spun around and hobbled toward the door. I took off.

I scampered along the porch roof to the chimney, which I had used to climb up the night before. Instead of descending on my own, I decided I had to find Doctor Morley. I rounded the chimney and rushed to the first window I came too.

It, too, was boarded up. I pounded my fists.

"Doctor Morley!" but there was no answer.

I took a look back. Behind the chimney I could see a hulking figure. Musa had made it onto the porch. I ran to the next window.

"Doctor Morley!" but, again, nothing.

Now Musa was working his way around the chimney, a big task for the big man. I scampered all the way to the corner of the house. With each step the porch roof groaned, making me wonder how much longer it would hold. I rounded the corner, coming onto the back side of the house, and kept at it:

"Doctor Morley! Doctor Morley!"

"Yes! Yes, I'm here!" came a call from inside.

And like a demon I ripped one board away, then another. Soon I saw glass, beyond it Doctor Morley. He was standing there, poised between pause and panic, when he should have been hoisting the sash. I had to do it myself, fearful Musa was only steps away.

"Come on! Come on!" I yelled, waving him out.

With a hint of hesitation he began to climb out. But as he did I turned and there, coming around the corner, was Musa, a mountain of muscle in the moonlight.

The goon smiled. Then he raised his arms wide and came toward us. At that same moment, Doctor Morley swung his last leg out the window.

KER-KRACK!

In an instant, a section of roof beneath us gave way. Doctor Morley and I fell down with it, crashing onto the floor of the porch below, unhurt.

We looked up: there was Musa, looking down at us. His section of the roof had held.

Then, from behind us, the most immediate door opened … and there stood Benito and Veronica, not more than ten feet from where we had landed. We all stared at each other for a brief second, then I yelled:

"Run!"

I pushed myself up, using one arm to pull Doctor Morley up with me. I held that grip as we sprang to the steps and rushed away. A few steps from the mansion, I turned to look back.

Benito and Veronica had come out the door to pursue us, but they were struggling to get over all the debris from the porch roof. At the same moment, Musa was approaching the hole that Doctor Morley and I had fallen through. He looked like he was going to jump down.

But just then there was a loud *SNAP*.

"Move back!" the she-devil warned Benito.

And I saw Benito, fake leg and all, dive back through the mansion's open kitchen door. He made it just as there was a final *CRACK*.

The porch roof collapsed. It all pancaked down, Musa along with it, onto the lower porch.

Doctor Morley was as shocked as I was. We both couldn't help but stop and gawk at Musa, half-buried in a pile of debris. Benito and Veronica stood behind him, in the doorway, two feet of rotted wood now blocking their exit.

That was all the head start we needed. I grabbed Doctor Morley by the sleeve and we started running. We ran around the carriage-house, down the perimeter of the property and out to the street.

I turned left at the first corner we came to, then right at the next. Then we cut through an alley and came onto a quiet side street, lined with cedar trees for hiding if the need arose.

"Slow down, slow down, my bad ankle can't take much more," Doctor Morley pleaded.

"We've made enough turns. We should be safe now," I proclaimed. "Stick close to the bushes."

He sighed and shook his head as he limped deeper into the shadows.

"Well, your second rescue attempt went better than your first," he remarked.

"Practice makes perfect," I replied.

36

An Impossible Dream

The streets were still dark but far from deserted. There were street-cleaners and delivery drivers at work, hours before the sun would rise. The shops were all closed, but I smelled bread, so I knew the bakers were already working, too.

Doctor Morley and I did our best to look like two typical American sightseers, out for a pre-dawn stroll. When we saw people, we would fake chit-chat and walk at a normal clip. When we didn't see anyone, we picked up our pace and scurried along faster. Soon we crossed an avenue and came into a well-groomed park.

"I believe we're on the grounds of the Royal Palace," Doctor Morley remarked. "Fitting."

After a quick discussion we decided that, since the current monarch wasn't home, it wouldn't offend him if we crossed his lawn. We made our way onto a wide path, then a narrower one. After a bit we were no longer visible from the street.

We continued to wind our way into the gardens. At one point we heard people approaching, so we turned onto a side-path to avoid them.

By and by we came to a clearing, at the end of which was a tall monument. We had a quick discussion and decided that it was time for a break. What better place for typical American sightseers to stop than a monument?

The monument's focal point was an imposing central tower, perhaps fifty feet tall. Upon this central tower was a large statue of a seated man. In front of the tower stood two smaller statues. One of these smaller statues showed a tall man on a horse, carrying a lance. The other looked to be a smaller man on a mule or donkey.

"Ah, Don Quixote and his faithful squire, yet again," I remarked. "If I didn't know better, I'd say someone upstairs is making a little joke at our expense."

"Which one of us is the sidekick?"

"I suppose we'll have to wait and see. My, they do love their Cervantes, don't they?"

We walked closer to the monument. First we inspected the statues, which both had a very realistic feel to them. We debated whether Sancho was riding a donkey or a mule and decided it was a donkey. Then we admired the statue of Cervantes, overlooking his dippy duo from the tower.

It seemed like a safe place for us. We found a decent spot to sit on the skirt of the monument and began to discuss our next steps.

***

We agreed it was too risky to throw ourselves at the police. To do so would guarantee a mad circus—two thieving, murdering Americans! Plus, we had scant evidence of our supposed innocence.

We debated at length going to the Embassy and ultimately decided against it. While it might preserve our personal freedom, at least temporarily, it would come at a cost. Namely, it would expose Doctor Morley's—and the Institution's—involvement in this bizarre scheme.

Next, I suggested he contact someone at Carnegie, someone he could trust. Perhaps Doctor Blom or even Tatiana. They could come help us. He rejected that idea, too.

I sensed he wasn't being forthcoming with me.

"You're conflicted, aren't you?" I asked.

He nodded.

"Did you ... see something in the map?"

He pursed his lips, then nodded again. Now I went back to my old ways, staying mum, hoping for more. It worked.

"It *is* Mani," he said. "I'm sure of it."

"Well, we knew that, didn't we?"

"No, no ... I mean it's not based on the Mani land treaty map," he went on. "But it's by the same artist, I expect that's why it jumped out at you."

Again, I didn't dare interrupt.

"It's a map of *the village itself.* The other marks correspond to roads and other landmarks in Mani."

"Other landmarks? Such as?"

"There's a cenote there, a hidden sinkhole, near the heart of the village," Doctor Morley said. "That's the little blob with the supposed letters by it. What was it, *v-t-v-a* ... oh, it doesn't matter. They're not even letters."

"They're not?"

"No. But I wanted Benito think they were, just as I wanted him to think that map showed a region, not a single village."

"If they weren't letters ... what were they?"

"It's a ladder. Chi was drawing a ladder. It must go down into the cenote."

A ladder. A ladder, in a cenote, in the village of Mani, in Yucatán.

"Do you think that's where the treasure is?" I asked.

"It might be ... or it might be gone already," Doctor Morley replied. "I'll give Howard credit, he called this one a long time ago. De Landa! I should have known."

"A priest took it? That's not very holy."

"I don't know if he took it or if it fell into his lap. But his scribe found out and, as near as I can tell, wanted to let someone else know."

"Who?"

"I can't even imagine."

Then we sat in silence. The sun was coming up, casting a warm glow over the treetops. A few early risers had strolled into the park for their morning exercise. A woman was walking a dog. I had a difficult question but I had to say it:

"I'm getting the sense you didn't want to be rescued."

Doctor Morley chuckled to himself.

"It's that obvious, is it?" he said.

"So ... now you want to see it through to the end? Even with a killer?" I pressed.

"Well, of course not. It would be nice to proceed to the end minus the killer, if that is an option," he said. "I'll need his magic sword, of course ... to unlock the magic door."

"Oh, stop. You don't believe that, do you?"

"The sword? Of course not," he replied, chuckling. "But I have become a believer in page fifty-six."

And then my former boss seemed to lose himself in his thoughts. I let him be, scanning my surroundings, my eyes focusing on a man who had come and sat on a nearby bench. He had a guitar case, which seemed peculiar for this early hour. He pulled out his guitar and began to pluck the strings. His first, sweet sounds wafted up to us.

Doctor Morley was staring out, past the statues of the man of La Mancha and his squire. He began to speak:

"It's an obsession. It's to me what Tut's tomb was to Howard. But at the same time it's more than that. This treasure, if it exists, could bring overdue attention to civilizations and cultures that history has overlooked."

He sighed.

"I've spent my entire career listening to fellow archaeologists belittle and downplay the contributions of the Aztec and Maya. To them, archaeology is all about epic finds in Egypt and the Holy Land. Well, if it takes a haul of gold to open their closed minds, so be it. And that's why I've got to beat Benito and Veronica to it. In so many ways it has become, as the writer sitting up there would say, my quest."

"Quest?" I asked. "What do you mean, quest?"

And at that moment the guitar player began to strum a simple Spanish melody. Doctor Morley began to explain, his voice becoming slow and deep:

"It's just … an impossible dream. To fight … an untouchable foe. A climb, steep as Kilimanjaro; A dare, where but bravest will go …,"

Was he singing? He stood up, then:

"… To right, what I perceive as wrong. To speak, and reveal the scar. To try, though it all might seem dreary. To teach, of the lies told thus far …,"

He became louder:

"This is my quest! It may sound bizarre! It all may seem hopeless, a bridge much too far. But I'll fight for what's right … I'll unmask all the flaws. And I'll put up with hell for the Mesoamerican cause …,"

He started walking toward the statues, his voice strong:

" … And I know, it may still prove not true; I'll still give it my best … so my heart can be peaceful and calm … and no longer obsessed …,"

Now he was next to the Don Quixote statue, so I took my place beside Sancho for his big finish:

"… And the world, they'll see what's been amiss. That one man, knew we must tell our youth … the glory … of the Aztec and Maya …,"

He spread his arms wide:

"To teeeach … the im-preg-nable … truuuuth!"

He held that last, deep word … a true baritone. The guitar player heard him and strummed out a big, explosive finale. At that, a flock of birds sprang from a nearby tree, their wings sounding like applause.

I let him bask in his glory for a moment. Then I said:

"I'm confused … are you saying you want to go *back* to Benito?"

37

A DEAL WITH THE DEVIL

That was exactly what he meant. Later that day, we began to make our way back through the park to the old mansion.

I had serious doubts about the wisdom, or lack thereof, of this move. It hadn't been easy to escape the damn place. To return ourselves to our captor—an admitted killer—seemed illogical.

But I had faith in Doctor Morley. I understood now, better than I ever had before, what this all meant to him. He wanted to see it through. For reasons I'm not sure of myself, a part of me did as well.

We had only the clothes on our back. I feared being recognized on the walk back, so I flattened my hair, trying to avoid looking like the monstrous woman from the newspapers. I insisted we stick to the side streets and the alleys. Eventually we made our way to a small hotel, where we secured a taxi. Doctor Morley had lost his wallet during our escape, but I still had my money-belt, so I fished a few coins out to pay the driver.

"You can run, you know," Doctor Morley said during our ride.

"What do you mean?"

"You can get out now. Walk away and not look back," he said, seeming quite serious. "You might not get another opportunity."

I thought about it, then thought about it some more, then said:

"I want to stay with you."

"I'm serious. You can go. I'll be fine. Go to Paris."

Paris. That almost won me over … but I resisted.

"I'll always have Paris," I told him. "Let's find your treasure first."

***

He repeated his offer a final time as we approached the run-down mansion we had escaped the day prior. Again I said no.

Together we walked to the door and, like guests arriving for dinner, knocked. There were footsteps. The door was unlocked and opened and there stood Musa.

He didn't seem all that surprised to see us. The big man waved us through the door then locked it. We went down the hallway and into the main sitting room, where we found Benito and Veronica sitting in armchairs. They both smiled as we walked in. Neither got up.

"Ah, sí, here they are, as expected," Benito said.

"Hmph. I sincerely doubt that," Doctor Morley scoffed.

"Oh, but I did, Señor Morley, I did," Benito went on. "It was a certainty you would return."

"Uh-huh. Why's that?"

"It's simple, is it not?" Benito said. "You are like me. You want to know if it's *real*."

Doctor Morley inhaled, then lied:

"My primary reason for returning was to make sure Howard was safe," my boss said. "Where is he?"

"Passed out upstairs," Veronica answered. "Sleeping off the distillery he poured down his throat last night."

"So …," Benito followed with a chuckle. "That's why the two of you returned? To check on the welfare of your companion? Mm-hm, of that I am sure."

"I said that was our primary reason, not our only reason," Doctor Morley said. "And yes, Señor Barataria … we did come back to talk about how we might move forward … temporarily."

"Perhaps I don't need you anymore," Benito said with raised eyebrows.

"You and I both know that's not true," Doctor Morley fired back. "The reality is you need me much, much more than I need you. You might think you can find a willing accomplice with my breadth and depth of knowledge … but take it from an expert, you can't."

Now Benito just glared at him. Doctor Morley continued:

"So I'd suggest you embrace this opportunity. With me, you just might find what you're looking for. Without me, you'll wander the Yucatán in vain, clutching that goddamn sword and wishing you would have listened to me when you had a chance."

***

So the deal was made. The rest of that day and evening were spent making preparations for our journey.

At first our plan was to take a passenger liner to Mexico. That would have meant going to Cádiz or San Sebastián, both of which had direct routes to Havana and Progreso. Then I mentioned that I no longer had my passport, which was back in my suitcase at the Palace Hotel. As I was wanted for theft—and possibly murder—going to the Hotel to retrieve my suitcase would not be wise.

My lack of a passport didn't faze Benito.

"There are freighters in Bilbao that will take us for a tenth of the price, no questions asked," he said.

"A freighter?" Veronica said. "I say we send Wendy back to the hotel to fetch her belongings."

It was not meant to be a joke, more of a kick in the shins. I glared at her. She glared back, then wandered my way. She came up to me and whispered:

"Just remember … we can turn you in at any time. Don't get cute."

I didn't make eye contact. I waited for her to slither away.

Suddenly, we heard a cry for help coming from the stairway:

"Ack! Erp! Hep!"

It sounded like a choking animal. We dashed from our seats toward the stairs, where we found Mister Carter staggering on the landing.

His face was purple. His eyes were bulging out. His collar was up and he had a finger in it, under his tie.

He looked like he couldn't breathe. Before we could reach him, he stiffened up and his massive frame toppled down the remaining steps.

"Help him, help him!" Doctor Morley shouted.

We sprang to his side.

"Is he choking?" Doctor Morley said, taking charge. "Howard, are you choking? He's got a finger to his throat. Howard, are you choking?"

"It's his tie!" I said, which seemed obvious.

I reached down and grabbed the knot in his tie. I pulled until it loosened. Mister Carter took an enormous breath in, then out. His color began to stabilize. His eyeballs returned to their sockets.

"*Wooh* ... oh, thank you, thank you ... this damn tie, does it every time."

"Every time?" Veronica asked.

"I must grip it wrong. This is the tie I wore in the Valley, you know ... that day we formally opened the tomb. Sentimental value, as you might expect."

"You should toss that tie, Howard ... it might be bad luck," Doctor Morley advised.

"Don't be silly, man," Mister Carter replied, still catching his breath. "The boy king is much more creative than that. He's not going to strangle me with my own blasted tie."

***

Before retiring to the bedrooms—the same ones we had fled the previous night—we inventoried our various clues. They would all accompany us on the journey:

Mister Carter had his two land treaty maps and he wasn't letting anyone else carry them. He kept them tucked inside a small notebook that he carried in his coat pocket.

Doctor Morley had been reunited with his portfolio, left behind during our escape. In it he had his collection of old maps and documents, the materials I had reviewed on the Orizaba. Doctor Morley's portfolio also contained my notebook, which contained my reproduction of the Codex.

Benito Barataria had his precious sword. I do not know if the blade belonged to Hernán Cortés, the second Martín Cortés or neither … but I do know that Benito loved his sword very, very much. He played with it, he fondled it, he stared at it, he played with it some more. When he wasn't touching it he would lay it down in its blanket then swaddle it like a newborn. At bedtime he carried it upstairs with two arms, like a doting father.

The proper storage of page fifty-six of the Codex generated heated debate. Eventually, it was decided the ancient page should be kept between two leaves of sheathing, secured inside a book. The book had been Veronica's, some smutty French novel. But it was the right size, so page fifty-six would be stashed there … and the book would then be stashed in Benito's bag.

That evening, as I laid in my smelly bed, I realized it was my final night in Spain. So I took stock of the clues in my own, personal treasure hunt:

I had gotten to see the Prado, which was good.

I had made new friends—Paris friends—which was also good.

I was returning to the Yucatán, which wasn't good … but was only temporary.

Then, as I inventoried my mind and body, it occurred to me that I had gone quite a while without any nightmares. I suppose meeting the Dead Writer in person had played a part in his banishment from my dreams … but that wasn't all:

I had started to act on the world, instead of letting it act upon me.

That was a good thing … I hoped.

38
THE RETURN VOYAGE BEGINS

Before dawn we departed, travelling in an arranged motorcar that drove us all the way to Bilbao.

It was an odd journey. Benito insisted on sitting in the front, on account of his fake leg. That meant the rest of us—Musa included—had to squeeze in the back. There were two uncomfortable jump seats, which were assigned to Veronica and myself. The remaining men occupied the back seat. Poor Doctor Morley was stuffed, literally, between the giant Musa and the portly Mister Carter.

Worse still, Benito instructed us to not discuss our voyage or our mission during the entire ride. He even told us to refrain from using each other's names. He seemed to think our driver—a stranger none of us had ever met—would betray us, which was ridiculous. Nevertheless, we kept up the act. We talked about the weather several times and politics once.

Just before noon we arrived at the docks in Bilbao. What few bags we had were unloaded and Benito paid our driver, eyeing him with suspicion during the transaction. Then the six conspirators made for the pier which held the only large ship in port.

Doctor Morley was studying our transatlantic conveyance.

"*That* rust-bucket freighter?" he observed. "It won't make it past the breakwater!"

"Nonsense, Señor Morley. These ships, they go back and forth all the time, no? Very safe."

"Well, it doesn't look very comfortable," Doctor Morley added.

"Comfort is subjective," Benito replied.

From what I could see, I doubted the freighter would meet anyone's definition of comfortable. The paint was flaking off its long sides, revealing its rusty skin. The peeling was so bad it had even stripped away the ship's name, at least on this side. The wheelhouse, a three-tiered structure set on the aft of the deck, looked like an amalgam of potting sheds. Above it rose a single smokestack, belching black.

"I say … slow down, man," Mister Carter pleaded. "It's not pulling away yet. And tell me, there is a restaurant on here, correct?"

"Una cafetería," Benito replied, without breaking stride.

"A cafeteria! Oh, my," Mister Carter moaned. "I *am* cursed, aren't I?"

***

There was little fanfare at the top of the gangplank. In fact, there was nobody there to greet us at all … we just walked on and wandered around until we found someone. Then some Portuguese man in a sailor hat led us around the deck, through a door and down a long dead-end corridor. There, we found our accommodations for our voyage.

It was a series of small cabins, set two by two. Each was equipped with a bunkbed. Benito began assigning rooms:

Doctor Morley and I were to be housed together, in one of the interior rooms with no porthole. Mister Carter would be in the cabin next to us. Benito and Musa would be in the cabin across the corridor from us. The she-devil would be next to them, in the cabin across the hall from Mister Carter's.

A rough-looking man, the captain, came and greeted us. He had the personality of a potted plant. He instructed us on how and when to get our food, then he turned to go.

"Perdón," Doctor Morley asked. "But can you point me toward the shuffleboard courts? Hoping to get some practice in."

Mister Carter and I giggled. The captain and our other companions did not.

***

An hour later the freighter pulled away from the pier. I wasn't on deck to say good-bye to Spain, as we had been told to stay put. So I collapsed on my squeaky top bunk, hoping for the sleep that had eluded me the night before. It occurred to me that if one's lot in life is represented by the comfort of one's bed, I was going in the wrong direction.

Sometime after that a few of us went in search of the cafeteria. There were three cooks on duty, each of them with a cigarette dangling from their mouth. The food was served like we were in a prison or an asylum: slopped onto metal trays, with a sprinkling of tobacco ash for extra flavor.

We carried our gruel back to our quarters and dined in private. Later, we reconvened in Mister Carter's cabin—which had been designated as our research center.

There, once again, we laid out our various clues. Doctor Morley pulled out a large map of the Yucatán and, ever the good actor, led Benito down the rabbit-hole. At one point I think Doctor Morley was simply trying to spout off as many village and site names as he could, to add to the confusion.

It worked, though. Only I knew what Doctor Morley thought of page fifty-six. The rest of them thought it showed a much larger region than it did. I knew it was a map of Mani itself.

It felt good to be doing some double-crossing, having been double-crossed myself.

***

The positioning of our cabins made them easy to guard. As we were all clustered into four rooms at the end of a dead-end corridor, Musa brought a chair out and set it down near the door to the deck. That meant to leave the rooms, we had to go through him.

He was somewhat friendly about it, though: he allowed us to venture out onto the deck without much bother. It wasn't like we could run off. I went out three times that day to smoke cigarettes, which Doctor Morley wouldn't let me do in our cabin.

Interestingly, Musa didn't seem to care where I went on deck, even if it was out of his eyesight. I suppose we were all on the honor system by then, an uneasy trust having taken hold amongst our gang.

So it came that on that first evening, after our gruel, I asked Musa if I could go out for a smoke. He waved me past, grunting something that was either a burp or meant 'hurry up.'

I walked down the corridor and then out to the deck. The wind was ceaseless, which led to several unsuccessful attempts to get my lighter going. I moved out of the direct wind, into a corridor between shipping containers, both stamped *Apples de España*. There, I got my smoke lit and leaned back to enjoy a peaceful moment to myself.

Suddenly, I heard voices coming from the other side of one of the containers:

"I cannot trust a word out of his mouth!"

It was Benito. He was not more than a few feet from me, unaware of my presence behind the apple containers. Then, Veronica:

"I'm quite sure he was rattling off random Yucatán places to throw you off."

They were speaking about Doctor Morley! I snuffed the cigarette, blowing my puff away into the wind.

"Señor Morley's value to us may peak sooner that we think, no?" Benito went on. "The closer he gets to Mexico, the more trouble he will become."

"I'll remind you that *you're* the one that wanted him back," Veronica said. "I warned you."

"I did not think he would play games," Benito growled. "He knows something and is not telling us."

"Well, stop letting him push you around."

"Qué? He has not pushed me around."

"He's cracking shuffleboard jokes and blatantly misleading you on the map," Veronica argued. "You know that, yet do nothing about it. Exert some dominance for a change."

"You know nothing of dominance."

"You'd be surprised," the she-devil shot back. "Benito, you have done what you promised you would do: you have brought order to chaos. Now, you need to show Morley who's in charge."

I was holding my breath. My entire body trembled.

"And Señor Carter?"

"Howard will be whatever we need him to be. Remember, someone will have to front all this at the end. He'll be good at that."

"But he annoys me."

"He annoys me too," Veronica responded. "At least he's better than the red-headed slut."

Me? My fists tightened.

"Hmph. You keep calling her that. If you are not careful you will slip up and say to her face, no?"

"Trust me, I've said worse to her. And she *is* a slut … she slept with you, didn't she?"

"Sí … but no woman can resist me."

"Uh-huh, right. But she *is* a woman, though? Not a man in disguise?"

"Ha ha. She is woman down there, sí? But up here, the chest … she more like boy, no?"

My instinct was to charge them and feed them both to the frickin' sharks. Every ounce of my will-power was being tested. I kept listening.

"She's a threat, too. Probably more than Morley is," the she-devil said. "At least an archaeologist brings value. She brings nothing."

"She found the map."

"No, she diddled you, so you keep her around," Veronica shot back. "You're like a cat playing with a cornered mouse. We'll have to dispose of her soon enough, you know. Let's hope we don't have to do the same with Morley."

Now a wave of horror washed over me. Dispose of me?

"That moment may come," Benito said. "But I give Señor Morley a few more days to ... see the light. Is that the term? Sí? He does have, as you say, the value."

"And the girl?"

"I will decide by Havana," Benito replied.

"Don't be sentimental about it," Veronica sneered.

Then they began to wander away. My feet wanted to scamper alongside the containers, to see what else they might reveal ... but my heart and brain said no. My life was now on the line.

I had to let Doctor Morley know, before it was too late. I waited until I was one-hundred-percent positive I could move undetected.

As I made for the door to go inside, I happened to glance up at the wheel-house. There, in faded letters, I finally saw the name of our rundown freighter:

Hispaniola.

39

OUR CABIN CONFINEMENT

I came off the deck and inside, acting normal as I passed Musa. I made my way down the corridor to Mister Carter's cabin, where I knew Doctor Morley was working.

I entered to find the two archaeologists bickering over maps:

"No, no, Sylvanus ... you're holding it wrong," Mister Carter said. "Turn it one-quarter clockwise."

"Stop call me Sylvanus, for the kazillionth time," Doctor Morley responded. "And I disagree."

They had page fifty-six laying on top of the small table. Mister Carter reached out to rotate it. Doctor Morley slapped his hand away.

"Don't touch it!" my boss said.

Mister Carter rolled his eyes. "I don't see why only *you* get to touch it."

"Because I'm more careful, that's why. And I'm a Mayanologist," Doctor Morley said.

"Then you should know enough to turn it the correct way," Mister Carter said.

"It is the correct way."

"Nonsense. If that's a little cross on top of a chapel, we need to orient the map horizontally." Mister Carter said.

"Nonsense yourself. If we do that, it doesn't line up with the land treaty map. Here, dammit, look again."

My former boss huffed and pushed through some papers and pulled out one of Mister Carter's maps. He held it next to the Codex page and looked like he was comparing the two. He was putting on a good show … but I knew confusion, not solution, was Doctor Morley's ultimate goal:

"See, that cross you insist is facing the wrong way … we orient that to Teabo. Good-sized mission there, that would make sense. Then these other marks on the Codex page line up quite well with the other towns on the map. This mark over here must be Muna or Sacalum. And way down here, in the corner, that must be Ticul."

"But look how many missions are on the land treaty maps!" Mister Carter responded, then guffawed. "I mean, come now … if we turn it my way I think it all lines up rather well too. Turn it, let's take a look."

Doctor Morley sighed, then reached out and rotated page fifty-six a quarter-turn.

"Aha, see? The cross is up the way it should be. Now, this smudged town along the page break … you said this is what?" Mister Carter asked, now pointing to the Land Treaty map.

"Tekit," Doctor Morley answered.

"Yes, yes, Tekit, of course. And that would make this bigger mark down here line up with … what's this one again?" Mister Carter went on.

"Ticul," Doctor Morley answered. "Or that's Uxmal next to it."

"I thought Uxmal was in a westerly direction from Mani," Mister Carter said.

I jumped in. "Doctor Morley ... could I speak with you a minute?"

"One minute, Wendy. Yes, Howard, it is 'westerly,' not due west," Doctor Morley deadpanned.

"Well, then, we need to turn this land treaty map the proper way now, right?" Mister Carter said.

The Egyptologist reached out and rotated his own map. The Mayanologist sighed again, in mock frustration.

"You realize we're right back where we started, don't you?" Doctor Morley said.

"No, we're getting to the point where I can understand it better," Mister Carter said.

I tried again. "Doctor Morley, it's quite important."

Now he stopped and turned around, looking at me over his glasses:

"Well? What is it?"

"Um ... might we go back to our own cabin?" I asked, a wary eye on Mister Carter.

Right then the door opened. Benito strode in, followed by Veronica. Musa stood behind them, lingering but opting not to enter the cramped space.

"Señor Morley, Señor Carter ... progress, I hope?" Benito asked.

"Still trying to orient the thing the right way," Doctor Morley answered.

"Ancient cartography leaves much to be desired," Mister Carter observed.

Benito approached the documents laid out on the bed. At this point I had not yet informed Doctor Morley of what

I overheard on deck. I tried to look calm, act calm and be calm. I sat down in one of the chairs to stop my knees from knocking.

"Señor Morley," Benito said, now sliding between the two archaeologists. "Sometimes I wonder … if the heart is in place, no? Of you?"

"You mean … you wonder if my heart is in the right place?" Doctor Morley interpreted.

"Sí … that is, we are like Musketeers, no? All for one, one for all?" Benito went on. "That means we are honest with each other at all times, ah? No holding back?"

"Of course not," Doctor Morley said.

Now Doctor Morley backed away from the bed and walked to the other side of the tiny cabin. He had his arms folded in disgust. Benito looked at him and smiled:

"Señor Morley … I must remind you of our first meeting. Your past, it may bite you in the back, no?"

"It's 'your past may come back to bite you' and yes, I remember the meeting well," Doctor Morley replied. "You're dredging that up again? Blackmailing a supposed partner?"

Benito took two steps toward him, which was about the entire expanse of the tiny cabin. He brandished his walking stick in his right hand, raising the parrot-head handle to Doctor Morley's face.

"Do not think you can keep secrets from us," Benito snarled.

"Put the bird down," Doctor Morley snarled back.

"Absurd! Your mind's gotten the better of you, Señor Barataria," Mister Carter jumped in.

Benito whirled around, now bringing his cane handle up to within inches of the Egyptologist's nose:

"*Enough* out of you … back to work. Speak only when spoken to … comprende?"

Mister Carter's face went white. The big man pivoted around like a beaten dog, returning to the maps. Benito turned back to Doctor Morley. He got right up in his face.

"And one other thing, Señor Morley," he sneered. "I know all about your game at the ruins, ah? And how it is all paid for? Señora Shitty, she has told me all about it."

"It's 'Shetty,'" Veronica interjected.

Benito shot the she-devil a don't-correct-me look. Doctor Morley was saying nothing, only staring at our lead captor with quiet rage.

"My point, señor, is that you have many, many secrets," Benito continued. "To have those revealed would not be good for any of us, no?"

Doctor Morley took a dramatic breath in, then:

"My conscience takes priority over my profession."

Which was a good comeback. But Benito didn't smile. The Spaniard leaned in and said:

"Sí. But … I hope I get these words right … do not let your conscience take priority over your life."

And that line took the air out of the room, even though I was the only one that knew the full extent of Benito and Veronica's treachery.

***

It was only late that night—after we had been locked up in our cabin—that I told Doctor Morley what I had overheard on deck. I leaned over my bunk—in case our captors burst in, unannounced—and whispered the entire exchange to him.

It was dark and I couldn't see his expression … but I could sense his worry.

"All my options are bad," he whispered. "If I help them, I've betrayed myself, my profession … and the great civilizations of our past,"

"Don't make it more dramatic than it already is," I advised.

"If I don't help them … well, then, I'm of no more use, am I?" he whispered, more to himself than me.

"We need to get away," I said. "Before Havana."

"Why before Havana?"

"Because I think he wants to get rid of me before we get there."

"Both of us?"

"No, just me," I whispered. "I hope that doesn't make a difference."

He chuckled. "Don't worry, we're not going to sacrifice you yet."

"Ha ha. So what do we do?" I asked.

"I want to talk with Howard, somehow," was the reply. "He's in as much danger as us."

"He'll spill the beans!" I warned. "Please, don't say a word."

"He needs to be warned."

"Let me talk to him," I said. "He likes me more than he likes you."

"Hmph. What will you tell him?"

I had no idea. "I'll think of something," I whispered.

Then we both tried to sleep, which was near-impossible. Throughout the night, waves crashed broadside into the freighter, sliding me back and forth across my bunk. It got so bad that at one point I even tried to think of the Dead Writer. I figured a familiar nightmare would be a welcome escape from my horrible new reality.

***

In the morning the *Hispaniola* was still tossing to and fro. I fell on the floor getting out of my bunk then smashed into the corridor wall on the way to breakfast. In the cafeteria, I spilled my water into my gruel, ruining both.

Doctor Morley was so seasick he appeared to alternate colors, like a chameleon. He asked to be excused so he could go to this cabin. The rest of us went to Mister Carter's cabin—with the exception of Musa, who resumed his post on a chair in the corridor.

The moment we arrived in the cabin I felt compelled to act useful:

"Benito … might I see the sword again?" I asked.

"Why?"

"I've never held it. Maybe I'll see something you all missed," I said, playing up my sole accomplishment.

He considered me for a minute. Then he nodded, hobbled out of the cabin and returned a moment later, carrying his swaddled sword. He had the proud look of modern-day Mary, showing off the Messiah.

He asked Mister Carter and Veronica to step aside so he could lay it down on the lower bunk. He unwrapped his precious poker and bent down and picked it up by the handle. He backed away from the bed and, setting his walking stick aside, raised it up toward me … point first.

I jerked my face back, the tip coming within an inch of my chin. I glared. He smiled, lowered the weapon and offered the handle to me.

I took the sword from him. I studied it intently, scanning the blade up and down, picking at and around the guards, twisting the handle.

"This orb, at the end," I said. "Is that typical?"

Benito studied the metal orb which fused the knuckle-guard with the handle.

"Sí, I suppose it is somewhat typical of swords with guards."

"Are the balls always this large?"

"Well, ah … sometimes, perhaps," Benito went on, buying what I was selling. "Why do you ask?"

"Well … if we can't unscrew it … maybe the ball was meant to be broken?"

"Broken!" he exclaimed.

"Perhaps there's something hidden inside, like an egg," I said, then tapped the ball. "I dare say it sounds hollow. Here, listen, doesn't it sound hollow?"

It didn't sound hollow, of course. But the act was holding up, so I handed the sword back to him. He held the handle up to his ear, then tapped the little ball on the end. His face was puzzled, his pose was laughable.

"I hear nothing."

"Give me some time with it," I said. "It needs a full inspection."

Now he squinted at me, which made me think I had over-acted. But then he began to nod.

He handed it back and for the next half-hour I studied the damn thing. There was nothing special about it, besides the stamped crest with the three crowns. There were no hidden chambers, no faded etchings, no codes or writing engraved anywhere. It looked to be, as Doctor Morley had first said, a mass-produced item, personalized as a gift.

But I did all I could to appear mesmerized, as if the blade's hidden message was always just around the corner. I picked at it with a penknife. I asked questions about it, made comments about it and tried to impress upon Benito that I, too, considered it special.

Soon he took the sword back, announcing he was going to get some fresh air. Veronica then announced she wanted to get away from the stuffy cabin as well. The two of them left, leaving me alone in the cabin with Mister Carter.

***

The Egyptologist eyed the door after our captors walked out.

"Is something wrong?" I asked.

"There's countless things wrong with those two," he sighed. "Never mind that. We've got a moment, let's have a drink."

I didn't argue. He went to the head of the top bunk and bent his big frame over to reach a back corner, coming up with a flask. He handed it over.

"Scotch?" I asked.

"Absinthe," he replied. "The first mate topped me off this morning."

"Absinthe. Has it been watered down? Or sweetened?"

Mister Carter scrunched his face up.

"This isn't the Queen Mary, my dear."

Indeed. I took a swig. It was bitter-tasting … but boozy, which rounded it out.

"Careful," he said. "This stuff will make you hallucinate."

"So I've heard," I replied. "Mister Carter, while they're gone, I wanted to ask you …,"

"About the sword?" he said, which had not been my question. "A monogrammed present from father to son. Probably purchased at a nice discount for three … appropriate for a man of dwindling fortunes like Cortés. He probably spent more having it engraved …,"

"No," I interrupted. "I wanted to ask you … how far are you willing to go with these people?"

"Who? The pirate or the wench?"

"Both," I said, happy we agreed on something. "They seem … angry."

"Well, yes, quite angry," Mister Carter said. "You do know they don't particularly care for you, don't you?"

"Yes, I heard."

"Indeed. But I'll go only as far with them as I need to know," he went on. "I may seem helpless at times ... but this old dog still has some spring in his step."

"Would you consider leaving, before they find it?" I asked.

"Me, leave? No, no ... but I'd consider them leaving, before *I* find it," he stated.

I began to think I shouldn't press the issue much more. So I changed topics:

"Tell me about the tomb," I asked.

"Tut's tomb? I'm sure I already have," he stated.

"Not that tomb," I said. "I want to know about Cleopatra's tomb. And ... could I have another belt off that?"

He agreed, on both points. Then the great Egyptologist told me all about his search for the lost tomb of Cleopatra and Marc Antony, while we traded shots of absinthe.

***

Through the rest of that day and into the next, nothing transpired to alter the worrisome course we were on.

Doctor Morley continued to mislead Benito on page fifty-six. At the same time, Mister Carter continued to mislead about his thoughts on the sword. Veronica continued to play everyone against each other, like the viper she was.

And Benito, for his part, acted like he wasn't about to kill most of us, which I'm certain he wanted to.

It was over the course of the next two days that a thought began to grow in my head:

My situation was dire ... and time was running out. Perhaps Doctor Morley couldn't appreciate that it was *my* head first on the chopping block, not his. He wasn't giving my predicament the emergency attention it deserved. Likewise, Mister Carter seemed in no particular panic ... he would go along to get along, to whatever end.

And that little thought grew more and more in me. I could no longer wait for someone to come to my rescue. If I wanted to live, I would have to save myself.

***

On our third night on the *Hispaniola*, during a storm, a sudden opportunity arose: I was left alone in Mister Carter's cabin while the others went to the cafeteria.

I waited a full minute. Then, from the top bunk, I seized Veronica's smutty French novel ... and with it, tucked inside, page fifty-six of the Codex.

I put the book inside my shoulder bag, along with my own copy of the Codex.

Then I seized Benito's precious sword, which the dumbass had forgotten on the lower bunk.

It was time to force his hand and end this, once and for all.

40

THE SWORD OF THE SPANIARD

I double-checked to make sure Musa had gone to the cafeteria with the others. The coast was clear. I hugged the walls and slinked down the corridor, being careful not to make the slightest sound.

When I came to the turn leading out to the deck I paused. I knew this was a risky move ... but I had no choice. I adjusted my shoulder bag, gripped the sword tight and made for the exit.

A stubborn wind was blowing against the door. I pushed hard to get out. The door slipped from my hand as I passed through, slamming shut behind me. Fearing someone might have heard, I picked up my pace.

It was gusty on the deck of the *Hispaniola*. The air was thick with salty spray. Beyond the railing, I could see nothing but the blackness of the Atlantic. Clouds obscured the night sky and it seemed like the darkest and loneliest place on earth.

I moved forward on the slippery deck, in the direction of the bow. I was still a bit unsure of what I was going to do ... but I knew it was only a matter of time until Benito returned to the cabin. There he would find no me, no sword and no map. He would be furious—beyond furious, really—and I needed to find a way to use his anger against him.

Afore of the wheelhouse were several dozen tarp-covered crates. I wound around and between them and then cut straight up the middle, along the spine of the ship. I found what looked like a decent spot and crouched down, sword in hand, and waited.

I didn't have to wait long. Within five minutes of arriving on deck I heard his first angry shout:

"*Vendy!*"

I stayed quiet at first, half out of strategy and half out of fear.

"You cannot hide!" he yelled, sounding closer. "Show yourself!"

Now I heard footsteps, followed by Veronica's voice:

"Maybe she's hiding below deck."

"No," Benito growled. "She's trying to lure me out. Vendy!"

A grunt came from farther back on the deck, indicating Musa had arrived, too. I wondered whether they had left Mister Carter and Doctor Morley alone. If so, I hoped the archaeologists realized and understood what I had done. Perhaps they would have the presence of mind to make a run for the captain's quarters.

But that dream was dashed in an instant. First I heard Mister Carter cough, then I heard Doctor Morley complain:

"Dammit, don't hold me that hard!"

They were all here. I had expected only Benito and Veronica and maybe Musa, but instead they *all* came. I tried to think up a new plan, as my current one wasn't going to work.

Then Benito yelled something I didn't like:

"Show yourself, you bilge-sucking whore!"

There were many insults I could let slide. Calling me a 'bilge-sucking whore' was not one of them.

I stood up, holding the sword firm in my hand. I walked out from behind the containers, revealing myself.

"Looking for something?" I said.

He wheeled around to me. He did not smile. He saw the sword.

"That should not be out here," he said. "Give it to me."

"No."

He was about fifteen feet away from me; Veronica and Mister Carter were a few steps to his rear. Further back, near the railing, I saw Musa and Doctor Morley. The goon had one of his big hands wrapped around Doctor Morley's arm.

"See here," Benito said. "Give me the sword, or I'll kill Morley."

"What!" Doctor Morley exclaimed … and then Musa inched him forward.

"You're not going to hurt him," I stated. "You're going to let him go."

"There will be no mind tricks here," Benito replied. "You're going to give me the sword. In exchange, the two of you live."

"No," I declared, my voice strong. "You're going to agree to let us go. *All* of us: Doctor Morley, Mister Carter and myself. You let us go … and then I'll give you the sword."

"No," the Spaniard replied.

I glared at him. Benito glared back. I decided to play my next card.

Keeping the sword raised toward him, I used my other hand to reach into my shoulder bag. I pulled out the notebook containing my copy of the Codex. Benito eyed me with suspicion.

"Woah! Is that ... *mine?*" Doctor Morley called.

I took a big step toward the railing, the sword in one hand, my notebook in the other.

"I'll toss them both," I warned Benito. "Believe me, I will."

"You wouldn't *dare* drop that sword," he snarled. "And as for your art-class project ... it is only a copy, no?"

That was my cue. I tucked the notebook under my sword-carrying arm, then dug in my shoulder bag for my final surprise. My hand was trembling. I kept eye contact with Benito as I fished out Veronica's smutty French novel.

I raised it up so they could get a better look. Benito's jaw dropped. Veronica gasped.

"You didn't bring the actual map up here, did you?" the she-devil asked.

I ignored her. I watched the other devil.

"She is not that stupid," he snarled. "She only has the book."

"No," I declared. "The map is in here ... and I'm willing to throw it away."

"I do not believe you."

"You don't believe I'll toss it?"

"I do not believe you have the map in the book," Benito answered, looking smug.

I was in disbelief. "Huh? Of course it's in here! It's between the pages, right where it's supposed to be."

"Prove it."

"Come again?"

"You heard me. If you have the map, show it to me, sí?"

Goddammit. I was running out of hands. I had the sword in my right hand and the notebook tucked under that same arm. My left hand was holding the novel up.

Then I did something profoundly stupid. So I could show him I had the *real* damn map, I took the sword and pinned it under my left arm. Then, using both hands, I flipped the book open to its ancient Mayan bookmark. In doing so, I took my eyes off of my opponent.

I heard his feet move first. I looked up, frightfully aware I had left myself vulnerable.

Benito took a strong step toward me and, at the same time, twisted the parrot-head handle on his walking stick. He pulled up on the handle to unsheathe his sword: a hidden rapier.

His eyes were alive with fury. "Drop it!" he demanded.

"Don't charge her!" Veronica yelled.

But his mind was made up. Benito rushed forward, sword drawn. Panicked, I reached for my own sword with my right hand. In so doing I dropped the notebook, which had been tucked under my right armpit. In the nick of time, I brought my sword up cross-wise, stopping Benito's first downward blow.

I staggered back, trying to keep my grip on the heavy blade. I was still holding the smutty novel in my left hand. Benito glared at me like a monster.

I took stock of my surroundings. Out of the corner of my eye, I could see my notebook on the deck … a few feet from the edge.

"Don't test me," I warned. "It's time for this to end."

"My thoughts *exactly*," Benito said … and on his final word, he charged.

This time he slashed cross-wise one way, then the other. I put my sword up, not knowing what to do but protect myself. I swung the ancient weapon around in front of me. Benito hobbled backward and tried to find his balance. I heard Doctor Morley yelling:

"Veronica! Grab that notebook!"

I looked up to see Benito charging at me once more. This time he brought his sword low, so I blocked low. He went high, I blocked high. While he was more skilled with a blade than me, I had two steady legs—unlike him—and I was able to push him back again.

But then, as he staggered back, he swung his sword up. The tip of his rapier caught my shirt sleeve. The smutty novel, with the real map tucked inside, fell to the deck.

In a heartbeat, Benito whipped his sword down and used the tip to flick the novel away from me. It slid across the damp deck, toward the she-devil.

"Someone get that!" Benito barked.

Veronica moved to pick up her book. When she had it, she stepped back with the others.

Now Benito had a wicked look about him. His evil eyes chilled me to my core.

"Well. This was a very bad decision, no?" he said. "Now, please … the sword."

"No. Not until you agree to let us go."

"Very well," he said, then called back to his man-servant. "Musa, get up here and relieve this silly girl of her weapon."

I looked back. Musa had been holding onto Doctor Morley, but now he let go and marched toward me.

"The sword. *Now*," Benito ordered.

"So he can kill me?" I retorted, then I looked to Musa. "Alto! Or trust me, I'll feed this frickin' thing to the fish."

Benito held up a hand to halt Musa. I scanned my surroundings. Doctor Morley was not being restrained any longer, but I saw no sign he was going to spring to my rescue. Mister Carter appeared to be confused … and I noticed he was now holding both my notebook and Veronica's smutty novel.

The she-devil began to slither forward, a serpentine smirk on her face.

"Give it to me!" Benito hissed.

There was a brief moment during which I considered handing the weapon over. Benito must have sensed my indecision … and in that moment, he charged again.

I stumbled back toward the center of the deck to avoid the thrust of his cane-sword. His blade missed me, clipping my shoulder bag. He turned and swung down at me again, but I brought my sword up just in time for another block. Then a big wave rolled the ship, causing Benito to lose his balance. He hobbled backward a bit, got his bearings and then planted his feet like a trained swordsman.

"Say goodbye, Vendy," he snarled.

And just as he said that, another giant wave smashed into the ship. The force of the impact made me lose my balance and stagger forward.

Benito, thinking I was charging him, held his sword straight out. Out of instinct, I brought my blade up in a similar fashion.

But I had no balance.

I stumbled right past him ... my forward momentum only stopping when my blade met flesh.

I let go of the handle and stepped back, disoriented.

I looked up and only then realized what I had done:

I had run the sword into Mister Carter.

The big man gurgled. He looked down at the sword stuck halfway through his belly. He coughed, causing a spray of blood to explode out his mouth.

"The notebook!" Doctor Morley shouted. "Oh, crap ... both books!"

Mister Carter had my notebook in one hand. In his other hand he held Veronica's smutty novel ... which contained page fifty-six of the Codex.

The ship rocked again. Mister Carter began to fall forward, away from the railing and toward Veronica. The she-devil lunged to catch him.

But then the *Hispaniola* rocked hard the other way. Mister Carter staggered backward, saved only by the ship's rusted railing.

The Egyptologist looked once more at the sword sticking out of his belly. He coughed; more blood came up. Then he looked up at the moon and stars and spoke his final words:

"I see ... *wonderful things.*"

Metal creaked. The railing buckled. The great man fell back, into the darkness.

There was an enormous splash. All of us, myself included, ran to look over the edge.

There were small crests of white on the black waves behind us ... but nothing else.

Howard Carter was gone.

My notebook was gone.

Veronica's smutty novel, which had held page fifty-six, was gone.

And the sword of the second Martín Cortés was gone, too.

41

BENITO BOILS OVER

Crew members came running out. There was lots of yelling. "Hombre al agua! Man overboard! Hombre al agua!"

Soon there was a shudder as the propellers were shut off. Everyone was peering over the railing for any sign of the poor man. Benito alternated between looking down at the black sea and glaring at me.

The captain appeared and started issuing orders. The *Hispaniola* was equipped with two large flood lights on each side and they were all turned on. Then there was a great lurch as the props were reversed, as the freighter was too massive to turn around.

With the darkness and the cresting waves it was difficult to tell if we were moving backward at all. Not that it would have mattered: there was neither sign nor sound from Mister Carter.

For many minutes everyone's attention was on the water. We watched and yelled and listened, all to no avail. I kept a watchful eye on Benito the whole time, for obvious reasons.

Soon the captain backed away from the railing. He clapped his hands to get everyone's attention.

"Qué pasó?" he bellowed.

There was silence. I told myself not to say a damn thing. The captain scanned over everyone and then his gaze came to rest on Benito.

"Señor, that was a member of your party, was it not?" the captain asked.

Benito took a deep, dramatic breath in and answered:

"Sí, he was."

"And did you see what happened?" the captain asked, walking closer.

I gulped and waited for his answer. It surprised me.

"There was ... a great wave. He staggered and toppled over," Benito said.

The captain considered him for a moment and then asked, "And why was he on deck during such conditions?"

"He was ... seasick," Benito said.

I glanced at Doctor Morley, who was standing a few feet over from me, with Musa looming over him.

"Mareado?" the Captain said, and for a moment I thought Benito's lies had caught up with him.

"Sí, sí. Oh, my poor amigo. He didn't deserve such a fate," Benito said. Then, ever the great actor, he cast a despondent look to the dark ocean and sighed.

The captain bought it hook, line and sinker. "Desafortunado," he said. "How unfortunate."

Then the captain looked back to where Doctor Morley, Musa and I were standing. He scanned our faces, then his attention returned to Benito.

"It was ... el gordo that fell?" he asked. "The big man?"

"Sí."

"What was his name?"

"His name was ... William," Benito replied. "William ... uh ... Bones."

"And you know this man's next of kin?" the captain inquired.

"He had complained of having none," Benito replied.

It dawned on me that neither the captain nor his crew knew that the man that had fallen was Howard Carter. A great and once-famous man had left us. Perhaps at the hands of a thousand-year-old curse ... or perhaps at the clumsy hands of me. Yet nobody outside our own bewildered party could appreciate this historic moment. As I considered this sad fact, a crew member shouted:

"Capitán Smollet! Sangre en la cubierta! There is blood on the deck!"

And that created a great murmur. The crew members parted and the captain made his way toward a series of dark drippings on the wet deck. He bent down and touched the blood and smelled it, like a detective would, then looked up to Benito, who said:

"Ah, sí, poor William. He had been coughing up blood for days. Consumption, no?"

And the idiot captain simply nodded and then stood up. He turned to us and asked us if that was what happened.

I looked at Doctor Morley, hoping he would rise to the occasion and turn on our captors. Instead, he looked down at his shoes. I wanted to say something myself ... but before I could, the captain turned and walked away.

Soon the flood lights were turned off. The crew members were ordered to return to their posts. Musa grabbed hold of my arm, then one of Doctor Morley's arms, and pulled us with him.

***

The man-servant manhandled us to the door that led inside. I looked back to see Benito talking with two crew members. He had his hand inside his coat, no doubt reaching for his wallet.

"Moo-va, moo-va," Musa grunted as he shoved us down the corridor.

"Watch my arm," Doctor Morley said to him. That made Musa stop. He glared at my boss and then he must've doubled his grip. Doctor Morley yelped out.

"Ow! Damn you, enough, I'm going!"

I didn't put up a fight. I was numb. I hoped that it was all a bad dream, another nightmare from which I would soon awake … but I knew it was all too real.

I felt awful about Mister Carter. Awful, awful, awful. I could see his face, frozen in fear, his eyes wide and shocked by his sudden end. And I never wanted anything like that to happen. It wasn't my plan, at all.

Musa dragged us to Benito's cabin. He shoved us inside and ordered us both to sit. We did as told. A moment later, Benito and Veronica arrived.

"Tie her up," Benito growled as he came in.

"Now, see here man," Doctor Morley said. "All she was doing was trying to get …,"

SMACK!

Benito slapped Doctor Morley across the face, hard.

"Shut the hell up," Benito said to my boss. Then, to Musa, "You heard me. Tie her up."

Doctor Morley fell silent. Musa looked around for something to tie me with. He spied a curtain tie-back and took it off the wall. He came and stood over me. I was scared silent. I sat there and shook like a leaf as he pulled my arms in back of me and bound my wrists together.

"Bueno. All tight?" Benito asked Musa, who grunted yes.

And then: *POW!*

Benito punched me … in the face, with a closed hand. Then he got down, looked me in the eyes and said:

"Do you have *any* idea what you have done?"

I didn't answer. I concentrated on willing away the pain of his cheap-shot punch. The villain took a breath and kept going:

"That sword was … very, very important to me. I have spent *years* trying to get my hands on it. Years! And you … and you …,"

He stopped trying to find the right words. He let his fist fly again: *POW!*

"Stop that!" Doctor Morley pleaded. "Dammit, Benito, you know she didn't mean for Howard to go like that."

"Keep out of it, Sylvanus," Veronica warned.

"And … the maps?" Benito went on, in some disbelief. "The Codex page? Even … your copy?"

"See? My copy *was* important," I grumbled.

SMACK!

Benito's open hand stung my face.

"This is no time for jokes," he said. "You … you have destroyed *all* the copies."

I corrected him:

"You still have both of Mister Carter's land treaty maps. Make do."

I felt satisfied at that … but then caught Doctor Morley's eye. He was gritting his teeth, as if I had said something wrong.

"Mister Carter's land treaty maps *are* still here, right?" I asked.

Benito and Veronica glared at me. Doctor Morley answered the question:

"Dammit, Wendy. Howard kept his maps on him, in his pocket."

"He did … what? Oh. Shit. Sorry," was all I could say.

"Sorry?" Veronica scolded. "You think this is something you can apologize for?"

"No! It's just that I …,"

Benito got in my face again, threatening me:

"It was *your* life that should have ended tonight, no? I have a mind to correct that mistake right now."

Now I rolled my eyes up to him:

"You don't have the balls," I said.

His eyes lit up with anger once again. He reached for his walking stick. I thought he might unsheathe it and impale me right then and there. Instead he raised it back, over his head and swung it down at me.

All went black.

***

When I came to, I found myself in the lower bunk of the same room.

My noggin ached. My jaw felt displaced. I wiggled it and looked around. I was alone.

I laid there a bit, healing, then got up. I went to the door and listened. Nothing.

Next I tried to turn the door handle. It was locked, from the outside.

I returned to the bed and sat down. It dawned on me that I was now a prisoner and this was my cell ... on Death Row.

Fortunately, the bulk of the day went by without incident. At one point I had to use the facilities, so I knocked on the door for several minutes. Then I knocked on the wall my cabin shared with the cabin of the dearly departed Mister Carter. With no answer, the room's washbasin became my chamber pot.

After the sun went down—and I had given up hope of ever eating again—the door was unlocked. It opened and there stood Doctor Morley, a tray of gruel in his hands, Musa lurking behind him.

He walked in, Musa watching his every step. My former boss set the tray down on the table and said:

"I had to fight like hell for this. Enjoy it."

"Is this my last supper?" I asked him.

"Would you prefer we jump ahead to the crucifixion?" he answered.

"I'll take the resurrection, if that's on the menu," I replied.

"You haven't lost your wit. We'll be in Havana in the morning."

Musa was standing right there. If he had not been, I would have suggested to Doctor Morley that we bolt on the gangplank.

"What's going to become of me then?" he said.

"I'm not sure," Doctor Morley replied. "Benito intends to knock you out to get you off the ship. He worries you'll make a scene or try to run."

"He knows me too well. He's gonna knock me out? With his fists?"

"No, he's got curare. A tribal toxin, as they say. He's trying to figure out how much he can give you without causing death."

"Well, I hope you're helping with that," I said. "And after we're off the boat?"

"That remains to be seen," was the answer. "I'm working on him."

"What do you mean, working on him?"

"I mean … I'm begging him." Doctor Morley clarified.

Then Musa grunted. It was time to go. Doctor Morley tried in vain to smile, turned away … but then spun back around:

"Oh, I almost forgot, a drink for your meal," he said.

He reached into his inner coat pocket. Out came a metal flask … the one that belonged to Mister Carter.

"This was part of the negotiations," Doctor Morley said, then left.

I sat and ate my gruel and drank every last drop of absinthe from Mister Carter's flask. It was a fine last supper.

***

We came along the Cuban coast then turned into the harbor at Havana.

From my porthole window, as I watched the spires of the old city go by, I contemplated my probable demise. I wondered if anyone from Bittyville would find out that I died in Havana. It seemed like such an exotic place for a Vermonter to die.

It was very slow-going as the freighter was spun around by tugboats, then pressed up against the pier. Workers rushed to grab the lines and tie the rusty vessel up. I was tapping on the glass of the porthole, trying to get one of them to notice me, when my door opened.

There stood Musa. Without warning, the mass of muscle came right at me, seizing me by both arms.

Now Benito and Veronica strode into the room. Veronica was carrying something in her hands.

"Tie her," Benito commanded.

Musa slid his big hands from my upper arms to my forearms. He pulled my wrists toward him. Then Veronica came up and wrapped a rope around my wrists. As she was doing so, I made eye contact with Doctor Morley. He was giving me a just-be-calm look; I prayed he had made arrangements to spare me.

Then Musa bent down and, respectfully, held my calves together. Veronica followed with the rope.

"I can't walk like this," I commented as they tied my ankles together.

"I know," Benito snarled.

"I ... I need my shoulder bag," I said.

It was on the top bunk. Benito looked at it.

"Why?" he asked.

"Because ... it's important to me," I said. "That bag and I have been through a lot."

Benito went to the bed. He picked up my shoulder bag. He opened the flap and looked inside ... the contents by now consisting of empty cigarette packs, a cheap lighter and my tin for spent butts.

Then, instead of handing it to me, he hung the strap over the bunkbed's top railing. He adjusted the bag so that it was hanging down, suspended between the beds.

The Spaniard stepped back. He glared at me.

Then he twisted the handle on his walking stick.

He unsheathed his hidden blade ... then turned his fury on my poor, innocent shoulder bag.

He slashed this way, then that. There were hideous sounds as my favorite accessory was torn asunder, its meager contents falling to the floor. Benito thrust and jabbed and tortured until the sorry bag was no more. I had to hold back tears.

"If you cause *any* problems getting off ... that will be you, sí?" Benito explained. "Get ready with the gag."

Musa pinned my arms again. The she-devil approached, holding a long, black piece of fabric with both hands. I had eyes on her when Benito reached out and grabbed hold off my chin.

He pulled my face toward him, his grip smooshing my lips together. I thought the scumbag was going to kiss me again, but then he brought a hand up and crammed something into my mouth. He cupped his hand over my lips, so I couldn't spit it out. I looked at him, wide-eyed.

In my mouth I could taste the horrible little gunk-ball. It was bitter and barky.

"Curare," he said. "The poison used in blow-darts. If you swallow it, you die. Sí?"

Veronica swooped in. She slid the gag under Benito's hand, so I had no chance to spit the goo out, and tied it around my head. I used my tongue to keep the toxin in the front of my mouth, away from my throat.

Panic began to wash over me. I was gagged. My hands and feet were both bound. I had blow-dart poison in my mouth. It can't get much worse, I thought.

But then Veronica came up and, without warning, pulled a dark hood over my head.

"Now, we wait," came Benito's voice. "Let it take effect."

Time seemed to stop. Nobody talked. I heard them shuffling their feet, but that was it. They were waiting for me to go under.

They lowered me into a chair. I was getting woozy. Then Musa knocked my knees out so he could lift me. I felt him carry me out the door and down the corridor. As we moved, I heard Benito exchanging some words with a crew member.

A moment later I heard hurried footsteps approaching, then a board being put down. Musa then laid me down on what I assumed was a stretcher from the freighter's infirmary. Someone draped a blanket over me.

Then I felt the stretcher being lifted. They carried me out of the corridor and soon specks of light filtered through my dark hood, indicating we were on the deck.

I could hear men yelling and cranes working and seagulls squawking. Then, as they carried me down the gangplank, I could hear more sounds from the pier.

But I stayed quiet. They all thought I was unconscious.

I wasn't.

42

IN HAVANA

They carried me away from the ship and took me directly to a taxi. I played dead as they hoisted me off the stretcher and placed me in the back seat. My captors were careful to make sure the blanket—which covered my bound arms and legs—stayed in place.

The curare was beginning to dissolve. I used my tongue to keep the bitter blister of goo away from the back of my mouth—lest I swallow it—and tried to wedge it against my inner lips. My gums and even my teeth felt numb. My throat had started to tingle.

Oh, how I wanted to gag, to cough, to spit that wretched stuff out! But it was a losing battle ... plus, I knew my only hope was to stay quiet, so my captors would think I was unconscious.

And perhaps I *was* going to be unconscious ... if not now, soon. My feet and my hands and my legs had a peculiar tightness to them. My neck felt swollen. I resisted those sensations as best as I could.

Just then there was a poke on my shoulder. I ignored it. Then there was an impolite shove, which almost made me break character.

"She gone?" I heard Benito growl.

"She out," Musa grunted back.

"I don't want any trouble here in Havana," the Spaniard said.

"No trouble," Musa responded.

Then I heard Doctor Morley's voice.

"Dammit, Veronica, stop jabbing that thing in my side," he said. "I told you I won't run."

There was a shuffling on one side. The other door opened.

"Don't shove me, I'm getting in, put that blasted gun away," Doctor Morley said, followed by: "Wendy ... Wendy, are you awake? Can you hear me?"

I remained silent. Doctor Morley barked at my captors.

"You all should be ashamed of yourselves, playing God with these jungle drugs," he scolded. "You're lucky you haven't killed her."

I heard the front passenger door open. There was some fumbling and I could tell it was Benito, trying to hoist his fake leg in. He shut the car door and said:

"Señor Morley, please use the jump seat, sí?"

"The child's seat. Lovely," my boss snorted.

"Enough. My man-servant is rather large-framed, if you have not noticed," Benito said.

"You think I give a damn about his comfort?" Doctor Morley shot back.

There was a grunt, after which Doctor Morley let go a sigh of surrender. I heard the jump seat squeak down. Then the motorcar shook and sank as Musa crawled in and worked his massive frame into the seat next to me.

Next I heard the trunk of the motorcar close, then the sound of more footsteps. The final door opened and I heard our driver get in.

"Hotel Sevilla-Biltmore?" the driver asked.

"Sí," Benito said. "Rápido, come on, let's go."

I heard some shuffling, then the driver said:

"Qué tiene de malo?"

"She's very sick and very sensitive to light," Benito responded. "And you ask questions below your status, no? Apúrate!"

***

As the motorcar started to roll I remained still and did my best to fight the encroaching numbness.

I was still alert. I considered trying to gurgle for help from the driver, or maybe to kick my seat. But I don't think I had the energy to kick, and I doubted my voice would work.

I heard the sounds of the port go by: trucks beeping, people yelling, a ship's horn in the distance. I could hear Doctor Morley muttering and sighing from the jump seat. Musa, next to me, was trying to get his enormous anatomy comfortable in a space that was much too small. Veronica was on my other side. She nudged me.

"Her head moved. I think she's awake," Veronica said.

I froze.

"Nonsense," Benito said.

Then I felt a pinch on my left arm. It was sudden and maybe I flinched a little bit, but I didn't make a sound.

Then there was an even harder pinch, closer to my armpit. It was awful, searing pain ... the single worst pinch of my life. I bit down on my gag to keep from yelping and I could feel tears streaming down my cheek.

The wicked witch cackled when she was finished with her torture. I vowed to myself that somehow, someday, I would get even with her.

The motorcar took a turn. I studied the pinpricks of sunlight filtering through the dark fabric of my hood; the holes were too small for me to discern anything beyond light and dark. It was like being only ninety-nine-percent blind, instead of one-hundred-percent blind.

As the taxi zigged and zagged, I played limp and allowed myself to slump from one side to the other. Veronica and Musa had to keep shoving me back toward the middle.

My act was holding up. At the same time—and despite my numb mouth—I kept using my tongue to press the glob of curare against the inside of my lips.

And then a miraculous thing happened: Somehow, the little wad of wretchedness squirted out of my lips. A second later, I could feel it oozing out of my gag and down my chin. It dripped off, down into the hood. I worked my half-paralyzed tongue around the inside of my mouth, to spit out any last remaining bits.

I was awake and, as near as I could tell, I still had my wits. That was the good news.

The bad news was that I was still gagged, my hands and feet were bound … and there was a hood over my head.

But I had new hope.

***

After several twists and turns, the motorcar slowed and then stopped.

"Sevilla-Biltmore, señor," the driver said.

"Sevilla. Isn't it ironic," Doctor Morley sighed.

Benito barked his orders to his crew:

"Señora Shetty, please escort the good Doctor into the hotel, por favor," he said. "Keep the other one here in the taxi."

"What!" Doctor Morley exclaimed. "Keep Wendy here? No, absolutely not, she stays with me."

"Impossible," Benito said. "You leave. She stays."

And he said it in a very nasty and angry way, which got the driver's attention:

"Hey, cuál es la problema? Huh?"

"Métete en tus asuntos," Benito snarled. "Mind your own business."

"Eh? No, no, no ...," the driver protested.

"Veronica, dammit, get Morley inside. Musa, take him and go, now."

"And what the hell should we do with him?" Veronica asked.

"Get him to the room and secure him, no?" Benito answered. "Do whatever it takes."

And then the driver said some very fast and very nasty words to Benito. Benito snarled back at him.

"Sal de mi auto!" the driver yelled. "You pay me, then you go!"

"Don't point at me!" Benito warned. "You'll bring my associate to un lugar privado and then ...,"

"Un lugar privado? No, no ... sal de mi auto! Out! Go!"

There was more yelling and swearing. I stayed motionless. Then Benito barked at Musa again. The goon got up to escort Doctor Morley out of the taxi.

"Ow! Watch the foot, you oaf! I don't want crutches again!"

"You. Out," Musa grunted.

"Not without her."

"Out. Now."

"You heard me. I'm ... *ow!* Don't grab me like that!"

There was more shuffling. The motorcar was shaking and Musa's big legs were banging into me. Doctor Morley was putting up a modest struggle. I assumed it wouldn't last long, and it didn't.

"Dammit, let me at least say good-bye to her," he finally cried. "Alright? At least give me that."

"You'll see her soon enough," came Benito's voice from outside the taxi.

"I want to believe you," Doctor Morley sighed. "Just ... just give me a moment, would you?"

And then I felt Doctor Morley come close. If there was a time for me to jerk my body, and let him know I was awake, this was it. But I was still unsure what my next steps should be. I didn't want to startle him and blow my cover with Benito nearby.

"Wendy ... Wendy, I know you probably can't hear me, but ... I ... I'm so, so sorry," Doctor Morley whispered. "You need to fight, alright? Don't give up. *Fight.*"

"Enough of that," Benito snarled. "Out."

"Don't pull me!" Doctor Morley spit at them. "Ow! Stop that, for Pete's sake. Show me some respect."

"I've shown you nothing but," came Benito's voice. "Veronica, take him inside."

I heard more shuffling and more complaining from my former boss. His complaints became distant as Veronica and Musa led him away.

And just like that, Doctor Morley was gone. I was on my own now.

From my left I could hear more bickering between Benito and the driver. Then, a yell on my right that must have come from a doorman.

"Hey, move ese taxi!" the voice called.

"Uno momento, dammit," Benito growled.

"Cuál es tu problema, huh?" the doorman asked again, his voice growing closer.

Benito said something I didn't catch. I was focused on the doorman's footsteps. Perhaps I could grunt to get his attention. Maybe this was my one and only chance to escape. I could hear the doorman coming closer:

"Qué es esto?" he said, near the door on my right side. "What is this?"

Then I heard Benito hobbling around the rear to cut him off.

"A very sick woman, that's what it is," I heard him say. "Esta ella enferma."

"Por qué lleva una capucha?" the doorman asked, still agitated but drifting away from me. "Why is she ... wearing this hood?"

"Sus ojos lastimados," Benito answered. "Eye surgery. Very, very sensitive …,"

I'm surprised the doorman didn't hear me groan at that.

"… And, I must say I'm quite displeased with the Sevilla-Biltmore thus far," Benito continued. "I've had to deal with this unpleasant taxi driver, a lost reservation and now ... this?"

"Lo siento, señor," the doorman replied.

"Apologies are useless. Una silla de ruedas, that's what I need," Benito shot back. "Inmediatamente."

"Una silla de ruedas?" the doorman asked. "A wheelchair?"

"You heard me. I'd like to get this poor woman out of the car, por favor."

There was a silent pause, during which I'm sure Benito stared the outmatched doorman down. Then I heard the doorman scurry away to get the wheelchair. After that I heard Benito's walking stick clacking back around to the left side, where he must have paid the driver. Then I heard his uneven footsteps walk back behind the taxi again. Another pair of much heavier footsteps joined, then all the different footsteps stopped. I could hear talking—and a grunt which indicated Musa had returned—but I couldn't make out what Benito was saying.

Then I heard squeaky wheels approaching. They were going to stuff me in a wheelchair? My blurry brain fogged up as I tried to figure out what to do. But before I could process this turn of events, heavy footsteps came close and a thick arm slid in over my shoulders. I played dead. Another big arm slid under my knees.

I knew who it was from the arm size, of course. Musa pulled me over in the seat and then lifted me up and out of the taxi. I let my arms fall limp.

"Ugh. Heavy," he commented.

There was more squeaking and then he lowered me down into the wheelchair. I felt the blanket start to slip off, but someone fixed it. Then I heard the voice of the person that had fixed it: Benito.

"Excellente, gracias," he said to the doorman, followed by the sound of coins changing hands. "Déjanos. Leave us, please."

Then there was a lurch as one of my captors—Musa, I deduced—grabbed the wheelchair's handles and started pushing. I could hear our driver hurtling one last insult as the taxi pulled away.

My head was slumped to one side. There were a few specks of bright light filtering in but I couldn't make out my surroundings. I had to rely on my ears. And what I heard next scared me to death:

"There's another taxi back there, near the other hotel. Fetch it," Benito instructed Musa. "Then take this little tramp somewhere, sí? Let's be done with it."

"Bang-bang?" Musa grunted.

"Don't make that motion with your hand, idiot," Benito scolded. "And no, of course not … not with a gun. This is a city, no? Roll her into the harbor or something."

"That not nice," Musa replied. I felt the same way.

"Silencio," Benito fired back. "Get the taxi. Now."

I heard Musa's footsteps as he walked away to find a new taxi. I could sense Benito was still with me; soon my wheelchair started to roll again. We went a short distance then he turned the wheelchair around and backed it up. I could hear people walking on the sidewalk in front of me. As we stopped a shout came from farther away:

"Benito!" called the voice, Veronica's. "Come here. They need you to sign."

"Uno momento," Benito barked from beside me.

"No, *now!*" Veronica insisted.

"Oy, this woman," Benito sighed. Then he placed a hand on an arm of the wheelchair. Through my hood I could smell his wickedness. He came closer and closer and then whispered to me.

"I do wish you could be here for this good-bye," he said.

Then I felt his fingers on my hood. His hands were looking for my chin. They found it and he grabbed hold and turned my limp face toward him.

He then tried to kiss me, on the lips, through the hood. But his aim failed him—much like it did during our first encounter—and I could feel his awful lips on my chin. He held them there for a dramatic, lingering smooch that was a full inch below my mouth.

Then he walked away, leaving me all alone on the sidewalk.

***

I was groggy. My body felt frozen. My mouth was numb.

I considered tipping my wheelchair over. My hands and feet were tied, but I could lean hard and make the chair fall onto the sidewalk. Someone would notice that, for sure. They would remove the hood, see my gag and realize something was wrong.

But what if Musa saw me, instead of a good Samaritan? He would realize I was awake. That would only speed matters up. I needed a better plan.

Maybe someone nearby could help. I did my best to listen to my immediate surroundings.

I could hear the cacophony you associate with a city: motorcars driving and beeping, people walking and talking. Across the street I could hear an energetic salesman:

"Coca Cola! Coca Cola aquí!"

And as he yelled I thought about yelling myself. Maybe I could force enough air past my gag to get someone's attention. Maybe they would hear me before Musa did.

I took a breath in as best as I could and tried to push a sound out:

"Unnnhgowwz."

It was not a loud noise. I was sure nobody heard me. I started to suck in a big breath, to try again with more gusto.

But then I heard footsteps come close. They stopped near me. Someone was just off to my right side. Whoever it was didn't have the lumbering gait of Musa or the awkward stride of Benito.

Then the person started to speak:

"Hola señors and señoras!"

It was a man. I kept listening:

"Coo-ant-ass vee-sees ha estando … Cuan-tase vee-kee ha …,"

It was an American man, with horrendous Spanish.

"Ah, beans to this," he muttered, then he began to yell:

"Ladies and gentlemen! How many times have you stood on the deck of a steamer, tossing in a rough sea … and enviously watched the gulls wheeling and dipping 'round the vessel?"

An American salesman? I had to get his attention. I tried to gurgle another sound but the man was busy delivering his pitch, with panache:

"What swiftness and lightness! What ease, while you suffered the agonies of the endless rolling and pitching of a spiteful sea. How you longed for the smooth, quick flight of the gull."

He had not heard my gurgling. He kept at it:

"Now you can rise above the water and travel the comfortable way, folks. That's right, amigos … get to Key West in a fraction of the time it takes to ride the ferry. Fly the skies and see the sights … only with Pan American Airways."

Pan American?

My heart jumped. It wasn't Oliver … I would have recognized the voice. But this person must work for Pan American. That meant this person must know Oliver … and Mister Trippe … and Moses.

Any one of those three would help me, so I figured this man would too. He was still shouting:

"Yes, friends … fly like a gull in one of our state-of-the-art, luxurious Sikorsky amphibious aeroplanes. See the Cuban coast and the Gulf Stream and the Florida Keys like you have never seen them before."

I gathered up every bit of energy I had in my numb, exhausted body. I strained into my spit-soaked gag and garbled as loud as I could:

"Ahh-vah! Ahh-vah!"

But the words got stuck in my locked throat. I started to hack. When I finished my coughing fit, I worried the man had run off. Then he started up again:

"Folks, do you wanna spend over four hours bobbing and barfing on an overcrowded ferry? Or would you rather spend forty-five minutes in a state-of-the-art flying machine, having a Coke and watching the birds ...,"

"Ahh-Vah!" I repeated, somehow able to get it out louder this time.

There was another long pause, then:

"What the ...? Pipe down, would ya?" he said. "I'm workin' here. Jeez."

He had heard me. I tried again:

"Ahh-vah Wee-wah!"

This time I tried to wiggle my head in his direction, which was as much motion as I could make. I said it again:

"Ahh-vah! Ahh-vah Wee-wah!"

There was a silence. I could hear him shuffling his feet. Then he said:

"Are you ... are you trying to talk to *me?*"

"Ungh! Ungh!" I said, wiggling more. "Ahh-Vah! Ahh-Vah Wee-Wah!"

And then lady luck smiled on me: He got it.

"Are you saying ... *Oliver?*"

"Ungh! Ungh, ungh!"

"Oliver ... *Wheelock?*"

"Ungh! Ahh-Vah Wee-Wah!"

"Well, shit ... I know Oliver."

I could hear him coming closer. The next thing I knew, he was right by my ear:

"Pardon me, but ... who are you?" he whispered. "And ... why are you all covered up like that?"

"Haal meh," I whispered back, my throat catching again. Then I repeated, "Haal meh. Nouh."

"Are you speaking English?" he asked.

"Ungh! Haal meh. Nouh."

"You want me to ... *help you?*"

"Ungh!"

"Like, right this instant?"

"Ungh!"

"Are you ... in danger?"

"Ungh! Ungh!"

"Oh shit. Alright, okay. Umm, let's see. You can't walk, can you?"

I tried to shake my head, hoping whomever it was would pick up on my nonverbal cues. But he was silent. I didn't know what else I could do to communicate. I tried to gather enough air to puke out another half-word when something magical happened.

My wheelchair shuddered. The mystery man was in back of me.

"Dang, does this thing have a lock? Ah, there it is."

And then we were rolling. Slow. Too slow.

"Fah-nah!" I mumbled. "Fah-nah!"

"Huh?"

"Fah-nah!" I repeated, and at that instant a familiar grunt let loose behind us.

"Hey! *Hey!* Alto!" came Musa's voice.

"Fah-nah!" I pleaded. "Gah! Gah!"

"Go?" asked my prospective rescuer.

"Ungh! Ungh!"

And then we took off like a shot. Suddenly the wheelchair was speeding down the sidewalk and the man from Pan Am was yelling at people to move out of our way. Then came another menacing call from behind, closer than before:

"You! Boy! Alto!" Musa yelled. "Stop! Alto!"

I felt us jump the curb into the street.

"Ah, pecker. Hold on," my wheelchair-pusher said.

I could feel us bouncing off the cobblestone streets, but I couldn't see a thing. We took a sharp turn and while we were still moving I could feel him using one hand on my hood. He fumbled with the cord, got it undone and pulled the hood off me.

The sunlight was blinding. I squinted as my eyes tried to adjust. We were on a narrow street, still moving at a good clip.

"Holy halibut, a redhead!" my rescuer said. "You're that girl, ain't ya?"

Then he realized why I couldn't talk: the gag. He stopped the chair and ran around to face me.

He was a tall man, youngish, not much older than me. He was wearing a blue uniform jacket and a white Pan Am cap. He yanked my gag out and let it drop around my neck. A stream of drool poured out and I started to spit, trying to get any last curare out of my mouth. Even without the gag, it hurt to move my jaw.

"It *is* you, isn't it?" my rescuer said. "I'm Danny."

At that very instant, a gunshot rang out:

BANG!

There was a hard plink on the street in front of us. A cloud of dust rose up.

"Did someone just fire a gun?" Danny asked.

"Ungh ... *coff, coff* ... Ye-ungh," I said, the first semi-understandable word I could speak. "Go. Go!"

He ran around to the back of the wheelchair and began to push again. Another shot rang out:

BANG!

"Holy shit!" Danny exclaimed. "Was that for *you?*"

"Ye-ungh!"

He pivoted again and we came up onto one wheel and then rocked back hard to the other side. He launched us forward. We bounced past some bewildered pedestrians then turned the next corner. I could hear yelling. My hero stopped to look back. He swore and we bolted forward again.

"That guy is as big as a house!" he panted. "What the hell ... should we do?"

"We ... need to ... keep run," I said. "They ... they wanna kill me."

"Yeah, I figured that part out," he said. "I'm gonna take you to the police, okay? Can you walk?"

"No ... feet, hands ... tied ...," I began.

He stopped and ran around in front of me. He pulled the blanket off and saw the ropes.

"Ah, jeez, look at these knots!" he exclaimed.

"Legs ... numb," I tried to explain to him, but he was looking past me and back up the street. Then, without a word—and without untying me—he ran back to grab the handles of the wheelchair. He started pushing again.

As he propelled me down the street, I had a three-second internal debate about what to do. Should I go to the police? That would save my hide ... but at what cost? I didn't know what Benito's plans were with Doctor Morley. I didn't want to take action that would put him in *more* jeopardy. If I went to the police, that's exactly what I would be doing. Doctor Morley was a witness to Benito's crimes ... and I knew the Spaniard wouldn't hesitate to kill someone to protect himself.

"Not ... not police," I said.

"Huh? Lady, we ...,"

"Get away," I told him. "We need ... get away ... from Havana."

Even in my somewhat drowsy state, I figured it out at the same time as him.

"The plane," Danny said. "We have to get to the plane."

I craned my stiff neck to say yes with my eyes.

"Hoo-boy, okay," he said. "We need a taxi. I gotta loop us back. Hold on."

I was in no position to argue. He spun us around one-hundred-eighty degrees, so we were facing the street from which we had come. There, running toward us, was Musa.

The goon had a gun in his right hand.

"Bad ... idea," I warned.

"Nobody expects a bad idea," Danny replied.

Then my rescuer roared, like an angry lion. He aimed the wheelchair directly at Musa.

The big man appeared bewildered at first, but soon his expression turned into a sinister smile. He lowered his gun. We kept charging forward ... but ten feet from collision, Danny let go off the handles.

Then, in a motion so smooth and fluid it must have been divine, my savior plucked me out of the wheelchair. He lifted me up, spun me away and jumped sideways.

Musa let out a half-yell, half-yelp as the empty wheelchair barreled into him. I heard onlookers gasp. Danny never looked back: he carried me, still running, toward the main avenue. I could see taxis.

"You're ... strong," I said to my carrier.

"I've lifted lots of mailbags."

I looked over his shoulder to see behind me. A small crowd had gathered near the spot Musa fell; suddenly it parted. The big goon emerged, gun in hand. He looked angrier than ever.

"Uh ... oh," I said. "Go, go ... he mad."

"This dude up here doesn't look happy either," came the reply.

I swung my head forward. There was Benito, a few hundred yards down the street. He was limping, but limping fast. His face was all scrunched up. He saw us.

"You!" he yelled, pointing.

"Ah, frick!" Danny exclaimed. He carried me up onto the sidewalk; Benito started to hobble-hop in our direction. But Danny was faster: he cut sideways, darted around a food cart then carried me into the street. A truck blared its horn at us, causing Danny to jerk to a stop. His Pan Am cap fell off.

Then he turned around and carried me the other way, in the same direction as the slow-moving traffic. He dodged motorcars and trucks and kept running until he spotted an empty taxi.

"Taxi! Taxi!" he yelled. "Oh, Pedro! It's me! Stop!"

The taxi screeched to a halt. Danny dropped me onto my feet and propped me up against the taxi so he could open the door. Then he shoved me, head first, into the back seat.

And as he did another gunshot rang out:

BANG!

The driver turned around, his eyes like saucers. Danny got in and slammed the door behind him.

"Pedro, aeropuerto! Rapido!"

"Por qué te disparan, Danny?" the driver asked.

"They're shooting at *her*, not me!" Danny replied. "Just go, okay?"

The driver hit the gas. The tires squealed and we were off.

At this point my hands and feet were still bound, but I was able to crane my head to look behind us.

A block back I could see Benito. He was standing in the middle of the street. He reached down and picked up Danny's cap and looked at it.

"Faster ....," I said. "He ... he won't give up."

Danny leaned over the front seat and gave instructions to the driver. Without warning, we took a hard right turn. I toppled into the next seat and then halfway onto the floor.

Danny looked down at me. I nodded to my bound hands.

"Oh yeah, sorry," he said.

Then he pulled me up and began to untie my wrists.

"Gosh, this is like something from a movie, huh?" he said as he fumbled with the knots.

"If this is a movie ... it's too long," I replied.

He got my wrists untied and I tried to shake some of the stiffness out of my hands. I still felt slow and sluggish.

"They knock you out or something?" Danny asked.

"Blow-dart poison," I answered. "My legs, please."

He looked at me in disbelief. I hoisted my legs up onto his lap so he could untie my ankles. I glanced out the rear window again. Now I saw a dark motorcar slicing past other vehicles; I knew in an instant Benito was in it.

"Here he comes," I said.

Danny looked, then spoke to the driver:

"We got company, Pedro!"

And the driver responded:

"Es no problema."

He stepped on the gas, maneuvered us around a truck then pulled right to pass a horse-drawn cart. But then we found ourselves boxed in traffic. The driver leaned on his horn.

I checked on our pursuers. The dark motorcar was stuck in traffic, too, and like us they were beeping their horn. I turned to the driver and said:

"Don't use your horn. They'll know it's us."

He stopped beeping.

"Get down," I said to Danny, and we both ducked our heads. We stayed there for a moment then I raised my head to peek out.

And my timing could not have been worse: they were no more than a hundred feet away. I could clearly see Benito in the passenger seat and Veronica next to him, driving. Had they stolen an automobile?

I tried to duck back down, but it was no use. I peeked up again to see Musa getting out of their vehicle and marching toward ours.

"We need to go," I said. "I mean get out. *Now.*"

"And what, run?" Danny said, and I nodded.

He considered me and then said to the driver:

"The sidewalk, Pedro! Or we're all goners!"

Our driver let out a laugh and shook his head. He muttered something I couldn't understand, then cranked the steering wheel and laid on his horn. Startled pedestrians jumped. He hit the gas. The taxi jumped the curb and we were on the sidewalk.

It was a crowded sidewalk, too. People were diving and screaming. Our driver had a hand out his window, waving people out of our way. We just missed hitting some old lady, destroying a churro stand instead. Then we came down off the sidewalk, squeezed between two stopped trucks and emerged in an open lane. We were free of the congestion.

"You're safe," Danny said. "They have no idea where we're going."

"He saw your cap," I told him.

"Oh. Then they know exactly where we're going."

Danny told the driver to hit the gas. We zigged and zagged, took a hard left and then a hard right. At the next intersection I looked back and, unbelievably, there was the dark motorcar, still after us.

"He's persistent," Danny offered.

"You have no idea. How much farther?"

"Two minutes. Pedro, rapido!"

We turned onto a smaller street, but traffic was backed up all the way to the next intersection. There was no way around.

"You said ... minutes?" I asked Danny.

"Yeah, the airstrip is right beyond those trees over there."

I looked ahead. At the end of the block was a line of trees extending between two buildings.

"I can carry you," Danny said.

"No. I can do this."

"Your legs feel okay?" he asked.

"Yes," I fibbed.

I opened my side door and slid over. As Danny spoke with the driver, I tried to pull myself up and out. My legs buckled; I had no balance at all. I toppled out and fell to the ground.

"Aw, frick," Danny said. He picked me up from behind.

Then, with a final apology to our driver, Danny began to carry me again. He was tiring and starting to stagger. But he kept moving, carrying me all the way to the intersecting avenue. We had just started to cross when there was a long, sustained beep.

We both turned. There were our pursuers, roaring down the avenue in the dark motorcar. I could see their faces. Benito looked furious. Veronica looked excited to run me over

Danny didn't flinch. He saw them, but he kept going trudging across the avenue toward the line of trees. We came onto the grass and through the trees and I could see the landing field in front of us.

Behind me, I heard Benito's motorcar squeal to a stop. "After them!" he shouted.

Then Danny tripped. I toppled forward and rolled. I heard Danny yelp in pain. I looked back and he was clutching his ankle.

I crawled to him. We helped each other up. I was still terribly unbalanced and now he was hurt ... but we were still going. Danny winced as we hobbled.

"Aw, not again," Danny said. I followed his gaze. Musa was behind us, coming between the trees. He had the gun in his hand.

"Let's go!" Danny said, grabbing my arm.

We both turned … and then I beheld a glorious sight: *A Pan American airplane.*

It was the same kind of plane that Lindbergh had piloted into the jungle. It was a weird-looking thing, with awkward pontoons and a long wing suspended above the cabin. It had that long, strange, swallow-like tail.

Given the circumstances, that odd bird was the single most beautiful thing I had ever seen.

We limped and lumped along, trying but failing to go faster. Then there was another gunshot:

BANG! A cloud of dust exploded right in front of us.

Then *BANG!* Another bullet whizzed by.

We both toppled over; I got back on my feet somehow and tried to pull Danny up. He gritted his teeth in pain and pushed himself up.

We looked back: Musa was no more than twenty feet away. The big man raised his gun and pointed it at us. At me, to be precise.

"Lo siento," the goon said. This was it.

And right then Danny threw something. I didn't see what it was, but I saw his arm whip around … and then I heard a hollow sound:

THOCK.

Musa had been looking at me. Now he went cross-eyed, trying to see the spot on his forehead where the stone had hit. His eyes continued to roll back until his pupils disappeared. His gun dropped to the ground. The goon tipped straight back and fell to the hard ground.

THUNK.

I couldn't believe it. I looked at Danny. He said:

"Sweet Jesus! Did I just kill him?"

"I ... I don't know," I said. "It's like ... David and Goliath."

"Yeah. But ... my name's Danny, not David." my rescuer said.

"Sorry. Danny and Goliath."

We stood there for the briefest of moments contemplating Musa's motionless, monstrous body. Then we pushed ourselves up and stumbled toward the airplane. My vow to never again fly with Pan American Airways was about to be broken.

The airplane was a good hundred yards away. It was facing away from us, its snout and props pointed down the landing strip. For a moment, I thought we were in the clear. That jinxed it.

"Look!" Danny shouted, pointing.

Roaring in from between two barracks was the motorcar carrying Benito and Veronica.

I know they saw us, but they spotted the sprawled-out Musa, too. The motorcar swerved and then slowed near the big man. Benito jumped out. I saw Musa move an arm: he was alive.

With Benito momentarily occupied, my eyes shifted to the motorcar. I scanned it to see if Doctor Morley was inside, perhaps in the back seat ... but I didn't see him.

Benito's angry gaze returned to us. He left Musa on the ground and limped back to the motorcar. Veronica revved the engine.

Danny and I tried to pick up our pace, but we were both broken and bruised. I could hear the motorcar gaining. My legs couldn't move any faster. My companion winced with each step. Then, at the top of his lungs, Danny yelled:

"Moses! Eddie!"

Moses? As in *my* Moses?

"Moses! Eddie! Emergency! Emergency!"

And then a head with a Pan Am cap popped up out of the top hatch of the airplane. Even from a distance I recognized him: Moses Hardwick, my once and perhaps future savior.

He saw me, too. The pilot shook his head, as if he couldn't believe his eyes. Then:

BEEP! BEEP!

It was the motorcar, closing in. I could see Veronica's hate-filled mug behind the wheel. Benito was leaning out the passenger window. He had something in his hand.

"Gun!" I screamed to Danny.

Saying that must have startled him. Danny turned, then yelped, then crumpled to the ground. I tried to help him up again.

"Come on, come on!" I pleaded.

"Just go! Leave me!"

I looked up to Benito's motorcar. It was right on top of us, slowing a bit as it closed in. Benito was still leaning out, gun in hand.

We couldn't outrun them. I looked down at Danny.

"I'm ... I'm sorry."

"Me too," he replied.

I gripped his hand. I heard a shot ... then a yell from the airplane:

"Duck!"

And Danny pulled my hand and yanked me down to the ground. There was a great rushing *WOOSH* and something flew over my head.

I turned just in time to see Benito's terrified expression as a flare rocketed his way. The passenger door flew open just as the projectile shattered the windshield. There was a short pause then:

KA-BOOM!

The inside of the motorcar lit up like a firework.

Benito was lying on the ground. Smoke was pouring out of the motorcar. The Spaniard scooted himself away from the vehicle and, as he did, I could see his fake leg was bent at a ridiculous angle. He reached down and looked at it. Then with a sharp *CRACK* he tore the remains of his prosthesis off. He turned to the motorcar.

I could only hope Veronica was dead. There was no movement in the vehicle. But then the smoke cleared and the she-devil's soot-covered face was still there.

"She *is* a witch," I remarked.

Veronica's glare confirmed she wanted to kill me. She looked back to Benito, who was hopping on his one leg back to the motorcar. He bounded onto the running board and, to my surprise, the smoking vehicle started rolling again.

And then I felt a big hand grab my arm. I looked back. It was Moses:

"Let's go!"

He pulled me and Danny to our feet. Then Moses did all he could to prod, carry and drag us toward the airplane. He yelled ahead:

"Crank 'em, Eddie! Crank 'em!"

A second later I saw one of the airplane's propellers start to turn, then the other.

I looked back to our pursuers. The motorcar was moving, but not as fast or steady as it had been before. There was smoke pouring out of the windows. Benito was still hanging onto the side, his one good leg holding him on the running board.

"*Faster!*" I heard him yell.

The airplane was still fifty yards away. Suddenly it started to move forward, away from us. I had a moment of panic then realized it was turning around.

Through the cockpit windshield I could see the other pilot. It was the same pilot that had been with Moses when they found us at Yaxchilan. He turned the plane; the propellers became louder.

Now the airplane and the motorcar were headed toward each other ... and we were directly between them.

"Hop, Danny, hop!" Moses yelled.

Moses knew his co-pilot wouldn't hit him with the rolling airplane. Veronica, on the other hand, had no such assurances; she swerved the motorcar to avoid a collision. That made Benito bang the top of the vehicle with his fist.

"What are you doing? Turn back, turn back!" he barked at the she-devil.

The plane slowed, some twenty or thirty feet away from us. We made our move.

"Now ... the hard part," Moses panted, doing his best to keep Danny and I up.

It dawned on me what he meant. This airplane was amphibious, built to land on water. The door to get inside was on top of the cabin, just behind the raised upper wing. Back at Yaxchilan, they had used a ladder to help us up and in. That wouldn't be an option now

"I've gotta let you go so I can push him up," Moses said. "Then we'll lift you."

He said it fast then let go of me. Right away I stumbled and fell. Moses and Danny looked back.

"Just go! Hurry!" I yelled.

Then, as I pulled myself back up, I kept one eye on Moses. He was trying to push Danny up onto the moving plane. He finally got him high enough so Danny could grab a strut.

My other eye was on the motorcar. It had made a short loop away from us and now it was roaring back. I couldn't believe what I was seeing:

Benito was riding on the hood, like a goddamn daredevil. He lifted a hand and pointed at me.

I looked to the airplane. Danny had wormed his way to the top. A hand—the co-pilot's hand—reached up through the hatch and grabbed him. My young savior wiggled to the hatch and dropped down into the cabin.

Moses turned and started running back my way. His eyes told me to turn around. I did.

Benito's motorcar was closing in. The one-legged killer was still on the hood. He was snarling.

Moses reached me first. He scooped me up and started carrying me toward the moving airplane. Danny was watching us from the hatch and yelled:

"Look out!"

And Moses didn't look back, but I did ... and the motorcar was about to hit us.

"Jump!" I screamed.

Moses took a half-look and jumped up. With me in his arms it wasn't much of a jump, but it was just high enough. His fanny came down on the hood of the motorcar, not a foot away from Benito.

The Spaniard was as surprised as us. His face twisted up into a sinister sneer. He reached to grab us, and as he did Moses commanded me:

"Now! Grab the tail!"

I looked up. The tail assembly of the airplane was no more than two feet above my head.

Veronica, had she turned the motorcar, could have ended the chase right then and there ... but she didn't. Moses lifted me up. I reached both arms high and grabbed onto a flat part of the airplane's tail. I heard Benito yell at Veronica:

"Idiot! Away from the airplane!"

Which made Veronica turn ... pulling the car—and Moses—out and away from me.

That left me hanging from the tail of the moving airplane.

I struggled to keep my grip. Danny was coming up out of the hatch to try and help me ... but he was too far away to do anything. I started to slip.

"Grab the strut!" Danny yelled.

He was pointing to the long metal support that extended from the tail assembly to the cabin. There was no way I could reach it.

"No, with your feet!" Danny yelled next.

I kicked my numb legs out once, twice and a third time. On the fourth try, I got a foot up and around the support. I brought one hand under the tail and grabbed onto a strut. Then I dangled there, trying to work my other hand under.

But I couldn't. I was stuck.

As I hung helplessly, I looked back to Benito's motorcar. Moses had jumped off the hood and was now sprinting toward the airplane. Behind him I saw the motorcar swerving, then accelerating. Benito was still on the hood.

I was going to fall. I couldn't maintain my grip on the tail anymore. Then, just as I started to slip, a hand grabbed my wrist: Danny's hand. He had stretched himself out over the long support.

"Don't let go!" he pleaded.

And then Moses caught up with the airplane. He ran and jumped on one of the pontoons and in no time pulled himself up onto the roof of the cabin. He reached out to me:

"Give me your other hand!"

I had to try. I had one leg wrapped around the support; Danny was holding one of my hands. I let go off the tail with my other hand, swung it down and then up to Moses.

Our hands met ... but the same exact instant, Benito grabbed my other leg.

The bastard had my ankle. He yelled to Veronica:

"Turn! Turn!"

And Veronica started to turn the car. Benito's grip on my leg was firm. They were trying to rip me from the airplane. Then, Moses yelled to his co-pilot:

"Faster, Eddie! Faster!"

And the airplane sped up. Benito's grip slipped as we pulled away ... but then he got a finger inside my shoe.

I looked back. Benito was bringing his other hand up. He still had his gun. He got ready to take a short-range shot at me.

And then lady luck smiled on me one final time: my shoe fell off.

In a heartbeat everything changed. Benito stared at the shoe, then threw it aside. Danny and Moses pulled me up toward the cabin. But then:

BANG!

A bullet tore into the support, right above my head.

"Get in!" Moses said, then "Punch it, Eddie!"

I tried to keep my footing, but tumbled knee-first through the hatch and down into the cabin.

BANG!

I heard wood splinter. Danny and then Moses hustled down the ladder.

BANG! BANG!

Those bullets missed the plane, and us. I felt that I was safe, or at least safer ... but I was mad as hell that this one-legged asshole was *still* trying to kill me.

And in that instant I realized I had to take another bold step.

If I was to save Doctor Morley ... I had to reveal my secret.

I pushed myself off the cabin floor. I steadied myself in the rolling airplane and pulled myself to the ladder. I started to climb up through the open hatch.

BANG!

"Whoa! Get down!" Moses ordered, but I ignored him.

I stuck my head up out of the hatch. The moment I did:

BANG!

I heard a bullet fly just over my head. I ducked, then stuck my head up again.

Benito pointed his gun at me and pulled the trigger ... only to find himself out of bullets.

His motorcar was falling further behind as the airplane picked up speed. But I could see Benito ... and I know he could see me, just fine.

I had to show it to him.

Without breaking eye contact I fumbled for my shirt button.

Benito's angry gaze turned curious.

I reached inside my shirt ... and yanked my money-belt around.

As I unzipped it, Benito's face sank. I reached in the money-belt and pulled out my surprise:

The map.

Well, it wasn't the *actual* map. The real page fifty-six of the Madrid Codex had been lost to the ocean. This was my copy, the one I had made at the Museum. Tearing it out of the notebook before my dumb stunt on the *Hispaniola* had turned out to be a very, very good idea.

It was folded in quarters. I was tempted to unfold it, so Benito could see the entire thing. But I didn't have to.

He figured out what it was. His expression went from shock to surprise to insanely mad.

As the airplane pulled farther ahead of the motorcar, I pointed to the folded page with my other hand. I gave him a yep-that's-right nod.

I was in control. I had the only remaining copy of the map ... and I was going to use it to get Doctor Morley back.

But I had one last message for Benito. The airplane was bouncing and we would soon be airborne, so I had to act fast.

I held the folded map tight with one hand. With my other hand, I gave Benito the old one-finger-salute.

I raised that middle digit high and proud ... and kept it raised until the airplane bounced up and didn't come down.

43

THE FLYBOY

We rose. The motorcar—with Benito still on the hood—became smaller and smaller. Soon we were over the city and the landing strip disappeared. We flew over the coast and then we were over water.

I was safe. Pan American had saved me … again.

I collapsed into one of the airplane's wicker seats. In my hand I clutched my copy of page fifty-six. I closed my eyes and took a deep breath. When I opened my eyes, Moses was standing over me.

"Hi. I have *so* many questions," he said.

"Hi … me too," I replied.

"Who the hell was that guy?"

"Benito. He doesn't like me."

"I can tell. Why?"

"Long story."

"I thought you were going to Spain."

"I did. We came back."

"We?"

"I was with Doctor Morley. They have him now."

"They … *have* him?"

I nodded.

"You mean like, kidnapped?"

I nodded again, a wave of worry about my former boss washing over me.

"What's that in your hand, the thing you showed him?" Moses asked.

I considered whether to tell him … and decided I should.

"It's a map," I said. "At least I think it is."

"A map. To where?"

"I'm not sure yet."

The pilot looked confused. "Well, where'd you get the map?"

"I made it."

Now he was even more confused.

"It's a copy," I explained. "But it's a damn good one."

***

Moses returned to the cockpit to check on his co-pilot; I turned around to check on Danny. He was sitting two rows in back of me, his hurt leg extended into the aisle.

"Are you alright?" I asked.

"Yeah. Just a sprain," he said. "You?"

"I'm not sure yet."

"Why are those people after you?"

"It's complicated. Thank you for rescuing me."

"Yeah, sure," he said, then paused. "So … you were with Oliver and Lindbergh, right? In the jungle?"

"Yes."

"Jeezum. And did you, umm …," he stammered. "Did you …,"

"Did I what?"

"Well, some guys have been saying that, umm, that you … well, that you *shot* Lindbergh."

I was tired of lying, so I told him the truth:

"Yes, I did. Twice."

And his eyes got wide and he nodded and smiled. Then he said:

"Good."

Soon Moses re-emerged from the cockpit.

"Did you see where those bullets hit, Danny?" he asked.

"Two pierced the cabin, right up here and then over by the stairs. One may have hit the tail support, too … but I'm not sure."

I confirmed that a bullet had, in fact, struck the support. I knew, because the bullet had been intended for me.

Moses took his cap off, went back to the ladder, reached up and opened the top hatch. Salty air whipped through the cabin. The pilot climbed up the steps, so his head and half his body were sticking up out of the airplane. A moment later he came back down, closed the hatch, and said:

"Looks like cosmetic damage back there. If any of the control cables had been hit, we'd know already."

Then he went to the two small holes where bullets had hit the cabin. He inspected them, sighed, then came back and sat down across from me.

"Well, you win the award for most interesting passenger of the week," he said. "Gonna be fun explaining this to the bosses."

"Let me explain," I said. "I know your boss, remember?"

"You don't know the one I'm worried about. Never mind that. Listen … I don't know what this is all about, but you gotta go to the police when we get to Key West."

"I can't," I replied.

"Huh? People shooting at you, trying to rip you off an airplane—by your legs, mind you—and you don't want to talk to the police?"

"I'll talk to them in due time. First I have to get Doctor Morley back."

"You should let the cops find him."

"They'll never find him in the Yucatán."

"The Yucatán? Wasn't he with you in Havana?" Moses asked.

"He was. But they'll be in the Yucatán soon. I'm sure of it."

"And so that little map in your hand … how will that help you find him?"

I looked down at the folded paper, then I looked back to Moses.

"I'm, uh, still working on that."

"Right. You don't *have* a plan, do you?"

"Of course I do! Or I will. Soon."

***

They offered me a Coca Cola, which was the only beverage they had on board. Then I spent most of the flight telling Moses and Danny about what I had been through.

I didn't tell them everything, of course. I didn't want to get into what, exactly, our dysfunctional band of thieves had been on the hunt for. I only told them it was something very, very valuable.

"Like … gold?" Danny asked. "A treasure?"

"I'm not sure," I answered. "But something valuable enough to kill for."

And while I didn't want to tell them all I knew about the Treasure of Tenochtitlan, I did tell them about the theft of the sword. I told them about the poor guard at the Archive, the chase at the Museum and how I was a fugitive from justice in Madrid. I told them about Doctor Morley's second thoughts. Finally, I told them about the incident on the *Hispaniola*, though I left out some key details.

"Wait," Danny said. "You mean to tell me that Howard Carter is *dead*? Who stabbed him?"

"I can't remember. It all happened so fast," I said.

Then I gave a stern look to both Danny and Moses.

"This is all secret information, alright?" I said. "I need you to keep your mouths shut. Promise?"

They both nodded.

"Have you heard anything more from Oliver?" I asked, trying to change the subject.

Moses shook his head.

"Not a peep since that first letter to his mom. She's worried sick. She even asked me to go track him down."

"You should. He's in danger, too," I said. "Benito knows who Oliver is, but Oliver doesn't know who Benito is. I don't want to think about what might happen if they bump into each other."

"Oliver ain't done nothin' wrong, has he?" Moses asked.

"No, but that doesn't matter."

"So … our boy needs rescuing, too."

"Yes. He just doesn't know it yet."

The pilot leaned back and gave me a hard look.

"Again, let me make sure I've got this right. A half-hour ago you escaped from a crazed one-legged psycho that wants to kill you. You're soon gonna be safe in the U.S. of A. But now you wanna be a hero and go to Mexico and rescue both your boss and Oliver from this same one-legged psycho."

"Correct."

"But … how will you even find any of them?"

"I don't know how we'll find Oliver. But I've got a good idea where Benito is taking Doctor Morley. That's a start."

"And where's that?"

"A small village south of Merida," I said. "It's called Mani."

"They don't have your map, though. If I was this bad fella, I'd come to Key West and try to find *you*."

"He wouldn't dare come after me here. Too risky, especially with customs," I said.

"But won't he be lost without your map?"

"Only partially lost," I replied.

***

As we descended into Key West, I was mesmerized by the long railroad bridge and the pale blue water and the little islands. I could see small fishing boats and big trawlers and even an old-style sailing ship with three masts. It was just as pretty as Oliver said.

I had expected beaches. Instead, we came in low over a rocky shoreline. Ahead, by the landing strip, I could see one of those big buildings for storing airplanes. Next to it was a little white house.

As we came in I nervously watched the ground grow closer, the memory of the crash in the jungle still fresh in my mind. We hit earth, bounced up, then hit again. We rolled past the big airplane building, the propellers slowed and we turned around. I heard a big sigh from the cockpit:

"Moses, my friend, for once I'm gonna let you do all the talking."

"What, you worried about a few bullet holes, Eddie?" Moses said. "Priester won't even notice. If he does, I'll blame you."

"Betcha five bucks they see 'em within sixty seconds," Eddie offered.

"Easy money, my friend. You're on," Moses replied.

As we slowed two men in greasy clothes came running out of the airplane building. One of them yelled, "Ooohwee! Lookie that!"

The other mechanic looked toward the tail of the plane. His jaw fell open. He hollered toward the little white house.

There was another big sigh from the cockpit.

"You owe me five, brother," Eddie said.

"Ah, peckersnaps," Moses growled.

There was a tap on my shoulder.

"Ma'am? Let me help you out."

Despite his injury, Danny helped me to my feet. He went to the rear of the cabin and slid the hatch open. He hobbled aside so I could go first. As I climbed up I saw the two bullet holes that had pierced the cabin.

"Oh my," I said. "That's not good, is it?"

"No, ma'am. Not good at all," Danny said.

I came up the ladder and through the hatch. There was a yell:

"Vaht? Vaht ees dees!"

I turned my head to see a little bald man storming toward the airplane:

"Der plane! Ees dat ... ees dat a bullet hole? Out! Out!" the little man continued, with a heavy Dutch accent.

From my perch I watched Eddie climb out the cockpit door:

"Nothing got hit, boss. Pierced the skin twice in the rear of the cabin and once through the tail ... but it missed the cables. All good."

"All good? Das ees not all good!"

The angry Dutchman marched toward the back of the plane. He looked at the hole in the tail then the two holes in the cabin. Finally, he looked up to me.

"Und ... who ees dees?"

At that moment Moses was coming around the plane. He answered the question:

"This is *her*, chief. The girl. From Slim's trip."

The little man's eyes got wide. He turned back to Moses and whispered:

"You mean …?"

"Yeah," Moses said. "This is her. Wendy."

"Und … did *she* shoot my plane?"

"No, no," Moses chuckled. "Your plane got shot by someone trying to shoot her. We saved her. Let's get her inside, we can explain everything."

A rolling ladder was wheeled over so I could climb down from the hatch. After the curare and the chase—followed by an hour of sitting—my legs had awful cramps. Those cramps—and my lack of a left shoe—made me stumble coming out of the plane. Yet again, a Pan Am employee broke my fall.

They helped me to the little white house. The walls inside were plastered with maps of Florida, the Caribbean and South America. Moses slid a chair under me, and said:

"Just wait here, okay? Let us talk to him first."

He and Danny left the office, bringing their boss with them. They were gone for a few minutes. When they returned, the little Dutchman kneeled down in front of me.

"Dey haf told me vaht happened, ya? Der man chasing you, he give you a drug, ya?"

"They tried. I spit it out."

"Und do you need der doctor?"

"No," I said. "I'm sore but I'm okay."

"You should go to der police."

"I … I can't," I said. "I don't have time … and they don't have jurisdiction."

"Der Coast Guard, ya? Customs?"

"No!" I replied, frustrated. "Doctor Morley's on foreign soil and he's in danger. It's up to me to find him. That's why I need to get back."

"Get back. To Havana?" the Dutchman asked.

"No. *Merida*," Moses said, answering for me. "She needs to get back to the Yucatán."

"Merida! Und … den vaht?"

"I'm still working on that," I conceded.

"So … you vant a lift."

I nodded again. The Dutchman sighed then got up and walked over to one of the desks. He lifted the receiver and dialed a number.

"Ya, ees Andre. Ees he een? Ya, I vill hold."

"Who's he calling?" I asked Moses.

"Mister Trippe," Moses said.

My heart leaped into my throat. I had dreamt of the opportunity to talk with Juan Trippe again … but I never imagined it would be when I needed his help. Then:

"Ya, Juan? Ees Andre. You vill not believe dees, but … I'm sitting here vit an old friend of yours," the Dutchman said. "Der girl from der crash in jungle … Vendy, ya?

I couldn't make out the answer from the other end.

"Vell, dat ees why I call. Oh, und …. one of der Thirty-Eights, she has a, umm, few bullet holes … ya?"

I did hear a bit of that response. Juan Trippe wasn't happy.

***

His employees spoke to him first. Then the receiver was handed to me.

"Um ... hello?" I said.

There was a pause, then:

"*Can't say I ever expected to hear your voice again,*" Mister Trippe said. "*The world works in mysterious ways, I guess.*"

"Yes, it does."

"*Listen, from what the boys have told me, you should go see a doctor ... then the police.*"

"I'm fine," I replied. "And I can't go to the authorities. I don't have time."

I heard him sigh. As I waited for him to say something, I thought about the irony of the situation. I had literally prayed for this moment: A chance to scold Juan Trippe about Lindbergh, about the cover-up, about the Dead Writer. But now, circumstances required me to bite my tongue. I needed his assistance ... so I swallowed my pride:

"Listen ... I'm not good at this, but ... I really need your help."

"*Right. You want a ride to Merida,*" Mister Trippe said. "*Just a drop off? So you can chase the bad guys down by yourself?*"

"Precisely."

There was another pause, then:

"*Tell you what. We'll get you back to Merida ... but I'm gonna send one of our boys with you.*"

"That's not necessary."

"*To hell it isn't!*" he said, growing animated. "*You're going after the butthole that shot up my plane, aren't you?*"

"Well, yes, but …,"

"*I don't like it when people shoot my airplanes. The prick needs to pay a price for that.*"

"It's going to be dangerous," I explained. "This man is violent and unpredictable."

"*Well, don't worry … my guy fought with Rickenbacker. He'll take care of you.*"

***

And like that I had a partner: Moses, my two-time rescuer and occasional spiritual guide.

It was a decision I was very comfortable with … to the point that I insisted I spend the night at his home, rather than at a hotel.

"Der hotel ees very nice!" the Dutchman said. "Come, I take you, ya?"

"No," I repeated. "I don't want to be in any more hotels or any more inns."

"Ve can roll out der cot in der office, ya? Vas good enough for Lindbergh."

"Then I *definitely* don't want to be here. I'd rather be with him," I said, gesturing to Moses. "I feel like I need full-time protection."

"Ya," the Dutchman said, nodding. "Hardvick, dat ees okay vit you?"

"Sure, sure, no problem," Moses replied. "But just so we're clear, my place definitely ain't the Waldorf. Truth be told, I'm a bit embarrassed to think of someone seeing it."

"I'm sure it's fine," I assured him. "When can we get going in the morning?"

Moses shook his head. "Damn, you're itching to get right back out there, huh?"

"I am."

The pilot looked at his boss. "What d'ya think, chief? Can we hitch a ride to Merida after the morning run?"

The little man shook his head. "Your Thirty-Eight must be repaired, ya? Der other must stay on der route. How about dat Fokker?"

I was stunned by the unprovoked profanity, but then realized they were talking about a plane:

"The Fokker!" Moses exclaimed. "You mean the *General New*?"

The Dutchman nodded. The pilot turned to me and commented:

"I hope you ain't in a rush. That old Fokker's slower than a sleeping snail."

"I don't care, as long as it gets us there," I replied.

Moses turned back to his boss:

"We'll try to get out a bit past sunrise. I'll have the fellas pull her out and give her a check-up."

"Ya. Make sure dat Fokker has der flares and der life preservers, too," the Dutchman said. "Now, Vendy, ees there anything else you need?"

I was still processing his line about flares and life preservers. I shook it off, then asked him an uncomfortable question ... one I had wanted to ask since I saw the little man's feet:

"You've been so helpful, thank you. And this may sound strange, but … what size shoe do you wear?"

***

The kindly Dutchman gave me the very shoes off his feet. A bit later, he drove Moses and me into town.

"Drop us off here, boss," Moses said as we neared a busy intersection.

"Vaht? Here?" Mister Priester said.

"Yeah, yeah, it's easier to hop out right here," Moses replied. "We'll be by first thing in the morning."

"Eet ees easier I pick you up, ya?"

"Nah, nah, we'll be fine," Moses said. "We'll catch a taxi."

He got out his door, then came back and opened mine. Before I got out I thanked our driver:

"Mister Priester, sir …," I began.

"Call me Andre, okay?"

"Okay, Andre … I'm sorry about your plane," I said. "And I'm sorry I dragged you all into this mess."

He looked at me and nodded.

"None of dees ees your fault, ya?" he said. "You sure no hotel?"

"I'll be fine. Thank you … for everything."

I scooted out and Moses closed the door for me. He gave the top of motorcar a double-pat and Mister Priester drove off.

Moses led me down a side street, lined with pleasant homes and shady oaks. The oak branches extended over the street and through the leafy canopy I could see the rising moon. I took a deep breath of the salty air; I think it was the first time I had taken a normal breath in weeks.

We came to a large Victorian with a white picket fence. He slowed, making me think we were going inside, but then he turned at the corner of the fence and kept walking. We followed a narrow footpath that led to the rear of the property, where there was a small outbuilding with a sagging roof.

"Like I said, it's ain't much more than a shack," Moses said.

"More like a shed," I said, unable to contain my inner wiseass.

Moses turned around, a funny look on his face, and said something I needed to hear:

"Ah, shut your pie hole and quit yer bitchin."

He winked, turned and opened the screen door leading into his humble home. He gave me the just-one-minute finger, disappeared inside and lit a lantern. Then he came back out and waved me through the squeaky screen door with great flourish.

"Your majesty," he said, correctly avoiding eye contact.

I paraded in and surveyed the kingdom. It wasn't much. A stove, a small icebox, a tattered armchair, a few crates and barrels posing as tables, a single bed in the corner.

"The, um, facilities are around the side," my host said from behind me. "The streetlights keep it pretty well-lit back there. I'll, uh, I'll sleep in the chair. But you sit there now, just let me get this ugly pillow out of the way. There, there you go."

I sat down in his chair. My ass sunk through to the floor.

"Shit, sorry, it sags a bit," he said, then he handed me the ugly pillow. "Here, put this back."

I did. It was much better. Moses tidied up his bed then sat on it.

"I ain't got ... I mean, I don't have anything to drink here," he said. "I'd offer you something if I did."

"I'm fine, thank you."

"Well, Bert's ain't too far away, that's my usual joint, we can go down there later if you need a nip," he said. "Again, I know this ain't much, but its home. Rest assured those sheets are fit for a queen such as yourself; they're from the hotel."

"It's all perfect, thank you," I said. "Hotel sheets are the best."

"Yeah, yeah, Oliver's mom gave 'em to me. She works down there."

"You said she's worried about him."

"That's an understatement."

We sat and talked about Oliver's mom. Next we talked about Oliver. Then Moses insisted we talk a little about what I had been through. That topic made me uncomfortable, but it felt good to know that someone else cared about me.

By and by, I loosened up ... and realized I was parched:

"The place you mentioned, Bert's," I said. "If it's quiet there I could use that drink."

Moses looked at me, and broke out into a big gap-toothed grin.

"Bert tries to make it *not* quiet in there, but it's usually still pretty quiet," he said. "But listen, if we're gonna go there, I should let you know I'm, uh, avoiding the demon rum at the moment."

"*Demon rum*? I've had enough pirate talk, thank you. Are you trying to tell me you're not drinking?"

"Well, yeah, I suppose that's a more direct way to say it," Moses replied.

"Marvelous," I said. "I'll drink yours."

***

I used his washbasin to clean up. I borrowed one of his white button-down shirts, tucking it into my skirt. I had grown to like Mister Priester's shoes, which were surprisingly comfortable.

We left his shed and walked a few blocks. Moses held my hand as we crossed a busy street. We turned between two houses and walked into what I first assumed was someone's backyard. It was actually the way to the bar, which had to be discreet for obvious reasons.

Moses opened the door with his customary flourish and I went inside. It was one of the tiniest establishments I had ever seen. A long bar ran down one side of the narrow room and there were only a handful of tables. A beat-up piano stood against one wall, with a beat-up piano player sitting in front of it. The bartender looked up and didn't smile and spoke to Moses.

"Well, well, the legendary Captain Hardwick."

"Evenin', Bert. Thought I'd class the place up tonight and bring in a real, live female," Moses replied. "Wendy, this is Bert. Bert, Wendy."

"Hello, Bert," I said, then to be friendly, "How's business?"

The bartender cast an angry glare at Moses, then looked at me with an arched eyebrow and said:

"It's be a hell of a lot better if all my regular customers hadn't quit drinking."

At that Moses slapped the bar, barked out a laugh and said:

"You're such an ass, Bert. You should be grateful for every damn customer you get!"

"Hear! Hear!" yelled the piano player.

"Shut up, Cricket, nobody asked you," the bartender growled. "Play the damn piano."

BUM-BA-DA-DUM came the notes of Beethoven's Fifth Symphony.

"Very funny," the bartender said, in a voice that suggested he didn't think it was funny at all.

The piano player gave the bartender a squinty-eyed look. Then, without breaking his stare, he broke into the next notes of the symphony. He was marvelous. The bartender cleared his throat to get my attention.

"Your bluenose escort is having a Coke. How 'bout you?"

"I'll have a ... a whiskey, please," I said, and then without thinking twice, "Widow Watson's, if you have it."

The moment I said it a wave of regret washed over me. I should be in a church, praying for Doctor Morley and giving thanks for a renewed lease on life. Instead I was sitting at a bar, ordering Widow Watson's ... as if nothing had changed.

The bartender came back with booze for me and a bottle of Coca Cola for the flyboy.

I stared at my glass. Moses noticed.

"You alright?" he asked.

I looked at him and said:

"I will be."

I lifted my glass to his Coke. We toasted and then drank. I finished mine first and slammed the glass back on the table. Moses still had his bottle to his lips. His eyes were wide. He lowered his Coke and said:

"Speed demon!"

"I'm not screwing around," I said. "Barkeep, another please."

As my glass was refilled with liquid courage I began to feel a good, warm burn in my chest. The Widow Watson worked fast, she did.

"Hey, I know it's none of my business," Moses said. "But over these past few months I came to realize that ..."

"Oh, shut the hell up," I warned him. "I need a partner, not a priest."

He laughed at that, which made what could have been a serious moment most un-serious.

Then, with classical music playing in the background, I told him more of my tale. It was hard to even know where to begin … but it felt right to talk with someone about it. And his letters had meant so much to me, so I told him that too. Then I told him about how I had felt so alone, to which he said:

"Well, you're not alone anymore."

It felt comforting to hear that … and I was about to tell him so when the piano player started a new song. I recognized it after only a few notes, and it made me forget whatever it was I was about to say.

The song was *Habanera*.

My thoughts spirited back to better, simpler time. That wondrous night on the ancient ball-court at Chichen Itza. The talent show, when I did my send-up of *Habanera*, dressed as Doctor Morley. Oliver was there, Lindbergh too, and everything was pleasant and normal. It was a good night, a happy night.

I snapped out of it when the bartender yelled to the piano player:

"Dammit, Cricket, enough with the classical shit!"

The piano player played a few more notes of *Habanera*. Then he played the first few notes of Beethoven's Fifth again. Then he stopped and in a calm way said to the bartender:

"I play the songs that need playing, Bert."

"Oh, don't give me your moody mumbo-jumbo," the bartender replied. "I swear, you were more fun when you were drinking."

"The fun was merely an illusion, Bert," was the piano player's reply.

"You're gonna be a frickin' illusion if you don't play something else," the bartender said.

"Fine," the piano player said. "What'll it be? *Tiger Rag*, again? *The Entertainer*, again?"

"I don't give a hoot," Bert said. "Just play something that gets people to their feet."

"There's only two other people here!" Cricket said.

"Do the job I pay you to do," the bartender grumbled.

The piano player looked at the keys and took a deep breath. Then he brought his hands to his instrument and started to play. Again, I recognized the song right away:

BUM-BUM-BA-DUM DUM! BA-DA-DA-DA-DA-DUM!

It was Stars and Stripes Forever.

BA-DUM-DIDDLE-DUM! BA-DUM-DIDDLE-DUM! BA-DUM-DIDDLE-DUM-BA-DA-DA-DUM!

Then I felt Moses tap me on the shoulder. I spun around in my stool to see he had gotten up.

"Stand! Stand!" he said.

"Why?" I asked.

"What do you mean, why?" he replied. "It's Stars and Stripes! Stand up!"

"But I'm tired."

"You *have* to stand for Stars and Stripes."

"Nonsense. This is America."

"Damn right it is. And in America, not standing for this song is disrespectful."

"Oh, fiddlesticks," I countered, quite content on my stool.

He seemed rather worked about it, so I stood up. I turned to him, and it struck me that I had never noticed how handsome he was … in a roughed-up, bruised-apple sort of way.

Moses was starting to hum along to the song:

"Bum-ba-dum-ba-dum-ba-dum-dum-dum!"

The pilot was holding his Coke bottle out, swinging it in time to the music. He turned back to the bartender:

"Hell, Bert, get on your feet! Ain't this what you wanted?"

Bert was still sitting in his stool, arms folded. "I'm not standing 'til you and Cricket start drinking again," he grumbled.

Moses laughed, smiled at me, and then resumed his humming:

"Yat-ta-ta-ta-ta-ta-ta! Rum-pa-tum-pa-tum-pa-tum-pa-tum."

I couldn't hold back any longer. I started to hum along with him.

"Tum-pa-tum-pa-tum-tum-tum! Baba-baba-tum-tum-tum!" we sang, together, though our words weren't quite the same.

And as we hummed along I realized I was smiling. A good smile, a real smile, one of those smiles that you just can't stop because it needs to get out.

Don't think I had forgotten about Doctor Morley. I hadn't. I knew I was going after him. And I knew that I would have Moses by my side. Maybe that had something to do with the smile.

As we were *ya-ta-ta-ing* and *rum-pa-tump-ing* I looked back at the pilot again. Wouldn't you know it, he was looking right at me. He was humming and bobbing his head along to this music. It was irresistible, as if the gods couldn't abide by me not humming along with the rest of them.

"Pum-ba-dum-pa-dum-dum-dum! Rumpa-tumpa-bumpa-dum!"

In that moment, with all of us humming Stars and Stripes, I felt somewhat normal. I closed my eyes and took a deep breath. I told myself that I was going to be alright.

Then the most remarkable thing happened.

When I opened my eyes, they happened to fall on the mirror behind the bar. Wedged into the frame of the mirror was an assortment of photographs. One photograph near the bottom seemed to jump out at me.

"Bert," I said to the barkeep. "That picture. The one on bottom. Can you hand it to me?"

The barkeep gave me a puzzled look. Then he turned back to the mirror and when he saw the photograph I was talking about he hesitated. He reached out and slid it out from the frame and turned to me. His face was somber.

"Don't lose it, alright?" he said. "Means a lot to me."

He handed it to me. Now I could see the faces. My heart jumped.

The photograph showed several men sitting at a table outside the bar. All the men were smiling and had drinks and they looked like they were having a wonderful time. I recognized two of them.

Oliver Wheelock was sitting in the middle. Good ol' Oliver, the goof whose appearance at Chichen Itza heralded the start of my adventure.

Next to him sat the Dead Writer. Ernie was his name. He had an exuberant smile and was holding up two drinks.

It looked like he was trying to pass one of the drinks to the photographer.

A wondrous thought struck: he was trying to pass the drink to *me*.

"Are you saying we're okay now?" I drunk-whispered to the image.

The Dead Writer in the photograph didn't respond, but his smile gave me the answer I was hoping for.

Just then Moses nudged me. "Hey, come on, big finale!" he said. "*Ya-ta, ya-ta-ta, ya-ta-ta! Da-da-da-dum, da-da-da-dum, da-,*"

"So this is how it ends?" I asked, very much enjoying his humming. "Strange choice."

"It may seem strange now, but later on you'll realize it was pretty darn clever," Moses replied.

He lifted his Coke bottle and clinked my glass. He said:

"Cheers. To you ... and to the road ahead."

We smiled at each other and took a drink. Then we resumed our humming, *rum-pum-pumming* and *ya-ta-tumming* to the end of the song.

TO BE CONCLUDED ...

The final tale in Michael Scott Bertrand's
Treasure of Tenochtitlan trilogy will be released in 2019.

ABOUT THE ARTWORK

The illustrations of Don Quixote and Sancho Panza were made by Gustave Doré (1832-1883), a prolific and multi-talented French artist. While he gained fame illustrating works by Lord Byron, Milton and Dante, it was his stunning drawings and engravings for an 1868 edition of Cervantes' *Don Quixote* that made Doré a legend. His depictions of the knight and his squire forever influenced our expectations of what Quixote and Sancho Panza should look like.

The cover art was created by Alan Flinn, an artist and illustrator based in Colorado. Flinn also designed the cover of *Flying Conquistadors*. The *Sword of the Spaniard* cover is a tribute to Spanish travel posters of the late 1920s. The city in the background is Seville, the tallest building is La Giralda, the bell tower of the Seville cathedral. The sword Wendy is holding is based upon a real-life sword of Hernan Cortés, currently stored in the Royal Armory in Madrid.

The illustration on the 'To Be Concluded' page is *Well of Bolonchen* (1843) by Frederick Catherwood (1799-1854), an English architect and explorer. Catherwood accompanied diplomat John Lloyd Stephens on several expeditions through Central America and the Yucatán. He used a *camera lucida* technique to make extraordinarily detailed drawings of Mayan sites that had been swallowed by the jungle. Among the Mayan cities "rediscovered" by Stephens and Catherwood were the legendary sites of Copán, Palenque and Uxmal.

While not pictured in this book, all of the artwork in Salvador's studio can easily be found online. The paintings described in Chapter 20 are *Face of the Great Masturbator* (1929), *The Anthropomorphic Tower* (1930), *Study for Don Quixote* (1956) and, of course, *The Persistence of Memory* (1931). The film is *Un Chien Andalou* (1929). The 'awful' painting Wendy sees at the start of Chapter 33 is *Honey is Sweeter than Blood* (1927) ... which sold in 2011 for $6.8 million.

www.ingramcontent.com/pod-product-compliance
Lightning Source LLC
Chambersburg PA
CBHW060209030726
47499CB00004B/970